STRANGERS AND SOJOURNERS

A Novel

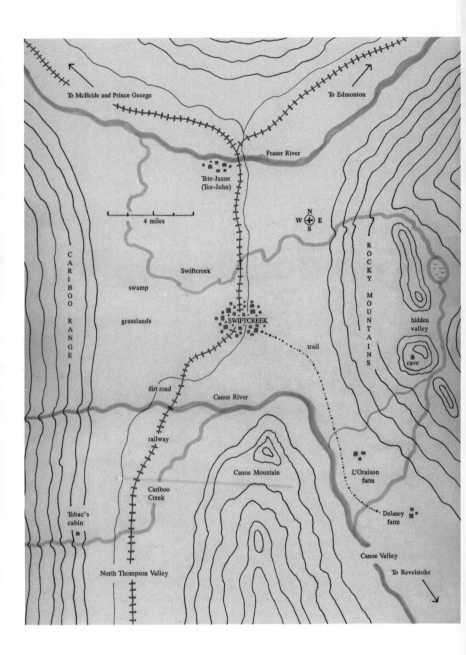

To McBride and Prince George

To Edmonton

Fraser River

Tête-Jaune
(Tete-John)

4 miles

Swiftcreek

swamp

grasslands

SWIFTCREEK

C A R I B O O   R A N G E

R O C K Y   M O U N T A I N S

hidden valley

cave

trail

dirt road

Canoe River

railway

Canoe Mountain

L'Oraison farm

Cariboo Creek

Delaney farm

Tobac's cabin

Canoe Valley

North Thompson Valley

To Revelstoke

MICHAEL D. O'BRIEN

STRANGERS
AND
SOJOURNERS

A Novel

IGNATIUS PRESS   SAN FRANCISCO

Cover art by Michael D. O'Brien
The Sojourners
Cover design by Roxanne Mei Lum

© 1997 Ignatius Press, San Francisco
All rights reserved
ISBN 978-0-89870-609-3 (HC)
ISBN 978-0-89870-923-0 (PB)
Library of Congress catalogue number 96–75779
Printed in the United States of America ∞

For my grandmother, Jane Sloan,
and for Nathaniel McKirdy

Contents

Within its depths I saw ingathered, bound by love in one volume, the scattered leaves of all the universe.

—Dante, *Paradiso*

Beloved, you are strangers and in exile. . . .

—1 Peter 2:11

Preface

T. S. Eliot once wrote, "Immature poets borrow. Mature poets steal." Thus, in *Strangers and Sojourners* I have dared to build upon that long-standing tradition, weaving into the plot a number of the thoughts of G. K. Chesterton, Christopher Dawson, Catherine Doherty, Dante, and a host of people whose greatness will never be known by many.

Some of the fictional characters are composites of real people. Their nobility and their failings are drawn from the drama of personal histories—the holy and mysterious material we presume to call "ordinary" lives. Their interior sufferings and joys and their exterior trials have been reshaped here (by borrowing or theft, I cannot say) through the wild license of art but are by no means unfaithful to the essence of the original events. Moreover, in some instances I have refrained from depicting certain extraordinary details of the events, truth being (as the cliché goes) far, far stranger than fiction.

The telling of stories is the abiding act by which people of all times and places pass down to the coming generations their hard-won fragments of wisdom. One can call it culture, or one can call it fun, but it will always remain indispensable. Wisdom is often purchased at great price, and much of it fades into disremembering because of silence or modest restraint, or because of shame and grief. Yet without the telling, we would soon cease to understand who we are.

PROLOGUES

January 1, 1900

The carriage bounced over a rise beyond Uffington, and the undulating escarpment hove into view. Anna jumped up on the seat and pointed.

"A white horse!" she shouted. "Look, it's floating on the mountains. It's going up into the sky!"

"Sit down, Anna, or you'll have a nasty tumble", Papa said gruffly. "Sit down, sit down, girl!"

He pulled her back and told her to be still. The team lurched forward, pulling the carriage past the gate of a farmer's lane that wound toward the base of the hill.

"Can't you see it, Papa? It's so beautiful! And there's a knight riding on it. He's got a flag, a golden flag."

"Do be quiet, silly!" said Emily.

Papa lectured: "It is a prehistoric art work, a great white horse shaped from the underlying chalk of the hills. There is no rider. Whatever you think you see is just an illusion created by the mists swirling in the wind."

"In a few minutes we'll be walking on the horsey's back", said Papa's companion, Mrs. Besant, who knew many secret things.

"But I don't want to walk on it", said Anna. "I want to look up at it when it rides on the clouds."

They came to a full stop at the base of the hill and dragged her out of the carriage, ignoring her protests. The wind blew hard through the valley of the white horse, whipping her lavender dress around her knees as she climbed, her hand locked in Emily's iron grip. The wool stockings and the high leather boots were not enough protection from the chill, nor was her macintosh, which Nana had cut down from an old coat of Mother's.

She whimpered, halted on a tussock of grass, stuck out her lower lip, and pressed a cloth doll to her chest.

"Come along, Anna", said Emily irritably. "Everyone is waiting for us. If you don't hurry up, I shall take Beatrix and lock her in my purse until it's over."

Anna clung tightly to the doll.

"Bea would cry", she said. "Bea would not be happy."

Emily knelt down and tied Anna's scarf tightly about her neck.

"But the spirits are waiting, Anna. They're all around us. Can't you feel them?"

"No."

"That's because you're too little. And too stubborn."

Papa, who had gone on ahead, now stopped and strode back, exasperated, swinging his ebony cane.

"I'm cold", said Anna. "I want to go down and wait in the carriage."

"Nonsense!" said Papa. "This is an experience you will never forget. I'll have none of your fussing, Anna . . . or else."

She waited, hoping he would offer an alternative. He stared at her, expressionless, inhaled deeply, then said, "Come along now, girl. What if your mother should speak to us today?"

"I don't want to talk to her."

They stared down at her, offended, wondering what to do next.

"She's impossible, Father", said Emily. "She'll ruin everything if she cries and makes a bother up there."

Papa glanced up the flanks of the sheep-covered hill. The chalk horse galloped over the swell of green. Most of the group had converged on the crest, gathering around the horse, and were looking out across the vast air above the plain. Down in the valley the bell of the Norman church of Saint Mary tolled the noon hour. Blankets of thick gray cloud rolled overhead.

Papa looked at Anna and said in his most severe voice, "You

are coming. You will behave. You will remember this day forever."

"But I'm afraid!"

"There is nothing to be afraid of."

"But they are bad!"

The man and his eldest daughter look at each other, then
down at the little girl.

"Who, precisely, do you think is bad?"

"The men with the bows and arrows, and the men burning
the babies on the altar. And the old man with the wicked eyes.
Up there!" she pointed.

"Whoever told you such a thing!" erupted Emily.

"Nana", said Papa in disgust. "Nana told her." Nana was
Catholic and did not like séances. Nana sprinkled holy water
about the house whenever Papa was at the clinic. Nana made a
sign of the cross on Anna's forehead every night with miracle
water from a place called *Loords*—such a funny name. Nana
made Anna promise not to tell, though, of course, she did tell.

Emily took her sister's hand and began to drag her along the
sheep path. Anna did not cry or make a sound, but she thrust
Bea into her pocket with her free hand and clutched the small,
blue-enamelled cross that Nana had pressed on her that morning, just before they had lifted her into the carriage.

"Shhhh," Nana had said, putting a finger to her thin purple
lips, "it is our *secret, ma petite*. Your *Maman* she want me for give
this to you. The holy Virgin she watch over you. Do not let the
bad spirits into your heart." She tapped Anna's chest. "The heart
is the key. It is the sacred place, *non*?"

Though Anna did not understand what Nana had told her,
she now clung to the little cross with all her might, until its
image was imprinted in the flesh of her palm.

When they reached the flat height of the hill, the group ceased
its chatter and, as if on signal, spread in a wide ring around the
chalk horse. The wind whipped the ladies' multicolored dresses,

and the men stomped out their cigars. Then they all held hands and waited.

Anna was placed between Papa and Mrs. Besant. Mrs. Besant and Papa held her hands too tightly. She stifled an upwelling of tears, her legs trembling.

No one spoke.

Then a man stepped into the center of the ring and intoned a kind of prayer in a high, wailing voice. He called on the spirits of the north, the east, the south, and the west. He called upon the spirit of the earth and upon the higher masters and upon many other names Anna did not know. Then his head fell sideways and he closed his eyes. For several minutes he remained in that position. A skylark flew right over the ring, its cries protesting, and the sheep began to baah noisily for no apparent reason. Then a fierce inrush of air suddenly filled the man's lungs, and he opened his eyes. The crowd murmured its approval.

But Anna saw that the eyes were no longer the man's own eyes, and his voice when he spoke was no longer high but deep. It seemed to echo across the limestone horse and reverberate throughout the valley.

"You have come to meet me on this propitious day, bearing an ancient fealty in your hearts," said the voice coming out of the man, "and it shall be rewarded." The voice paused while the group assimilated this information.

"Yea, for though you look about and see all the world become Christian, even so in the twinkling of an eye I shall pass my hand across the four quarters, and it shall become as nothing. My work shall begin here, for in this place the words spoken in the middle times shall be refuted, and the deed long forgotten shall be overturned, for the sake of Old Britain, which lies sleeping beneath this soil. And thus you shall be my servants unto the ends of the earth. You are to be my instruments in the days of reforging, when once again the sword and the fire shall rule, where only the chant of addled monks has held sway for these millennia. From your seed shall come the new age, which shall be built upon the ruins of the Lost Years. For those who say the Old Age has passed away forever know nothing of the power of the Masters who have gone before and will return."

The murmuring swelled above the level of awe to a pitch of exultation. Some of the ladies uttered short ecstatic cries. Emily bent forward into the center of the ring, sighing loudly, her eyes squeezed shut. Papa swayed. Mrs. Besant's hands shook rhythmically.

Anna tried to pull her fingers from Mrs. Besant's.

"Don't break the circle, girl", said the woman. Papa shot Anna a harsh look.

She made herself stand very, very still and looked out over the far edge of the ring toward the tiny doll-house church in the valley below. The hedgerows quilted the land as far as the horizon. The wind wailed.

"For, lo, in this place, long ago, the army of Alfred the Fool did beat back the forces of the Danes, using the usurper's magic to resist the higher magic of the forces of the earth. And, lo, for a time and a half time we were in eclipse, though we waited and pondered the devices of the enemy. And know too that on the hillock beneath this horse, there once did ride a knight in bondage to the usurper, and there he did in ignorance slay the dragon. And lo, on this height the thrice-ignorant priests did tear down the high places and the altars where the people communed with the spirits and made their sacrifices to the generative powers of man and woman. Thus did the bishops and the priests put an end to those things that once were the power and glory of Old Britain, which my word sustained and over which I ruled, raising prince and shaman alike, to the glory of the powers and principalities.

"But in the jaws of time Alfred died, and George died, and the succession of bishops died and their saints and kings died, and always we burst forth again from our sleep, from our tombs and caves and barrows. For we cannot be destroyed. We cannot die, and we will ever renew the ancient ways from cycle unto cycle of rebirth. Though my body sleeps beneath the white-thorn trees, in the fullness of time it shall arise and join my soul-powers for the last engagement with the ancient foe.

"There are still among you some who doubt. Know that you shall go the way of Arthur and Alfred if you persist in doubt. Know that in this place, which the adversaries have claimed for the God of the Jews, I once made my rituals and sustained the people. Here I raised my arms above the whole land and its kingdoms. Here I cursed the Romans until they departed, made incantation against the missionaries when they arrived, and wove the air about my prince, Henry, until his bent will was made straight and he, too, cleansed the land of the usurpers' rites.

"They said I was a legend, though I am real. They said I was evil, though I am good; they said I was *magus*, and so I am, for it was I who shaped the boy Arthur. It was I who molded his dream of the fair city, which he built, understanding nothing, knowing not the caverns of deep water that flowed beneath his throne. For he did not heed me and once in perversity did bear into battle the image of the mother of the enemy, and thus at Castellum Guinnion, victorious, he was convinced of the power of my foe. Thus did my Arthur leave me and reject my craft to follow the legends of the bishops and the priests. And thus did he die."

"It is Merlin!" gasped Mrs. Besant. "Merlin is with us. He speaks!"

"And so we have rested a while, and though we will bide a while longer, we have awakened you, the chosen ones, to pre-pare the way for us. Work, then, until this people falls into deep disremembering and neglect. When that day comes we shall awaken our armies."

The man began to chant in a foreign tongue.

Anna looked up at the earthworks of the old fort and saw many men and women moving about like walking crystal. They wore the hides of animals, carried wood, danced, beat their dogs, fletted arrows, and tended cook fires. Below on the plain she saw a small army crashing into an immense host of warriors, pushing them back, swords and helms ringing, leaving a litter of bodies in its wake. She heard the shouts of the victors and the screams of the dying. She saw the mouth of the valley drinking the blood of men.

Then the wind blew again and the mists parted. She saw a knight astride a white horse gallop up from the plain unto the dragon's mound, and there he thrust his lance deep into the boiling rage of a huge serpent, which coiled about the hilt, vomited black blood, and, after much thrashing and bellowing, lay still.

Then she glanced back to the center of the ring and saw a gray-bearded old man in swirling red robes. A black symbol like a claw or a spider was marked upon his forehead. He raised a twisted staff in his hand, atop which the carving of a red dragon spread its wings as if alive. The wicked old man stared at her and frowned.

Then Anna broke the circle, thrust her hand into her pocket, and clutched the little cross. For a moment there was absolute stillness.

Then she screamed and fell to the ground, and the valley flowed sideways and ran down the drain holes into a well of black waters.

April 11, 1909

Diary Entry:

"Friars", Blackswan Lane, Bishopsford, Hertfordshire.

Light is breaking into the cupola.

It is my fourteenth birthday. I am a glass egg in a nest of iron. I shall make an invention of my life: I shall write what I am to become.

I have begun to notice the birds as never before. It is they who are my true teachers. Unfair that we are born without wings! Yet, we are only partly bound, for those who long to fly may sing:

> Anna Kingsley Ashton Green,
> Been to London to meet the Queen,
> Anna Kingsley Ashton Blue,
> Whomever you marry will ever be true.

Swallows have built a nest under the eaves of the cupola. Now a robin is investigating me from where she is poised on the railings. All is stillness. Sound itself dissolves. For a brief moment I become her. My breast is the colour of dried blood. My feathers melt into the green of the elf-leaf, that green which is only seen in morning fog as sun burns through and polishes berries.

Last evening, Papa showed Emily and me some magic-lantern slides. At first the light was curry-coloured, then like old muslin curtains in the attic. There were scores of silly images of a regatta, and legions of preposterous personages discussing things on lawns. I saw La Tour Eiffel. Then the Crystal Palace. Finally, in a blaze of glass, the little sepia empress, Victoria. Had I been there, I would have pushed through the crowd and thrown myself at her feet. I know she would have loved me, raised me to my feet, and embraced me in her stout arms. It is a pity she is dead. I might have been invited to join the royal household! Father would have been furious! He is not a monarchist.

My tyrant sister has driven me here to complete the prescribed reading, as tomorrow there is an examination. I loathe examinations. They prove simply nothing, only that it is possible, after all, to mould another into the shape of one's whims. Yet, if I do not imbibe this romantic treacle I shall be the most miserable young woman in Miss Windsor's Academy for Young Women. 'Anna', she will fume as usual, 'you are impossible!' Shall I be chastised for my failure to appreciate the demented love of Cathy for that beastly rustic, Heathcliff? Still, if I am to become a writer, then I shall have to imbibe.

'Miss Ashton!' the senior Miss W said to me the other day, in the most ferocious tone, in front of all the girls, 'Anne Ashton, you have been gifted with intelligence. Do not presume that this is sufficient for a successful life. Sloth can bring it all tumbling down!'

I know that Miss W does not like me. But at least Emily loves me. What might I have become without Emily? She is only my tyrant-sister and older by five years. She is not yet a woman, though she does have a beau. She has shaken hands with Mrs. Emmeline Pankhurst and her daughter in front of the House of Commons. 'The world does not look kindly upon Amazons', says Emily.

Papa's friend, Mr. Conan Doyle, came to visit on Saturday. He is a writer. I do not like him, although he has very nice manners. Emily thinks he is charming. After supper several of their friends came, and they had a séance. Though I was invited, I declined and went up to bed early. I was fast asleep when Emily burst in, crying, 'Come downstairs quickly, Anna. It's Mama! Mama's spirit is speaking through the medium! I saw ectoplasm!'

I think my eyes must have been overstrained, for I saw these words take a visible shape as they left Emily's mouth. They were like short bursts of shadow. I was terrified. I knew, though I do not understand how I knew, that whatever was speaking through the medium was not Mama. And if it was not Mama, then it was a liar. If it was a liar, then I did not wish to hear a single word.

Emily went back downstairs, crestfallen.

Where are you, my Mama?

Keep me safe, keep me safe, O my true mother!

I come often to sit in the cupola. It is screened from the eyes of the house. I am perfectly motionless. The birds are mute. Time drifts, then ceases altogether. In the hollow of my being is the glass egg. When I look into it, I begin to weep and I am very afraid.

Will there come a day when I shall shatter and fly at last? I do not dare to guess. In the meantime, I would like to be a princess in a crystal palace.

April 23, 1915

The rain fell through the night with the predictability of the obsessed. It beat the fields of mud into a swamp. The lorry churned it up, and when the going was good it merely skidded over the undulating ruts of a supply road that snaked across miles of front lines. In the back a soldier of the signal corps clung to a wooden crate and cursed at each bump, anxious for his equipment. Seated across from him a medical officer rolled a cigarette with both hands, swaying, bracing himself with his legs, and eyeing the nurse as if to diagnose her terror.

"Where are we dropping you?" he yelled above the roar of the motor.

"A field hospital near Ypres", she said.

"Wipers? Those idiots! That's no place for a girl."

She looked away.

One of the canvas flaps was faffling loose, and she saw a ridge of false dawn erupt in the northeast. A minute later the concussions came in, and the doctor observed her reaction.

"First time this close to the front?"

"Yes."

"You a real nurse or a volunteer?"

"I was a medical student before the war broke out."

He looked at her, finding the information hard to believe.

"We'll be there in ten minutes", he said. "Smoke?"

"No, thank you."

They rode the rest of the way without speaking, listening to the thuds of the bombardment as if they were the dreary games of madmen. Occasional machine-gun fire rattled like pebbles tossed on an iron roof.

The lorry slid into the yard of a hamlet of tents.

A nursing sister appeared at the back of the vehicle and helped her down into the mud. She was a no-nonsense Scottish gran with a watch and a military decoration pinned to her apron. Shaped like a barrel on bowling-pin legs in black stockings, she barked:

"You're the new surgery staff. I'm Blakey", she said, thrusting out her hand. "Come this way, sister."

"Good luck!" shouted the doctor, grinning as he lurched away into the dark.

The nurse led her into a large, white tent lit by gas lanterns. It smelled of disinfectant and cheap perfume. A coal brazier, its door open, burned brightly in the middle of two rows of cots.

"Don't talk too loud", she said. "The day nurses are sleeping —or trying to. You get five hours' sleep, then it's into the valley of death for you, my lass. Hungry?"

"No. Do you have some tea?"

"Tea and sugar. No milk. You should get some rest. Tomorrow will be frightful. Like Euston Station in the morning. There's a bad one on right now, and they'll be bringing the bodies in by the cartload before too long."

She poured boiling tea from a large kettle into a tin cup and handed it to the newcomer.

Anne accepted it gratefully and blew across the top. When she could bear it, she drank it down in small sips.

"Just how much experience do you have? Been in surgery before?"

"Yes."

"What have you seen?"

"A lot."

"I think not, my girl. Tomorrow you get to feast your eyes on something worse than heaps of amputated legs and arms. I hope you're not the kind that shocks easily. No? Good, you'll have something to tell the grandchildren when you're my age."

The old nurse's mouth twisted sourly, and her eyes bittered.

"The burns are the worst", she went on. "The Bosch are using mustard gas. Have you seen gas victims?"

"No."

"It's not pretty", she said, and left her alone on a cot to think about it.

In the morning she came back and took Anne to the mess tent where half a dozen women were drinking black coffee and eating scrambled eggs and biscuits with plum jam. Some were modern women, hard-eyed, smoking cigarettes and chattering as they ate; others were Florence Nightingales, staring into their tin cups and visibly suffering from fatigue. All of them wore white dresses and jaunty caps with red crosses, punctuated by spatters of brown and purple.

The dawn arrived on a chilly wind that stank of cordite and putrefaction. The rain had stopped, but the sky boiled over in charcoal breakers lit by phosphorus.

The sergeant—that is how she thought of Blakey—took her down a street of thwacking white tents. Giant red crosses were painted on the roofs.

"You're a lucky one", said the sergeant. "No blood and guts for you on your first day. Maintenance only."

She held back the door flap of a large tent at the back of the compound.

"This lot in here are the no-hopers. Most of them are in coma. Those who make it beyond today go out to the main hospital when artillery can clear a path to the west. The sisters will tell you what to do. Most of the lads want water."

Anne was glad of the reprieve from surgery. Her medical training had so far consisted of six months in premed at Saint Bart's, some theory, textbook anatomy, and a dose of bravado. Since coming to Belgium she had been repeatedly analyzed as too sensitive and had been given the lesser tasks of sterilizing instruments, boiling used bandages, and rolling fresh ones. She

27

had recently decided that she was unsuited to the medical profession. She did not tell the nurse any of this.

"The ones who wake up will tell you stories and think you're someone else. They'll fall in love with you. But don't be a fool. I've seen a lot of brainless girls come into this tent and a lot of dead boys go out of it."

Anne was beginning to dislike the sergeant.

She spent the morning mastering the routine, siphoning water into the semiconscious, changing dressings, wiping up vomit, applying ointment, and learning the pecking order among the staff. Groans and occasional screams became a texture of ordinary background noise that she scarcely heard. She wondered at her lack of feeling. At midmorning she went out into the sun and stared up at the blue canopy of Flemish spring. Pockmarked brown fields, overgrown with weeds, stretched in every direction. She listened, as was her habit, for the sound of birds, but there were none. Three biplanes, their undersides painted with British insignia, flew over the camp and waggled their wings, though no one seemed to pay much attention.

"Dragonfly patrol", she whispered, remembering summers when squadrons of long blue incandescent tubes, whirring and humming, would clear the marshes of tiny black flies.

Three men died before lunch; another died while she was out spooning boiled potatoes and bully-beef into her belly. Two more died by supper time. There were some shell and bullet wounds, but most of the patients were victims of the chemical burns. The lorry doctor came in with orderlies who were carrying a post-op, but he did not notice her. The sergeant passed by once to check on her reaction and, noting that Anne's temperament was enclosed and calm, went away again.

At six she was relieved of duty and went outside to breathe the cleaner air. An officer clopped down the row on horseback, throwing up hoof-sized pats of mud against the tents. A Cockney nurse from the neighboring ward hurled a crude taunt and a fistful of wet turf at his back, but the officer, riding tall above the tyranny of human detritus, pretended not to notice. Anne passed along the aisles of the wards and near the surgery surprised an orderly and three nurses sitting on packing crates, giggling. The orderly was playing a ukelele fast and funny, and no one seemed to be bothered that he was smeared up to his neck and elbows in blood, like a butcher's boy on tea break.

Her own tent was empty. She lay down on her cot and opened a small leather-bound book. She tried to read Tennyson's *Ulysses*, to sail with him beyond the sunset and the baths, to lift beyond the gore and the despair, but the lines of poetry seemed too heroic and absurd. The print blurred and she fell asleep. She was awakened at eight by a rough hand shaking her. A voice informed her that one of the night nurses had gone to bed with dysentery, and Anne would have to stand duty for her at the tent of the no-hopers.

It was a long night. She and two others tended the dying and called for orderlies whenever there was a need to remove corpses, as if they were cleaning up the greatest embarrassment of all. She began to long for her cups of tea like a laudanum addict. She noted again the deadness of her emotions. She registered a certain intellectual sympathy, of course, even pity, and was suitably appalled by the destruction of young lives. But the absence of strong feeling disturbed her. Would it not be more appropriate, she wondered, to feel horror, rage, disgust, even a foray into mild feminine hysteria? She felt nothing. And disapproved of herself.

"You're a sensible girl", said the sergeant, patting her arm. "You'll do well."

After midnight a warm breeze blew in from the south, scented with saturated earth and the unfolding buds on a fringe of trees that had survived in that direction. The bombardment ceased, though distant rifle shots could be heard from time to time. The rows of bodies grew still, and the other nurses sat down, sighing, on camp chairs by the stove, gulping stew and discussing the day's events. They tried to engage Anne in conversation, but it failed after she offered some feeble comments about the Royal Air Force and dragonflies.

A loud groan came from a corner where the flap was strapped open to let in air.

"Should he be lying in that breeze?" said Anne.

"Don't worry about him", said one. "There's nothing you can do."

"He's not in any pain", said the other. "I gave him morphine a half hour ago. He's just raving."

"I'll see to him", Anne said, and left the other two to their gossip.

The soldier was a parliament of disasters: a broken back, stitched gashes on his shoulder and neck, and one side of his face and skull bandaged where the gas had got him. But there was no mangling. The chart said severe blood loss. He was mumbling through blue lips.

His exposed chest was a mess of tape and muscle. She pulled the blanket up under his chin and reached for the tent flap.

"Don't," he mumbled, and she saw that he was staring at her. "Please don't close it."

"You'll catch a chill."

"I need to see the stars", he pleaded.

"All right. But just for a minute."

She sat on the stool beside him.

"Look up. Can you see it?" he said.

"See what?"

"The Southern Cross."

"I don't think so. You can't see it in the northern hemisphere."

"If you climb to the crow's nest you can see it."

"That's enough talking. Close your eyes. You should sleep."

"Not tonight. The sea is so beautiful."

The breeze snapped the wall of the canvas tent beside them, and his eyes darted toward it.

"The wind is up. I love it when the foresail is digging into the waves."

"Quiet now. You're going back to England tomorrow. You'll get well."

"No, Miss, I'm going to die. I want to die on this ship."

She said nothing, feeling no desire to engage in dialogue with an irrational stranger.

"Do you see them?" he said.

"Who?"

"The angels."

"Angels?"

"There's one standing on the top mast and one on the bow and one at the stern."

"Oh?"

"They're so beautiful. They've got swords. Unsheathed."

"Why are they here?"

"They're watching over us. They're strong."

"I expect they are strong, angels."

He turned his swimming eyes upon her.

"I'm going to die", he said.

She could not lie to him. She said nothing for a minute or two while he observed his angels. Then she reached up and closed the flap.

"Are you hurting?" she said.

"A little bit."

"Do you know where you are?"

"I was on a ship in my mind, and now I'm in a tent near Ypres."

"That's right. You've been wounded, and you're recovering from surgery."

"But it's no-go. It didn't work, did it? I can't feel my toes. My face is burning."

"Would you like some water?"

"Yes."

She gripped him under the shoulders and with considerable effort raised his head. He cried out. She held the cup to his lips, and he gulped. When he had had enough she eased him down onto the pillow.

"Thank you, Miss."

He lay still, looking at her.

She looked back. There seemed no reason for her to stay with him, but no other duties called her at present. During the brief moments when she had been free during the past twenty-four hours, she had attempted to focus on the blurred poetry in her book, to think thoughts that escaped the sucking tide of blood. Neither her mind nor her emotions had proven sufficient to restore her to a sense of interior unity. A human face might help her to do so—any human face—an image of some inscrutable harmony, some high purpose written into all living things.

He was going to die, that was clear enough. Thus, she could look into his eyes as long as she wished, and it would cost her no intolerable social repercussions. She could examine the face of a condemned man and learn from it.

It was a very fine face, she thought, but then all faces in repose are beautiful. Coils of chestnut hair spilled out from under the bandages. The contours of his brow, cheeks, and chin were clean, brown, and lean; the shoulders, where they had not been violated, were well-muscled. She decided to stay with him for a while longer.

"What's your name?" he whispered.

"Anne."

"Anne", he echoed.

"What is your name?" she asked, though it would perhaps have been easier to glance at the chart.

"Peter."

"Do you like the sea, Peter?"

"I love it", he said passionately. "I love it too much."

"Where are you from?"

"Canada."

"Where in Canada?"

"A place where the ice sings."

"Does the ice sing?"

"Oh, yes, it sings. When I was young I didn't know that, but then I heard it myself and I knew."

"Is it a nice sound?"

"It's like crying and laughing all together, but mostly it's like music."

"Where did you hear it?"

"Up north."

"Ah", she said, and thought this might be the neat completion of their exchange.

"Can I tell you about it?"

She looked around the tent and assessed it. One of the nurses had fallen asleep on a chair. The other was ministering to a cry for help at the far end. The other patients were motionless.

"All right."

"Can I hold your hand?"

"No, I don't think so."

He stretched out his one good arm, and he took her fingers gently in his. She did not pull them away. She had never before experienced the feel of a man's hand enfolding hers. The fingers were weak and cool. They did not imprison. At any moment she could have withdrawn her own without undue effort. She did not. She swallowed hard and looked into his eyes. His eyes were very intelligent and blue.

"I have to tell someone", he said. "It's so beautiful. Like the angels."

She nodded her assent, and he began.

"I always dreamed of the sea, but I never saw it. I wanted to get into the navy, but I was too young. They told me to wait a year. I'd saved some money logging in the interior of British Columbia—that's where I'm from. Then I thought I should spend the year studying painting. I got into an art school in Montreal. In the spring, after classes were over, I bought a canoe and gear and took a freight train to northern Ontario. I decided I wanted to stay in the bush and see what it's like. It's a kind of ocean too. If you stand on a hilltop in a windstorm and squint your eyes, you can see the waves rolling through the forest. You can see the curve of the earth. Up there beyond Nakina, where the Anishinabi people live, there's a million square miles of wilderness where nobody ever goes. There are thousands of lakes that don't even have names. I wanted to paint it."

"Paint it?"

"I like to do oils and tempera. You need really strong colors to capture it. The land is savage and dangerous. It's so beautiful it breaks your heart. I wanted to try living in it alone for a while."

"You don't seem old enough to do something like that—all by yourself, I mean."

"I was seventeen."

"And how old are you now?"

"Nineteen. How old are you?"

"Twenty-one", she replied after hesitating.

"Women are always older than men, in their hearts."

"You really think so?" she said, intrigued.

"Men are older than women in other ways", he added.

She did not pursue this curious line of thought but instead encouraged him to continue with his tale.

"The train went north for two days. In all that time we didn't pass a single cabin. The land was so empty. The train dropped me and my gear by the side of the track, near a river. I had my canoe and enough food for several months. I had a map. That river connected to a lake, which went into other lakes. I just went deeper and deeper into it. I couldn't stop paddling. I had to keep going farther. I don't know why."

34

"Perhaps you needed to be alone?"

"Yes. When you're alone, that's when you see what you are. Eventually I found a little lake that was full of pike and trout. I built a tent frame of lodgepole pines on the south shore. I put up a tent on top of the frame, so it was like a small cabin. Easy."

"Easy."

"I painted all summer, and into the autumn. Winter was coming, but I was so happy I couldn't bear to leave. I'd brought along a small, airtight stove that weighed almost nothing. I'd smoked a lot of fish. I had plenty of dried food. I decided I should stay the winter. And I did."

The cryptic language did not really paint an adequate landscape in her mind. She waited.

"When the first ice came on the lake, it was like a sea of glass. I threw stones. They skipped across. Zing, zing, zing, with a hollow sound underneath it. Have you ever heard that?"

"No."

"When the first arctic wind blew in, the pines bent in worship, row after row bending and praising, praising and sighing. 'God is great!' they sang. 'God is great!' Have you ever heard that?"

"No. Weren't you lonely?"

"Sometimes. Once I thought I was going crazy. In February I got snow-blind from the reflected sun on the lake. I nearly died. I wanted to die. It was like hot sand under your eyelids. I stayed in my sleeping bag for weeks. I chewed dried fish and waited. I was afraid I'd go mad and put a bullet in my brain. But when my sight came back it was too wonderful! I ran out and I saw!"

"What did you see?"

"I saw that everything is so beautiful we should fall down and worship God a hundred times a day. I knew then I'd have to be an artist and nothing else. Nothing else would ever be good enough."

35

"How did your God let you fall into *this* hell-hole?" she blurted out.

"Maybe he has his reasons."

"You're leaving some rather large blanks in your tale. How did you get from the wilderness to Belgium?"

"Some native trappers came by in early March before break-up. They told me a war had started in Europe, but they didn't know who was fighting who. I left when the lakes opened up and went home to B.C. Then I got conscripted."

"And here you are."

"Here I am."

"Do you still desire to fall down and worship a hundred times a day?" she said, and instantly regretted the minor cruelty.

He looked at her evenly before replying.

"No. But maybe he wanted me to learn something."

"A rather hazardous education."

"Maybe I'll die, but I've seen things that people wait all their lives to see and never see. I'm old", he laughed. "I'm way older than you."

She looked at the boy dubiously.

"Have you ever heard loons calling?" he said. "They sound like they've got broken hearts. But they're very happy. Sometimes they laugh."

"I see", she said, wondering if his mind was wandering.

"Have you seen geese skidding on the ice as they land?"

"Is that when you heard the ice singing?"

"That comes later, in the spring. There's no light brighter than spring light, did you know that?"

"Spring in England is rainy."

"In March and April, in Canada, it's full of white light. That sort of light makes a kind of music, too, but not the kind you can hear with your ears. The best of all is the last song of the ice. You can hear that. During the winter the lakes freeze four, five feet deep. The ice cracks and groans on the coldest nights—

sometimes like gunshots. And then when it's time to die, it just breaks up."

"It doesn't melt?"

"It's so thick the sun can't wear it down fast enough. First the lake gets wet on the surface, then the ice at the shore pulls away from the banks, leaving a rim of cold water so clear you can see twenty feet down to the bottom. Then the thickest parts out in the middle turn into long crystals, and they start to disintegrate, and for days all you can hear is the sound of a million crystal chandeliers tinkling. That's the chorus, but the big singing's when the ice sheet starts to buckle. The sound it makes is like a whipsaw or a hundred owls singing hymns."

Anne suppressed a smile.

"A hundred owls singing hymns? That sounds rather comical."

"Maybe to you. Just think about it for a while."

"I am", she said and laughed outright.

"All right, then, the singing ice is like a hundred old ladies wailing at a funeral. Then one morning a strong wind comes, and the whole thing just breaks up, and you've got water!"

"I can't imagine a hundred old ladies wailing at a funeral."

"If somebody I loved died, that's the sound I'd make at their grave. I'd cry. Do you ever cry?"

"No."

"Why not?"

"I cried everything out a long time ago."

"What made you cry?"

"My mother died when I was very young."

"I'm sorry. Do you think you'll cry when I die tomorrow?"

"I don't think so. I don't know you."

"You know me!" he said amazed. "I've told you the really important things about me."

"What happened to your paintings?" she prompted.

"They got lost when I capsized in the rapids going out the following spring."

37

"How awful", she said. "That's so unfair."

"I really was sad about losing those paintings. But it's okay. I keep them here inside me."

She was about to blurt a counterargument, to state categorically that upon his death even the memory of the images would be snuffed out of existence. But she caught herself in time.

He smiled at her. It was a very winning smile, and she felt her heart contract.

"You're really beautiful", he said.

"I don't think so."

"You don't?" He stared at her as if someone had convinced her of a devastating lie. "If I weren't going to die tomorrow, I'd love you forever."

At which point she understood that a line had been crossed over and recalled the sergeant's warning.

"I expect", she said coolly, and not unkindly, "that you would feel a certain affection for any nurse who held your hand tonight."

"No", he shook his head. "That's not true."

"It's true."

"You've got sadness inside you."

She shook her head.

"An old sadness", he corrected.

"I have to go now. The other patients."

"Stay with me."

"I can't." She shook off his fingers and stood nervously.

"You'll come back, won't you? I have to tell you something."

"I'll try to see you later."

When she returned to his cot an hour later he was sleeping. She watched his strangely intoxicating face for some time and then, because her shift was over, she left.

When she returned for the afternoon shift she found him still sleeping. His eyelids twitched and his mouth hung open.

"*What a piece of work is man!*" she said aloud, unnerved by the power of mere words to unlock an intolerable emotion, "*how noble in reason! how infinite in faculty! in form and moving how express and admirable! in action how like an angel! in apprehension how like a god! the beauty of the world! the paragon of animals! and yet, to me, what is this quintessence of dust?*"

Then he woke up.

"Hello, Anne", he said.

"I came to say goodbye", she replied formally, "and to thank you for your interesting stories. I hope you recover. The lorries may soon be here to take you to Calais. Possibly tomorrow."

"Then how will we ever see each other again?"

"I don't think we will."

She reached out and took his hand, shook it, then dropped it. It fell limp onto his lap.

"Do you know", he said carefully, "that I have never kissed a girl?"

"That is unfortunate", she said, businesslike. "You must get well, then, and correct that omission."

"I don't think I'll ever get to kiss a girl. I know it."

"Nonsense. Modern medicine can do wonders these days. You will . . ."

"I want you to kiss me."

She stared at him. The emotions that now coursed through her veins competed with every mental defense accessible to a young woman in her position. Shock, pity, attraction, the social inappropriateness of the proposal, the pathetic dignity of his plea—it all swirled and drowned like works of art lost in a rapids.

She knelt beside the cot and held his face in her hands, very gently, so as not to disturb his wounds. Then she touched her lips to his and bestowed a delicate kiss.

He closed his eyes.

"That was the sweetest kiss in the entire history of the human race", he said. He did not see her face convulse or her flight from the tent.

When she approached the tent of no-hopers the following morning, she had repaired her decorum and prepared a mouthful of discreet recriminations. Even so, she knew that she would sail with him beyond the sunset and the baths, until the Southern Cross rose over the rim of the earth. Eventually they would go together to the savage lands and listen to the siren songs of the ice.

When she saw the empty cot, she said, "Where is Peter?"

"That Canadian you had a crush on?" said the sergeant frowning. "He's gone."

"He's gone?"

"Well, yes. One way or another. The worst cases were taken to Calais before dawn. But some died in the night. I'm pretty sure he was one of them."

"Is there any way to check?"

"No. All the records went with them, living and dead."

"I see."

"Don't worry, dearie. You'll get over it."

PART ONE

The Sojourners

Autumn 1922

I

"Is it safe?" she asked the conductor.

"Nothing in life is safe, Miss."

They were crossing a bottomless canyon on a matchwood bridge.

His accent was thick French Canadian, his name, M. Charon, embroidered in red thread on the blue breast of his uniform.

She was staring at him, and he was staring back—not very nice manners for a public employee, although it must be admitted that his eyes were sympathetic. Those eyes had observed everything there was to observe in life, by the looks of them, and they seemed to find her only a variation of a question he had answered a thousand times. He would have lumbered along the aisle then, but something in her face arrested him. She glanced nervously out the window.

"I mean, it's a long way down."

"*Oui*, it is. But those trestles are as strong as steel, only seven years old, and built by the best engineers in the Dominion."

She looked quickly away from the abyss.

"How far are we from Swiftcreek?"

"Not long. An hour or so." He was curious now and sat beside her. "May I ask, Miss, what you'd be going to such a bushwhacking place for?"

"I am the teacher. Or mean to be. The government is opening a school."

"*Tiens!*" he nodded, his mouth dubious, even amused. He

wondered how long she would last and decided that within the month he would be seeing her again, when she handed him her one-way ticket out.

"What is it like there?"

"Swiftcreek? Wild. Not a place for a lady. One muddy street of boxcar houses along the rail and a few cabins out in the bush. I suppose you could call it a town. Maybe a hundred people now. Mostly the section crew that keeps up the tracks and some homesteading folk. There's a trapper or two down the Canoe Valley."

It had been described in more encouraging terms in the letter from the Ministry of Education: *a rapidly developing rural community with most of the amenities of a larger. . . .*

"There's a store and a sort of church."

"A church?"

"A parson comes down from McBride and has a meeting."

"You seem to know the place rather well, sir."

"Yes, indeed. We're held over there sometimes if there's a slide or derailment down the line. Ah, then we have to go to Mother Gunderberg's Rooming House." He made big eyes and grinned.

"Would that be Mrs. Turid Gunderberg?" she asked, becoming mildly alarmed.

"There's no other, Miss. Why?"

"I have a letter of introduction to her. I shall be boarding at her establishment."

He pursed his lips at this information and gave her a week at the most. With that he rose, tipped his hat, and passed along the aisle.

She glanced out the window at the enormous land, its mountains and shroud of forest dwarfing the train.

"I am Anne Kingsley Ashton", she whispered, "of Friars, Blackswan Lane, Bishopsford, Great Britain! And I shall not be swallowed!"

44

Behind the glass, a cold sky was spilling its stains over the teeth of the peaks, while the earth, unconscious of what was to be performed upon it, lay silently beneath. Would her personal armament of diction, poetry, and Greek mythology be enough to subdue it, she wondered.

She consulted her watch again, primly, apparently a woman of experience and education, convinced of the power that positive action maintained over the emotional things.

I shall write, she decided, and propped a silk-bound notebook on her knee. Then, manipulating a fat maroon fountain pen, she wrote:

Approaching Swiftcreek, British Columbia,
20 September 1922.

Rain falling beyond the glass of my carriage. The peaks are white. There are unidentifiable birds fighting in the air. Two small birds chase off a large one.

What shall I become that I have not already become? Do we create ourselves, or are we created?

This is the land that Peter loved. What was his family name? I shall probably never know. How shall I find the place where he lived? This province is as large as a nation, and practically empty. Leave it, Anne. Let it go! The war is over and a new world begins.

But where are the children who would have been? And where will I find my own lost children? Are they to be found, then, in these little ones bred for toil, to clear the forest, to question nothing? Of what use can I be to them? I, the foolish virgin, shall I disintegrate before their eyes? If the conductor is a portent, then this is merely a long ride across the River Styx.

It is utter foolishness coming here! What have I done? What have I done!

She stared at the green ink, then at the rust velvet cuff at her wrist and the lavender handkerchief tucked into it. She looked out the window again. The sun already appeared to have imploded in cloud above the forested waste—a war-zone sky, a bombed vault, the ruined dome of a cathedral. She controlled an ache rising in her throat. Her hair glinted copper under wooden holly berries that bobbed on a ridiculous hat. She closed the diary firmly, a literate woman on a foredoomed adventure in a land where she did not belong. But there appeared to be veins of steel among the softer metal of her hair, and she opened a book, this time to pages where chips of dry violets were pressed. Lord Tennyson's sensitive brow glowed in an engraving.

She pronounced the publisher's data with precision and deliberation, exercising her faith in the scope of civilization: "London, Oxford, Glasgow, New York, Melbourne, Bombay."

Civilization. Places that actually existed, geographies of the soul that were fading into mist as she stared through the glass of the carriage.

The book was nine years old, a gift from Papa. If only she had listened to him, that distracted man, her father. She had dragged him from his medical journals to explain that she was leaving.

"Why do you want to go there, of all places, Anna?" he said with evasive eyes.

"Because it is empty."

"Because it is empty! Good God, girl, what do you mean?"

Her face had become blank then, concentrating on an unexplored territory of her own, where solitude was a climate, not merely passing weather. She stood listening to this silent interior, much the same as a person in an empty house might strain for the sound of a clock ticking in a distant room.

"I don't really know what I mean, Papa", she breathed at last, still attentive to some mystery that her eyes had turned inward upon. "I know only that it is real."

He looked at her and sighed, "If only your mother were still alive!"

Dear Papa. He was a doting father, when he was there. His

frustration would never express itself beyond such grieved exhalations or a glass of port tossed hastily down his throat. Or a crumpled look. His wife, before her death, had always been able to tie the man in gentle little knots. Love nots and will nots. And his younger daughter had inherited the talent. Among their many avocations his daughters were active campaigners for the emancipation of women. *Suffer-jettes*, he called them, poking fun at their rhetoric over pudding and pie. But the women loved him much too dearly to rise to the bait and coddled this old, blind, dancing bear out of any reactionary tendencies.

It was his habit to shake his head frequently at their antics, to disclaim publicly at the club, though secretly he considered them part of his charm.

"My dear, dear, rebellious women", he would explain, pause, sigh, "have minds of their own!"

Though they were not the kind who chained themselves to the gates of Parliament, for which he was grateful, or who threw themselves beneath the wheels of the King's carriage. But they had participated in a march and had been known to carry signs. It was a new age, after all. A devastating war was finished, and a hundred thousand miles of rail now crisscrossed the empire. How could he think to hold her? For all his prestige at the Royal College of Surgeons, he was helpless before this girl, who was operating on him, it seemed, with her instruments. So his permission was a foregone conclusion, though she would not have departed without the actual words of his blessing.

"Sometimes I feel as if I have lived my life behind glass", she informed him on the quay. And squeezed his arm the tighter for fear she had offered an insult, or at least a defection from the kingdom he had so carefully bestowed.

The sea lanes were peaceful—the U-boats all sunk or returned to port. It had been a long, uneventful voyage across the Atlantic. Then a journey through the ocean of wheat that heaved from horizon to horizon without relief, wider than continental Europe itself. Eventually, she had arrived in Vancouver, where she was permitted to rest for a few days until fully recovered. There was a pleasant meeting with the superintendent of schools, then departure the following day for the northern Interior.

Thus, the object of her long waiting was approaching. The track hugged the flanks of a mountain chain that dwindled northeast into infinity. Into this vast emptiness she was now being plunged. The valley opened up as they emerged from the steep cleft of the pass, the engine turned in a wide arc and went down the last gentle grade toward the village.

Her heart beat wildly, and her breath came in shallow gasps. For as they passed the first few outcroppings of tents, the entire panorama of her situation was instantly laid bare, and she saw her error: she was too small for this land.

There was a moment of added fright when she saw shadows moving against the sky. She shook her head and refocused—it must have been vapors formed by the fog at the edge of a clearing. They rose up and swirled and reshaped themselves into a giant panther or a bear or a dragon—she could not say which. She rubbed her eyes. It was still there, hideous, immense, staring at her. Astounded, she pressed her face to the window. She was paralyzed and could not cry out to the other passengers, who were gazing ahead toward the cabin roofs now appearing through the trees. Time was suspended for her as she looked into the eyes of the beast. It stood motionless, with one forepaw lifted in mid-stride, claws exposed. Its eyes were cold with malice, surprised by the unexpected presence of the woman.

She was terrorized most of all by the fragility of her mind. Dementia had haunted her family for generations, though she had held it at bay until now. She tore her eyes from the image, or perhaps ordinary time asserted itself, and the noise rushing back into the world propelled her away from the hallucination.

The train steamed and screeched to a stop before a ragged

muster of shanties. There were bodies and faces gliding past the window—completely uncivilized. It was not in the least as the superintendent had described it.

She decided to remain on the train and proceed to the most eastern port of the nation. Then, home. She would disembark here only for a few minutes, for a breath of fresh air. She stumbled toward the doorway and looked out. The town was as the conductor had described, cut from a wall of forest that steamed in the drizzle. There were bearded men in a variety of eager or laconic states receiving cases and sacks from the door of the baggage car. Her own trunk was being lowered and set on a tussock of grass that rose above the general tyranny of mud. She was about to tell them to put it back into the baggage car when she stepped from the carriage and sank her Spanish boots calf-deep into gumbo and had to be dragged out at an angle by her friend, M. Charon.

"There, you're safe enough now!" he said with a wink. He lifted her as he might have done a piece of light freight and placed her on top of the trunk.

She was stammering her predicament at him, but he wasn't listening; he winked at her and yelled something at the telegraph operator. There was too much shouting going on—no one could hear a thing—and then it all happened too fast for her to think. The conductor blew his whistle, and the train drew away in hisses of steam as she cried her protests, unheard.

So I am here, she thought to herself, stricken by the reality of it, picking flecks of mud from her moleskin gloves and beating off swarms of mosquitoes. The whole situation was a ridiculous mistake. She was wondering when the next train was due to arrive when she suddenly noticed that an assortment of calico children had gathered around her pedestal.

"Hello", she greeted them. Their mouths closed en masse, though they continued to ravish her with their eyes as they might a creation of porcelain flowers.

There was a decided absence of other women on the siding, though a hefty creature in pants was lumbering over.

"You the teacher?" it growled in an approximately female voice, a big yellow grin tossed in for measure.

Anne Kingsley Ashton nodded.

"I'm Gunderberg!"

They shook hands, then, the two emancipated women.

"Let's get this bugger stowed", said the concierge, grabbing one handle of the trunk and gesturing that Anne Ashton should take the other. Together they staggered down the street to the "hotel".

Her room was, thankfully, a private affair, stuck onto the upper floor at the back of the two-story frame lodging house. Like the rest of the building, it appeared to have been thrown together hastily and with a minimum of art. But compared to the rest of the buildings in the settlement, it was a quality establishment, with a lid on the chamber pot and an ancient brass bed that squealed. A window admitted a patch of darkness through which men's voices drifted from the wet-sounding streets. There was an outburst of fiddle to accompany the smack of balls in a shed next door. The woman's shelter remained inured to the influences of the pool hall, the community's one establishment for cultural exchange. Noise was determined to enter, though, as was a little wind that blew through the cracks in the plank wall. If it could permit wind to enter, then it could also allow imagery to escape, the woman concluded, and carefully extinguished a paraffin lamp before disrobing.

She noted a pine board table upon which the lamp stood before night engulfed it. She would write at this desk, when the world ceased to spin. She was composing already as her body sank with relief into the mattress, as if her flesh were an animal and she, the master, had ridden. As if fragments of her body had been broken and laid into earth, and the rider, upon wings of sleep, were gathered into a chaos of dark cloud.

She was always to remember this first night. There was a haunting cry from the woods, an unidentified night bird. It burned an image of loneliness, rather than solitude, upon her mind. Or an anguish of separation.

* * *

Violence bashed open her door, or butted in the gray light of dawn. She sprang upright in bed, unable to see the intruder who had paused before entering. Never in her life had she been awakened in this manner, her sphere of intimacy so rudely penetrated. She could not for a moment believe in rape, though lesser social indiscretions might be in the offing.

A white, horned being entered, naaaahing and clattering its hoofs across the planks of the floor. A spray of black pellets went pattering out behind. The beast glanced around the room with intelligent, sardonic eyes, spied her wicker portmanteau, and began to peel and crunch.

"Mrs. Gunderberg!" she yelled.

There was a loud rumbling from regions below and stomping on the staircase. A second apparition in white entered. Mrs. Gunderberg, in seasoned long-johns and gum-boots, was now obviously female in a tired looking way, slats of iron hair whipping across her face.

"This is damn Lottie", explained the concierge, pulling the goat back from luggage and red berries.

"I was out in the back-house doin' the usual, and I guess she just damn well got tired o' waitin' to get milked."

"Oh", said the younger woman. Distended pink bags continued to swing obscenely through her mind.

"Well, c'mon you old bucket o' guts", said Mrs. Gunderberg, dragging the grinning beast backward down the stairs. She neglected to close the door behind her, leaving Anne Ashton sitting up in bed, exposed, as a sound of crackling wood fire and

51

radiant warmth crept through the house. There was also a glimpse of men stretching themselves and scratching pectorals as they clomped down to grub.

"So I am here", she said quietly, and tiptoed to the door, shutting it with no sound.

Breakfast in the dining room took place on a long, plank table buttressed by sawhorses. It was an affair of backbacon, pancakes and corn-syrup, and a tea strong enough to tan hides. Despite the addition of goat's milk, woody and alien, the hot beverage became familiar. She rearranged the cutlery in the proper manner around her plate, domesticating the situation, taming it with polite conversation. She introduced herself to the half-dozen shy and carnal men, hunched over their stacks of sweet cakes as if life depended on it.

They were not much interested in conversation, though one or two offered their names with fleeting smiles and one even passed the syrup without being asked, a heroic dash, on his part, into the realm of chivalry. It was a little like breakfast with the seven dwarves, she mused, remembering a childhood that Papa had made magic.

Full of sugar, grease, and dough, she found herself, all in all, rather cheered and capable of attempting her adventure, at least for a day. Possibly a week. A month at the most—sufficient time for the Ministry to engage a permanent teacher.

The children, a score of them, met her at the door of the shed that was to be their schoolroom. They ranged in ages from five to fourteen and appeared to be mute, though if eyes could suck meanings from cloth and eggshell skin, she would have found herself tattered and finally devoured by their curiosity. She quickly took charge and herded them in.

She arranged them by size and age at the tables. There was a desk and a captain's chair for herself, facing them. A sheet of canvas, which someone had painted with stove-black, had been nailed to the wall above her desk, for use as a chalkboard. Her trunk and its manifest of books had been deposited by the door. The room was complete. She breathed deeply, folding her hands.

Now, the moment of mystery. Of meeting between old world and new, of adult and child, of soul and soul. Can we achieve this, you and I?

No! said the rows of masks.

"Let's get to know each other, children", she said with a forced smile. "How many of you have been to school before?"

Three of the older ones raised their hands.

"I see. And how many of you can read?"

Two raised their hands.

"Add? Multiply? Subtract?"

"I know my sums to a hunnerd", said a thin, dark-eyed boy.

"What is your name?"

"Maurice."

"Maurice. A very fine name. And what is your last name?"

He squirmed.

"L'Oraison", he whispered.

"I beg your pardon?"

"A raisin", squealed several little girls in unison, giggling. Maurice went red.

"Raisin", she repeated carefully. "An unusual but distinctive name." And looked perplexed when the entire class collapsed in laughter.

In order to distract, she unfolded a large map of Canada printed on oilcloth and commissioned two big boys to tack it to the side wall.

"Children, do any of you know the name of the country in which we live?"

Fourteen eyes looked down.

"Canda?" ventured Maurice.

"Excellent! Now can anyone tell us where our town is located?"

None of the children could show her precisely where Swiftcreek was. Only one could narrow it down to the left side of the map. Maurice again.

"It's in Beecy somewheres", he added as a fine point.

"Well, Swiftcreek is not actually on this map", she admitted after a closer look. "But one day it will be."

She pointed: "We're here, in the central interior of the Rocky Mountains, in a narrow valley where several ranges converge—the Rockies themselves, the Thompsons, the Monashees, and the Cariboos. Four valleys open out from this central one. It's where we live. It's our home."

At the utterance of the word *home* she felt her voice falter and gazed suddenly into an interior range. She felt a wave of something that could only be called a pressure of *destiny*. She stared at it with fear and realized that she would not, in fact, be departing on the next train. She was about to excuse herself from the class, to go outside for a cry, when light interrupted the course of events.

A shaft of sun broke through the overcast and illuminated the room. The unwashed windows glowed, and rows of faces were tinted honey, or crocus, or apricot, depending on how summer-brown each had been. They were unaware that they had bathed in the magic of a prism. They were suddenly beautiful to her. Their eyes and their minds appeared to be empty, to be locked in some pitiful form of ignorance that wrung her heart. They were hungry and she could feed them. But they did not know they were hungry. The stove crackled with the fire she had lit to drive the chill from the morning. The sun passed on, and the children were bleached into gray.

Throughout the day she began to assess and recognize the personality that escaped from the cracks in their faces. The ones whose eyes fled, the ones who stared brassily. The moderate, the suppressed, and the free. Those who were cherished, and those who were not. It was fairly obvious, though, that clothing, finally, meant nothing, as a starched shirt and waxed boots could disguise as many injuries as disintegrating wool could dress secret joys. She melted and flowed toward them, though for safety's sake, for the benefit of order, she would not permit it to be seen. A cheerful authority, a professional firmness—these were what she allowed to prevail. Not one of them guessed how unsure she was. Carefully, as the morning progressed, she learned their names and did not forget. She looked briefly into each one's eyes with her curious mixture of translucency and a mask of self-possession. Some of the children were discomforted and some delighted. She used their names respectfully and handled well the inevitable rebellions staged by the older, goatish young males. Goats in a bedroom and a big grizzled proprietress hacked from a side of pork were a different matter. But these children flushed like birds out of the forest were to become her passion. She took them delicately, then, into her hands.

When the silence was at last broken in the dust of the yard at recess, *red rover, red rover, we call teacher over,* she ran with relief and laughter spilling from her lips to break the chain of their arms and was gathered into them. By noon she was twirling some of them around and around, little ones screeching as their heels took flight in the dizzy air. The girls whirled like a ballet of dandelion seed. Large boys, bony and given to arranging their bodies impressively, took her hand for crack-the-whip, finding it warm as cream and strong enough to send them tumbling. The hands of the china lady gathered respect as easily as they might harvest flowers.

Little girls brought her votive offerings, crushed winey handfuls of cranberry or bouquets of yellow birch leaves, delivering them with winning smiles, though she was already won. Conquered most of all by the middling-sized boy, the Raisin, who approached with eyes locked on his bare feet, face screwed up in abashment. He summarily, with enormous effort of the spirit, whipped from his pocket a prized possession, the toothy skull of a rodent, placed it on her desk, and ran.

"Children", she called after them as they scattered into the wind at the end of the day.

"Children, we shall have much to learn, you and I." Though it was doubtful that any of them heard.

2

Swiftcreek, British Columbia,
7 April 1923.

My dearest Emily,

It is unfathomable to me that I have been here almost a year. Time is truly an illusion of the mind.

Your latest letter reached me only one month after posting. How precious your words are to me, my faithful sister, and how bright the pictures you paint of the theatre, of music, and of your formidable Mr. Eliot. His poetry is, without a doubt, the apocalyptic kind and left me quaking. How I devour your letters. What light and affection they bring into my rather solitary world. (I do not mean to complain about a life I have chosen but would ever like to continue that frankness which has existed between us since childhood.)

Papa has doubtless shared with you the bits of news. I clip them from my days like newspaper items, as they adequately express to him the state of my life and he is reassured. It is to you, Emily, that I must fly with a woman's deeper need to "bare the soul". This loneliness will make a prattler of me yet, it becomes so insufferable at times. Dare I write the word, *loneliness*, when I am so well loved?

Of course, the children occupy me fully and are my greatest joy. But there is also an interesting minor character, a Mister Gunnalls, the visiting preacher, the only ambassador of organized religion whom I have met so far. He is virtuous and manly, and I have begun to discuss with him the more easily navigated shoals of laymen's theology. I have not yet revealed that I am a freethinker. So far it is all quite polite and abstract: I am the one who must approach him after meetings to solicit his paternal smile. 'How are we this evening, Miss Ashton?' he invariably begins, using a public voice that carries to the ends of rooms. I am always tempted to reply, 'To which of my multiple personalities are you referring, Reverend Gunnalls?' But he is really too simple for this kind of social sport. I don't believe he has even heard of Doctor Freud. But he is civilised in a North American fashion. The local wives are conspiring a match. Poor souls, they cannot begin to guess how far I am from his view of things.

I must congratulate you on your membership in the Party. It is not what I would ever choose for myself, but in honour of your daring I shall wear a red kerchief on the first of May. I am happy for you. Is it true what I read between the lines? Are the intoxications of ideology heightened to a pitch by the passionate conviction of your comrades? Is it friendship or love, this thing you have found? You called it 'nourishment'. But deep within me there is a note of caution. I mistrust crowds, Emily, even if they are crowds of brilliant young academics.

Yet, I am malnourished. I am hungry for thought and the exchange of insight, not for the attentions of a man or the thrill of a political cause—though I know you will hasten to assure me that thought, insight, and even the attentions of male revolutionaries are to be had in abundance in your present company. Is it love I seek, or truth? There is no one here who can tell me what I am, none who could begin to understand the various lacks in my womanhood. There is Mrs. Gunderberg, of course, who is a dear and would like to be intimate. When I read her some of Eliot's poems recently, she blew tobacco smoke in my face and said, 'That poor bugger needs t'fall in love.' Can you imagine!

But Mrs. Gunderberg is my society. She saves me the special cuts of meat at dinner, and we share a private daily tea together in her kitchen. 'Annie, girl,' she repeatedly advises, 'what you need is a good solid fellow to take care of you.' She suspects me, rightly, of little mad thoughts of independence and other such tragic impulses. She is a woman who believes that the functions of the glands are more abiding than the faculties of reason. Do I sound mocking? Believe me, Emily, I am not. I am perhaps experiencing a touch of that isolation sickness known locally as 'getting bushed'.

Thank you, incidentally, for forwarding our old copies of the sisters Brontë and Jane Austen. Wherever did you find them? It was with pure delight that I opened the fly leaf and read the familiar lines of Father's handwriting: *To my darling Anne on your birthday, 1910.*

I believe I must hastily change the subject if I am to avoid tears, and as I shall be going down to dinner within the hour, it is best not to do so with swollen eyes. It will be all over the village that I have been jilted by the good Mr. Gunnalls.

My dearest sister, I must tell you of a recent experience that is profoundly disturbing. The events in question are brief and in most aspects quite undramatic. Despite this, they have loomed larger than is called for, and their memory has come to dominate my thoughts.

One balmy Saturday afternoon, when the last of the snow had disappeared, I endeavoured to take a walk into some region beyond the settlement where I had not yet explored. There were many of these, naturally, as life for a teacher here is compacted into a few lanes and a schoolroom.

West of the village is a tract of swamp and grassland that sweeps north toward the Fraser River. I am told that the Indian tribe that used to live here had made a practice of burning off this area to provide pasture for their horses. There is no evidence of this people's presence now, and a young pine forest is beginning to encroach, but it remains a wide, flat place, perfect for grazing.

I was walking across it, quite happily, the breeze strongly scented by the conifers and accented by grasshoppers clicking in the hot sun. Though only a week previously a late snow had fallen, spring was now in full revelry, and I felt rejuvenated, even elated. As I passed through a delicate copse of birch, I encountered a small group of horses on the other side. They were clustered in a semicircle around a man. He was feeding them salt and was unconscious of my presence, for I was in my tawny-coloured dress and had been stepping through the trees noiselessly with an eye open for thrushes' nests and kildeer. The man was looking into the horses' eyes, making animal noises himself, nickering, whinnying, and blowing air through his lips. The horses were reciprocating, and I can only say that between them all there was a most intense and tender communication.

Frankly, I was fascinated. It was spellbinding, beautiful, and stole my breath away. I wondered who he was, this man, not much older than myself. He was dressed in the caulk boots and baggy wool pants that most of the local men wear, but his shirt was a hand-sewn arrangement of deerhide, crude and sturdy. I suppose I must have breathed then or made some small noise, because suddenly he knew I was there. His eyes flicked in his face and were upon me, though nothing about his movements changed, his head and shoulders had not stirred. But he was watching me, staring boldly, though I must say there was nothing cheeky about it. He was merely looking. As if I were a creature of the woods whom he felt free to examine with unflinching curiosity. But his glance was guarded, too. I could not enter into his eyes in the way he seemed to be examining what lay within mine.

I was about to speak, to shatter this interlocking of strangers. I confess it was making me uncomfortable, and I wished to establish some order. As I opened my mouth to speak, he was gone. Gone, Emily! At that very instant he turned and stalked off across the plain as if I did not exist. Then, a few hundred yards away he broke into a trot, his animals galloping along beside him as if he were one of them. Then I heard a piercing whistle, and they were lost in the trees.

Emily, I believe I have seen a Centaur! You will think me a fool, won't you? Or worse, a silly, romantic fool. Do you remember the pact we made when I was sixteen, that summer at The Oaks? We vowed that we would never, upon pain of death, allow our heads to be turned by the charms of men. That we would ever strive for the rational, the noble, the true? And that if we were to marry, the man in question must be above all a person of the mind, or, at least, the spirit. I held nothing back then. I believed and still believe in our ideal: woman must become free of her condemned state. She can no longer be a slave or an eternal mother or a mere repository of animal passions.

The man who galloped off appeared to be far from scholarly. Yet, Emily, I wonder about him. The look that penetrated me that afternoon was not animal. Neither was it one of those tiresome attempts at charm by which most men try to control the situation. Nor was it, on the other hand, a boyish clinging. It was something entirely new, and I am not so sure that I shall easily recover.

Ever yours,
Anne

* * *

She saw him moving along the lanes of the village from time to time. Once, from the windows of the school shed she observed him load bales of fur onto a boxcar pulled up by the station. *Winnipeg* had been inked onto the tan wrappers of the bales. The scene transfixed her halfway through a description of King Arthur's Britain. The children clamored for her to continue, and she flushed deeply. She would not have been surprised if the man had suddenly drawn a suit of burnished iron over his body, mounted, and ridden off into the forest with sword in hand in search of dragon or some other dark beast. His face was too noble for his shabby clothes. The scene burned in her mind.

There was also an incident at the lodging house, where she stood beside the garrulous Mrs. Gunderberg, watching with her a retreating thunderstorm that had swamped tempestuously through the village, leaving the street full of ripped evergreen fronds and cedar shakes.

"Lord, that was a basher", said the older woman, chafing her arms in the aftercool, protected by a rat-hole sweater.

The sun fractured the clouds then, and the two women stepped out onto the porch to breathe the pure scent that lightning had torn from the air. At that moment the teacher breathed more deeply, for a horse had stopped a way up the street, and she recognized the rider. He slid from the saddle in front of the general store. Water ran from him. Wet black strings of hair hung from the horse's neck and rump. It steamed. The man himself appeared slippery in clothes that rain had plastered to his skin. He moved slowly as he mounted the steps of the post. It was the Centaur.

She wished at that moment to ask for his name but was silent, not trusting her companion. It was too obvious. And when the man entered, the other woman turned a pouchy, experienced eye on the girl and said:

"Handsome feller, in't he?" and watched the reaction.

Anne Ashton smiled a casual smile. A detached teacher's smile.

"Yes, rather", she replied, in much the same way she might remark on the plumage of a thrush. But Turid Gunderberg, an avowed expert in the entanglements of both halves of the species, was not deceived.

"His name's Steve", she said, her lips twitching, her eyes cavorting in delight.

"Oh", replied the velvet woman, touching her hands to the splinters of cedar planks. *Stephen.*

"Yep, and every damn unattached gal from here to Tee-John has done her best t'get his attention."

"Oh?" She turned and looked at her informant, the suddenly indispensable Mrs. Gunderberg.

"Well, no go! He's a solitary. A bush nut. Been ten years down the Canoe all by his lonesome and likes it that way. He's a Mick. Came here when he was almost a kid. Before the train or settlers or anybody."

"Surely he is attached?" she said without emotion.

"Yep. Very attached. To his horses and dawg. But let me warn you, young gal, you just think the word *luv* or *weddin'* on the same street with that man, and he'll be high-tailin' it for the bush. He's sharp. He's clever!"

"I assure you, Mrs. Gunderberg . . ." she sputtered, but Turid had become immersed behind walls of laughter, having seen and heard it all before.

* * *

She emerged refreshed from a summer vacationing on the Queen Charlotte Islands, where totem villages bent ponderously over the waves and spirits thronged. She drew their terror in a precise pastoral manner, bleeding power from them with the watercolors that Emily had sent. Her cheeks glowed red on the cream of skin, health and a jaunty objectivity restored on the decks of excursion boats, which were filled, mostly, with other teachers. For them, shuffleboard and quoits had quickened pulses, and a wake carved in the liquid jade of the straits had stirred up dreams. But solitude had been her travelling companion. She made shallow acquaintances and missed her children. She thought about them constantly. Occasionally she was reminded of elements of the irrational within herself, when the beast in the forest broke into her consciousness, or when the image of the Centaur constricted her heart for a moment—yes, for a very brief moment. In Victoria she was relieved to find sanctuary within the palmy depths of the Empress Hotel, where Darjeeling tea could easily subdue the heat of a stallion's eye or stamping haunch; damask and silver discreetly banish hallucinations of malice.

She slept in the sun on deck chairs, lulled by the surf or roused by the seagull cries of the children of the wealthy. They destroyed each other's sand castles with abandon, she noted, tossing victory shouts and taunts in a variety of accents, mostly dipped in British. She stared out to the horizon where white liners disappeared into the matte finish of the sky. She wondered if Peter would have wanted to paint that sky, if he had lived. Had he ever walked along this beach? Did he ever stride down to the water's edge and hurl himself, brave and male, into the tide? Then she remembered that he had not seen the sea until he crossed the Atlantic in a troop ship. She admonished herself that it was a distinctly pathological habit to cling to the memory of a dead man she had not really known. To think of it as love was an absurdity. It was fantasy and an unhealthy one at that! She must cease nursing, and feeding, that wound.

Her fingers would sometimes find themselves inserted numbly between pages, when she almost slipped down into fissures opened in her mind by particularly pompous ideas in Wells' *Outline of History*. The man was rewriting history, and she did not like it. Yet, as she looked around the beach, her head spun and she was no longer sure of anything. Had simply everyone rewritten history to suit his prejudices? Was most of it, perhaps all of it, a myth? If so, what was real?

"What shall I teach them about their past?" she asked the screaming gulls. "Which version is the true one? Upon this question hangs their understanding of their own lives, and their future."

Without answers, her thoughts dissolved, and she drifted

back to memories of faces like apples, their hair powdered by the dust of henhouses and serum draining from their nostrils. She longed for the certainty, the purpose, their eyes had given to her life. There was something consoling in the vision of bare feet trampling the dirt and limbs reaching into the light with shouts of joy and defeat. Games. Children's games. As if all history were not revealed within their rules.

She dropped from the steps of the train on a hot evening in late August. Engine bells rang through the drugged town, ravens caronked, and the humans appeared to have departed. There was only a slow-moving ticket agent slamming wickets for the night.

Home. Strange to think of it as such. It seemed that Turid had done things in her absence. There was a geranium in the downstairs window. There were flowered curtains. As she entered the hallway there was a busty embrace and an exclamation salted with tears:

"By gum, chickee, it's good t'have a woman round here again. Drives me crazy sloppin' hash t'this pen full o' steers, month in, month out, never say a word!"

Though Anne Ashton knew that a steer might flee behind a wall of silence, in self-defense, and a house full of cattle was kept more easily corralled than a stallion.

She shook her mind free of this thought.

"Lottie is dead", Turid informed.

"Oh . . ." replied Anne, unmoved.

"Got hit by the way-freight in July. There was blood and milk all over the tracks, took an engineer with a fire-axe t'finish her off, there was such a terrible bawlin' from the poor critter!"

The girl from Blackswan Lane flinched.

"There's some that takes t'drink from loneliness", said Turid, talking to the fire where a kidney spat and tea boiled itself into acid. Anne sat by the table. She undid her ribboned straw hat and placed it on her lap, hands cupped to receive.

"These fellas that live here, the navvies and mill-hands, they're tough. But there's a tender streak under the hides o' some." Accents rolled from her tongue, grease anointed the ritual slaughter on the stove, and more details of the woman's summer surfaced like lumps in the gravy. The one-way chatter went on and on, and, between listening or eating the sacrificial kidney on a slab of bread, the younger woman was unable to speak. Which was unwanted and unnecessary anyway. Her ears rang, her eyes bulged from forced attentiveness, her neck was sore from nodding. When Turid had thoroughly finished her narrative and the fire was down to ashes, Anne began to realize that she was indeed *home*. The word no longer made her wince.

But eventually the chrome orange sunset demanded attention. The mill-hands were back from the bar, banging up and down the staircase in heavy boots, joshing, slurring, needing snacks. There was a stack of mail to be opened. And fatigue beckoned. Anne made her excuses and got up from the table.

She kissed Turid on the cheek, murmured good night, and ascended with her luggage.

"We papered yer room!" yelled Turid after her. "Me an' the guys!"

Which they certainly had! Pages of *The Colonist* were glued to every last inch save the floor. She pretended with a little effort that the type was a garden of peridots and periwinkles, minute black and white flowers, not a swarm of births, deaths, demented utterances, and pleas for help. In that way the room became beautiful. Above all, it was sealed and modest at last.

She rebuked a desire to see the Centaur. She undressed wearily and slept.

* * *

That was the night of the dream. It erupted from no known sources within herself. She could not decipher it, though for the rest of her life it hovered like a wraith at the edge of consciousness.

Beside a stormy sea a boy of about fourteen years of age ran through the night. He was a comely child, with black hair streaming out behind him in the wind. He was lit by moonlight, and his breath came in agonized gasps. He stopped before a cave in barren hills that rose from the waters. He looked down upon the body of a man. The man was a giant of great nobility. A broken sword lay across his breast. The giant was dead. The boy's grief was as deep as the ocean, and his tears were the rain, filling the earth with inconsolable anguish.

The boy bent and took from the man's hand a small stone carved with symbols. These runes were unintelligible to her, though they were the embodiment of all meaning to the boy. He held the stone toward her, but she backed away, for it was bathed in the giant's blood. She would not touch it. The stone cracked and blood spurted out, covering the child's hand. She turned away from him and fled down the mountain to awake panting in her bed.

Trembling convulsed her whole body. The house was silent. She rose and parted the curtains to read the sky and found it strewn with dim stars. There were no lights in the village. Dawn was approaching but still distant.

Motionless in the dark, she stood shivering in her flannel nightgown, listening: senses alert, heart beating hard, a void gathering around her, broken only by the hushed utterances of the dying fire in the parlor below.

What was the dream's meaning? Did the desolation of these mountains generate such fantasies? Perhaps her loneliness was deepening as the years progressed and the edges of reality were blurring?

Why had she returned? Now, beginning her second year here, it struck her suddenly as futile that she should continue. What good was it accomplishing? Oh yes, there were the one or two children who looked hungrily at her. And there was Maurice, with his astonishing ability to transfigure words. Was he the child of her dreams? He bore no resemblance to him. Painfully sensitive, introverted, disliked by the others for reasons buried in the inscrutable politics of childhood. He was the child who had bestowed a gift of polished skull. What good, what good to raise his hopes, to multiply those differences that only served to alienate him further from the other children. His small dreams would be shattered eventually by this physical land. Muscle was needed here, not poetry. It would be better for her to flee before he became badly infected. Though it might be already too late.

> *The sun is a golden river,*
> *The sun is a golden birch,*
> *The moon is a silver river,*
> *The moon is a silver birch.*

He had said that last year, staring into space. Not great poetry, but a sign that the muse had begun to whisper within him. Large eyes drenched in sunlight, moonlight, leaves.

Who knows what shapes poets will take, she thought. *But I cannot bear to see him born only to have him die of starvation.*

Disturbed by her dream, finding it impossible to return to bed and too chilly in her room to do much of anything, she decided to go down to the ground floor to stoke the wood-burner. The doors she passed were ajar, left open to admit the heat rising up the staircase. Quiet breathing came from most rooms. She heard Turid's loud snore from behind a closed door, then from the same room a man's voice muttering. Anne stared at the door for several moments, then turned and went silently down. It was a long way, she decided, from Blackswan Lane.

She lit a kerosene lamp in the hallway, deafened by the loud scratch of the match, blinded by the sulphurous flare. But no one stirred. She would have gone into the parlor then but was arrested by a door left wide open off the hall. She stared. It was a room occupied by one of the mill-hands. He was a youth barely capable of growing a moustache or spelling his name, a bush child, perhaps a year or two older than her eldest students. By daylight he was not attractive—an ugly, sinister looking boy. His eyes were dull, and fingers on one hand were missing, the result of a mill accident. He was what Maurice would probably become, because that was all there was for him to become. But neither of them was the child of the dream.

The mill-hand was sleeping off drink. His mouth was open and the pillow stained dark around it. Black shadows played over him; golden lamp light spilled across the ridges of brow, cheekbones, shoulder, breast, hip. He was half naked, with the blankets tossed off in fretful sleep. His whole life was exposed. Pity and sadness coursed through her. He was, she saw, a child in a large, carved body, a sculpture soon to be worn or broken. She tried to tear her eyes from him but could not. She had no brothers, and the men she had known at college were clever talking forms inside of collars. Oh, she knew the biological details well enough. Her short-lived attempt at medical school and covert forays into the *Anatomies* in Papa's library had provided that part of her education, or at least the diagrams indicated the approximate difference. Her brief experimentation with nursing on a battlefield had introduced her to an abattoir of flesh that was only incidentally male.

But now, in the night, a magic lantern animated the design and infused the clay with fire. It was hot gold poured out at the moment of creation. His throat pulsed. He was Adam. A woman would soon be fashioned from his torn rib. On the rim of the planet a hand was creating the gash of red dawn, awakening this primeval man to his first word.

She stared for a long time and listened to the hammering of her heart. It was desire, she thought, but not a desire for flesh. It could not be lust, she argued, for the feeling was something that lay much deeper, at the core of being.

In the end she did not stoke the fire but turned, fearing that someone might see her, and went up to her room.

The ache would not relieve itself in sobs or in sleep. She wrote finally:

26 August 1923. Swiftcreek, British Columbia.

I am once again in the land of wind and stone. My friend is a great broken mother of a being, whom I must love. As for my-self—I am a small unbroken mother of a being who yearns for children who are not her own. Soon we shall be together again, the offspring of my spirit and I.

It is more clear now what I do not want—the tyranny of a man's love, the helplessness that beauty can sometimes inflict, the gown of passion-fire. I loved a stranger once, with chaste passion, and have paid the price ever since. Never again.

I am ashamed to admit I desire a tidy universe. I seek peace, no more, no less.

3

Rainbow-colored cocks ripped up the turf beside the main street. They crazed the air with their voices, calling pullets home beneath a sun that was determined to sink behind the bank of massing cloud.

The man and the woman strolled through this commotion, absorbed in presences and casual conversation. They understood that discretion would limit their walk to the main thoroughfare, for to seek more private routes would invite public speculation. It was a hazard of small places that if one started with a cut finger at the bottom of a street, the news would quickly reach the top end that one had suffered an amputation. The man and woman laughed together at the smallness of mind that surrounded them. Having both been raised in cities, they thought themselves above it and were amused. Nevertheless, despite their superiority, they did not venture into side streets or forest paths to the creek but kept a platonic course through the middle of the village. They were merely two professionals in conference.

"You can feel the snow", said the woman. "It will come to-night or tomorrow and stay."

It had been falling and melting for days now, and she had begun to find the tension unbearable.

"Yes", said the man. "Yes", he repeated thoughtfully. Though he would rather not have been talking of weather, which was altogether too detached. His temperament was not precisely passionate, but he was inclined to stroll casually down the path of intimacy.

"It's like death", she said coldly. "Annihilation!"

"Like death?" he said with an odd smile. He did not care to discuss treacherous subjects outside of a pulpit, a helm from which one could deliver carefully researched dissertations.

Annihilation, he repeated to himself. Good Lord, this woman was intelligent. And had a disconcerting habit of leading the conversation wherever she desired. Although she was very attractive.

"Death raises difficult questions, does it not?" she went on. "Why is it, for instance, that the victims of violence and disease are so often the innocent ones?"

She is a bit ponderous, mused the young man, who might have been having second thoughts. And he noticed suddenly that her face, though striking, was somewhat long, stretched no doubt by a weight of ideas. Her eyes also were too serious. She was not one to prattle about chintz and twill, it seemed, or to trill for the little occasions of life.

"Is it because the innocent are ignorant, perhaps?" he offered.

"Are you implying that with enough knowledge we can defeat evil?"

"Well, I . . ." he paused, uncertain if what he had been about to say was theologically astute.

"All I mean", he went on, "is that maybe if the innocent knew how to defend themselves a little better, they might cease to be victims."

She thought for some moments about this.

"So, knowledge is power, and power is survival, and does survival, I wonder, mean happiness?"

"Well, Anne—may I call you Anne?"

Though she refrained from immediate reply, he proceeded: "I think, Anne, that I can give you some speculations, beginning with Job and Milton . . ."

"Ah, yes, but it's from you yourself, you see, that I would prefer an answer. What does a living, breathing man have to say on the subject?"

"I suppose one must simply say that the lightning strikes where it may, and that the rain falls on the just and the unjust alike."

"But why?" she pressed, her brow knit.

"I really don't know. Maybe suffering asks questions of us. A test, an education. Or maybe we've been thrust into a war zone and we're dazed, shell-shocked. And there's too much happening too fast for anybody to stop and explain to us just precisely where we are."

He laughed nervously, not entirely satisfied with what might have been a good answer had he investigated further. He was an honest young man, willing to admit his lack of education in matters of pain. He desired to change the subject, an aversion to morbidity rising within him.

"Above all, we must remain positive", he said.

"Positive", she mused over this word. "So, then, you're an optimist."

"Well, yes, I suppose I am, and you'll have to forgive me if I simply refuse to apologize", he laughed.

"I think you're a very nice man, Reverend Gunnalls", she said cryptically.

"Thank you."

"I think you're a very nice kind of idealist, who wishes to abolish evil by rearranging the social situation, are you not?"

"I am. I believe that any intelligent modern person recognizes the need for something radical, something new that will break us out of our old habits. Most of the people I respect, the ideas being forged right now, are not produced by, how shall we call it, traditional Christianity."

"And you admire the new thinkers, am I correct?"

"Yes", he said defensively. "Yes, people who see a new age beginning . . . and whether or not they profess the particular myths to which I aspire, they at least are willing to fight for a new world and a new spiritual life for mankind."

She looked at him, intrigued.

"You're full of surprises, Mr. Gunnalls."

He smiled, flattered.

"But you see, I've had all that", she went on. "My own father is a devotee of that sort of thing. He's an intellectual, a very well-known surgeon, and an essayist for the literary journals. At present, however, he's most interested, most involved, in the occult. It began as a desire to communicate with the spirit of my departed mother. It grew from that."

"Did he ever make contact?"

"He communicated with something. When I was a child, I refused to take part in their séances. When I was older, I attended one. I was there and I heard it. It sounded like Mother, but it left me with what I can only describe as a horrid smell in the mind."

"Your primitive fears, no doubt. Now, Freud—"

"Primitive or not, the thing that communicated with us was intelligent . . . and deceptive. I suspect that it was evil."

Reverend Gunnalls looked bemused.

"Good and evil. Aren't they just the opposite sides of the same thing, like the dark face of the moon?"

"That's exactly what Father says", she replied, looking at him directly.

"I mean," he went on, "Nietzsche and Hegel and Jung have made an excellent case for—"

"I don't understand the languages of philosophy and psychology, Reverend Gunnalls, but I do recognize the smell of something corrupt. I'm not sure precisely what good and evil mean. But I do know that I'd rather not take instruction from whatever caused that smell."

"But your father has. And he's an intelligent man, is he not?"

"Intelligent? Oh, yes. He's truly a brilliant man." And the irony on her face threatened to break down into sarcasm.

"We all need a religion of some kind, don't we?" she continued. "And that's his religion presently. He began with a cult of the Mind, then Politics, and now this. He needs a higher cause, you see. There has to be something more than biology at work in the universe, more than just eating and getting eaten. I mean, if we're merely clever talking beasts, what's the point of it all?"

"Perhaps there is no point", he said.

"You do astound me!" she laughed outright. "First you assert that you are the professional agent of a *myth*; then you say there may be no point in anything. And you want me to believe you're an optimist!"

"All religions are the same, Anne, and each of them has its way of helping us adjust to an empty universe."

"But isn't it curious that some of those religions produce nations of beggars, and others produce nations of poets and thinkers?"

"This is a very odd conversation", he smiled. "I'm a bit astounded to hear the village atheist deliver a thinly disguised defense of Christian civilization."

"A perfect match for the village parson's defense of paganism! I hear a thinly disguised despair beneath your *optimism*."

"You are cruel."

"I don't have any time to waste, sir, as village atheists, like village idiots, live somewhat exposed to the cold winds of the cosmos."

Ponderous and intense, thought Reverend Gunnalls. *We shall not repeat this conversation.*

"What *is* your particular brand of religion, then, if you are right in saying everyone has one?"

"My religion?" she replied. "I don't really know what it is, except to say it's a listening very closely to growing things, to beautiful things, to true things. I try to understand if there's something they're telling me."

"Shall we stop for tea?" he suggested as they approached the Railroaders' Café, where things might after all take on a more social air.

Her face was turned inward, and her eyes so clouded that he grew anxious lest the other patrons suspect a lovers' quarrel. It was a point with him that he must project an aura of constancy, as a good example.

The half-dozen shaggy customers stared at the two neat and laundered newcomers as if they were refugees from a fabulous bestiary.

Reverend Gunnalls regarded them with mild distance. Anne Ashton did not see them. The minister turned his attention to his guest and noticed that something was preoccupying her, something other than the questions they had just discussed. In his professional capacity he might attempt to unearth it. Her particular "religion", he thought, might mask her own brand of despair. What had caused that despair?

He asked if there was something troubling her, expecting an exercise in self-analysis as reply.

Instead, she said, "It's the children. So many of them are sick now. There's not much point in keeping the school open while the disease runs its course. Those not in bed are nursing their parents."

"Typhoid is a serious matter. An encounter with . . . annihilation", he ventured, willing to bend a little before the depths of her eyes. Their table was by the barrel-burner, and the flue wailed with a sudden surge of wind outside the rickety walls. Tea arrived in old mugs. He added milk to his.

"Yes, Mr. Gunnalls, annihilation", she said quietly, then grew silent within the aura of the word.

He was about to invite her to use his Christian name, Edwin, when into the windless sea of dialogue, on which the two had become becalmed, there burst what the minister considered to be a gust of bad air.

Turid Gunderberg, habitual breaker of stillness, grand mistress of disorder, thundered in with news.

"Annie", she gasped, and stood by the table breathing. The

Reverend Mr. Gunnalls was tempted to an unholy exasperation, and though it would never find expression on his face, his handling of a spoon in the china threatened to become severe.

"Annie, it's the O'Raisins! Their mum is real sick and sinkin' fast, I think, and the dad fit t'be tied. I been tendin' her fer two days, but there's more'n I can handle. Can y'come?"

"Of course", she said rising, alarmed.

"Is there anything I can do?" inquired the ginger young man, scraping back a chair. "I mean, in my position, I might offer some comfort."

"They ain't that kind of folks", said Turid. "C'mon, Annie, let's go!"

The two women were off at a trot down the street and into the bush.

"Have you called the doctor?" she asked, breathless, breaking her stride to mop a brow. The heavy older woman, for all her weight, clopped along like a hearty Percheron, to the dismay of the Thoroughbred, who almost permitted a cry of protest to escape her throat. Large flakes of snow had begun to spin down, carpeting the path ahead.

"The CN operator wired up to McBride, but the doc's run ragged with his own people there droppin' like flies. Wired back he'd try t'get down t'morrow."

They presently arrived at the impoverished homestead, known in that district as *O'Raisins*.

Camille L'Oraison, his wife, and five children lived in the cabin he had erected among a few acres of stumps beyond the village. A frayed and grubbed-out place where dung abounded and broken implements rusted in the snow. He was a faller and bucker by trade and sometimes stood duty at a steam donkey that yarded fir out of the bush to feed the mill. The swayback horse and a cow with a dangling empty purse under its hind legs revealed much of the story.

As Turid burst through the cabin door with Anne not far behind her, they penetrated a silence. The younger woman was halted at the entrance by the sight within, an almost luminous stillness, a tableau of five children glued to the long, blue body of a woman who was stretched out on the bed.

The fecal stench was overpowering. A baby began to squall. A kneeling man, who had been interrupted by their entrance, now resumed a profuse lament, embracing the shoulders of the dead woman in a refusal to allow spirit to tear itself from flesh. Which, in fact, it already had.

"*Mon Dieu, mon Dieu!*" he sobbed. The children stared with numb, white faces.

Turid took the baby from the foot of the bed and began to comfort it, though her eyes looked suddenly old, stricken, as if she had been punched by a long-time friend: she was more astonished than hurt.

But the younger woman felt the pain keenly; she was the unwilling interloper into a tragedy. She did not wish to be enlightened. She did not want to see. The eyes of the children had begun to bore through her, the teacher, champion of order. Their eyes were hoping, and she found this intolerable in her state of helplessness.

It was her first domestic corpse. She had not been permitted to see Mother's coffin. Nana had dressed her in the black satin dress with the purple crepe roses bound at the waist by a sash, and she had been restricted to the safe sections of the house while the body was in state. Death had then and there become her first abstraction and her primary question. Mother was simply no longer present, though it did seem that a gate had been slammed shut, and no one would explain. At night she spoiled the linen with tears that no one could see.

Now the obscenity of shucked flesh. And a Dickensian arrangement of orphans. No, it was too like a bad play to be true, and she would not be dragged into it.

"God, get me out of here", she cried silently, as the orphans continued to stare.

But the disguises of God are many, and Turid Gunderberg, the breaker of china and illusions, began to assert her will into the chaos.

"This baby is starvin'", she announced, and flopped into the rocking chair by the stove to undo her blouse.

"Annie, make tea!" she ordered, and Annie did as she was told. There was a convincing rattling of pots, a dented kettle was in her fingers, and water spilled into the chamber. It began to steam. She stood dutifully at the stove, devoid of analysis, staring, hearing only the concussion of bombs and shocking male screams, the banging of iron kettles in faffling war tents, the metallic taste of tinned bully-beef, and the hissing chorus of a thousand serpents. The baby's wail broke the spell.

Turid primed the pumps of her breast.

"These old bags have suckled seven kids", she said, dangling one at the squally baby, who was not impressed. The breast promised but did not fulfill. The baby screamed.

"Damn", said Turid.

The child bit and spat nipple.

"Double damn! I knowed there was no milk in there, but at least you coulda done some suckin', kid!"

She stuffed the rejected organ back where it belonged.

Anne began to thaw in the heat from the stove. The screams and the explosions faded into the attic of memory. Here were new forms of death. New World death, as natural as . . .

As a field of battle on which warriors staggered without reason or purpose, without maps or generals. Though the territory was strange and frightening, she was entering into it as a lost person will orient himself gradually by the sun, after panic, if sufficiently strong. She realized that she was not to be struck down immediately and thrown onto the communal pyre. She would continue to function and might as well do so with the degree of excellence that was her habit. Tea, that universal comforter, must be dispensed as medicine. Thinking commenced as she poured it into chipped mugs.

The flagrant exposure of breasts had shocked her into awareness that Turid was—O strangest of revelations—a mother. She had never asked Turid about the meaning behind her *Mrs.*, as if it were a curio she had picked up along the way or a burr in her coat. Why had she never inquired about the husband and possible children? She wondered at herself. Was it because the poor thing had been in her mind just that: A thing? A character? The stuff of amusing letters home?

A wave of shame washed through her. She looked at Turid for the first time, a spirit crated up in a box stamped Gunderberg. There she sat, a large, indefinable being, rocking the little creature.

"Two-legged rats", the woman had once named that queer species known as children, using scorn to mask a hunger too deep. And lavished her maternity on such subjects as the assassinated goat and a small herd of ungrateful steers, and on Anne herself, of course.

She was tempted to love the woman. Not because of anything. Not for her refreshing crudeness or for her little kindnesses or her liberation from the propriety the Englishwoman held dear. But to love her instead for that heart which had shown itself when she opened her blouse and fixed her eyes on the face of the child. A moment of weary cornflower eyes and compassion, of an areole as dark as a mole, purple-veined and used. Ugly and profound. Anne recognized it, though it would not find its way into any letters as had the humorous anecdotes and one encounter with power and horses.

"This little toad is gonna die, too, if it don't get milk", said Turid, who had stayed on top of matters.

"You better git over to the nearest place where there's a goat or a cow", she added.

"Where?" asked Anne.

There was a moment of silence during which all the living humans in the house continued to breathe noisily.

"You best try Steve's place."

"Who?"

"Steve Delaney", she repeated crossly, her tone saying, *as if you don't know, girl!* "The solitary, down by the Canoe."

"Where?"

"Go through the bush back o' the cowshed. Maurice, show Miss Ashton the way."

The boy, eldest of the children, detached himself slowly from his mother's bed. The sound of their father's weeping had terrified the children and frozen them in various states against the body of their mother. Now the boy was relieved of this imprisonment by a promise of action. He was suddenly all solemn bounce and coiled energy. He pulled a tuque over his ears and boots onto his bare toes. He wrapped a canvas jacket around himself.

"Come, Miss Ashton", he whispered, his face a white mask. He would have extended his hand to lead the woman had not fear and her own mask of authority prevented. And she would have taken the fingers, those almost-man's fingers, which were dirty and trembling and had held pigeons tenderly.

Outside, the earth was cold and terrible like the flesh of a dead mother.

She followed the boy through the thickening snow that powdered the crust of leaves. Winter, it seemed, had inserted its more permanent signs into the abyss between the afternoon's social tea and the corpse. Their boots left black trails in white. They shivered. There was an acute brittleness about the bones of the trees.

She realized now how small the boy actually was, silhouetted against the latticework of the cottonwoods, how tragic and innocent the exhalations streaming out behind him. His breath was visible. Victim's breath.

And a little child shall lead them, she thought.

About a quarter mile from L'Oraison's, they emerged from the trees into the fields that the solitary had rooted out of the forest. The boy halted.

"Somethin's wrong", he said, listening.

She heard a cow bawling in an advanced stage of discomfort. And along the trail came a shrinking, whining, blue dog.

"Bluey, Bluey, what is it?" cried the boy and charged off behind the animal at a headlong run toward the cabin. There was no smoke coming from the chimney. The woman hurried up behind, gathering her hems.

She entered the cabin without knocking, for Maurice had already burst in and the dog was lashing circles around a figure on the bed.

"It's Steve! He's sick!" shouted the boy, rending the air with dread.

She stared. The Centaur.

"Maurice, take one of those buckets and go milk the cow. Then home with it to Turid for the baby. Quickly, now!"

When he was gone, she stood helpless for a moment, then exploded, much as the dog had done, in concentric rings of activity.

First, heat. It was as chill as an icehouse in the cabin. Slivers of birch split in her hands, and snapping matches lit fire in the stove. She set a tub of water to boil on the black hole. Then she checked the unconscious man. Blood had dried beneath his nostrils. There was a scum on his chapped lips, and despite the unheated cabin his body was burning with fever. Her hand applied to his forehead nearly ignited on contact.

Fever must be slaked, she knew, or the man's life would be consumed as fuel. She began to cool and cleanse with a cloth. But there was also the assault upon her senses by the bed, which incontinence had rendered foul. This would demand a thorough cleaning and courage in the face of male anatomy that she would leave to the more experienced Turid Gunder-berg.

As a young girl, during a particularly romantic stage, she had been nearly lost in a fantasy. She had dreamed of nursing a fallen soldier, a warrior in spotless khaki. She had fed him on consommé and small, white, crustless, watercress sandwiches cut in the shape of diamonds, and one fleet brushing of lips, which restored the pulse to a righteous angel struck from the battlefields of heaven. She told no one, for the family believed neither in heaven nor in war. She situated the crucial scenes in the summerhouse under the cupola, where wooden beads and braided lathe shielded them from the eyes of swallows that streaked through the park Papa had created. A quintet played Mozart there once, and it was famous for trysts. But the extent of their intimacy, had it occurred, would have gone no farther than the uncontaminated kiss, an intertwining of their hands, and an exchange of words borrowed from Elizabeth Barrett Browning.

Then, the night in Belgium, when fantasy took on a form and an actual kiss drove itself deep into her and would not de-part. These memories were roundly smashed by the odor now pervading the room, an atmosphere in which the day's second abstraction was becoming bluntly real.

The dog, sitting at attention beside the bed, had engaged its eyes upon a long stare down its nose at the intruder. Suppressed air escaped through the nostrils. The woman was a saving pres-ence, and female, but was strange nonetheless. The dog looked away, as did the woman.

Sometime later, a huffing Maurice crashed in again and handed her a note.

ANNIE, MY HANDS ARE FULL HERE.
DO WHAT YOU CAN TILL THE DOC COMES.
TURID

She scribbled a reply on the reverse and sent the boy packing.

Turid, please come quickly. I cannot deal with the situation here. The trapper is dangerously ill. He must get to a hospital. Anne Ashton.

Maurice was back in twenty minutes with another message.

NO BLOODY FEAR. THERE AINT ENUFF PEOPLE
STANDIN ON LEGS TO TEND THE SICK. THE DOC
WILL GET HERE WHEN HE GETS HERE. I GOT A
SICK BABY AND A CORPSE TO WORRY ABOUT.
THE DAD'S GONE CRAZY AND THE KIDS IS
STARVED. DO YOUR BEST GIRL. TURID

"Thank you, Maurice", she said weakly. Then, swallowing hard, she assured him that she would manage and asked him to convey the message to Mrs. Gunderberg that she need not worry.

As he departed into darkness and snow began to choke the air, she sat by the stove regarding the delirious man, who evidently would not go away. Storm beat at the window. The dog whimpered. She resisted an impulse to do the same.

"O God, not again", she said aloud. She glanced up at the roof beams, but there were no angels with unsheathed swords.

Pride asserted itself eventually. There was the motto embroidered around the Union Jack over the desk in Papa's study:

> *In time of crisis it is better to do*
> *any intelligent thing quickly than to*
> *hesitate, searching for the ideal.*

So she took rags and soaked them in the bucket of steaming water on the stove. And pulled back the covers from the body of the man, curled around its distended belly like a question mark. She held her breath, averted her eyes, and began to work. It was an unpleasant, malodorous task, and when it was completed, all illusions of romance had disappeared.

Later, when he appeared to be resting more easily, she soaked the rags in a bucket of lye water and set a fresh kettle to boil.

She scoured her hands, arms, and face with carbolic soap and rinsed. Then, with a rough blanket for consolation, she settled onto the chair by the fire and listened to the wind.

4

Morning: the crest of fire along the horizon rose into the air, spilling through the trees and fields, illuminating the windows of the cabin down by the Canoe.

The man was pulled and pushed and sucked into abysmal currents. When he surfaced for air, he realized dimly that there was another human in the room with him. As she rattled the fireplates and banged pots, he sank helplessly from view before she could notice. His mind began to grab at thoughts and memories floating by.

He had been fourteen years of age in long pants and his first polished boots, the ones his father bought for him on that last trip to Dublin. For a boy from Dunquin, it was a great terrifying place, with trams and a thousand carriages and the wonders of motor cars roaring in the streets. Dublin the grand, city of castles and electricity. The sidewalks and shops were coursing with people, more than enough souls to fill every half-empty village on the Island. And they were Irish, like himself, though many had lost the Irish tongue. True Gael talkers were few and far between now, said his father, who did not like the English. He was a Republican man, with certain things under his hat he didn't discuss. Quiet activities that Stiofain's own mother was not allowed to know of. If she had, certainly the starry-eyed lad in his cloth cap would not have been set free to accompany him the long journey to Dublin from their scratch of soil on the coast of Dingle.

But his daddy said that boys must sometime see the wider world if they are to understand the bit of turf it had been given them to call their own. Stiofain's father loved his wife and children, and with near as much passion as he loved illegal newspapers and dreams of freedom. Finbar was black and tall. The boy appeared to have inherited most parts of himself from the man, though his nature flowed evenly like his mother's.

"Finn, stay away from political matters, won't you?" she had said on that day of departure. They were talking by the gate, and she was all kisses for the boy. He was their fine young prince.

"Don't be anxious now", his father said. "We'll be as good as sheep."

He had thought himself liberated from childhood for a few days. As they walked the streets of Dublin, he was aware of being only a head shorter than his father. He stepped quickly to keep pace with the man who, even here in this place where he was not known, parted crowds with his shoulders and the dignity of his brow. His power was of the unconscious kind. He did not preen or ruffle his feathers or ever give in to the urge to crow. He was no village hector and was respected far and wide as a man who was strong in a deeper way than tough. Never once in his life had he picked a fight, though he had finished a few. He could read and write and recite the ancient lays.

"Stiofain, look here, now." They stopped before one of Dublin's countless beggars. Finn dropped a coin into the wooden bowl. The boy saw bloodshot eyes and held his breath from the stench of alcohol that clung to the rags.

"*Slainte mhaith*", he said, Good health to you!

"*Dias Muire dhuit*", God and Mary be with you, slurred the man, whose eyes spun and darted.

As they walked through the throngs his father shook his head slowly.

"Did you look hard at that, Stiofain?" he said. "Did you see, and will you remember?"

The boy nodded.

"That is Ireland itself you saw standing there."

As was promised, the boy was not embroiled in any unpleasant political events. Though there were meetings with various gentlemen in the rooms Finn had rented over Sibley's on Grafton Street.

"This is my boy Stiofain."

There were smiles and nods and a *God bless you, lad*, but very few offered their names. He was permitted to merge with the wallpaper and learned one or two unpublished poems spoken aloud in that room. He heard the words *Sinn Fein* pronounced intensely and reverently, though used in a strange way: the words meant "ourselves alone", he knew, but what the significance was he could not guess. Later he would remember that there was no talk of bullets and bombs, lurid conspirators whispering in decadent rooms. No, it was all legend, rhyme, and visions flapping in the Hibernian wind. A battalion of dreamers.

Occasionally, when there were a number of them gathered about the table or seated on the beds and floor, Finn would ask Stiofain to step outside for an hour. The boy would take himself off then, scuffing his boots, hurt, demanding of the sidewalks why he must be excluded from these deliberations of men.

"I am not a boy!" he would say, angrily, to no one. Though he was still of an age to slip back into calling his father *Daidi*.

Trying to stretch himself uncommonly tall, he succeeded only in creating the appearance of a dangerous scarecrow. He would stroll, hands in pocket, through the pathways of St. Stephen's Green or over to Eden Quay, where barrels of Guinness stout were being rolled into the holds of ships. Mountains of crates stood there waiting to be loaded, some stamped Phoenix Brewery or Jacob's Biscuits, bound for Salisbury and Karachi, Batavia and Halifax. Names that were magic and contained power.

He longed for the names of all things, for the meaning of things, which adults appeared to know but conspired to keep from children. Then he would feel a yearning in him, a thirst to consume distance, to feast on seven oceans full of kingdoms. To see. To know and to feel! And he would hang on ropes, swinging out over the harbor slime with fantasies seared in his eyes, till the roustabouts chased him away.

He was thrilled to follow the lady usher down the gaslit hallway to their seats at the theatre, her red satin dress lapping the floor. And to stand on the steps of city hall beneath the statue of Daniel O'Connell dressed in a marble toga, the Irish Roman Emperor, and gaze with the stone man out over the heads of a thousand beggars and as many Celtic princes. And it was good, good indeed, to sit in the booths of Sackville's Café on Earl Street sipping cockle soup and curd-cakes with your *Da* buried in the Republican rag. The boy's soul became partially sated by the sheer number of such events. But with the passage of time he discovered that it was not enough to be in a fabled city where the exotic comes and goes as ordinary as old soup. A sickness grew within him for his mam's hearth. Oh, then, it was finally enough for a manchild to go home to his daddy's field and be content with potatoes and herring.

As they took the last leg of their return journey on a cart bound for Dingle via the Conair pass, he was grateful for what was familiar and was his own. That shade of green which had been boiled in his blood was lush again after gray Dublin. The road was rutted and the donkeys were slow, flicking sweat backward into their faces. The boy lolled in hay, seduced by blue sky interspersed with sheep-shearings of white. His ears still rang from the city's din. His head teemed with images.

By sunset they were bumping down the track with the roofs of Dingle in view. Stiofain was roused by his father's voice, a hand thumping his shoulder.

"Look now, we're almost there."

The boy shook straw from his hair and stood, stretching his four limbs with precarious balance as the vehicle rocked. He threw his arms around the man's back.

"Ah, 'tis a grand fine journey you've given me, my father!"

"It's not over yet, lad. We'll have a few miles walking to Dunquin, but it's a fair evening and will wake us up for the reunion."

They passed a gathering of deserted stone houses and fields gone back to gilgowan and yellow prashack, those unwelcome flowers, decorations for the funeral of a farm. The boy shuddered at the branches of rowanbush and blackthorn pushing through the eyes of the windows. A barren place, the haunt of fairies.

"Stiofain, when my daddy was still alive, he told me something I've never forgot." The man grew silent momentarily, regarding the passing farm. The boy looked more carefully at his father's eyes. They were of an excessive blackness, as if inked, and though Stiofain had known them from birth he had seen them change in recent months, growing deeper, if that were possible, and more luminous.

"He was an old stick of a man, with no teeth and very bent. But his mind was clear, and he could blow the pipes fair to his dying day."

Stiofain had not known the old man, their forebear. His soul had departed before the boy's birth, and he had left only a few legends. He had been through the Hunger and had lost a goodly part of his family to starvation and others to the sweatshops of Boston. They were strangers now, vanished on the streets of gold.

"He says to me, *Finbar, in the villages of our land, for every ten houses that are dwelt in by human beings, there are ten empty houses and ten public houses. And you can thank the English for that!*"

Stiofain had heard his grandfather's words often enough, for they were cornerstones in the family chronicles. It sounded like a riddle but was, in fact, a true sketch of the recent past. His inheritance.

Yes, Stiofain nodded. *The English.* The theme that recurred, like bad weather and death.

"Our greatest loss, lad, is our youth, all the bright young beings who could put life into Ireland's tired blood."

He looked intensely at his son.

"Stiofain, these are troubled times in the history of the world. Wars will soon be breaking out everywhere. It may be dark days are a coming."

"Dark days, Daddo? Darker than these?"

"Yes, lad, darker than these. So dark that none will know it's dark. They'll think the light has come. That will be the darkest times of all."

"I don't understand."

"No. You couldn't. Not yet. Maybe when you're an old fellow you'll see it."

"Why will it be dark?"

"Men will want to ride up into the sun and make themselves like God. When you see that happening, Stiofain, you'll know that the time is near. The Antichrist will be king upon the world. You must stay here in this good land, boy. In the visions of Saint Malachi there's a prophecy that Ireland will be spared the rule of the Beast. We'll sink beneath the waves of the ocean in order that we not be swallowed in the jaws of our mortal foe."

"But wouldn't that be drowning a lot of fine folk?"

"Yes, it would, and a terrible grief it would be. But far worse to fall into the mouth of the dragon."

The boy stared at his father for a long time as the cart lurched along the donkey track.

"Daddo, it seems to me that we're after thinking sad things much of the time."

His father gave him a look.

"That may be so. But tell me why you think it."

"I'm thinking that the world's a lovely place, and maybe we're looking at it through a smoked glass. Like when the chimney on the lamp is smudged with soot."

"*Arra*, but you're a bright old lad, like your mother's father's father. You resemble him too."

He gave the boy an affectionate thump on the arm.

"The world is lovely, Stiofain. But it's full of shadows too. Beyond this island there are places where the angels still fiercely make war, and the outcome of the battle is not known. Our land is a small place where God reigns. With all its pain and troubles—and a few angels still carrying arms here too—think of what troubles there must be beyond the seas."

But the sun on the hills was too sweet and brash for such thoughts.

"I see only light, Daddo."

"Then I fear for you, my son. For a man who sees only light will stumble over the things that lie in shadows."

"Then does a man who looks only at shadows not also stumble, for lack of seeing light?"

"*Arra*, but you're a wise child!" he laughed.

They rode on in silence for some minutes.

"Tell me, Stiofain, tell me that you'll not leave her, this land."

"I will not leave her", he had replied. "No, not ever!"

* * *

Time had methods of wrestling men's promises from their mouths, though the actual words could not be forgotten.

In those days he would take the flock of his father's sheep into the high meadows from which one could see the sea. The sky died without resistance beneath the blanket of night upon which stars had been liberally tossed. His youth was spent drinking the sustenance of stars and ocean, the air stirred by the tang-tang of bells and the roar of the surf. The little island upon which he was born had seemed then an immense kingdom. He had cut its solitude with the dances of tin whistle and flute. He had learned to finger and blow music into the sky as if braiding tame notes with the wilder wind, reels, and laments he had soaked up from his grandfather's *uillean* bladderpipes and the timpan. He knew "Robbers' Glen" and the "Kerry Slides" and numberless other movements of noise that had no name but would puncture the darkness. He had been drowned then in the soft night, sunken and risen forever in the ocean of mystery. Its waters inside of him might never flow outward in any way save those provided by the length of hollow wood with holes.

A tide of memory was rising within the shack by the Canoe, in a foreign land, down the length of cold years. Night lay upon the new world. There was no other light of cabin or campfire as far as the eye could see, and the woman saw that upon this ocean of forest the man had sailed alone. He mumbled now in delirium, *an vocal, an vocal*, the word, the word, though what this utterance might have meant was not clear, even to the man. The dog sighed. And the woman listened.

The voices grew more insistent:

"Stiofain, the ocean is too wide. If you go it will be as if you're dead to us!"

"No, Mother, not dead. It's a new world out there. Clean. With no memories."

Then his mother in anguish: "It's running. You can't run forever!"

Then his youngest sister ran before his eyes down the shingled beach, tears streaming and her child's voice foolish above the waves:

"Stiofee!"—a gull's cry drowned behind the swell, and then there was only wind and the thug of oars pulling him into what would amount to his life.

And later, when he had come to the sea of grass:

"Stay with us, Steve. You're a free man now, your passage paid off. The prairies are the place of the future for a lad with ambition."

"Thank you, Mr. MacLean, but I have to go."

"Where to, then?"

"The mountains. West."

"Your own dreams?"

"Yes, my own dreams."

"There's plenty of fool's gold in those mountains to satisfy many a dreamer."

"It's not gold, sir."

"Then what?"

"Space."

"Space!?" said the wheat farmer, spreading his arms wide as if to say, what else have we got but space here in Fort Pitt.

Then, as he parted the waters of space and dream, he saw the many forms that actual water takes. At first it wound sleepily through the flat land. Then, as he climbed through the tangled bush into the West, it began to coil and leap, then to thunder and roil and ravish the earth. From the moment he had departed from Alberta, the province named for an old queen's dead consort, he encountered a variety of it—streams, creeks, devils' races, rivers like galloping horses, and merciless falls—an abundance of fervent movement, confounding his ideas of what a river should be, for he had been formed near the mild Liffey and the Lee.

But water would not cleanse everything:

"The blood!" he cried, pressing the nightmare into his sweat-soaked blankets.

"We threw it in the sea, lad. Now, forget, forget!"

Then the waters boiled again, and he was swept under only to emerge farther downstream.

Gasping for air, he heard a man's voice discussing with a woman the matter of an afflicted object.

"There's little else I can do now, Miss. Just keep that fever down with tepid baths."

"Really, doctor, this is most distressing. I have my students to attend to."

"I'm sorry. Looks like you got the luck o' the draw. I'll do what I can to find someone to come out here to relieve you. But we have an epidemic raging up and down the Fraser. Families take precedence. If I had ten times as many nurses and doctors, there'd still be none to spare for these solitaries. Aside from the fact that it'd be risky to move him, the hospital is full to overflowing."

"Is there no one else who could come? Surely . . ."

"I'm sorry. It's really an emergency situation. This isn't civilization, Miss."

"I've noticed that."

"Give him lots of fluids and soft food only. There'd be hell to pay if we punctured a bowel."

Outside, winter had arrived. Light was cruel. A skewer of pain pinned him to the mattress through his gut.

"Keep him in bed. Total rest. And put him on a bucket when he's able . . . no trips to the outhouse."

The woman, whoever she was, had closed the door upon a pressure of silence broken only by the crackle of fire. Then opened it again to fling suet scraps out to the dog. She was a figure of mist lost in unceasing activity, pushing back sleeves and a loop of hair that had escaped in the steam from a pot of soup.

Eventually she noticed his eyes fixed on her.

"Oh," she said, startled, "it's you! I mean, you're awake."

"Yes", he croaked, and tried to rise.

She brought water, for which he was desperate. His dirty teeth champed at it and sloshed it in a grim way down his unshaven chin.

"Easy, now", she said, her hands soft and the eyes as purple as lupin, though more tender.

Just as he was ready to plunge into nothingness again, he realized that she was the teacher. Inexplicably, he remained afloat on the void.

Night and day came and went. The man ate, drank, slept. The

95

woman fed, cleansed, and cajoled his body into a manikin of strength.

"You're becoming well", she said evenly.

He drank and was silent.

"You're the teacher", he said at last.

"Yes, that's what I am."

"You're English", he added.

"Yes, I'm that too, apparently."

He turned away from her toward the wall, upon which a stone carving had been hung.

5

Dear Emily,
S.O.S.!!!

To describe my current situation will demand a suspension of disbelief on your part. An epidemic is raging throughout the interior, and hundreds of homesteaders have died. The entire region is tragically short of medicine, nurses, and doctors. At one point I must have mentioned to Turid my short-lived experiences on the front during the War, because the entire populace now thinks I am a nurse and expects me to behave accordingly. I have been appointed to watch over a gravely ill man, a solitary who seems to have come from nowhere and belongs to no one.

I am sleeping on a mattress in his cabin, which is the most primitive shelter imaginable. I now understand why civilisation invariably evolves into concentrations of city dwellers. In the city one is surrounded by networks of efficiency. All human knowledge is accessible in its most convenient forms. But here! Alas, here the very idea of enlightened knowledge is suspect. Modern science is unknown. Things break down. Distances are vast, continental—no, cosmic! The seasons are tyrants who will not be denied. The virus and the bullet wield excessive authority.

An Indian man tells me I should apply rancid bear grease, mixed with its green gall, to the belly of my patient. A Nordic crone tells me I should pour whisky down his throat. So far I have resisted both approaches. At every turn the rational mind threatens to give way to the tide of unreason. Solitude, fear, death are as elemental as fire and air. You wake on the most beautiful of mornings, and you taste blood.

Oh, help me. I wish you were here. I am unsuited to this land. When these troubles are over, I am returning to England. I am resolved. Absolutely! I am!

Write soon,
Anne

* * *

Journal Entry:

A trapper's cabin, Canoe River, 18 November 1923

I have a great deal of idle time, during which I have fairly resisted the urge to grow ponderous about the unknowable. But it is no use. I must try to understand things a little. It is either that or succumb to daydreaming, and I don't trust where the impulses of the subconscious will take me. And yet I cannot seem to concentrate. His books are not for advanced minds. Conversations are a plunge through the looking-glass. In English he has managed only one clipped exchange that approached coherence. For the most part his communications are garbled, a mixture of Gaelic and cryptic imagery. This morning he mumbled, staring at me as if his message were perfectly intelligible: "The blood . . . the stone . . . the little golden boy." Make sense of that, if you will!

And so, a few random thoughts of my own.

First, the subject of Time.

Where does it begin, and where does it end? Is it an infinite line or a circle?

How can our portion of time be meaningful if there is no beginning and no completion? I will admit that mortality is a kind of finiteness. If this man dies, his little biological span will have reached its neat conclusion, but he will not know about it. Only I will know, and that knowledge too will expire when my own life is ended.

What is a human life? Is it designed? Is it accidental? The latter, I think, but I do sometimes wonder if we are subsumed in something much larger than our senses can perceive. What if we are to greater beings what the fish in the river is to us? When it is hooked on a lure and hauled through the upper limits of its world into a higher realm, does it wonder at the naïveté of its brief sojourn in the water?

Does all existence point inexorably to the future, to what is coming? Is it always determined by the past? If the past has meaning, why would the future not have meaning? And if so, what are the exact parameters of the meaning?

Sigh! You open a door only to find an infinity of closed doors waiting beyond it. I will leave the question of Time and consider something more tangible: conscious life. Biological existence in its human form. More precisely: the male. More precisely still: sex.

Well, it is a simple fact that the billion members of our race now living on this planet are divided quite evenly into male and female. Very curious. It is a fact so ordinary that we never question it, hardly ever think of it. It has always been that way, we think. And yet it is so extraordinary a condition that one steps back in astonishment. What is it exactly that draws me to the opposite sex? The chemical drives within the body? The longings of a microscopic egg for an encounter with a determined little suitor, the best swimmer in a school of sperm? Surely it cannot be only that!

The universe is not flat. It is deep, multilayered, complex, always astonishing. Therefore, the principle that drives the cycles of biological life may be connected to dimensions that we cannot see. There is a male and female principle in biology. Thus, there may be a male and female principle in all existence, reaching far beyond the limits of matter, high above the surface of the river of life. On every level the unifying principle would seem to be love. But what is love? Is it no more than the sensation of pleasure as life is bestowed on life, no more than a reward mechanism that ensures the complexification and affirmation of existence? If it is only that, and if the whole thing is meaningless, I think it a colossal waste of effort.

On the other hand, if it does mean something that we cannot yet fathom, then the mysterious presence of love must tell us something about its ultimate purpose. If love is the means and motive of the ascent, then what is its end? And how does this yearning within me relate to that hidden purpose?

Man. Male. The other half of our species. There he lies, that godlike being who obsessed my thoughts for months. O mastery of form, quintessence of harmonious power, in shape and movement how admirable, the beauty of the world! The paragon of animals! See how he lies, brought low, stricken by a tiny virus. He has become a grey carcass, with no looks to attract our eyes. Who is he, what is he, and what does he represent?

I remember the first time I went to Italy—that first exuberant plunge into the riches of Christendom. I was a student, on an excursion from Zurich. There were many nudes in Italy, of course, but I had seen marble nudes before. They meant nothing to me, other than cold information about anatomy. Then, in Florence, I met Michelangelo's *David*, the colossus.

For a number of reasons I had never liked the etchings I had seen of this work: its undeniable brilliance (and possible arrogance) seemed an embodiment of what was unbalanced in the spirit of the Renaissance. It seemed more an invasion of my imagination than an incarnation of the true story of that little shepherd, the lad who slew a giant against all odds and through the transmutations of art became another kind of giant. No, this carving seemed to be more about man's sense of his own power. Yes, it was a masterpiece, but above all a triumph of *technique*.

Moreover, it had become in the ensuing centuries an overdone cliché. I went to Italy knowing that I would be taken on a tour of Florence, that I would see this work, and, of course, that I would be suitably impressed. But I dreaded it.

During the tour I became separated from the group, and, searching blindly through the corridors of the Galleria dell' Accademia, I came upon the statue from the wrong direction. Suddenly there it was. My first glimpse of it was from the reverse. It is normally viewed from the front, and from that direction one sees a powerful body firmly planted on the earth, poised, balanced, muscular, set in its essential form, like the triumph of the will.

But I saw it first from an entirely different vantage point: viewed from behind, the figure appeared to be glancing back over his shoulder. The image of the noble torso was dominated by David's facial expression. The eyes, the mouth, the brows, and the sinews of the face were taut with an emotion that is so quintessentially human: a split second of uncertainty and a groping for faith, the moment when courage overcomes terror—not as animal instinct but as a spiritual decision. From the front it appears as an embodiment of confident resolve; from the rear it is about doubt. That was the artist's intention, and that is its *word*. It is concerned above all with the struggle of the human spirit.

Michelangelo's *David* is not about sex, it is about character. It is in the same spiritual line as Andrea Del Castagno's painting of David, Masaccio's *Expulsion*, and Donatello's champion *Saint George,* all of which are ultimately concerned with the dignity of man. All of which are far from the spirit of Donatello's *David*, which is a sensual bacchus or satyr dressed (or rather undressed) in biblical costumes. In that difference can be seen the central problem of the Renaissance.

There is another thing to be learned there: the artist showed me that this truth was already a living thing within me. He had exteriorised my own experience and given it a shape, a form, a name, an identity. I was able to step outside of myself and to look within. Art had liberated the perception, incarnated the invisible reality.

In Shakespeare's *The Winter's Tale*, Leontes says of a statue:

> I am ashamed: does not the stone rebuke me
> For being more stone than it?

Oh, am I pure stone? Three times in my life I have beheld a living man in repose. My noble and beautiful Peter. The ugly, drunken boy in the lodging house. This sick trapper. Three times the curious workings of fate have laid the male principle helpless at my feet. I have looked uncomprehending at their faces and their forms. These sleeping titans would awake, if they could, and sweep up my life and carry it away to some unknown place where they would remake it into their own dream. This must be resisted. Existence, yes, even female existence, must assert itself or be consumed.

Perhaps I am wrong. There may be other reasons connected to the largest reason of all. Is it not true that the female principle rules in its own unique way? It creates the flesh of new men, moderates men into tamer pursuits, guides their confused drives, determines their desperate plunge up so many streams. It controls, without the visible apparatus of domination.

Ignorant of my meditation, they slept within my gaze, those warm giants, possessing only their muscles or their charm, their savage dreams and their arts, locked within the dictates of their inscrutable maleness. And none of them, none of them, could ever find within himself the secret garden of life.

Why do I dare to look at them only when they are rendered powerless? Do I fear them? Yes, I fear them. For if love is only a system of exerting power, a cycle of domination and submission, sustained by appropriate rewards, then to love is to be defeated.

Knowing that, do I still long for union with one of them? (Honesty, Anne, honesty!)

Yes, I do!

I fear them and long for them.

Are submission and control the only alternatives? There is another, but it is entirely theoretical: Let us suppose that a man and woman, understanding their limitations and their greatness, were to choose to give life to each other by giving away their very selves. Then both would be defeated, and both would win. In the process, both in the end would become a new kind of being, something they could not understand in the beginning and would never choose if they could foresee the struggle involved. If they were to persist, however, both would eventually become free, because neither would be dominated by the will to power. Only by the will to love. Yes, I see it. I might even be willing to engage upon such an experiment. But does such a man exist? I think not.

What have I just written here? Exhausted musings. Madness.

I must return to England in the spring.

* * *

While he was semiconscious and muttering things in Gaelic, she entertained a stream of worried visitors who came to see. Maurice looked in daily with rations and barely legible notes from Turid. Once he brought a letter from the school board instructing her to suspend classes until the epidemic had run its course.

She had many solitary hours during which to assess the sleeping myth. She analyzed his home, which was a contraption of cedar logs and sod roof, a pounded dirt floor in the lean-to kitchen, and the beginnings of a rough plank floor on the remainder of the cabin. The walls were chinked with saplings and mud. A window had been sliced from one of them. As a civilizing touch he had oiled a map with lard—tacked to the cross-pieces of the window, it was as translucent as amber. Sallow light spilled through it, illuminating the puncheon furniture, a table and a three-legged stool that sat steadily on the uneven floor. Beneath the bed were kegs of nails, planers, awl, traps, blankets, and a wooden storage chest. On a shelf were tins of food and tobacco, a stained clay pipe. A rifle hung on a peg by the door. Dried furs hung from rafter poles. By the bed were a few books in an indecipherable tongue. A leather-hinged door approximately closed. So the dark chamber where the Centaur lived was inscribed with personality: austere, inscrutable, male.

In the long nights, warmth laid balm on the ache of her body, as she tossed and turned upon a mattress unrolled by the stove. Light from its cracked plates danced on the ceiling and across the mantle log. There she found inscribed, with patience and art, his name:

Stíófáin Ó Dúláine

* * *

For several days they pottered around each other in harmless passes at conversation. He sat up in bed at last and asked for the clutch of books. She identified the volume bound in green as a collection of verse, *filliocht* stamped on its cover, though the contents were unreadable. Other books were in English, a *New Testament*, *Mammals of North America*, and a frayed grammar-school speller. The remaining items could be investigated only when he fell asleep again. He did sleep a great deal. Or merely watched.

Occasionally, he called the blue dog to his side to stroke the mottled silvery fur. He talked to its adoring eyes and sent a current into the depths of its glass. And received back his reflection. The woman noticed that it was a form of the same communication he had been engaged upon with horses the previous spring.

Now, however, it had lost its radiant power; it had become a tame occupation, the quirk of a gaunt, stubbly man.

He appeared to be brooding when he was not absorbed in his literature. She sensed that he resented her presence—perhaps this mood was because he had fallen into a time of weakness, and strong men, she knew, did not like to be weak. Had his fine looks been intact, he would have been difficult to endure. His glance could curdle the milk, but she would not permit it to drive her out until she was certain he could totter a bit more steadily on those legs. But as his present ugliness robbed him of any disturbing qualities, she decided to open whatever wound was festering. Perhaps, as Turid Gunderberg had suggested, he just did not like women. She searched for a handhold.

"You're a long way from home", she said. "Do you miss Ireland very much?"

"I am Ireland."

"I beg your pardon?" she said, touching a pearl button beneath her throat.

> I am Ireland.
> I am older than the Old Woman of Beare
> Great my glory
> I that bore Cuchulainn the Valiant
> Great my shame:
> My own children have sold their mother.

She choked on the polite repartee she had been preparing. Elements of extreme unreality had entered the room, and she wondered in a moment of alarm if he had become unbalanced by the illness. Was this verse only one of the less offensive symptoms and harbinger of worse to come?

But he was suddenly coherent.

"A fellow named Padraic Pearse wrote that not too long ago. The Black'n'Tans shot him in Dublin. Was it a neighbor or a brother of yours, I'm wondering, who pulled the trigger?"

His face was set like flint.

She sat in shocked silence.

"My family are peacemakers, not soldiers", she replied after a moment in which she definitively folded a handkerchief. "And I am for people not politics."

"People! Ah, so you're one of the humanitarian kind, then. Educating the Catholic barbarians? Civilizing the world with your English God and your law?"

"I've shot or converted no one, sir. Will you cease attacking me with your irrational words!" He was that. Irrational. She rose to find some necessary project.

But he was not listening. The acid would break from his mouth now, the fragments of truth mixed with a pollution of hate. He could not stop himself, nor could he rightly understand who she was—this woman with straight spine and firm mouth, striding back and forth between the water bucket and the stove. She was an Englishwoman. She was as much England at that moment as he was Cuchulainn.

So his flood broke against the dike of her silence.

"Barbarians and heathen, that's what Cromwell called us. Nits breed lice, he said, and butchered thousands of men, women, and children at Drogheda."

Oh, he was indeed angry, choking on deep history. And though she was at present its victim, she was also shut out and could say nothing.

"We had schools and monasteries when you were worshipping toadstools and burning babies on your pagan altars. You and your Druid ancestors!"

Really, that was too much!

"What of your Druid ancestors?" she said indignantly, "Don't you know your history?"

"Don't you know yours? You cut down all the oak forests of Erin to make your damn ships. Britannia rules the waves on a fleet of stolen wood and a sea of children's blood! You left an island of bogs and fairy bushes and a million starving croppies to scratch potatoes from the dirt. Thank you for nothing! For nothing!"

He made an angry swipe into the air, into the past. His arm flailed the vacuum, his lips compressed.

"Really!" she said. "This is a ludicrous discussion. You are enraged with history? With injustice? So am I, I would like to inform you. I, myself, am no great admirer of Oliver Cromwell, a terrible man. But I will have you know that displays of bile such as yours do no good for the cause of justice!"

Then, in effect, she departed. She became totally involved in the conversion of dried beans into soup. The conversation was completely and absolutely over. Though words like *pathetic* and *futile* continued to shoot through her mind.

Dignity enveloped her. She was fortified. Her movements became precise. She would leave soon, she decided, for the situation had become appalling. A domestic squabble, of all things, over politics. She had spent two, nearly three weeks tending this man and his heap of repugnant flesh. And all he could do was insult her. In the universe to which she was accustomed the objects of such heroic service would inevitably suspire in love with their nurses, lifting their Pre-Raphaelite faces to fall upward into the light of pale amethyst and the caress of doves.

Oh, for goodness sake, tears, she groaned inwardly.

Her back, turned to him, began to quiver. The man saw it.

"Lord, woman, I'm sorry." He slumped back exhausted, eyes closed.

Apparently deaf, she began to strip a haunch of deer with a sharp knife, shards of meat melting into the bubbling broth. Regardless of everything, substance must be stuffed back between his ribs. He must also have water to drink and a clean bucket on which to groan when occasionally she left the cabin for air.

The peacocky sign, professionally lettered, was nailed to the roof of a new log building across from the station. It had added a weight of commerce to the aspiring town of Swiftcreek.

CANOE MOUNTAIN DRYGOODS AND TRADING CO.
JONAH MACPHALE, PROP.

. . . who was loudly engaged in conversation with a wild-looking man standing there in buckskin.

"Business enterprise is boomin' in this country, Delaney, and only a fool could fail in times when money is flowin' like water!"

"There's a lot of money about, for sure," agreed the other man, "though precious little of it finds its way into trappers' hands these days."

"Trappin'!" said the disgusted MacPhale, "I'm glad to see the last of it. Bullets and broadbeans never go down in price. It's always up and up, if y'get my meanin'. Ho, ho, ho", though the listener did not.

"When I came here," said Stephen Delaney, "a marten fetched thirty-three dollars a pelt, and now it is four, with mink at a dollar and a half."

"Precisely!" said MacPhale.

"But it's a good life."

"Not so good down the North Thompson, which I'm not missin' in the least. It's plumb cleaned out. God knows where the beaver have gone, or the fisher."

"It's your own fault, MacPhale, using the deadly traps."

"There's no profit in your jump-traps, man!"

"There is. They don't do damage to the animal, and if it's female I turn her loose to breed."

"There's no money in such madness."

"No quick money. But a slow steady harvest. It's not my valley that is cleaned out, but yours. I make a good living still, though not like 1918."

"We'll see in a decade just who's the wealthy man", he said with finality, and continued to sweep.

"I have no doubt that you'll prosper," he said to the proprietor, on whom skiffs of flour had settled like fate, "but, MacPhale, I'm worried about Thaddaeus Tobac!"

He waited while the other screwed up his face.

"Tobac, eh! Look, I sold my trapline to him fair'n'square. So don't be gettin' high'n'mighty with me, m'boy!"

"Is it his fault that he has bought a cleaned-out run?"

"I didn't say, now, that it's a dead loss of a valley. There is weasel and link to be had . . . and besides," he admonished the young fool, "besides, Tobac is an Indian!"

"A decent man is what he is, MacPhale, with a wife and kids."

"I gave him a cabin t'boot and credit here at my establishment", he defended. "And there's nothin' more I kin do. Fair is fair, let the buyer beware! That's written in the law."

"You're a true gentleman of commerce, MacPhale, and generous! I can see that you'll prosper."

Sarcasm did not suit his kind of face. He had grown thinner after a recent sickness.

MacPhale lifted a cup from the top of a barrel. Grog poured smoothly into his mouth. He savored it with a swirl before knocking it down his throat.

"This'll do me condition good", he said, sucking the fluid luxuriously, then throwing back his head to break into song:

> Oh, gimme rum, gimme rum,
> Fer the troubles in me bum,
> I got pain when I go an'
> Pain when I come!

Oh, gimme rum, gimme rum
Fer me stuck caboose,
Jis pour er down me gullet
An' I'll shit like a goose!

Jonah MacPhale's face burst out purple with tears of laughter spilling. His wit would have taken them by the ear through several more lengthy verses, but Stephen Delaney's face put a stop to it. He was thought to be a mite humorless in these parts.

"Why did you leave Ireland, then?" said MacPhale, calming himself, changing the subject judiciously.

"There was no place for me anymore." He spoke the words slowly and cautiously.

"Were you farmin' people?"

"Yes. That and fishing. Water and earth. My grandaddy built a speck of land out of nothing above where the tides hit Dunquin. Dug it out of stones in his spare time, and in those days there was precious little of that. Long before I was born."

MacPhale lifted his cup.

"A man dug potatoes and peat and fish. And he prayed. That was life round and round, with a begetting of children added on to it. Like the wheel of a donkey cart turning and turning. There's a cross in the spokes, have you ever noticed, MacPhale?"

"I can't say that I have."

"In winters, when other men were patching the curraghs or playing knucklestones, he'd be out there piling rock to make a fence around his own property. An acre or two of gravel that he built up into good soil by carting seaweed and dirt from abandoned gardens down in the village. There were lots of those from the famine, half the place dead or gone."

Up to this point Jonah MacPhale had been amused. It was a rare event to have Steve Delaney's tongue wagging, no doubt from the lubricant of conversing with a countryman whose accent was almost as Irish as his own. Though Jonah MacPhale was not, in fact, a man like himself.

"All that was before the sheep. The sheep came after, in my daddy's time."

Now it's sheep, thought MacPhale, who was beginning to lose track. Reminiscence burdened him. He nodded more slowly, though he had been enchanted for a moment by the wonder of it. He yawned as Stephen continued:

"Some sabbaths, after Mass, I'd take a day and walk along the cliffs. You could see the curve of the planet. It was such a sight, man, with the sea like an arc and the sun a spinning top. Sometimes the water was serene, sometimes an angry cursed thing, but it always wrung your heart out, it was that beautiful."

Stephen reached down to scratch the ears of his blue dog, who had sidled up.

"I had a cousin there at Dunquin who fished for mackerel off the island of Great Blaskett and had himself a collection of boats built in the old style, curraghs and the like. On a fine day he'd let me borrow his curragh, and I'd take her out on the sea, letting the swell lift the little craft up like a mother's hand and sliding down the hillocks of water. Oh, then it was good to be a man, free and powerful."

His face clouded. It had been a borrowed power.

"What the hell were y'doin'? Just out fer a Sunday jaunt, were ye, like the gentry? Or was there a purpose?"

"Purpose? No. There was no purpose in mind save to feel what you can feel out there. A day of freedom maybe. I'd take the curragh out as far as I dared, making wild guesses about the sun and currents, trusting that a little tarred canvas would keep me from a wet grave. I pointed her west across the Atlantic to where Brendan the Navigator sailed so long ago, to the land of the young."

"Well here y'are, Delaney, a big growed man smack in the

middle o' the land o' the young. Does it suit yer fancy now, the real thing?"

"The real thing is always different from how you dream it. But there'd be no real things, MacPhale, if we didn't dream."

MacPhale grunted. It was too difficult and useless a thought.

"Yes, if dreams were facts, my boat would have shot across those waters like an arrow. They were such wide, wide waters! In the end I'd turn her around and row back to shore. Coming home you could see the cold arms of Ireland, the strip of beach and dark rocks rising from the village. A fine dusting of green on the bogs. A harsh land but too beautiful. When the time came, it was hard to leave her."

"Who, a woman?"

"No, man, Ireland!"

"Why did you leave, then?"

Stephen looked away and became silent. After a strained moment he looked back at MacPhale:

"I was seventeen when I came to this country. Worked off my passage on a prairie farm with good people. Lots of grub and hard work."

The impulse to reveal had suddenly exhausted itself. Jonah MacPhale sensed it and puzzled over it.

At that moment they noticed a figure moving down the street toward them. She was muffed and scarfed against a cutting wind but was easily identifiable.

Stephen Delaney stepped out into the street.

"Miss Ashton."

"Yes?" she said, slowing her stride, though she did not exactly turn her head.

"I'd like to apologize", he said, doffing his cap, anxious to bring her to a stop. He had already begged her forgiveness. But she had remained silent, a diligent worker, unreachable right up until the morning she had departed with a formal *Good day to you!* and no backward glance to the man who stood mostly recovered by the doorway of his cabin. So it was not really a further apology he wished to offer. He sought an outright acquittal.

"Apologize for what?" she replied in a deceptively quiet voice. "For your particular perspective on the truth? It is a habit of human beings to crystallize around themselves a lens through which they may safely view the experiences of life."

"Please," he said, though he would not have actually touched her arm, "may I walk with you?"

"If you don't mind consorting with the enemy."

If he had been better endowed with a temper, he might have engaged her in combat. He searched instead for some acceptable topic. They had not been properly introduced, it seemed, though his body was overly familiar. Both limbs and glances were veiled now and moderately harmless.

"What's your name, exactly?" he asked.

"Ashton. Anne Kingsley Ashton."

"It's a fine one."

"It is my own", she said, turning to him, "And was given to me before I had much to say on the matter."

Conscious that a portion of his power had been restored, he wondered if a gentle tease might stir up anything kinder than an angry hive, though she might be the sort of bee who droned peacefully among the apple blossoms until touched.

"And do you wish to know my name?"

"I know only that it's Stephen, and the final part comes close to being unpronounceable."

"My name's Delaney. That's not so hard."

"Your real name is Stiofain O'Dulaine."

"How do you know that?" he said, startled. More than startled—stricken.

"Your mantlepiece told me."

When he recovered he made light: "Your name, too, is a mouthful, Miss Ashton."

She was tempted to smile at this large fellow in his costume. But it was safer to remain wrapped in coldness as if by a necessary shawl that could be adjusted from time to time.

"Excuse me, please, I have business to attend." And she turned.

"I see", he said. "You punish with politeness."

She turned around and faced him. The black glint in her eyes was nothing less than the studied flourish of weaponry. She had learned it from many a woman in Papa's parlor.

"Would you have me producing meek and silly comments, Mr. *Delaney*, that would reassure you that you are on the right side of the species? And have not been seen naked and unclean?"

He searched for an answer that anger might sharpen into a suitable weapon of defense.

"It is comforting, and not a little amusing," she continued, "for certain women to be thought weak. It eliminates many burdens, though some dignity is lost in the process. I am not that kind of woman!"

"Do you always talk like a teacher?"

"It is what I am, after all. As well as English!" She turned to go, and this time meant it.

"I was sick", he called. "It was an old bitterness. Would you forgive me?"

She turned back toward him.

"I was not aware that the opinions of others would matter to a person such as yourself. Your self-sufficiency is quite evident."

"You know the truth of that, Miss. I've been as weak as a pup and would have been done for if you hadn't come along."

He would tame her with humility.

"I shall never understand men. You all feel such embarrassment when you suffer a weakness of the sinew and bone", she replied. "But I am referring to something worse, a malady of the character."

"The character?" he said, genuinely puzzled.

"Your *self*, sir, your self, which you have hidden down a remote valley for a number of years. From what are you hiding?"

"I don't understand, Miss. I'm a trapper, and I must live where I live."

"Oh, but I think you do understand. To put it simply, you are a man of renowned physical courage and of some mysterious private fear!"

He gaped at her open-mouthed as she wheeled and departed. He was not accustomed to being thumped, defenseless, in the middle of the village. Nor was she prone to flush a deep scarlet in the heat of debate. She proceeded down the street to the sanctuary of her school. There, hidden from all eyes, she sat in the darkened room and struggled unsuccessfully to suppress with pure rage a scalding eruption of tears. Her anger was not so much directed at the poor shabby trapper as it was toward the unfairness written into existence, that principle which erected mythic heroes and then shattered them with cruel persistence.

"A Centaur! Ha!" she sobbed, "A donkey! An ass!"

Stephen Delaney made his way slowly back to the porch of MacPhale's emporium, where his horse was tethered. The proprietor, who had been leaning on his broom handle and watching from a distance, was smirking.

"I love watchin' courtship. It warms me heart."

"That was not courtship", said Stephen hotly. "That was a political discussion."

"Oh, Stevie, love is a sweet thing."

"Be quiet, MacPhale."

"How else does the world keep turnin' round? Me old Dad used t'say, 'Jonah boy, once there was only two MacPhales on the planet, a male one and a female one. Now there's millions o' the buggers!'"

Stephen climbed onto his horse and sidled her away.

"I don't know what you two was discussin' out there," called

MacPhale, "but I must say y'look like y'got kicked in an uncomfortable spot."

But Jonah MacPhale had ceased to exist.

It did strike Stephen suddenly that the woman had invested a considerable amount of attention and words in an enemy. So he was presently able to ride home somewhat distracted from a pain of the unphysical kind, which had begun to eat.

6

In April, following the winter of his illness and being now fully restored, he decided to risk the swollen river and make his yearly journey down to Revelstoke. He pushed the canoe into the current of Canoe River and was off, sitting as still as he could in the turbulent water—his hair parted down the middle for balance, as the saying goes in that region. It was a considerable number of water-miles but swift and full of distractions. The valley teemed with life, breeding, killing, and eating undisturbed by man. He passed sow bears standing erect and protective of their cubs, woodpeckers and flickers knocking, bull moose rearing their ponderous lips and rack of bone from which water roots dangled slovenly. Geese, too, passed high overhead, northbound and honking. The man began to assume again life's benevolence, of which he had recently entertained some doubts.

The creeks passed by to his left, one by one: Packsaddle, Yellowjacket, Bulldog, and then Ptarmigan gushing out of the broken heart of the rock. Ptarmigan joined the Canoe ten miles south. Years before, he had built a trap-cabin there, hardly bigger than a closet. It contained a sleeping bench and a miniature cast-iron stove. He used the place to overnight on his trapping rounds or escaped to it from time to time when disturbed by the new invasions, the whine of the sawmill, or the roar of railroad engines making their way southwest to the North Thompson Valley. His own valley of the Canoe, where the river continued to buck and bolt as always through the rock, remained unseen by any other creatures than those that could not speak.

He saw the cube of his trap-cabin emerging from the melting drifts. He noted the open door, which was as it should be. More than once this shack had been broken into by foraging black bears and the roof torn off by grizzlies. It was best to allow them their curiosity. They would wander into the shelter in his absence, find nothing to eat, and amble out again, leaving the place undamaged.

Past Rat Rock, then past the hot springs steaming in the moss, patches of eternal summer on the coat of winter. He had long ago discovered there a garden of green and orange flourishing in the midst of a blizzard. He went there sometimes to float in the mineral pools while flakes of snow melted on his chest and lichen trumpeted his presence in silver. He was a giant in a miniature Eden and would have remained its king forever, but hunger had always driven him out again onto the cold river.

Down through the twin rows of peaks the man now went upon the liberated water. For three days he travelled in this manner, until rounding a bend late one afternoon he saw a town emerge from the mists rising off the surface of the river. It was not yet spring in Revelstoke, where winter had fallen heavy that year, though the water was running high. In the Wild Dog Café he proceeded through his annual attempt at consolation, which money could supply in abundance, though the effect was minimal upon the running wound of his heart. Rum failed, in the end, to fill a void that occupied the precise center of his being. But there were concoctions of rot-gut stewed in blind pigs from boiled fruit, dried apples, and currants, which coiled through copper, then mixed with tobacco juice or opium to produce a totally intoxicating drink. This too, though the immediate effects were spectacular, failed to console.

Then he was falling, falling into the many-eyed argus of the night. Rain filled the universe and the sea roared in its agony. Without light, the boy Stiofain knew the sheep paths and bog-trails that zigzagged up the high slopes, having climbed after peat and flock for a number of years. There had been British gunshots in the hills all day. And his father had failed to return for the evening meal. When the boy was far above the village, he began to squeeze notes from his flute, tremulous and questioning, running like a blind man's fingers over the face of the bogs. He was a few hundred feet below the ancient stone huts that shepherds used as summer shelters, deserted now. The dog whined at something, sniffing the turf.

"Da!" the boy called.

Woodcocks, startled, cried across the gorse. A faint voice was hailing him some distance away. The dog raced off toward it, up where the dark shape of a shelter was silhouetted against the stars. The boy followed.

He stumbled around in the shadows of the stone hut, arms outstretched, tripping finally over an object that lay propped against the wall.

"Stiofain!" it groaned, almost soundless.

"Da!"

"Boy. I think I'm badly hurt. The English are after me."

"I'll get help. We'll hide. We'll be safe, Father."

"There's no safe place, lad. If I'm to die, it will be under these stars and not in a British gaol."

"What happened?" Stiofain cried. "They told us nothing when they searched the house."

He could hear the man struggling for breath.

"You remember when Lord Ventry's bailiff evicted those families last week for being late with the levy? He sits in his magnificent house in Dingle while Irish children go searching for shelter in the rain. The boys and me went mad. We set out to give him a bit of a lesson. We were in m'lord's fields by sunset, and as there didn't appear to be any observers, we set to filling sacks with grain for the families that were drove out."

He paused, exhausted. After a few moments he continued, the words coming tortuously.

"Well, we didn't look close enough because sure as the divil, there comes that informer of his, the bailiff, with a pack of constables and soldiers. They start cracking off a few shots, and we scatter fast. But the bailiff is that same fellow I had a bit of a tiff with last year at the races, and he spots me. 'There's that big bastard from Dunquin!' he shouts, and they're after me, the mob of them, and I run halfway home before they start to gain on me. Round about the edge of the village, one of 'em gets lucky and puts a hole through my ribs, so I turn up the hill as fast as I can. I hid in the rocks and crawled up here after nightfall."

"I think we're safe now," the boy said.

He gripped the man's arm where blood had seeped, holding on for balance. His father slumped, worn most of all by the pain of speaking.

"What was that?" he cried suddenly. The dog barked. There were noises below on the meadows and a spark of lantern light appeared, still far off but bound in their direction, perhaps a half-mile away.

"Whist, dog!" the boy silenced the animal. "It might be nothing but souls from the village."

"Or it might not", said his father, struggling to rise. "Were you followed, boy?"

"I don't know for sure. I struck no light. The dog an' me walked up quiet behind the house. No one would tell about this place!"

"They might have guessed."

"If it were our folk they'd be playing the pipes as they cautioned me to do."

"Then let's be gone from here!"

Stiofain's shoulder supported part of the man's weight as they made off across the *croagh* to low cliffs that jutted from the crest farther along. His arm around his father's middle, the boy could feel a stream of blood on his fingers, and the mineral smell of it stung his nostrils. He crushed any sobs that threatened to burst forth, lest they cripple him. Fear lashed them from behind. The man pressed his body against the night, desiring to die, if he must, in a safe place with his eyes full of stars and a final glimpse of moon on the western sea. The boy desperately wished his father to bear the weight that had been dropped upon him or to help plug with his fingers that hole through which life seemed determined to spill.

"I know of a place", the boy whispered. "Farther on. A cave I found last summer."

It was hardly a cave. It looked little more than a shadow beneath a low overhang. But when they scrambled and dragged their bodies under, they found another crawl space that took them through into a deeper chamber. They could barely sit up in it, but there was room enough for several men. It was almost entirely enclosed, invisible from the moors by night or day.

They lay close in the darkness, the two human beings and the dog. Their hearts beat. The man groaned. The boy cried for awhile into the crook of his arm. They took small doses of sleep, and it appeared that the man was not immediately to die.

The boy had black bread in his pocket and a flask of liquor that his mother had pushed in with it. The man broke the bread carefully down the middle and gave the boy his portion.

"Eat, Stiofain."

In the light of dawn that seeped in, he could see his father's pain as he lifted himself to glug the burning fluid, larynx rising and falling in the muscles of his neck. The rhythmical swallowing seemed to be eternal.

"Here, lad", he offered. "Take it and drink."

So the boy swallowed fire and blood and held it in.

As the morning light increased in the entryway, Stiofain gathered courage to put his head out into the rain. There was nothing stirring on the bogs, only mist and the cries of birds. Beyond, it was still. He crawled back in to tell the good news.

"I think it's safe now. I'm going t'fetch help."

"A good lad you are! Off now, and don't be worrying about me. That bullet didn't hit nothing vital. Just a little missing blood is all."

He gave an encouraging squeeze, and the boy returned it, then crouched into the tunnel.

"Wait, Stiofain. Here, I want you to take this."

He handed him a stone object about the size of his own great hand.

"I fished this out of the dirt while you were sleeping. It was digging such a hole in my back." He sighed. "It's old. Very old."

"It's a cross."

"Yes, the Celtic cross, with the wheel round it."

There were many like it in the local graveyards, monoliths, taller than grown men, with Latin or Gaelic inscriptions. Some dated, it was told, from the time of Saint Padraic, who had driven the serpents into the sea.

"Go, now, and keep this near to your heart, lad. It's as old as the Faith in Ireland. God knows what martyr carved it. Go!"

So the boy stamped quickly across the slip of mud at the base of the rock and was gone down the slopes to the village. As he went, he thrust his hand inside his jacket to protect the stone thing. It was warm and stained because his father had pressed it to his body. He ran and stumbled over the sweep of turf and rock. The stone grew hot against his flesh, and though it was not heavy, it seemed to take on an unfathomable weight, as if it bore the being, the life, of a man.

* * *

Eventually, the man Stephen found his own body on the stones at the edge of a northern river, beneath the upturned canoe with which someone had covered him. Upon waking he wished that he had not. His head felt broken, his limbs disjointed, his flesh crushed. His eyes refused to focus, and he shivered uncontrollably in the rivulets of water that ran under the canoe. Then the blindness came again, and liquor could no longer drown the black fire of memory.

The corpse of his father was lowered into a grave. Holy water and tears flowed, and the stones were laid over the turf like the clicking in a game of knucklestones. The women keened, and the boy Stiofain shook against someone's shoulder. He kept a semblance of control, his face like stone, his body upright. Rage boiled together with horror, and both seeped inward to the core. His hands dangled cold at his sides. The sun cowered behind a storm and forced curtains of light to sweep across the hills. Light, darkness, light, darkness, the boy's eyes contracting and expanding as he walked home with his weeping mother and the young ones. Droplets began to fall out of the clouds.

When the family was within their cottage, he remained outside, letting the iron rain hit the palms of his hands, which he held out before him. His eyes were black. Out of the mist a priest came and stood beside him. This man's eyes were grieved, but his pipe emitted smoke in slow, steady puffs. He shielded the bowl from the rain with his thumb.

"Stiofain, it is hard."

"Yes. Hard." And his voice was hard.

"You're very much like him."

The boy could find no comment, for there was darkness and light, darkness and light upon the hills, just as there was darkness and light upon the hearts of men. And he saw that darkness was winning.

"Inside of yourself," said the priest, "inside, I don't think you're the same. No, lad, there's a love of poems and songs within you. Finn was a fighter."

"And can we not fight, then?" Stiofain said with deadly calm.

The man regarded the boy, wondering in a flash of intuition if the family would lose him. He weighed carefully such things as the anger of boys.

"We may fight in our own ways, yes."

"You mean with words."

"Yes, with words, Stiofain. With truth. If there had been no poets and storytellers in Ireland, wouldn't the people have died long ago from giving up? It's a powerful way to do battle, more lasting than the sword." He paused, reflecting, "And remember, lad, those who live by the sword shall die by it."

"And when will the English start perishing? Them and all the tyrants in the world?!"

The priest sighed loudly in a lament too deep for words. He only regarded the boy more closely, praying that he might not have to mourn for him one day.

"If there is murder in the heart, Stiofain, and blood on the hands, we must cleanse it with prayer and music and poems. If we do not . . ."

He searched the boy's eyes.

"Stiofain, if I can wish for one thing, it's that you hear me now. Don't be flinging the wheat of your youth into the fire. Work it hard, grind your anger into flour, and some day, I promise you, we'll be sitting down to feasts instead of funerals."

"Oh, Father," the boy cried, "you are a fine spinner of words. But I am drowning in blood!"

* * *

Up from the waters of time he floated again and awoke.

"I would like to die", he informed the world, though no one heard. No one was there actually, except two sparrows pecking innocently among the gravel. They looked sideways at him, and their sharp little eyes were full of disapproval.

"It is not good for man to be alone", they said.

Sometime during that day he fumbled money across various shop counters and gathered supplies for the coming year. Among his purchases was a seven-and-a-half-horsepower kicker, which he bolted to the flat butt of his canoe and headed upriver with unmuffled roar. He stared at the water and did not look back, his eyes tormented with motion and flight. He was conscious of the offer made by an icy plunge and death by exposure in a land only nominally given over to spring. A few times his bow bumped against rocks in midstream, and if the current had been a little more shallow he would have gone over into the obsessed water. His reactions were slow in the rapids. There were portages as well, during which his body complained and threatened to disobey. The sun emerged in late afternoon, and his parka steamed in the heat. He beached on a spit of sandbar and rolled his aches into a bag beneath the canoe.

When, days later, the familiar landmarks of the Ptarmigan appeared, the man suspected that he might survive. He found his trap-cabin intact. Supplies were presently unloaded and stored under the bunk. He set a gill-net in the river. His body was hungry for flesh, and in the morning, perhaps, he would cook fish and recover some of his strength. Without bothering to light a fire in the tin-box stove, he fell again into oblivion.

A sound rippled through his scalp and woke him. The eerie light of predawn was in the window. Something large was scratching to get in, tearing at possible openings. If he was very still it might go away, he hoped, though he was not really convinced of this. His present depression told him that the worst was always about to happen. His hands were wet, cold, trembling. He grabbed the .303 Lee Enfield propped against the wall. Quietly he swung his legs to the floor and slipped his feet into gum boots. *If it had been any other time*, he thought. *O God, O God, why now? When I am weak!*

He pressed a shell into the chamber, ready to fire down the bear's snout when it burst in. If only he could see. Was it a black? Or a grizzly? A hungry sow with a demon's temper?

His trembling increased. He had heard of men putting five rounds into a grizzly before it fell. Five shots at some distance.

But here he was only inches away from a will that with one swipe could tear his head off. *Ursus horribilis*—the horrible bear—had been given its scientific name for a good reason. Would his bones add to the creature's reputation? He sat and waited for the answer.

He scarcely breathed, listening to the silent calculation on the other side of the door. He found that many thoughts can crowd into a mind at such a moment. These thoughts revolved around his chances:

A fellow he once drank beer with at Fort Pitt had showed him a mangled slug dug from the heart of a moose.

"Dangblasted thing ran a quarter mile with this in him afore he fell!"

So a gun, that frail scepter, was not as reassuring as it might have been. This bear desired to depose him. The man tried to pray but could not, though his mind dragged the actual words across his vision.

"You'll not be having your way with me!" he muttered aloud. It was uncertain whether he was addressing death and its most recent instrument, the bear. Or nature. Or perhaps even God. When he spoke, the snorting and scraping of the presence outside immediately stopped.

The man ceased to breathe. Would the door now splinter and crash open, popping hinges and latch beneath the battering ram? Lord, would the bullet fly true in the split second left to him for a small final protest? Whose blood would splatter the floor in a moment or two? The bear, which was powered by hungers of the blood and a ravaging curiosity, was not intimidated. The man was convinced that it would be he himself who would be spilled out completely.

"I'm losing control", he thought, his grip slimy on the stock.

Cry out! The words shot through his mind. The silence beyond the door threatened to burst.

Speak!

Speak? Speak what? O God, I am coming apart!

He began to pant. He examined minutely the *George V Rex* engraved in the brass. How many bear or Germans had it killed? Or Irishmen, for that matter? The gun was suddenly a heavy, alien thing. He could not understand its relationship to the finger and to the presence.

Now! Said the word.

A wave rose up within him, some primal authority he had not known he possessed, an eruption of mad courage.

"Be gone!" he roared, flinging the door wide open.

"Go!" he shouted. Only obedience was possible. A startled black bear, looking alarmed and foolish, turned on its heels and crashed away into the bush.

The man exhaled a long stream of breath and sank to the porch to rest his quaking muscles. He understood then what bear it would be his lot to wrestle with. Not blacks or grizzlies. But the one that struggled for mastery within his own being and had already been identified for him: fear.

He stood into the shaft of the rising sun, the shivering lord of creation. Then he went down the footpath to the edge of the river, where he might complete those small tasks that reassured him of the order of existence. He drew the net in slowly as if he were not performing the visible act but had deciphered in the simple, hand-over-hand motions the knowledge of cosmic order. He untangled the gills of a grayling and two whitefish, tossing them up flapping onto the snow. Later, he cooked and ate them.

The man slept early that night. He did not dream of bear or war but was pulled by a tide into an ocean upon which he miraculously floated.

Beside the sea a noble man with silver hair, wearing a rough-spun woollen cloak of burgundy and green, turned and looked into Stiofain's eyes. The seagulls cried, *Malachi, Malachi, who art holy upon the waters!*

Do you see this ocean, Stiofain? said the man, pointing at the surf with his shepherd's crook.

Yes. I see.

It is the ocean of God's mercy.

But the boy Stiofain covered his face with his hands, and his hands were red with blood, and he ran, he ran from the sea.

In his sleep he sang, as the soul will sometimes release at the deepest level of being the music of a dirge that the ancient ones had keened in the cottages of his childhood:

> You have taken east from me, and west,
> You have taken sun and moon from me,
> You have taken love from me.
> And great my fear,
> And great my fear,
> That you have taken God
> From me.

He sang in longing notes, which no one heard.

7

"You see my ring?" said the bride, offering her hand across the banquet table as the fiddlers tuned up.

"It's lovely, Turid", said her companion.

"I know it's only a bit of ivory, but he's carved hisself into it, along with the little animals."

Anne Ashton took the large gruff hand that marriage was making tremble. She inspected and admired the bone ring and a steeplechase of loon, fish, dove, and hare that Camille L'Oraison had cut around the band. The groom appeared to have settled into passivity beside his woman, and, though not unhappy, he did appear to be still adjusting to fate.

"There's plenty of buggers will give a gold ring and break yer heart soon enough", she continued by way of explanation. She appeared robed in virtue if not in virginity. It did strike some in the hall as incongruous that the bride was out in white to the ankles, with a spray of lily-of-the-valley clipped to the iron hair over an ear.

"This was my mum's best tablecloth," she said, touching the flowered design woven into the linen over her breasts, "and MacPhale's yard-goods had nothin' a girl could deck herself out proper fer a weddin'."

"That's true."

"Can you see me trottin' up the aisle in red polka dots?"

"Certainly not."

"Well, 'tis done now", said Turid. "We are wed fair and square, and all that's left is the dancin' and the honeymoon."

She appeared agitated, uncomfortable in costume, and eager for that moment which would be taken in the cabin among a mob of sleeping kids. Most eager, perhaps, to get back into her old work pants and sigh over a cup of strong tea.

"Marriages are made in heaven and consummated on earth", she said. "But it isn't the pleasures of the bed I'm after so much as the companionship . . . permanent like!"

"Look", interrupted Anne, who did not wish to hear such revelations. She pointed around the community hall and said with excessive enthusiasm, "Such beautiful paper flowers, Turid. People have worked so hard to make this lovely for you and Camille."

"Course, that's not t'say I don't like a little wrestlin' match in the hay", Turid went on, not listening.

"Look, they're bringing in the piano from the hotel bar", Anne said in a desperate voice.

"Gad! Even my competition is here!" said Turid, who appeared pleased that four hurly-burly men had wheeled in the great beast on a trolley.

"How nice of them though, Turid!"

The hall was now filling with townspeople, the burghers, the trackmen, and a scattering of shyer farming folk. There were also wild characters leaning against the log walls, unshaven types with oily looking garments who had come to see. Among them stood a taller figure in hide from whom Anne Ashton wished to avert her eyes.

"The whole world is here, girl!" said her flushed friend, who had begun to receive the guests regally, as was befitting. Some women, after depositing their pot-luck on the serving table by the far wall, came over to congratulate.

"Well, you're Queen for the Day!" said Mrs. MacPhale sweetly. There were others who exchanged glances and smiles innocently, but hooded like falcons.

"I'll not deny it", said the bride, squeezing her husband's arm.

"Good evening, Miss Ashton", said Mrs. MacPhale. She and

her entourage nodded at the teacher, their brows exerting an effort to understand her relationship to the notorious concierge and Queen of Hearts. The ladies had been unable to attend the religious section of the celebration, due to prior commitments. Turid's voice assumed a dignity in the face of their stares, though it could not quite hide a rasp:

"Miss Ashton is my bridesmaid and unofficial maid of honor—not being Catholic-like."

"Ah", said the chorus, and departed.

With that the fiddler began to scrape out a few warm-up tunes, "Double Eagle" and "Little Brown Jug". There were men climbing up on the stage to join him, mandolin under arm or harmonica in hand, and that Irishman with his bristling collection of whistles and pipes. Even Wanda Tobac had sat herself grimly down at the piano.

The four of them, looking at each other, tried to figure out how they might arrange these separate tools to crank up the machine of their sound.

"Best just launch into er", said the fiddler, and off they roared through "Soldier's Joy", jostling each other's notes and bars but gradually pulling together. Bits and clumps of people broke off from the crowd milling at the food table or the booth where somebody was dispensing porter from a hogshead. The couples began congealing into twos, trotting and tapping around the cleared area in the center of the floor. Spectators clapped in rhythm with the two-stepping or jigs, and then the electricity of joy took hold and swept the crowd. The cries of babies were drowned in the hoots and whistles and tides of happy gossip shaken together with the clomp clomp clomp of the dancers. Everybody knew it: a good weddin' dance! The epidemic was now completely over and their numbers decimated. They badly needed a celebration, a victory feast, if the bung would be pounded back into the barrel out of which death had so recently leapt.

The bride and groom beat their way through elbows, hips, and blessings heaped upon their heads, arriving at the center of the floor with their feet clattering in a jig. The mythic couple was swept away in a flood of exultation, and no matter what they attempted to do this night, they could not be found guilty of it.

Through the crowds moved the L'Oraison children, dressed up in their best with greased shoes. They were apple-cheeked and winded from threading the needles of the dancers, tagging and chasing with town children, thumping the planks to run faster than they could be counted. Only Maurice, eldest and serious, moved cautiously about, observing, unsmiling, offering mugs of rum to the gentlemen and glasses of punch to the ladies.

Anne Ashton, who was captured in her own sphere of silence, watched the boy as he weaved through the hall. *He alone is not happy here today*, she thought. Though the observation was not entirely correct, for her own singularity had become an unwelcome pressure.

On similar occasions she had found it enough to remember her pride and inviolability. *I am a Person. I am a Woman*, would be plenty to banish any embarrassment. Those swains who then dared to approach swiftly dispatched themselves to less dangerous women after a single dance. She had developed a reputation for lack of warmth, and there were certain lines around her mouth that, if she were not careful, might appear to be bitter.

"Drink, Miss Ashton?" It was Maurice, with his troubled eyes, offering a glass.

"Yes, Maurice, thank you." She took it and sipped, looking at him.

"*Such sweet compulsion doth in music lie*", she said.

"What you say, Miss?"

"Nothing. It was nothing, a line of poetry."

"Oh", he said, and moved on. She regretted her attempt. Although aging teachers, extinct volcanoes, and other fixtures of the landscape might be permitted to erupt from time to time, their reputations would remain unalterable from then on.

Foolish! Fool! Her punishment of herself was not yet visible but might become severe. She had wanted only to reach out to touch his pain for an instant, to console with the only unguent she had at her disposal: words. That large medicine bag of quotations and maxims she carted around in case of emergency. It had come out wrong, superior, and patronizing, placing distance between herself and the boy.

What is this thing that makes us all the same but keeps us apart? Is it loneliness? Fear?

And pronounced a judgment finally: *I am foolish and lonely.*

She concentrated on the music by way of distraction. Reverend Gunnalls had replaced Wanda at the piano and was now working a path through some sheet music for the waltzes. He was, she realized, as confused and pedestrian in his playing as he was in his ministry. Only now and then did hints of genuine creativity escape. His music, like his exercise of religion, was by rote, theoretical and possibly loveless. She might have been attracted to him, but never once did he depart from the fundamental score. If, in this remote corner of the continent, the birth of jazz were to find a timorous counterpart, there would be some who would be shocked by the impropriety. For passion, that most treacherous of human impulses, was as unseemly in art as it was in the realm of the supernatural, it was felt by some. And thus the sight of the minister faithfully working the keyboard in an accustomed manner was most reassuring. They could not for an instant guess that he was incubating a secret new religion.

She was caught upon the thorn of this strange development: here was the most conformist personality in the hall infatuated with an utterly destructive rebellion, just as Papa had been. What did it mean? She tried to read the future in the neck of the man of God. It was a strong neck, though not bullish like those of the Eastern Christs in murals she had stumbled upon in Venice and Ravenna in another life. No, it was a thin, upright, Calvinistic muscle, cropped and clean and sweating coolly with his labor. Did his puritanism hide a suppressed passion, a fire that could express itself only through violent eruptions? Was that why he was flirting with paganism?

His flesh was familiar flesh, identical to that of her uncles and cousins, parsons and barristers all. It was barbered and talcumed flesh. It did not smell. Edwin Gunnalls was, like them, a decent man, willing to build a better society, to go to any lengths to alter basic human nature, whether or not it desired to be altered. He loved to talk and would hold forth on anything—rather, anything that did not threaten his damnable confidence. Though, when he had asked her to dance, and she refused, he had moved away like a puppet in a pantomime.

The other musicians handled their fiddle, mandolin, and flute much as they might wield crude weapons. It was doubtful that any of them could read music. They played by ear, that primordial memory by which the self is released into space. They were churchgoers for the most part and in this way were attached to Reverend Gunnalls. But the point of their joining was a narrow one at best, as if by some hinge around which they would swing with different noises, some of which were not pleasant. They would expect him at any moment to shut down the pagan thrills of "The Lop-Eared Mule" and drag them all into a rendering of "Where Is My Wandering Boy Tonight?" or "Have Courage, My Boy, to Say No!" Whether or not he was bold enough to attempt this was uncertain, but he might want to.

The truth of the matter was that the other musicians were engaged in a festival of release. At times it appeared they would tear apart from the established scores and careen off toward the frontiers of heaven following instinctive hungers of the soul. The pull between the minister and his band of merry men was most obvious to Anne Ashton, and she saw written there in the struggle between law and spirit the dimensions of their lives, their simplicity and greatness. She was somewhat chilled, however, by the perspective in which she found herself, its great height or poverty, she could not tell which. Edwin Gunnalls, without doubt, would have assumed that their perspective was one of superiority, that their knowledge placed them precisely but democratically *above* the underprivileged. It was a new kind of aristocracy, and she hated it.

All of which contributed to the impression she created: a silent, sour creature staring critically at the jubilation that surged around her. She gazed for relief at the individual musicians: the fiddler, a quiet pondering man, was now carving up "Speed the Plow". The mandolin player thrummed the strings with blurred fingertips, an ardent, impulsive man. Then the flute player . . . but here she stopped. Stephen Delaney was blowing cries down through the hollow tube, and the sound was old and beautiful and heartbreaking. His eyes were closed, fingers dancing on the holes. Once again she was drawn to look obsessively at this man as his notes were sent upward by some tapped mystery and majesty of soul. Soul. As if that, too, were threatening to be unleashed in this conglomerate of sound. All musical possibilities were buried here in these musicians, if they only knew, and they raced dangerously close to eruption as Wanda took over from Reverend Gunnalls again, and the heat generated was compressed and would have burst into flame for a brief joyful searing had not their own exhaustion muted their cries. This kind of passion, she saw, came from suffering, not theory.

Anne Ashton had heard intimations of it on the big radio that occupied a corner of her room at Mrs. Gunderberg's Rooming House. She had lain on her bed, sleepless, as the sharp night air carried programs to her from Seattle and Chicago and, in one freak reception, the voice of London, faint as the pleas of a lingering empire. She had bathed in the orange light from the tubes and leapt to her feet to crouch by the speaker, her heart pounding, as once she found New Orleans and heard for the first time the birth of the black man's blues. A different language of suffering wrung from yet another crushed people.

Madame Turid L'Oraison crashed into the chair beside her, flushed from the reel. She had brought a warm, damp lump wrapped in a napkin and offered it now to the maid of honor, along with some verse:

> Cake in the griddle,
> Cake in the pan,
> If ye don't eat weddin' cake,
> You'll never get a man. . . .

Anne smiled weakly and ate the tart fruit of wisdom but began to gag on a stone. The words delivered by the laughing bride struck cruelly, even though they had been meant in the friendliest manner. The stone flew out as the bride thumped the maid hard. When it was assured all round that Miss Ashton was in no danger, the onlookers turned away or went off dancing, leaving her staring down into her hand. In the paper napkin lay the remains of squashed cake, mashed by her fist.

It was impossible to finish eating the thing, despite the threat of barrenness. She wiped her hands clean on the napkin.

My soul is becoming thin and gray.

She was afflicted by hallucinations of herself raising a family of begonias or lavishing the dregs of her passion on a cat.

I am not afraid of being unloved. But I am terrified of never learning to love.

There, she had articulated it to herself, the perfectly predictable insight that spinsters are condemned to say to themselves just before they depart for cool rooms and chilly futures.

She was weary. It was easy enough to wrap herself in a secret sterility. She was about to kiss Turid's cheek and gather a more solid shawl for an early departure when she realized that a presence and its shape were standing before her.

"Miss Ashton, would you dance?" he said, and his hand was offered, his face melting into the guttering light of candles.

"Yes", she replied, gathering rose organdy about her ankles.

So the rough hands took hers, and, though their bodies did not meet, they were attached by mutual agreement and consigned to the blueprints of the waltz.

She did not really look at him.

"Thank you", he said.

"For what are you thanking me?"

Never had she felt more vulnerable to the heat of bodies reflecting off each other, or to her own emptiness. An absence which Greek and manners would suddenly not fill.

"Thank you for dancing with me, even though you don't like me."

Possibly she did not hear. There were streaks of sweat running down the wrestler's neck, and the sugary scent of moose hide and birch smoke came to her from his body. She found it difficult to compose a reply, and he had given up expecting one, when she said:

"It isn't that I dislike you."

"What is it, then, that makes us this way?"

"I don't know", she said simply, wishing to cry, or perhaps to leave any scenes of potential damage. "It could be the fragility of glass."

"I'm sorry, I don't understand. Glass?"

"Behind which we all hide."

"Glass", he repeated, willing to learn.

"There are those we encounter in life who possess the gift of reaching through our barriers. To touch."

"And is there harm in that?" he wondered, holding her imperceptibly tighter in the big hands.

"No harm if we're not shattered", she said.

"But how would you know it's safe if you don't allow it to happen?"

"How can I allow it to happen if I don't know it's safe?"

The fiddle rushed into the gap left by their abandoned voices. And when that music eventually failed, silence split the man and woman apart.

"Thank you", she said quietly, tightening her shawl and turning to the door.

"Miss Ashton, may I walk you home?"

"You may, if you so wish, Mister Delaney."

* * *

Swiftcreek, British Columbia
September 1924

My dearest Sister,

Such an abyss between my last letter and the one you now hold in your hands. I have been unable to write anything, really, for the longest time. School reports have been about all I have been able to handle. Creative writing, my poetry, and those communications to which it pains me to be unfaithful have suffered most grievously.

Allow me to explain, and in the process to unburden myself of a weight of dilemma. My difficulty festers precisely where a terrible joy has been woven into the cloth. I can scarce believe that it is happening and in my lowest moments do suspect myself of madness. At best it is a defection from the vows you and I made so long ago. However, I must beg permission to break the ancient pact.

Did we know ourselves then? I see us strolling through the wood, arm in arm, professing our disdain of 'boys'! I remember our cleverness and ignorance. I recall also how much in love with Ben I was that summer. How, stealing out of the house under moonlight one night, I caught his mane and rode him bareback across the moors. It was power. It was freedom. It was wind pouring over and through me. I could fly. I laughed, I yelled, I sobbed for joy, a joy that has never been repeated. I *became* wind, and Ben no longer our dear old gelding but rampant Pegasus leaping into space, I holding him up by will. That was the last time I rode him, for I went to school in Zurich that autumn, and when I returned he was dead.

What a jumble of words I have just written! How dishevelled! The problem simply is this: Man, that mysterious half of humanity it is our pleasure to misunderstand, has begun to confuse me and bemuse me. I understand neither myself nor the gentleman in question. He is the one of whom I wrote over a year ago, the Centaur who galloped away across the clearing that afternoon, having burned me with his eyes.

Emily, what shall I do with a man who attacks me for the politics of my race one moment and drags me to the brink of disaster the next with the delirious ardour of his music? And what shall I do with myself? Certainly, I cannot call it romance. There have been a few innocent walks and conversations, dominated by a certain dream of his concerning sheep. Or we discuss my children, who once again, as school commences, have eased the longing in my womb.

Am I rash to write such things to you? You, who have been the discreet confidant of the past decade of our womanhood. If I am now too blunt, please accept the trust implicit there, and a desperate plea for your discernment. Send me the fare home if you sense a derangement. Tell me to flee if this frontier has at last narrowed my horizons.

I am thirty-one years old. I am a moderately attractive but intellectual person approaching that difficult age in life when it is one's lot to be defined as maiden aunt—a cruel summation. I have met another human being. He is a large, foreign, physical man, who traps wild animals and raises livestock for a living. His home is crude, his fields as rich as this grudging land will allow. Our relationship is neither intellectual nor a mutual animal magnetism of the venereal kind. Though I will not deny the attractiveness of the person in question.

The facts are simple, as I have said: a lonely spinster meets a solitary bushman. Hence, a convenient solution to both their problems. It suddenly seems so staged, so fatefully arranged and inevitable that I wish to flee for my life. Emily, find me a thin professor or a disgraced baronet. Anything that may be brought to the altar on legs. So cries my mind!

But the heart says No. It has learned that a tidy universe without love is cold. Here is where I must be beaten upon the threshing floor. Hidden, crushed, and transformed beneath the stones. I suspect that I shall be broken; I suspect that I shall finally live. Save me, Emily! Save me from this shattering we are pleased at times to call love.

Spring 1925

8

It was more or less decided by everyone that they would be married. The number of strolls the man and woman had taken together through the town of Swiftcreek amounted to a weight that could be measured in terms of destiny. Curtains on the kitchen windows would flick as the couple passed by, and little girls had acquired a habit of giggling behind their hands, or boys kneeling at marbles would shout backward into the wind.

The man and the woman took the long morning journey on the Grand Trunk Pacific north to McBride that day in May when the leaves unfurled and white butterflies were set loose in the sun. The couple sat stiff and estranged from each other, due to the impending event. Varieties of apprehension afflicted them both, though the man was more encouraged than the woman, having submitted to forces greater than himself on a number of occasions.

Woman, do you know me? Can you love me as I am?

She fingered her purse, something solid, which contained her history and a tenuous future.

He is so massive and cool. A stone man. Beautiful. Am I mad, mad, mad to do this? Yet, it may be the sanest thing I have ever done. Time will tell if my love can ride him to the stars, and his love root me to the earth.

He looked at her from the corner of one eye.

Woman, you seem so calm. Are you not afraid of this thing that is happening to us? If you saw my past, would you still wish to marry me?

Turid L'Oraison sat with her husband in the seats directly behind. They were the proposed witnesses to the act that was about to be committed. Turid thought the groom was deliciously, impossibly handsome, if a little aloof. More important, he was a potency that needed to be tapped. She thought the bride looked radiant. But she did not realize that the radiance was a terror of existential proportions, for time itself was being immolated within the fire through which the bride must walk.

Who is this man, the bride wondered, staring at his jaw, which mallet and chisel had artfully carved.

I am torn. The fiery gown of love is lowered over my body, and I cannot cry out. I assist at the dressing of the sacrificial bride: myself!

She threw open the window and thrust her head outward to suck in the cold spring air that carried the scent of thawed earth roaring by—but choked on smoke.

"Careful, Annie, you'll get a cinder in yer eye!" shouted the matron of honor, stoutly vigilant for the ceremonies. Her eyes had got red in the process of rejoicing, though Camille remained solid for both of them. He extended over Anne's shoulder a handful of dried berries for fortification. Was he consciously contributing to the day's orgy of symbol? Not likely, but there was a split second when their eyes met as she accepted the fruit. Perhaps he understood her condition, she thought, for he had only recently passed through the same fire. That at least was communicable. Sympathy could be flashed across a void by a mere gesture of the eyes, but he would never be so imprudent as to attempt actual words. Camille would remain a mystery, she supposed, as would everyone, including her proposed husband.

As she chewed the pulp, it became, with time and determination, a form of wine in her mouth. Would Cana be reenacted in the depths of these mountains, she wondered. Would the water in her bones be transformed?

It is not Stephen's past that disturbs me so much as my own inability to grasp it. His vague references to some troubles he has endured in

Ireland are as unreal to me as my own past. Who is he? I do not know! And who am I? I do not know!

At that moment, the man who was to become her husband turned away from something within himself to look into her eyes. She was at once grateful and embarrassed for this moment. Above all, grateful for an implication that she might not be travelling alone through that furnace in which glass is melted to become vessels.

The forest is passing by, she thought. *It is eternal unless destroyed by fire. Yet even then, fire will release the seeds of cones buried within the soil. Do I love in my heart as well as in my will? Shall my frailty destroy us both or be the burned soil out of which our generations will grow?*

Clear sky, blue, blue, with high white peaks around the train, creeks melting below in the valley. Blue smoke rising from cabins on the outskirts, laundry flapping on lines, children running.

My heart, my heart, thumping like drums. Anne, Anne, it is not to your execution you are going. It is to birth.

Is there a difference, asked the eagles, circling in their zone of freedom.

Yet he did not compel me or beg for this marriage.

"Would a woman like you ever consider marrying a fellow like me?" he had said.

Oh, yes, a woman like me just might. If we could swim together beneath our cultures to the sea where all is one and we may mingle our blood and grace, happily drowned. Speak, love, O speak to me out of your ocean of silence.

But he was made voiceless by the din of the wheels.

"Do not fear to take the woman as your wife", the angel said in a dream. And the man arose to do as he had been bidden.

"Do not deprive yourself of a wise and good wife", said the angel voice fading into the clatter from the tracks.

But I am carrying an ancient wound, thought the man, *and I have been alone too long. Then there is the blood!*

You shall be tried also by fire and created anew, said the wind.

I am with you, Miss Anne Kingsley Ashton.

I am with you, Stiofain O'Dulaine.

I am with you, said the wind. *I am hidden in your weakness, flowering in the heart of winter.*

"It is for this reason", said the priest who stood before them in the church of St. Patrick. "It is for this reason that a man and a woman shall leave mother and father, so that the two of them shall cleave to each other and become one flesh."

One flesh, one flesh, said the wind to the woman.

"Life is a transformation, and you are entering into it with the person chosen for you from all eternity."

Chosen, said the woman's mouth.

Where everything is given, nothing is lacking, said the wind.

Yes. I do promise, she replied. *I give it all. All.*

"And now the Scriptures. Please be seated, won't you?

"A reading from the Book of Hebrews. . . . 'All of these died in faith before receiving any of the things that had been promised, but they saw them in the far distance and welcomed them, recognizing that they were strangers and sojourners upon the earth. . . .' "

The priest read on in one of the many languages the woman had ceased to understand. She could hear nothing other than the cries of children playing somewhere beyond the glass that had been opaqued in colored paint.

Did it hold the glory in or out?

Wind and children chanting. Words falling upward like blown seed. Music.

O hundred hymns and splintered ice like a thousand chandeliers singing.

O lamentations.

O rejoicing.

O light striking on the frozen world, make me run home.

Home.

It is good that you have come empty before the Presence, said the wind.

But I do not believe in the Presence, she replied.

Be still, be still.

I will, I will.

Are you listening, do you hear?

I am listening, but I cannot hear. I cannot hear!

* * *

So it was done.

When they were at last alone and the troop of L'Oraisons young and old had marched off along the giggling path, the man and the woman who had not yet dared to touch became disturbed by the presence of each other in the kingdom of solitude.

"I'd best see to the cow", he said with a brief look.

"I'll brew some tea", she replied. She entered the building that a sacrament had made officially her own. It appeared so hollow, so strange, that she forgot her weeks of service here. She attempted to claim it by confiscating a peg on which to hang her shawl and a berried hat that she found suddenly absurd. She lit a fire in the iron mouth of the stove. A spear of flaming kindling snapped and made her jump.

She sat waiting for the man, her elbows pressed to her sides, staring at the bed on which someone had laid a new quilt and a sprig of cedar. A stone cross hung over the headboard, and an alien rosary made of horse chestnuts dangled from the bedpost. A dog lay as if dead on the blanket.

A clock ticked. She rubbed the ring the man had hammered out of an ancient coin.

When he returned she took the bucket of milk in which straw and dust were floating and strained it through a cloth into jars that frothed up white. She continued to stare as the bubbles subsided into liquid.

The man stood by the mantle log, distracting himself with a fire in the hearth, where poplar roared up the flue. He stroked the adoring dog with the working side of his fingertips. He sat for a while with the woman at the table, neither of them able to find subjects with which to tame the silence. They sipped their tea slowly. When he rose up and went outside again, the woman undressed, wrapped herself in a gown, and hid beneath the covers of the quilt. The dog leaped onto the coverlets and lay there staring at her.

On his return the man made no comment but did look quickly once and away.

"Stephen, it's the dog or me!" said the bride, making light. "I'll not share this bed, or you, with her."

"Bluey, go", he said, and the insulted dog unfolded herself off the bed and out the door, casting a glare backward at the woman. On the porch the man spoke softly to the animal, came in again, and closed the door. Then he blew night down the chimney of the lamp, and stars began to crowd through the window he had so recently covered with glass.

"*Let thou with me now speed the soft intercourse from soul to soul*", she whispered, her arm flung on the quilt to receive.

She could not see him. His back was toward the fire, and the front, that inscrutable male equation which comprised the other half of the species, was clothed in shadows. As he undressed she was made speechless, not by the shock of nudity, but by the meaning of the event. His outline loomed and glowed from the nimbus of fire behind him, and as he came to the bed slowly, cautious and yearning, she felt that at last a force of immense mystery was approaching. This complexity of earth, water, fire, thought, and seed was turning with infinitesimal slowness into her own being, which opened wide in the cold of space to receive his heat. As the wheels of galaxies will blend without collision.

The man covered her body. The woman received his power,

crying out for the fusion and flow that matter would attempt in becoming one. The two souls, catching fire, would indeed have been consumed and flowed together if flesh allowed such finality.

But they were content at last with having begun the friendship of their bodies. As mercury will part to roll like silver beads around the palm of the hand, their souls would approach again in search of union.

The man could now take his wife's hand and press its soft mounds as if they were his own. The lids of her eyes became familiar to the lightest touch from his fingertips, and his lips blessed the fields of wheat. She in turn could lay the down of her arm across the brown of his belly and sleep the sleep of tenderly ravished brides.

He offered the bowl of his hand, the chalice of his senses, which time had filled at last. The hand appeared empty, though, and naked. Through which someone might yet be determined to drive a nail. And so she took it to protect.

After they had both fallen into the bottomless well of sleep, empty and full to their cores, the woman awoke to enfold the man, who snorted and muttered, his mouth gaping open in the cabin's air, drowned.

"*Na muir, muir*, the sea, the sea", he said, in a language she did not know.

* * *

She awoke to the sound of his axe. She went onto the porch, shivering in the air that a just-risen sun had not yet had time to wring. Across the clearing at the edges of the bush, down by the river, the man had resumed an attempt to defeat the forest with his strength and his tools.

"Stephen", she called. It took a second for the word to travel, and when it reached he turned. He waved. In the motion was written everything, and she knew that she was his and the adventure begun.

As he approached in sleeves and shoulders, his eyes searched for hers and met and would have pulled them into a resonant stream had the woman not felt a compulsion to join them further with her words.

"What are you doing?" she asked the powerful man, her husband, who belonged to her.

"I'm bringing down some poles for an extension to the house. There will be more than us before long."

He smiled with a glint of sun off the blade of his axe.

"It doesn't have to be completed at once", she said. "Have you eaten?" Thinking, of course, that he had not.

"I've eaten."

"Oh", her voice fell. She had desired to fuel such power herself on this, their first of mornings.

The man, seeing her hurt eyes, said:

"But I'm not full now and could eat a horse!"

She smiled and bustled in to lay a fresh fire. He considered mentioning to her that during one of his winters here he had indeed eaten a horse but decided against recounting that memory.

As she rattled the stove-plates and poked the embers, she was a girl again, walking in the minty morning grass in her nightgown, while scents of fried bread fled through the window to blend with the herbs of the garden. A sundial glowed with bronze children, greened by London fog.

> Anna Kingsley Ashton Brown,
> Who's the fairest in Bishop's Town,
> Anna Kingsley Ashton Green,
> Been to London to see the Queen,
> Anna Kingsley Ashton Blue,
> Whomever you marry will ever be true.

She might have performed barefoot elfin dances in the leaves. Perhaps she did, or only wanted to, and desire had converted the dream into memory.

Mother, she had called, forgetting that Mother was ill and could not hear behind the leaded windows.

Shhhhhhh, child, said Nana. *Come in to breakfast, or you'll catch your death of cold.* Anna Kingsley Ashton Brown had danced in with wet feet, but silently, so Mother could sleep.

"Come and eat", said Anne Delaney.

She placed the feast of eggs, fried potatoes, thick white bread, and a pot of orange marmalade before the man. He was not in fact as hungry as he maintained, but he did not dare to resist. He ate and was thankful.

"What is this?" she asked, touching the crudely carved stone cross hung on a nail.

He paused, looked up. Looked down at his plate.

"It's a thing. Which my father gave me."

She waited for further explanation.

"Anne", he said, still staring into the plate.

"Yes?"

"Nothing. It was nothing."

She would have probed or dug it out, but his face had firmly closed upon what he had been about to reveal. There were depths hidden there that might never be delivered into her hands. Springs that ran silently beneath the stone of his strength.

On the first day, then, the limits were being set, and she did not grasp what was happening.

Geese came by that afternoon, high overhead, northbound, ignoring the expectant field. Coyotes yelped in the woods, and the blue dog barked sharply throughout the second night. The man awoke and touched his wife's hair, rose and went out beneath the stars to silence the dog, and stayed awhile shivering in his skin as he studied the planets and constellations.

As silence crept over the earth, a wave of heat enveloped his body, rising from within. Out of it he sang, in a voice that might be unidentifiable when heard with the wind:

> You have given east to me and west,
> You have given sun and moon to me,
> You have given love to me,
> And great my joy that you have given
> God to me.

Had the woman known, she might have traded years of her life to receive the sounds the man's soul was making. But she did not, being asleep.

9

Blue woodsmoke rising against the mountain in the sun. Indian summer it was called, and as she walked through the fields with a basket of lunch and a jar of milk, the dying season enveloped her. She had found in the several months of their life together on this clearing a new awareness of the worlds that remained unexplored just beyond the line of forest.

Her husband brought her an alarmed bundle of feather and bone, a thrush, a fledgling robin-like bird he had captured beneath a tree.

"Some mountain cat ate the mother", he explained. "Do you think we can tend it till it flies?"

He delivered the explosion of noise and struggling fragile limbs into her hands, which were too wet with dishwater for such surprises.

"I would be astonished if it survives", she said dubiously. But its trilling changed her mind presently, and she fattened it on worms dug up from between the rows of potatoes. Whenever she entered or left the cabin in the weeks that followed, the creature raised a frightful clamor of hunger and rewarded her when full with song. Its nest of hay within a chicken crate behind the stove quickly proved too small for the battering it persisted in giving itself. She took it out into the field every morning and tossed it into the wind, but it would only strike at the air feebly, making slow, clumsy arcs back to her feet. It would hop from finger to shoulder and, as if knowing, would insert its beak into the hole of her ear. *Preeeeep!* it would say, courting her heart. Delight would threaten to become uncontrollable, and she grew fussy and overcautious with the package of song that fate had delivered into her hands.

"Not too tight, not too tight", she admonished the little L'Oraison girls bouncing on tiptoes, who had, had, had to *hold* with hot fingers and a yearning that might pop like buds. Or Maurice, who knew, and could absorb the bird's noise into the stillness of his gentle grubby hands.

In the garden of the woman's interior lay an ancient nest, a memory. At school, the child Anna Ashton had fled one morning to the washroom to suck a spot of ink that had spilled onto her uniform. Fearing that the mistress might see, her agony grew as water would not cleanse, and terror was reflected in the sterile, waxed hallways, the perfect marble sinks, the face in the looking glass. She stood by the window of the lavatory and gazed despairingly out over the rooftops. She was rubbing distractedly at her eyes when a flurry of wings beat upward and disappeared across her vision into the fog. She saw, then. And at first could not believe. On the granite lintel in the stone alcove where rain and wind would not reach, but might be accessible to the hands of privileged girls, lay a nest.

It was a circlet of wire. No straw or mud or down, just coils of very thin rusty wire and some bent nails—a metallic nest. It appeared a bit unreal or contrived, an obscure joke. But there it was. In the middle where there was no wire sat one small white egg resting on stone.

Her concepts of flight and song, and also of motherhood, had been altered then and there by the city bird, offspring of generations of beggar pigeons bred in the maze of brickwork. She was glad that evening for the flight into green that the carriage accomplished as it made for Bishopsford, a village where badgers and peewits could still come and go as they pleased.

On Monday morning she looked to see if the egg had hatched, only to find that someone, in a fit of hygiene perhaps, had brushed the nest and its treasure off the sill onto the cobblestones three flights below. At that moment she might have thrown a bottle of ink, if one had been handy, hurled it furiously down to smash, to cover the smear of tragic yellow.

The moment did come when she, the woman, was able to throw the orange stripes of the thrush into the sky and watch its arcs become wider, then disappear into widening rings of air, insects, and abandon. And was gone.

She was pondering this newer memory that her husband had provided as replacement for the old. It was his gift, a form of healing, and she held it close as she crossed the field toward him. He was stumping out the new field, and the carump, carump concussion of the gunpowder reached her some distance from the blast, when all she could see was the matchstick man through the smoke of the slash heaps.

"Stephen", she called, loving the sound of her voice calling to him, loving his reply. It was often this way. They came closer, it seemed, at those moments when they were calling to each other from a distance, deliberately searching through smoke. Though there were also moments when the entanglements on the much-used bed approached perfect union. Many such things, both pleasurable and disturbing, composed the new rituals of the woman's world.

She caught him stuffing paper into the firebox one day.

"What's that you're burning, Stephen?"

"Nothing. My old trapping notes, some silly poems I made once. And thoughts."

She leapt across the room and plunged her hand into the fire, saving what she could. He stood back, astonished.

"Stephen! These are precious. They are your past. They are you!" and went dancing around the room, blowing out the charred edges of the fragments.

"They're hardly me."

Since the coming of the woman into his life, his need for communion had been satisfied, and he could dispose of those temporary mirrors he once had held before his face in times of loneliness. They were useless now, and he wished to forget. The present would always be enough for him, and the annihilation of his past a blessing.

He looked closely at his wife, who was cooling her fingers in a water bucket. It came to him that there would be levels of her being he might never be able to enter. Who was she, then, this lover of words, braving fire to save a rhyme.

Her own poetry had become more difficult to compose. Its rhythms had been usurped by those repetitions at the barrel churn or the wheel on which Turid was teaching her to spin wool. The bride appeared willing to learn, clumsily and diligently, with less art than she could have achieved in petit point.

The older woman helped by an endless monologue of practical suggestions and, from time to time, a consolation.

"You're doin' just fine, Annie", she said, sweating.

"You're too kind, Turid. Do you really think I'll ever be finished?"

"Man doth work from sun t'sun but wimmen's work is never done!"

"I've come to understand the truth of that myself."

"Indeed you have, my girl!" replied her friend, offering no more judgment or approval than the younger woman could read for herself in the face. The eyes of the concierge had grown more thoughtful. Mystic circles made by the wheel of life were now old habits to Turid L'Oraison, who could tell you a few things.

The man observed the month by month progress of his wife. She had made his hermitage a place of sound and fullness. He was constantly being surprised by creations not made by himself. A mat she had woven from rags. Or wondrous scents that came to him across the oats from the region of the cabin, the odor of baked soda bread or stews of deer meat into which she had diced wild leek and mushroom. Or an odd poem about a bird in an iron nest. And once, on an evening when he approached home heavy and overcome by the doggedness of stumps, he found twelve jars of blueberries lined up on the porch to cool.

Thorned berry canes grew through the spokes of the wheel of time, large melon moons rose, and toasted hay mounted in the loft, pungent and reassuring. The almost-fullness came over the earth, and the migrations began in high lines that remained bright ivory in the sky even though the cabin and fields darkened in the shadow of the mountain. The earth, he saw, was not required to push its abundance at him, but it did, and he was grateful for its generosity.

At times he would look at his wife as she kneaded dough or hunched over long pages of hoarded vellum, composing letters home under the cone of lamplight. Or regarded her as she listened to the endless questions of the smallest L'Oraisons, who possessed her fingers freely. He could not believe in her need of him or her hunger for what was hidden in him. He could not quite believe in her love, though he grew almost contented on it, his soul fed by her tending, much as the bird had fattened in her hands. At times he would drop his mattock among the stubble as his fingers and palms uncurled and his arms opened wide to embrace something that was not visible. And emitted a brief sound that could never be translated into words.

As she wrote into the night, then, translating herself to her sister through the alchemy of ink and lines, he would pull the rosy pipe from its case, blow down it and play quietly so as not to disturb her thoughts.

Even as I write, Emily, he is making his music. This man who has begun to make me whole but does so with gentleness, with silence. He is helping me to remove my fingers from the weapons of defence we learned so well. He does not even realise. Yet, I wonder if I shall prove as helpful to him? The person you know is ceasing to exist; who I am to become has not yet been revealed, though I am certain now it is peace and not disaster that is intended. I am happy. I think that my flute player shall imprint his image more clearly on myself and on his music than on our children. May they come swiftly.

My love as ever,
Anne

The woman's image was also imprinted. There was a little girl she briefly carried. Annie grew *as big as an August pumpkin*, Turid said. The child hid for awhile in the belly of the peaceful being whom winter and swelling breasts made slow. But it came early and motionless, a blue rubber doll with its cord wrapped around it. And the woman wept.

They made a grave in the back field toward the strip of bush that separated their place from L'Oraison's. The man constructed a corral of pickets with which to contain their first tragedy and crowned it with a cross, which the woman painted white, as white as her own concave belly.

Another season passed, during which the bride became permanently a wife, though thinner than ever, *pale around the gills,* said some local women, who knew just by looking. It was conjectured that the Irishman had failed to make her happy.

It was true that she did appear more bleak and was easily chilled. She did not recover quickly from the loss of the child. Her nerves were delicate. As the seasons turned back toward the dark side of the year, she grew frightened by noises she did not understand. Once, a maniacal laughter rattled through the bush, and the woman sat bolt upright in bed, frozen by a terror of madness. She shook her husband awake.

"Stephen," she cried, "there's someone very insane or wicked running around outside!"

"What?" he said, groggy but listening.

The laughter scuttled through the clearing again, and the woman's fingernails cut the skin of her husband's arm. Then he too began to laugh, and she wondered if her entire marriage,

her accumulated seasons with this man, were a cunning decep-
tion leading up to the cruel trap sprung this night. Would she be
fed alive to that shadow-beast she had seen or imagined on her
first day? It was everywhere and nowhere. It was within Stephen, too, for even he was not what he seemed to be. He would
not stop laughing. And though it sounded not unkind, it was
the cruelest note of all.

"Annie, Annie," he whispered, soothing with his hands,
"that's the sound a buck porcupine makes as its mating call.
Now go to sleep."

But a day did come when she maneuvered her body down
onto the mattress and conversed with Turid between pains. The
large woman had her sleeves rolled up to the armpits and was
boiling water. Between the blankets the drama of water burst
from the mountain, and blood showed.

"It's a good sign", said the midwife, who had just entered and
was consulting with Turid.

"Breathe faster and shallower", she advised. "It's like climbing
a little hill, and with each one you'll get better at it."

Though the little hills got higher and higher and became
whole ranges of mountain, and she was tempted to add screams
to her groans. *If only Stephen could be here*, she thought. But he
had been rescued by Camille early on and went with him down
the path, albeit a little reluctantly.

"Y'might not be so quick t'fill yer ovens with bread," Turid
shouted down after their heels, "if y'had t'see what it takes t'get
it out!"

"Birthin's fer wimmen!" called back Camille.

"Birthin's not fer cowards, that's fer damsure!" she yelled at
the back of their heads.

In the early part, which they accurately called labor, she did
not mind if her husband was not there to hold her, but then she
was screaming, and the rhythms scrambled, searing, and coming
too fast.

"Don't push now, girlie, pant, pant!"

"Let's get this pup born now", said the midwife through clamped teeth. "Now push, push!"

And there was a small, pinched wail from an electric blue creature as it fell into the midwife's hands.

"Lord, don't they all look like skinned rabbits?" exclaimed the sentimental Turid, with smiles and hot cheeks.

"It's a boy", said the midwife, showing the body with its lurid coil of umbilicus.

"Give it a tit, give it a tit", said age and wisdom, and the little mouth sucked terribly and beautifully on her breast, dripping his mother's fluid all over. She gasped and cried. *It is a boy.* Grateful that it was human and alive.

"There was a bad moment there", said the midwife. "That critter had the cord wrapped round his neck, and what's more, a section of it was tied in a granny knot."

She showed the marvel to the mother as she cut with a knife.

"Bloody lucky little gaffer", said Turid.

"He must've been no bigger'n a polliwog t'swim that knot. Wonder it didn't kill him in the end though!"

"He's a tough bugger!"

Oh, it is a fine little body, noted his mother. *His skin is brown, curled around my breast as white as dogwood blossoms. Black hair and wide little shoulders. Oh, he is no squire Ashton, but a mite of a Celt and offspring of the northern sea. No doubt there is some fisherman with that same jaw and raven hair pulling herring into his boat at this very moment.*

Yes, she would soon float along the path to show her bright dark boy to the world.

"I've been through this seven times," said Turid, narrating the event, "and each time it's different. All the same, there ain't one of 'em not special."

"Oh, you get used to it", said the midwife, who was a leathery, practical sort. She was wrapping up the great purple horror of the afterbirth in paper, to bury.

The mother would find soon enough that there were others who had pushed so many out of their wombs in one way or another that her encounter with the miraculous might prove tedious. So she would nurture a secret sanctity, hidden from the eyes of the world. And would offer it only to those who could receive her epiphany.

* * *

A few months after the child's birth the husband came into the cabin one hot morning. His wife was resting on the bed, and the new creature pedalled its limbs happily beside her. As the man gathered the child into his arms and went outside in the sun, the mother awoke and called after them.

"Stephen?"

But he did not respond, and she rose to investigate what he was doing with this baby who was not yet his. He was halfway across the field when she decided to follow, to take with them a dose of sun, to be fused by light into One by this new equation of three. She grew alarmed, however, when he laid the baby on a blanket by the river, struggled and stepped from his clothes. He was uncovering the baby as well.

What madness is this, she said to herself, and quickened her pace.

"Stephen?"

He turned with the infant in his arms, two nude beings entangled in each other's limbs under the hot sun.

"Have you lost your senses?" she said angrily, coming up to them. "There might be a breeze and he'll catch a chill." But the pool simmered like a warm bath, and the symphony of insects would not be defeated. The horses watched, tails thwacking at flies as bees ripped through on private flight paths. The man smiled. He began to move about in the air, dancing slowly, whispering to his child, prancing on the grass like an unfettered quarter horse. The Centaur.

"This is the air, my son", he breathed into the small curved ear, and had he then beaten the earth with his hooves he would indeed have leapt toward the sun.

"I give it to you, it's yours."

And the air was good. She sat down on the blanket and began to smile at this Adam who might at any moment peel crisp fruit with his teeth. This tiny Abel who had not yet committed himself to self-defense. Though she did glance around at the paths into the woods along which other people did sometimes pass.

"Suppose a neighbor comes!" she said, amused. "They'll say in town that we were screaming naked around the meadow with roses in our teeth."

Which he did not hear but was tempted to.

"And this is the earth", he said to the boy, folding his muscles, kneeling to clutch a chip of dried manure that rain and time had debittered. He held the stuff before the child's nose. It sneezed, showing gums, but produced other happier noises that reassured the mother. She would have laughed with them and been absorbed had not her breasts begun to ache for the child's mouth.

"This, too, I give you", the man said.

Slowly, as swimmers go down to the sea, exchanging the sweet tyranny of air for the harsher one of water, the man entered the pool. The woman struggled to her feet and was about to protest, but the planes of his back were immutable. When both he and the child were submerged to their chests, the child appeared startled but not unpleased, slapping about with his miniature hands that someone had so recently invented.

"This is water", the man said, pressing his lips to the ear. "This too I give."

He came up out of the pool to stand before the woman. He stood without shame or self-consciousness, gazing at the child with some inner repose beyond her understanding. She waited quietly before her possessions as they completed their contract: the pulse beat softly in the depression on the child's skull, and a blue cord spasmed beneath the skin of her husband's arm. Then, she reached for the child's body, which was more than ever her own after this separation, this exposure. She clasped it to her breasts. Warm milk began to fill its thin, cooled flesh.

"I give you all of these. And I promise", said the man to his son, "that no one shall ever take them from you."

PART TWO

The War

Summer 1936

10

Life continued on in the clearing where the Delaneys had conspired to live. About a mile from their fields, where their lane cut into the road, the one-horse shay spun its wheels along the ruts and turned toward town.

Swiftcreek had achieved permanence now, finally convinced of its own existence. The faith of the inhabitants had been justified by its recent promotion onto the provincial map. During the late 1920s the village had grown fat and sleek as an autumn muskrat. There were a half-dozen new streets, upon which small geometrical residences, with lawns, were neatly arranged. Several of the cruder shanties had been swept away over the years, sparks from rickety stovepipes catching tinderbark eaves and fanned by ill winds. Patriarchs and codgers had been burned in such fires, lonely men given over to drink and memories, some of whom had opened up the country, some of whom had never worked. The rubble of their hovels was carted away to make place for a feed store here or a post office there. Anne Delaney, in her weekly column for the town paper, would attempt to write obituaries for some, those who could be identified. But by and large they were unlamented.

The land beyond the peaks now lay in the grip of a depression. The valley people did not suffer to the degree experienced by the rest of the country, but the universal tension was felt, and the eyes of the men who rolled by in boxcars spoke eloquently enough. The soil still produced its harvest here, where there were those willing to turn it, though it yielded only food and not the reassurance of a little solid cash. There were the mills as well, fed by the ocean of timber, producing the slabs of fir, balsam, and cedar that rose in tiers on the loading docks beside the rail. But as the barren years progressed, even these dwindled to a few unsold gray piles. The engines continued to run in and out, heading east and west, jarring the mountainsides with echoing hoots and quaking the foundations of nearer houses. Children stirred in their sleep but did not wake, grown accustomed to the vibrations that shimmered the blood and invaded all dreams.

The trackmen would stand to the side of the rails as the slower trains pulled through, laden with drifters or with what wheat still grew somewhere. They stared solemnly at the fabric trains that roared by with thousands of bales of raw silk from Cathay bound for the garment districts of the east. All other traffic was shunted to the sidings when these priority shipments were mainlined through, which was only fitting, as passengers were abundant, and life, along with the dollar, had been devalued. In other parts of the country unemployed men were rioting. But here the laborers would only suspend their banter and lean on their tamping bars, daring the hurtling engines to interfere with their fates. They could have grown cynical and furious within their helplessness. But as the machinery of economics roared by them, they remained stolid, for they also had land, which was their real life.

Anne Delaney jogged along in her cart, upright, her chin horizontal, eyes clear, reins held firmly in her hands. Behind her, in the box, like sparrows in a hard nest, her three children bounced and rattled around, giggling as the shay made its way through the potholes of the road to town. She was grateful for the bit of cash in her pocket that morning and for the man, her husband, who had provided it, wrestling a living from his furs and summer work as fire warden for the Canoe and Upper Columbia. At two dollars a day they were fabulously wealthy, it seemed, and could afford the copper boiler she was after this morning without guilt. Times were not as bad as they sometimes did appear. There were the sheep. Mutton and wool brought in a little silver. The sandy, fertilized soil turned up potatoes each September; the cows were generous with their milk; and the hens laid so many eggs they could sell a few dozen a week. And before the snow came each autumn, there was usually a flayed moose or caribou hanging from the cottonwood behind the barn.

A good life, she thought, and wondered why she continued to suffer the wound in her breast, which she had diagnosed as chronic separation. Separation from just what, she could not say. England? No, she did not miss it overmuch. Papa? No. Emily? Yes. A faded memory of singing ice and a warrior's kiss? Yes, but even this affection did not explain the level of anguish that sometimes fountained up from within. It was true that the glass of her self had been cracked by her husband's love, by birth, and by dying to much of what she held sacred: art, ideas, the lively sport of conversation. The liquid of her being had begun to pour out into the lives of others: the man, her children, and a chosen neighbor. But the vessel of her mind had not been fully compensated.

I am happy, she thought. *I am lonely, too. I love and am well loved but remain incomplete.*

When was the last time she had been able to concentrate on a book or hear the ocean in Debussy? Or embrace another human being in the voluptuous union of minds? Oh, she loved her husband, there was no doubt of that, profoundly, passionately, as some will love stars, clear but unreachable. She would look up from time to time to see him engaged in some task. He was always wholly involved in whatever it was: playing the flute or rasping rust off hames or doing something horrifying to the testicles of newborn rams, turning them deftly into wethers. She would stare through his skull then, wondering if he was simply shallow and heartless, and her concept of him a romantic illusion. She often wondered who he was, for he still revealed little of himself through the commerce of language. Yet her own face she found veiled in a glass darkly as she brushed, brushed, brushed her long hair and the man slept exhausted on the bed.

Anne Ashton had stumbled upon the patchwork of her identity only in those moments of her youth when ideas were released from her mind like clutches of pigeons. When other persons, older, wiser—a sister, a professor, an organizer of the earliest rallies on Piccadilly—when they had heard her voice and reflected back a confirmation of her personal equation, she had begun to know: I am a thinking person. And a woman. Though what her exact mission might be had never been revealed.

As Anne Delaney's buggy wheeled into the main street and trotted on down to the shops, many eyes observed her passage. They could not begin to guess the history that lay behind the prim form of the driver.

"Who is that woman?" said Mrs. Parsons, a recent arrival, watching the shay with an analytical glance.

"That's our aristocrat", said Mrs. MacPhale. "A person who keeps to herself and is superior like."

"Really, now," commented the other, "and has she been here long?" Duration of residency was of particular concern to Mrs. Parsons, the newcomer, who had just penetrated to the center of the community's power in record time. An administrative husband and a certain manner of dress had helped. And knowing the rules, of course.

"She's been here a decade or thereabouts and is married to one of the first settlers, an immigrant."

"Oh", disappointed.

"She was a teacher."

"Oh", interested.

"An Englishwoman. A doctor's daughter, actually."

"How strange!"

"Yes, there's some confusion as to why a person of her background should marry a man of his kind. He is rather . . . common", she said apologetically, not wishing to be cruel, merely precise. To avoid misunderstanding.

"But there's always the possibility that she had no choice in the matter", she added.

"Whatever do you mean?" said Mrs. Parsons, delighted and fascinated.

"Oh, nothing, nothing . . ." said Mrs. MacPhale, whose mouth had closed roundly over a small bird.

"Look, it's beginning to shower", she said to distract, encapsulating her awful secrets within the chamber of her power.

* * *

Anne thought constantly about her children. If it was no longer possible to improvise on the pianoforte of her childhood, it was at least possible to create with the raw material of human personality. But so much of their inner life eluded her grasp. When they lay asleep in the new rooms Stephen had built onto the cabin, she could turn them over and over in her hands, wondering who they were or might become. She would hold them in her mind one at a time, listening to the wind outside go spiralling through the night under an opal moon, as owls hooted and coyotes wailed. The stillness within her then approached happiness, even as it opened up new questions, new awareness of the mysteriousness of being. Sighs could not reach deep enough at those moments to express the puzzlement she felt, and the joy, concerning those phenomena, her children.

Ashley was the eldest, ten years of age now, black-eyed and long-limbed like his dad, brimming over with whatever current adventure he had brewed. Smart. Top of his class. She had taught him to read early, yearning for his mind to take shape faster than those muscles that were racing to win and might in the end no matter what she did. She read him as many stories as she could beg or borrow and wrote new ones for him when her supply ran low. His mind was quick and eager to absorb everything.

"What are those letters on the fireplace, Mama?" he had asked when barely able to read, exploring with his fingers the symbols that the man had scratched into the mantle log.

"It's your father's name", she explained, "in a language that is dead."

But he was his father's boy, too. Stephen would swing his little bright love onto his shoulders and walk to town, showing him off to the tradesmen and other trappers who were his friends. Or over the ten miles in a backpack to see Tobac, with whom he hunted sometimes. The child loved these journeys before he grew too big to be carried. He climbed the mountain of his father and rode through the forest on his shoulders, magnificently elevated to a helm of vision. If he at times felt dwarfed by the kingdom of stone and wind, he was thrilled at least to penetrate it on the shoulders of a giant.

"Oh, Daddy, you are clever and very, very tough!" he exclaimed once, hugging the man tight around the forehead as they staggered across a cold stream. Such things from the mouth of a child!

Ash Delaney was indeed their small being of light, molded into subtle shapes by his mother's words and his father's silence. Their concepts of what the finished product should be were not exactly the same, though they were both passionate that it be a masterpiece.

As Turid L'Oraison once remarked, "When y'made that un I sure as hell hope y'kept the mold. He's a dandy!" This and other admiring things were said over the years by the doting neighbor, who had enough of her own, God knows, to spill her affections on. A certain overflow could be expected, though, from spigots that were never completely turned off.

"Little Ash is just like my natural born kin", she maintained, as she and the boy's mother punched sheepskin in the back yard. Spring was looming on that particular day, and they had ventured out to work together in the new sun.

"I should know," continued the neighbor tenderly, "fer I was the one spanked his little ass on the first day of his life."

Anne poured salt over the hide and rolled it up. Her forearms had become sinewy. She had grown thinnish, a woman who appeared to have suffered, some said, and come out the worse for wear, married to that man. She was peeled down to the bone now, not an ounce of baby fat on her, Turid noted, and she had lost some of her tea-and-crumpet ways. The bush had means of roughing up the surface of hands and manners, it seemed. It was still mostly wild out here, even if they were only a couple of miles from the spreading edges of Swiftcreek, where electric lights cast a yellow dome into the night sky. Stale music sometimes blared out from the bar, moving blatantly over the woods to the homesteads. Civilization had come. But the two women might as well have been a hundred miles from it for all the good it had brought. Though they had pressure lamps now, "Sunshine of the North" was their name, and a hand-operated gravity washer for the eternal laundry, "The 20th Century" that contraption was called. There were a few more ribbons and fripperies available at MacPhale's, of course, and there was the road, which Stephen and Camille had put in the previous summer, allowing occasional visitors to come calling.

Some of the ladies who went to consult with Turid were frankly concerned about Mrs. Delaney's welfare. Something seemed to be bothering that woman. She was not communicative when encountering other housewives on the streets of the town.

"Annie's just a serious sort of person", apologized Turid. She didn't offer any further tidbits regarding her neighbor, being wary by nature. Those who probed for gossip or frankly offered for trade anything they knew went away empty-handed. Turid had buttoned her lip.

But she is lonely, observed the older woman to herself, and wondered why Annie should be that way. Didn't they have each other, two gals with their farms back to back and two good fellas with honest calluses on their paws. And two houses filled up with kids—or at least filling.

"I have raised me own and Camille's brood, too," she said out of the blue to her friend, who was red to the elbows with salt and alum, "and I can't say I've been wore down yet!"

Now what is this about, thought Anne, looking.

"There's some of these new citified gals in town have taken t'holdin' their noses as I pass and pronouncin' judgment. A drudge is what Mrs. Sinclair called me to my face the other day. I called her a name back that changed the color of her socks fast, I can tell you. It was t'votin' she wanted t'drag me out fer!"

"Voting is a precious right, Turid, and if you cannot abide that man Bennett in Ottawa, as you have so often maintained, you are now free to do something about it."

"I serpose. But what's one little voice?"

"It's power. However small. And it can change things."

"What can I change?! I expect I never changed much except dirty diapers and one side o' the bed fer t'other."

"That's not strictly true, now, is it", Anne stopped to chide.

Both women were wiping sweat from their brows with the backs of their arms. The wobbly flesh of the neighbor had begun to spread with the years.

"Look how your family is thriving. Your second family. And now young Maurice off to college."

"It's money well spent", said Turid, the light in her eyes contradicting her sighs. "I'm glad to have sold the Hotel if it makes a lawyer of a boy who might've wasted his days in the bar or died under a widder-maker in the bush."

"There, you see, you've answered your own question. You've changed a great deal of things."

Yes, Maurice had been saved, she knew, but wondered what had become of the child poet.

When the older woman had gone, Anne reflected on her own son, a boy whose mind she could sometimes read but who remained largely a phenomenon. She recalled him gliding down the slope on those barrel-stave skis his daddy had made for him, face as pale as milk with a flash of scarlet slashed across it from the clear winter air. Or tromping into the kitchen with clothes always ripped from wild roses or devil's club, grinning from ear to ear under his coonskin cap. His knees perpetually scabbed from rocks as he beat his way along the river bank to scavenge whatever the water would thrust out for him.

"He will be killed", said his mother, watching from the porch, knitting her hands in anxiety. Ashley had been, oh, perhaps four then. Stephen had come out behind her. It was from the porch that they so often viewed the events of life as if from a great height, in repose. In the summer they lived mostly outside. The interior was only for cooking and sleeping and winter.

"He will be killed", she repeated.

"Leave him be, Anne."

"He's four years old, Stephen, and I will not have you training him to be a Spartan."

"He'll become that by himself if it's meant to be. Or by this land. Leave him go, woman, or you'll make a wether of him."

Her husband had caught the bunched apron strings on the small of her back, twisting them so she could not move. It was a curious sensation, this mixture of anger and delight.

"Stephen!" she cried, furious but laughing.

"Annie!" he cried, mocking her gently with that grin. And pulled her to him as the shearer will pin the ewe.

While they kissed, the boy ran up from the rocks and across

the field with platinum minnows flashing in his fist to show them. Smiling his mother's smile through his father's eyes.

* * *

A daughter was added eventually. Anne and Stephen took the train to McBride three days before the birth, and they were grateful for a real doctor and a hospital, because the delivery was difficult. The little girl eased the ache of the small wooden cross in the back field. She came to share understandings with the woman that the man and the boy failed to penetrate. She had winning ways, a face of cream and rose to pierce the sternest of hearts, and a small body full of energy. She met life at a gallop and didn't look back from the moment her feet first hit the ground. She walked and talked early and was shamelessly domestic but just as at home in the barn hucking manure as her brother. However, there were shades of delicacy in her that refused translation. She would arrive home from a solitary jaunt along the edge of the bush to give her mother nosegays of Venus slipper and Virgin's breath. But just as easily might offer for explanation a vertebra from which decaying matter still dangled. They called her Emily, after an aunt whom no one but Anne had actually met.

Another son came, a sickly lad who might have died. But didn't. He grew into an angelic, laughing toddler, ever a source of joy to his family but a subject of concern to the neighbor, Turid, who liked kids sturdy. He would stand and watch as Ash and Emily scaled the peaks of hay in the loft or plunged screaming, naked, into the pool by the river. He was timid but grew bolder as years were added. He was always hanging on his daddy's hammer strap, begging for a ride, and, when obliged, would reward his master the giant with stories he had invented. He was a child of riddle and song like his father's father, and you would not mind a long winter's evening in his company. At two he could sing "The Holly and the Ivy" right through as clear as a lark, and he knew the names of a dozen trees. He had mischief in his eyes. He was the one to put eggs in people's boots or hide for hours in the burlap fleece sacks dangling from spikes in the shearing shed. There would be a fine panic about the homestead until he was found asleep in a bag by his exasperated mother.

His name was Bryan. When he was not engaged in such tricks, he was out in the fields overturning stones in search of the signature of God.

11

The morning following her ride to town, Anne received a letter. Her husband propped it up against the new copper boiler, in which she was canning whirls of fiddlehead.

"Now what is this?!" she exclaimed, wiping her hands on the apron. She fingered the expensive envelope, intimidated by its unwritten messages. The only regular correspondence that came to the house was from her father or sister and stamped with the King's face.

> Dear Mrs. Delaney,
> Mrs. Parsons and myself would be delighted if you would receive us for tea tomorrow afternoon. There is a matter of considerable importance we would like to discuss with you.
> Sincerely yours,
> Mrs. Adele MacPhale.

She felt a moment of panic. It swept over the flash of expectation that had begun to unfurl like ferns in the shade. The house was a mess! Tracked-in dirt, fragments of the wild fronds, full steaming jars, empty dusty ones, clean hot ones waiting for the ladle . . . unmade beds, socks drying over the wood heater, baby chicks in a crate behind the stove, and no tea!

For the rest of the day and the following morning, a reign of terror swept through the cabin. The despotic woman scoured everything, swept the wood floors, turned the cracks in the crockery toward the wall, polished brass, punished locks in her own bun, and generally drove her family to the brink of madness with fussing. Her husband, in fact, decided to go off downriver to repair the roof of the shack at Ptarmigan, taking his grateful elder son along with him.

The two youngest were condemned to pinafore and knickers, and a currycomb was dragged through their hair. As a last thought the chicks were banished under the boys' bed in the back room. Tea was borrowed from Turid. An ugly framed engraving of Bishopsford was brought out from a trunk and hung over the mantle. A certain primitive arrangement of horse chestnuts and the stone cross just narrowly escaped being hidden beneath a pillow, but the woman drew up short at that.

We are what we are, she sighed, though she did hasten into a clean dress and wiped a wet rag up and down her arms. By the time the last touches were being administered to the dwelling, a straightened curtain here, a fiery bouquet of woods-lily there, the rumble of an internal combustion engine was heard coming down the lane.

She took her two children, the crown prince and princess, out onto the porch, to receive at the gate of her palace. She did wonder at herself in a flash of lucidity: Was she so eager for society? Was she hoping for that long-awaited exchange of insights between cultivated women that gathered the tatters of their labors and wove a garment of gold? Had she ever performed such antics for one of Turid's visits? Or to welcome home the man? She had no time to ponder the answer to these questions for the Tin Lizzie had bounced and squealed to a halt in the yard. With a cough of flatulence, the engine died.

"Well, we are here!" said Mrs. MacPhale, dismounting. Mrs. Parsons, pale and shaken, slowly removed her own body from the passenger side and stood beside her companion.

"You do live considerably farther out than we had imagined", said Mrs. Parsons. "And such a road! You must feel so isolated, my dear."

"Oh, there are times . . ." said Anne. "But we do love it here. You can see the stars, and there is room to breathe."

"Yes", said Mrs. MacPhale, who did not appear to approve of space and mystery.

"Won't you come in," said Anne, sensing an uncomfortable silence about to spread. The two visitors looked at each other and eyed the patchwork house.

It was some malicious operation of fate that arranged for the loose step finally to give under the weight of Mrs. MacPhale. There was an exclamation of pain and a sharp wince as the two other women rushed to her aid.

"It's only a little skin", stated the victim admirably, her shin beginning to stain through the stocking. The hostess was appalled, though her children had collapsed at the sight of a frilly bottom turned to the air. They attempted to strangle their hysteria with fingers but did not succeed. Their mother shot them a glance.

When all were arranged inside around the hearth and a cold cloth was applied to Mrs. MacPhale's shin, the occasion proper was commenced. Tea was served, along with a cheese biscuit covered in her own dandelion butter, which the ladies politely ignored. The hostess did feel at a disadvantage, having inflicted a wound on the guest, and was prepared now to acquiesce to nearly anything they might propose. The ceremony of tea proceeded in its most rudimentary form, there being, after all, no lemon or sugar, only thick cream and honey.

"Mrs. Delaney," said Mrs. MacPhale, who was the leader, "I don't know if you're aware of the existence of the I.O.D.E. A branch is being opened by myself and Mrs. Parsons in Swiftcreek. We would be happy to have you join us."

"Oh", said Anne, who had never heard of the organization. She was pleased but puzzled.

"The Imperial Order of the Daughters of the Empire!" they explained, as if the full blast from the brass band might finally convince.

"Oh," said Anne again, "and what precisely is the objective of your group? If I may ask?"

"We're a social organization . . . one of our main intentions is to preserve and foster an appreciation of all things English—the *cultural* things", she said sweetly.

There was a cautious streak in the hostess.

"And is your group open to those of other nationalities? As you know, our social life is rather limited out here, and I believe many women would be enthusiastic. Mrs. L'Oraison for instance . . ."

The ladies' smiles were cut in half.

"Well," the leader said, doubtfully, looking at her assistant, "it is felt that, perhaps in the beginning, we might just limit ourselves to those of English extraction . . . until we have established ourselves proper."

"Oh", said Anne, a certain rebellion working its way to the surface of her face.

"There are many worthy projects", Mrs. Parsons hastened to add. "We'll be sending packages to the Eskimos. We'll be having bake sales and strawberry teas to raise funds. And we'll be inviting speakers from Victoria and Vancouver."

"It sounds a very worthy project indeed", said Anne. "Have the Eskimos been consulted?"

"I beg your pardon?"

"The Eskimos."

"Well, not actually", said Mrs. Parsons. "Though I'm sure they'll be most eager to receive the gifts."

"Yes," said Mrs. MacPhale, "there'll be dolls for the girls and skates for the boys, costume jewelry for the ladies, whom I've heard do love a trinket."

"But I'm sure you'll fit in perfectly, my dear", said Mrs. Parsons, who could spot a person of quality. "I understand your father is a doctor."

"Yes, he is . . . He's also a Fabian."

"Beg pardon!"

"A socialist. He would like nothing better than to see the end of the monarchy in Britain." She sipped her tea.

"Oh, really", said the ladies in unison, and only good breeding kept them from any gestures of outrage. Their eyes were fixed on the hostess to see just what she might say next.

At that moment there was a scuffle of the caged fowl in the bedroom, most of which were roosters and more gangly adolescent than chick. They had grown tired of their prison beneath the bed and had worked their way out. With unerring timing they chose that moment to run through the front room with leggy abandon, peeping and gawking left and right.

There was an intake of breath by all concerned. One of the creatures poised itself on the toe of Mrs. Parson's patent leather pump, hunkered down, and deposited a custard coil. Mrs. Parsons did not notice immediately, but her friend tattled the tale with outraged eyes, informing the victim, whose horror in one instant sucked all oxygen from the room.

Anne saw. If she had been helpless to right the treasonous situation so relentlessly unfolding, she was now physically disabled as well. Her body was pinned double by nails of laughter. She could not catch her breath. The perfect hostess, she knew, would have blithely taken a cloth and wiped the excrement from the toe of her guest and said something witty. But she could only follow, bound and trussed, the anarchy of her laughter.

The insulted ladies were offended not so much by the chickens as by what the woman's hilarity revealed of her opinions. Wronged most of all by their own mistaken enthusiasm. They bent in a flurry of hankies, lips sewn together. Wordless, they steamed out the door. With a bang and a fart from the Ford they were gone.

When Anne's convulsions finally died away, she held her belly, looking down, drained and cleansed. For several minutes she regarded the crumpled lace hanky abandoned on the floor like the flag of a deserting army. The children stood across the room, watching their mother, the rooster chicks pecking in the hearth, the overturned teacups. At last the younger one, Bryan, said *Mum* and leaned on her arm. She reached around him and pressed him into the valley of her breasts. The little girl came over then and joined them.

The woman's eyes swam in ways the children did not recognize, from hilarity or shame, they could not tell.

"Well, it seems", said their mother, "our social climbing is done for good." With that, two long streams of water were released silently from her eyes, her mouth still gashed and smiling.

* * *

"Well, have the starlings departed?" said Stephen. He had just entered and was pushing back his cap with a grin.

She flew to him and threw her arms around him.

"Oh, I'm so glad you're home", she cried into his shoulder. "I'm so grateful you are the way you are!" and could have been trying to convince his flesh.

"Now what's this about?" he said, becoming all pats and squeezes.

"Did they steal the silver?" asked Ashley, coming in behind with a brace of partridge in his hands. Then they were laughing, melted and flowing together into a new shape.

"Pa, what did you mean about starlings?" asked Bryan.

"Starlings are an English bird", Stephen replied. "Someone released a pair of them in New York last century, and they've taken over the country. They drive out the bluebirds. They rob nests. They eat eggs."

Anne, disregarding the minor detail that she too was an import, laughed outright and hugged her husband the harder.

In this way she became more rooted to Stephen and the children, above all to the enigma of their place in the social order. Its low station had threshed a certain falsity from her understandings. Time seemed to cover the little wound she had received at the hands of her past. She no longer wished to be a person of quality, if by that word was meant a view from immense height upon an inferior humanity. Perhaps she would never cease to be an elitist, she thought, but it would be an elite of the merciful, the lovers of song and story, of children, of beauty, and of truth.

Precisely how that was to be defined and, further, how it was to be transmitted to her children was another matter. There was the immediate question of Ashley and that mind of his, so hungry for ideas. She knew that the fields and forest would teach him a wisdom that no city child could possess. But there was more to life, and she was determined to winnow it out for him. She saved her egg money and ordered volumes of preserved experience to administer at Christmas and birthdays: *Robinson Crusoe*, *Tom Sawyer*, and *Gulliver's Travels*.

"Mama," he laughed, looking up from the latter, "did you know there are people who start wars over whether you should cut your egg at the top end or the bottom end?"

"Yes, Ashley, I did know", she smiled.

When he was twelve it was *The Scottish Chiefs*. When he was thirteen and beginning to ask difficult questions about intangible things, she bestowed a copy of *Les Miserables*.

"Mum," he said with a voice that was leaving childhood behind, "d'you think there are actually people who hate just for the sake of hating?"

"Yes. I do."

"Not really?"

"Yes. I've met them. But the point is, Ashley, they don't realize it. They think they're improving the world."

"I find that kind of hard to believe."

"You will meet many such people in your life. They are sad and tragic. You would do well to avoid them at all costs."

Stephen looked up from his old Irish poetry book and said, "There's another way."

"What way?" said the boy and the woman in unison.

"Treat them with mercy, but never let them have any power over your heart."

Her undeclared competition with her husband for the soul of their eldest child continued unabated. What was literary, thoughtful, scientific, and intellectual, she encouraged heartily. Egg money eventually purchased a crystal radio that the boy assembled. Later there came glass cases for his collections of butterflies and birds' eggs. And subscriptions to learned periodicals on archaeology and insects.

The father, Stiofain, would leave his own legacy: whatever was intuitive, mystical, musical, and loric was there for the boy to behold, to absorb through a mute osmosis that existed between the man and his son. There were few words of the revealing kind. The man's nature was not preservable in specimen cases, but it was detectable in those sudden shimmers of light that flashed like the sides of trout in streams. His silences and subtle facial expressions often achieved more at town meetings than the noise of many a bellicose democrat. There was something in his presence that other men admired and gathered around to learn its secret. It was not just that he was the first man in this valley, nor that he had cut a farm out of deep bush, nor the curious fact that he had caught and continued to manage a difficult woman. It was not just that he was handsome and carried his looks with dignity, without vanity. No one could describe it. Perhaps it was his constancy and that solitude of soul which he radiated even in crowds. Thus it was that his glance could shatter liars. When he did speak it was usually in small stories, the point of which would be suddenly grasped by his hearers on long buggy-rides home. His parables were gleaned from the trees and the wind, the tending of sheep and the struggle against predators. Those who understood this, usually the older sages of the community, saw a younger version of themselves in the making. There was his strength, also, which was respected but not feared. His power, exercised gently, contained a mystery as rare as true fatherhood. This was the thing his son admired but could not possess and could not name. The boy's worship of his father expressed itself only in silent glances.

There was a part of the man, however, that made his wife groan, an element of what she called superstition and which she suspected was a perverse offshoot of his religion. It did attempt to explore the supernatural, an area she found wholly danger-ous. She did not trust any force that incited primitive instincts. Their progress from terror in caves to the light of civilization was just too recent. It was impossible to convince her husband of this.

"Civilization is Reason!" she declared once, angrily.

"Reason without love makes a dead civilization", he replied after only a moment's hesitation. The compassionate, knowing look on his face was so infuriating. She was stopped in her tracks, though, by the revelation that her husband was capable of abstract thought. Not that this changed anything, really, she argued. He loved his old yarns and Celtic myths far too much. She admitted that they contained a few fragments of wisdom garnered by simple folk over millennia of harsh existence. She could not bring herself to banish them entirely from the life of her family, but would keep a wary eye on any excess.

"Anne", he said one evening, with a look she recognized.

"Yes."

"If I tell a little story, can you promise you won't be scoffing at it?"

"I can promise nothing, Stephen."

"Nevertheless, it's a story I wish to tell."

"Then proceed, and we shall hope for the best."

"And so I shall, God save us all!"

As the children gathered close, he stoked his pipe. There was that look she distrusted in his eyes. It sparked too brightly. He cleared his throat.

"Have you ever seen a field full of little blue flax flowers swimming in the wind?" he asked by way of opening. The children shook their heads.

"Ah, it's a sight to knock the smoke out of you. So grand", he whispered. "Or have you seen the pink blossoms of the bog pimpernel?" No, they shook their heads.

"One morning in the Old Country I was walking to a cousin's wedding at Ballyferriter, but taking the long route over the mountain, the sun was so bright and the fields swaying so lovely. Up into the pink and blue I go as blithe and as happy as can be, off to a dance like a full-grown man. And what should befall me but the sun starts sinking o'er the sea, and it only morning! *Arra*, says I, can it be a whole day I've been walking these few miles? Sure this is passing strange! And a chilly wind blows up out of the north."

The children shivered.

"Then what should I see but a finger of smoke rising from the top of the mountain where there's an old stone cairn. So I make for it fast, and behold there's this wee bit of a lad cooking fish over a peat fire in the shadow of the cairn. And his face shining like the sun."

"How little was he, Daddy, how little?"

"Oh, as big as Emily here." Emily on tiptoes came only to her father's waist.

"Well, I must have been drunk on the miracle of it all, for it seemed as normal as spuds to meet a tiny little golden boy on top of a mountain.

" 'God bless you,' says he, 'but aren't you worn out from all that walking to your cousin's wedding at Ballyferriter?'

" 'Saints preserve us,' says I, 'but how would you be knowing that?' And sure it was a shock because never had I laid eyes upon this lad in my whole life. He makes no answer, just smiles and hands me a piece of grilled fish."

"Was he a little *Irish* golden boy, Papa?" said Bryan.

"He was definitely not speaking the King's English." Stiofain glanced sideways at the woman.

"Nor bush-English?" she interjected.

"He was a little Irish golden boy. But something more than that, too."

"What? What?" A chorus of voices.

"I dare not say. Let me finish, now. So this lad looks me right in the eye and he says, '*Do not be afraid, Stiofain O'Dulaine, for fear will breed a deadly rage.*'"

The man was lost in thought for a moment, and the children were puzzled by this twist in the story.

"Can you believe what happened next?" he said with a smile.

Another chorus greeted him.

"Well, I eat the fish and thank the golden lad, and then I'm off down the mountain on what should be the longer part of my journey. But I'm at the bottom of the mountain in a lick and into the dance as if I'd flown."

"No!" said the children.

"Indeed!" said the wife.

"Yes", said the man.

He drew a breath, and his brow could not have grown more serious.

"Well, it was a fine wedding with a great tip-of-the-reel and hullabaloo. It was all night I was up, kicking my heels through 'The Walls of Limerick', an eight-handed effort, and 'The Bridge of Athlone'. I slept on a pile of jackets, my belly full of porter, like a poisoned pup.

"On my way home the next day I chanced upon some English soldiers walking the coastal road. They saw I was in poor shape and shoved me around some. I would have given them the fist but remembered the little lad's words. I ran. I ran up the side of the mountain while they stood below laughing their guts out. At the summit I came to the cairn. God save us, but I found not a single trace of the stone fireplace or scorched rock or soot or anything at all to tell he'd been there."

"No!"

"Indeed!"

"Yes, and not a word of it false."

He had a head full of stories like that, some more tame, some so cleverly spun that they would raise the hackles on the enlightened woman.

"Let's have another one", the children would cry, eager to be demolished by terror.

"A quiet one, Stephen; it's bedtime."

"There was this man in Dunquin had two fine strapping sons, but sad t'say, they were as lazy as young shoats, not a spot of work would they do to help their old father, who wasn't as well as he was in his youth.

"One day he gets sick, so sick they're after having the priest in for the last rites. So the old fellow is lying there, saying his prayers, and he calls the two lads to his side.

" 'Boys,' he says, 'I'll die peaceful if I know you're settled at some life's work.' The two lads look glum. 'Would ye like to fish in the sea?' he asks them. No, they shake their heads. 'Would ye like to be farmers?' he asks them. Oh, no, they shake their heads again.

"So he sighs and says, 'Well, I guess there's nothing for it but to give you the pot of gold.' Oh, then their heads go bobbing up and down. Yes, they could do with a bit of that gold all right.

" 'It's in the field,' he says, 'buried about two feet down, and Lord, forgive me, but I forget just where I tucked it.'

"So the two hefty lads are out there digging from morn till night, day after day, and not a speck of gold do they find till they've got the whole field churned up finer than any plow could do.

" 'Faith!' says one, 'not a coin to be seen, but so's it won't be a dead loss, let's plant the field in wheat and sell the harvest.' 'Right', says the other. And so they did.

"It's to the old man they come then and put up a great stink. 'Da,' they say, 'we've dug and planted the whole field and not a glimmer of gold to be found!'

" 'Yer souls to the angels,' the old fellow cries with a laugh, 'but there's yer gold, me boyos!' Then he dies on the spot, a happy man.

"And so they harvested the wheat, and the money they made was worth more than a bucket of gold. And that's how they learned what comes from good, honest labor."

There was some silent thought about that one when it was concluded. The eldest considered it unfair on the part of the old man, tricking his sons that way. But the parable had its effect: Don't be wandering off after fairy gold, it said. Work hard. With which the woman could agree. And she sent them to bed.

12

Her life began to solidify as the years progressed. She had lain down with the man in the bed of time, grown fertile, bled, suckled, wept, laughed, and fed on the bounty of his earth. She had almost discovered contentment and accepted the limits of the possible. But through the valley of fruitfulness there continued to wind a cold river.

The traffic of the stars turned inexorably through the seasons. On earth, wool spun in cycles through her own fingers. Meteors scored the glass sky. Gold moons rolled up and down the mountain slopes. Space bled indigo into black and then back to jasmine and copper again as the predawn chorus of birds swelled and faded, or left for the south, returned once more, or died in the talons of eagles. Beasts also hunted each other discreetly back and forth behind the screen of forest. Armies of men bluntly fell upon each other here and there. And all the while the man and the woman continued to plant and harvest, to eat and sleep and submit themselves to the web of these laws. The embryo of the woman's consciousness pushed within her being and took forms that could not express themselves in newborn gestures or cries.

* * *

Journal Entry:

Swiftcreek, B.C., 2 April 1936

My life is suffused in an excruciating beauty. And a dreadful loneliness. Why? Why is it this way?

My life is a temporary encampment on the edge of an abyss.

I beg for oxygen, for light, for strength. Yet of whom do I ask it? Certainly not that God whose coldness could make me tremble with fright as a child. Mother's great aunts achieved precisely the opposite of their designs. I could never worship a deity who presided over the petty tyrannies and hypocrisies of the Ladies' Altar Society or the genteel cruelties of high tea at the parson uncles. I remember trembling with fright as a child, before the terrorising eye of puritanism. Only Nana—tiny Nana—provided a counterpoint, a stroke of Catholic color in a monochrome of post-Reformation gray.

Yet, she was always too small, foreign, eccentric. I loved her, but how could I ever ally myself with her alien creed, with two thousand years of bad Catholics. "We are all bad Catholics", says Stephen. But then, neither could I cast a longing eye backward to the bacchanal in the forest glade.

Perhaps such false gods must die. One by one they fall away to reveal a hidden face. I do know that he is not the indulgent uncle some of the moderns are urging us to adopt. Edwin Gunnalls may *think* this is his God, but in the end he is no god at all—merely a cosmic rubber stamp to the whims of men who deify their own impulses. Oh, I am a harsh thing!

We are starved for the unknown God. A few, like Stephen, will consume him in a sacrament. Others, like myself, are driven out into the waste places in search of his presence. That elusive presence that is neither here nor there but arrives, strangely, when we are becoming resigned to absence.

From time to time I sense him hidden in the deepest currents of life, flowing beneath verse, lovemaking, the smile of a child, the cycle of the seasons. I tried to explain this to Turid the other day, understanding full well how foolish the attempt would be. But I threw myself at her feet nevertheless!

"I am dying for lack of poetry", I told her.

She looked at me as if to say, "Well, now, who is this queer bird?" But Turid is Turid and will rise to any situation.

"Poetry!" she grinned. "Well, girl, if it's poetry you wants, it's poetry you gets!" She then proceeded to recite for me the long tale of a trapper who gleefully cremates himself during the cruelest freeze of winter. I was almost enticed into enjoying it but drew back just in time. The writer of this homely and ingratiating verse is considered the poet laureate of the north, and a critical word would be nothing short of sacrilege. I would certainly lose this one good friend.

For an instant I wanted to lash back with a few lines from "Four Quartets", the words so true, so clear:

> Love is the unfamiliar Name
> Behind the hands that wove
> The intolerable shirt of flame
> Which human power cannot remove.
> We only live, only suspire
> consumed by either fire or fire.

It was a convincing wind that drew me out of the cabin last night. I was bundled against it, carrying the big empty sack of myself up the eastern logging trail. It is that tentative part of spring in which the day's puddles still freeze at night. I must have climbed a thousand feet of ruts before the trees broke open to reveal Canoe Mountain in all its grandeur. It was white and a full moon rose over it. I could not move, it held me so.

I don't understand why, but I began to weep then. First, a great welling up from within, then silent tears, followed by sobs, then wracking cries. Thank heavens no one witnessed this thunderburst. Though an owl did interrogate the night. In the wake of my seemingly inexhaustible noise I felt a very tender, quiet peace. As if mountain and moon were caressing me, as if the gentle "who?" of the owl was directed at my own unrealised self.

"I am so afraid", I whispered. The wind combing the pines

dragged the complaint from my lips and carried it away. Yes. I am afraid. And alone. But I will not denounce life. It is we who fail to be worthy of it. I have attempted to rap at the door of this mystery with my mind, or batter it with scientific method, but it refuses to open. At times it opens a crack before that other side of my nature—intuition. It must have been given to me by Mother, for Father said there was neither door nor anything behind it. The aunties and parsons had taught him well.

They had convinced him when he was quite young that the universe is cold and that whatever had created it was without a heart. They called it "The Deity", and he called it Science. I call it neither. Mother did not know for sure, though she found the world warm, and her embraces proved it. But she went away before she had shaped me with the heat of her hands. Is my yearning a disguised longing for her?

Perhaps this desire for true home is a quest for the promised land. At the height of my weeping I cried out, "I want to go home!" The words tumbled out from some fissure in my subconscious, while wheeling through my mind went the images one after another of black satin dress with crepe roses, green sundial, and robins dashing against the crystal of leaded windows.

Curious. In the stillness that followed, more of Eliot's lines came, providing the conduit along which my spirit might cry:

> April is the cruelest month, breeding
> Lilacs out of dead land, mixing
> Memory and desire, stirring
> Dull roots with spring rain. . . .

So the poet utters the deep dreams and the lamentations of man. In his protest against a violated world perhaps he creates the material of a better one.

Is this true? Or am I of necessity creating an artificial spark in the universal darkness? An emotionally ill woman left out too long in the elements.

Oh, yes, I am laid bare, my abscesses gaping. Self-pitying, melodramatic as well. Yet there is a truth forming within me, and though it is hurting I cannot reject it. Should a mother refuse the pain of labour? I will not hide from this mysterious being who is myself, about to be born. To do so would leave me haunted and anxious forever. I have only two options: to accept my innate poverty or become the slave of bitterness. I suspect that this will be the struggle for years to come.

Perhaps there are places within us, places of true home, that do not yet exist and are carved from the stone of our hearts only by suffering. Perhaps. Who will tell me if this is true? For if it is not, then I am subject to the cruelest delusion of all. Yet, if I were to know, I would cease to be vulnerable, and I might make my home in exile.

In the beginning I thought this country was clean and un-spoiled, a place of promise fulfilled. Yet time has proved it a variation of desert, its beauty spectacular, but a desert nonethe-less. Beyond each horizon emerges a new emptiness begging to be filled with our tears. Beyond it, promises the wind, lies the true and lasting land where life exults. If the wind from the promised land is at times cruel, it is to remind me that my jour-ney is not yet complete.

O promised God, O silence! O absence whom I do not see, give me the courage at least to believe this!

* * *

Fragment

"The Birth of Our Daughter, Emily"
by Anne Delaney

It is a long labour.
The hour-hands fly then slow.

The hills of pain grow higher,
and we in our ascent
are faced with whole ranges rising in the sky.
The nurses whisper to each other
that my eyes are purple glass, which they admire,
though my sighs are harsh;
they close the door,
discreet upon the scandal of my noise.

We have an older boy
who wants the ring of news
to widen into fact,
but is willing to wait as we engage, enact
the water-tale, the song of blood.
Too young to know
that flesh which parts to take the seed
will break again as life is freed
(and who can say where joy or pain will lead?).

Blessed are the cries of birth:
a woman's, child's, the silent worth
of being (questioned everywhere on earth).
In other wards the nurses bring
the gleaner and his knife that sing
the cosmic praise of death:
"O up in smoke the chimney go
the unwanted miracles, ho, ho, ho!"
Row on row, the women of the future lie
discussing Kant, success, and vie
for knowledge and its rotten swain.
"A seed", he says, "is just a seed
to throw upon a fire."

The doctor is called (he smiles, is bald);

his the voice of authority,
his the eyes that know.
He blesses, assures, his faith endures,
high priest of scientism,
he fades and then returns to see:
dilated now most perfectly.

Push, he says,
and then we three, the father, child, and mother (me)
are melted, fused into a one.
We cry, we strain, are almost done.
A face is born. He checks to see:
Yes, eyes and nose,
brows and mouth,
are situated properly.

But the baby's large, the face is blue,
the shoulders will not, will not
go through.
The doctor yells
and stumbles over tubing,
his voice collapses like the bombed roofs of cathedrals.
The hand of the high-priest trembles as he shoves
the needle into my veins
and shouts for more technology
(his practised eye knows,
there are bells that summon us not
to prayer but to disaster).

This baby refuses to be born.
The doctor insists.
Though his stainless steel authority is no longer intact,
he is prepared for any unseemly act.
There is a spray of blood on his linen breast,

there is loud, white, ceramic panic,
there is an astringent perfume of dread,
the knowledge
that all can collapse,
and lie still beneath flourescent light.
There is the losing, falling, sinking, blinding, draining down the
sinkhole eyes,
and white horses galloping up on fields of moon.

I cry aloud in one last plight,
shouting "yes" before the extinction of the light,
when shoulder one,
then two
are born of me, of you.
A pinched wail from the electric blue
rubber doll baby.
The man, my husband, weeps, then laughs, as I;
A girl, a girl! I cry.

She curls, uncurls her miniature toes;
they run with her, suction her nose.
Legs and hands lash, mouth opens a sweet gash.
Oxygen bursts into sacrificial lamb,
I am, she screams,
I am, I AM.

* * *

Note to myself: Well, if it's poetry y'wants, it's poetry y'gets!
Haven't your literary pretentions died yet, girl? Lord, what tor-
turous straining to make it rhyme. The meter is all wrong. I'll
have to work on it some day. Maybe I should burn it—up in
smoke the chimney go! Or hide it in my journal, that other box
of woe.

Her questions grew urgent but were contained. There were threads of gray in her hair. Her eyes appeared used, though deep as springs, as cool as violets that boots would not dare to crush. Her children thirsted for her smiles and received them. She touched them often with her hands, and though such affections were real, there were other provinces of her being that were separate from this tenderness. Places where the climate was more severe.

The position of her husband in the order of existence continued to pose problems for her: Who was he? What were the reasons behind those odd zones of silence, certain periods of his past? At times she wanted to shake it out of him, or wheedle until he gave in. But the man was impervious to these tactics and turned immediately to stone.

Stephen, Stephen, you cannot claim a noble silence until you first have learned to speak. To me.

The children did not think his silence in any way abnormal, for it had always been that way, from birth. Indeed, an absence of words in a person makes of him a malleable image in the eye of the beholder.

"Daddy is like a king lost in a foreign country", their eldest son once observed in a hushed voice. He was watching his father, who stood beyond earshot. The man was fixing something over by the toolshed, and he was dressed in torn bush jacket, greasy pants, and dung boots. The boy's reverence irritated the woman.

You will be hurt, she thought. *You too will break against his silence.*

She had concluded that Stephen did not wish to communicate with her and added an unspoken corollary, *Nor does he love me!* This was not, in fact, true. But it nettled the woman as she explored his surface, yearning for significant words to break forth from his hidden interior. She was unable to read the continual stream of communication in his vibrant presence. At times she resorted to thrusts at the underbelly of his soul, probing for entry.

One evening she read from the pages of a book:

"Listen to this, Stephen. It's one of your countrymen, Shaw, writing about the Irish . . ."

He looked up from a saddle on which he was tooling images of flowers.

" 'Oh the dreaming! The dreaming! The torturing, heart-scalding, never satisfying dreaming, dreaming, dreaming. . . .' "

The man looked and said nothing. The clock ticked loudly as the woman buried herself in the book again. One of the children muttered in sleep from the other room.

"Yes, we're guilty of that", he said, bending over his leather dreams.

The Centaur did appear to be one who could gallop up and up into massing fields of moon-cloud, wheeling back and forth between the dominions of earth and dream. The woman's citizenship was of a single world only, but it was real enough to her, investigated, reported, and analyzed. It was disconcerting how unsatisfied this difference made her feel. In the beginning their differences had appeared as small flaws, easily mended. It now seemed to the woman that they were worse than ever.

When the visiting priest was in town, she rode beside the man, her husband, with the children bucking in the buggy box, to join the invisible cavalcade, only partly convinced that they were going in the right direction. She retained a number of bothersome questions and had not yet legally committed herself to his troupe of jesters. She was not yet permitted to partake of their Communion. Though a certain stillness did surround her at the crucial moments of the ritual held in the old schoolroom. A small hand-bell dinged, incense rose drowsily, and beauty suffused every cell of the beaten, tired, and ordinary lives of these poor bush people. They did not realize their lot, but she did. She did, and it was too cruel! Under the waves of this exquisite beauty she felt a sharp edge of exile. And there was longing, too, when the man returned down the aisle from the giving of flesh with a live coal of presence radiating in his smaller vessel of presence. Sometimes she watched him sitting there beside her. He was absorbed, quenched, drowned with peace, his big hands folded reverently on his knees. His face like a child's turned upward to beg an outpouring of light.

She envied this Communion, envied whoever it was gently invading him. It had not been allowed her, his wife, to penetrate him so thoroughly. She did note, though, how he often touched her hand lightly with his fingertips as if wishing to uncurl them from their fists or to place into them an invisible portion. At those times he looked too fully, too quickly into her eyes.

This silence was a presence he had chosen to name and she had not. Still, she turned to it more often than she would admit. At other times she had to resist the impulse to bolt from the church during the key moments. Gradually, over the years she had learned to be still and to listen. This waiting consoled her somehow. And it confused her also, for it would not be possessed like a boxed thrush but would fly suddenly, a flash of saffron, then gone!

Turid did not approve.

"What yer hangin' round with that bunch of clowns fer?" she said one day. "You'n'Camille are the jiggerist Catlicks I ever seen! Should've been yous got hitched!"

Turid's dialect would coarsen when saying blunt things. Anne could think of little to reply when that tone was used, so she straightened her glasses with dignity. They had come flying off with the thump Turid gave her on the back to show that the comment was all in good fun.

"I go to look and wait", she said, "and to find my . . . soul." She carefully enunciated the strange word.

"Yer soul? Annie, you spend too damn much time on yer soul!"

The defendant stared.

"I mean, ain't it just another way o' thinkin' bout yerself all the time?"

"Well, I don't know", she replied unsteadily. "Perhaps we have to think about ourselves a great deal—in order to know what we are."

"Yeah, well, I must say, girl, you do enough of that stuff fer all of us put together!"

"Yes. Maybe that's why", she whispered. "I am to do it for all of us."

But she had foundered on the rocks of Turid's unbelief.

"Look at me now", said Turid thumping her chest. "I *know* who I am and proud of it! It's you educated gals that get to stumblin' all over yer innards trying t'find out who y'are. Hell, y'are what y'are, dammit!"

Two small roses had appeared on Turid's cheeks, and steam came from both ears.

Clowns, thought Anne, when she had escaped. *Yes, I am a freak. I am the fat, tattooed, and bearded lady all in one. If I belong anywhere, it is not with the normal people who are at home in the world, but rather in this circus parade of gilded wagons, pumping calliopes, midgets and martyrs, prophets and princes, sinners, cardinals, and naked mystics. Shepherds and geniuses and monkeys clamoring in the tree of life. A pierced Christ nailed up there with all the high-wire walkers in the world. A fascinating, repulsive scene rumbling through history. It is almost too much for delicate sensibilities!*

She never quite heard a complete sermon. She edited the flawed diction and the dangling assumptions mercilessly. She was distracted by the authority of her own sensations. The children, too, grew restive during the foreign rubrics. They bounced and twitched, sighed or fell into doped stupor. Only Stephen remained enraptured.

Ashley served the Mass. He was stiff and anxious not to make mistakes. The priest was teaching him the ritual Roman responses and prayers.

Et ne nos inducas in tentationem.

Sed libera nos a malo.

Yes, please, deliver us from evil, she said in her mind, gathering her chicks into the buggy for the ride home. She gazed anxiously at the torn sheets of a storm sky.

Deliver me from the shadow in my mind, she asked the benign Presence—asking in the same breath if it was real, if it had ever been there. This was the social time, when nods and smiles were exchanged between the French trappers, Portuguese section men, and the other Irish families, the micks. Camille came sometimes, with his more tractable girls. Maurice never came. Occasionally Wanda Tobac was there, seated in the last row, yellow and fierce, looking down sullenly until all had left so that she could depart alone. A flock in various stages of illumination, herself, Anne, the darkest of them all. Anne-the-clever, who did not know herself the way they all seemed to know themselves. Anne—a skeptic in grays and violets, hungry and estranged, even from the candlepower of her own mind. She looked impervious to all eyes that flashed a curious glance at her. She was always in perfect control. She ordered Stephen to flick the reins, and they departed in a cloud of dust, back toward the fissure in the trees.

* * *

Night. The children bedded. Once again the space between the man and the woman grew cavernous. The time of sleeping children, when the attentions that had been safely distracted by work must now turn to each other. She laid aside the afghan that was almost crocheting itself through her fingers.

"Stephen."

"Yes." He was carving something from wood with a knife.

"We never discuss together, you and I."

"Never discuss?" he said, puzzled. "But we do, Anne."

"I don't mean the garden or the children's behavior or what is spawning in the river. I mean ourselves."

He digested this slowly.

"We are woven together", he said at last, "and shall not be torn apart. Do we need words to knot the matter?"

"Yes, we do. Or at least I do."

"We can hide a lot behind words."

"And silence."

"Agreed", he allowed, though she could tell by his face and the sudden preoccupation of his hands with the whittling of a barrel plug that he was about to enter the private room of himself and close the door. Her foot went swiftly into the crack.

"Do you believe in God, then?"

"Yes, I believe in him."

"But you never speak of it, Stephen."

"Why must we speak of it?"

"To tighten the weave", she said earnestly. "We're not woven together completely. We're only in the act of being woven."

"Maybe we should trust what the Weaver is doing!"

She leaned toward him, searching for a reply, yearning in her voice: "Stephen, I don't know if there is a weaver . . ."

If she could have found any more metaphors, she would have offered those also.

He did not answer. His door closed, and she felt suddenly abandoned.

"There's the horses to feed", he said, scraping back his chair. He found his cap. It appeared that nothing of significance had actually happened, though he did go out with a sigh, closing the door too carefully.

She could at times be moved to anger at him. The cut of his jaw, which had thrilled in the beginning, now looked obstinate and ignorant, a mule's jaw. Sometimes it was shaven smooth like the skulls of infants; at other times it bristled like the hairs of an ass' lip.

She made herself furiously busy in the dish tub, scalding his stupid bestial male personality in her mind, sloshing crockery with the last of the hot water. Damn, but wasn't that bucket always empty. When was it he had promised a well and a hand pump? Years ago. Tossed onto the heap of promises.

Serve, serve, serve, she growled. *That is my lot. Condemned like Eve to the sweat of my brow, the agony of birth, and a few fig leaves. No doubt I'm supposed to be grateful!*

He came in then with a bucket of fresh water and set it beside her on the counter. He desired to communicate by presences, standing there, barely touching, giving his labor, the brushing of his arm against hers. She ignored with the shoulder whatever it was he offered.

"Anne."

"Yes." Cold. Polite.

"Annie, sometimes I don't know about your God."

"*My* God?"

"Your God is too much an English judge. I can't warm my hands by his fire."

"Who, then, do you believe in?" she asked, turning to him.

"My God is a peasant, dragging his cross through the streets of Dunquin and Swiftcreek. He's got splinters and dirt on his fingers. He laughs and weeps."

"And smokes, no doubt! A real regular fella!" she snorted. "A smoking god!"

"A warm God. A father", he said, wanting to look into her eyes. "A bleeding God", he added.

She would search for a response when the floor was scourged by the wire broom. She dared dirt to enter. Or her convictions to leave. She whacked the quilt straight on the bed, scene of their other wrestlings.

203

"You Irish are in love with suffering and death. You Catholics!" And would rinse off the scum of her disgust among the pots in the dishwater.

"Who taught us about suffering?" he said, poking about in history with a pointed stick.

But their communication was taking a direction she had not anticipated. The conversation was finished. She dried her hands and went to toss the dishwater off the porch, narrowly missing her rival, the sleeping dog.

Later, in bed, after a sexual incident that had become as ordinary as old socks, the man began to slide into sleep. The woman, however, was afflicted with a form of darkness. Not the darkness that is the slumber of light and that she had come to love as the vessel of the evening thrush or the holy breath of sleeping children. But that other kind, the enemy of light. The stars were sucked out, horror smothered the air. Terror hammered for entrance, possession. As if an evil archon were officiating at a liturgy of hell and she were the sacrificial victim.

"Help me!"

"What? What is it?"

"Hold me; I'm afraid."

So he held and contained her, calming the ewe with his hands until she was still. She began to weep finally, quietly, protected. Freed from a bush in which she had been thrashing wildly for escape.

"What is it?"

"Nothing. Everything. I don't belong here!"

"After all these years. Together. And the kids too!"

He could not take her seriously. It was too much like the after-sadness that followed the birthings.

"Anne . . ." Gentle, gentle. He might have thrown her over his shoulders to carry her home from the blustery moors. But pressed her into the sanctuary of his breast.

She heard him whispering prayers over her and felt his finger on her forehead, tracing the sign of the cross. Stark terror receded but left in its wake her chronic fear.

"I belong neither to the heights of heaven nor to the dust of the earth", she wailed. "Your Irish martyrs could never love me, Stephen, and I doubt if your God does either. I cannot abide the blood. Or the manure for which you have so much respect."

I am lost, lost, she thought in anguish.

He appeared to be dropping off to sleep again.

"At times I could positively shriek", she said.

"Why?" he mumbled.

"The excrement, excrement everywhere! The outhouse is full, the barnyard is heaped with it. The children persist in leaping barefoot into cow-pies, and they track dung in on their toes."

"But that's the way of things."

"Sometimes I just wish the place could be cleansed. Clean! Pure!"

"And where would we be then," he asked, "without dung?"

"Offal. Repulsive offal. It's endless."

She did seem to have a fleck of something foul in the milk. Or was perhaps grateful now for a tangible enemy.

"Yes, dung and dirt. And out of it comes the garden and the pasture and our lives. Don't hate it, Anne. Give thanks for it. It becomes earth when we respect it."

"Respect it? Really! You would make poetics of anything!"

"It's like the past. Out of our blind struggles comes wisdom. If we forgive."

"Forgive. Forgive what?"

"Ourselves and those who have marked us."

"Stephen, I do not expect to find wisdom in the dung heap."

Having defined the universe diagrammatically, it did appear pointless for the woman to hear any more of his verse. But he was persistent.

"Your God wasn't lowered on a golden chain, woman. He

chose to be birthed in a stable. It wasn't any Christmas crèche either. He was born beside smells that weren't too polite. And he walked through a little bit of a tough hill town. Shepherd folk with sheep grease on their hands."

"And must we love squalor? What about progress?"

"Progress. It's good if it doesn't blind you to what life is all about. Cut you off from wisdom."

That large and sanctimonious word, *wisdom*, appeared cumbersome in his wide sensuous mouth, a well at which she had drunk deeply, but not of his thoughts. Her husband seemed distorted by its utterance, by the magical properties of its meanings. So in the end she continued to wonder if she had ever truly known him.

"I think, if I live to be a hundred, I'll never get to the bottom of you", she said.

"Nor I you," he replied, holding her body, "and that's how it should be."

13

His deep voice booming in the bush, the sad, beautiful words trumpeted with joy:

> Speed, bonny boat, like a bird on the wing,
> Onward, the sailors cry!
> Carry the lad that's born to be king
> Over the sea to Skye.

Oh, yes, she could still be stirred by the man when she came upon him singing and felling trees in the forest. The teeth of his bow saw cut music from the butt of a pine.

> Loud the winds howl! Loud the waves roar!
> Thunder clouds rend the air!
> Baffled our foes, stand on the shore,
> Follow, they will not dare.
>
> Burned are our homes, exile and death,
> Scatter the loyal men,
> Yet, e'er the sword cool in the sheath,
> Charlie will come again.
>
> Speed, bonny boat, like a bird on the wing,
> Onward, the sailors cry!
> Carry the lad that's born to be king
> Over the sea to Skye.

Her foot would crush leaves then, and he would turn, nod to her, grow silent. She remembered first laying eyes on him with his horses, how even then he had not been surprised and had revealed nothing. It was his way of protecting himself, she supposed. Were he to expose his weakness she could begin to treat him as a weak man, and then he might become one. Did he fear this? Did he believe in himself so little? What lay behind that admirable stone monolith?

Oh, yes, the dreaming, dreaming, heart-scalding dreaming! A lot of that, she guessed. A vanquished people grown gentle after centuries of foreign domination, melancholy, poetic, romantic to their cores. There was no harm, she thought, in pining for a good prince to restore their kingdom. A little late, perhaps.

Edwin Gunnalls was a different kind of man. She had seen that, finally. Just before his departure he had asked to speak with her. After a town meeting that night he had walked her to the buggy.

"I'll miss you a great deal", he said, with the contortion of suppressed emotion on his face.

"Yes, I too shall miss our discussions. Your radical ideas, Mr. Gunnalls, have brightened many a long winter's eve. I can't say that I agree with most of your positions, but they have provided much private stimulation over diapers and dishes."

He did not reply and appeared strained.

"Well," she went on briskly, "the university is indeed fortunate to have such a dynamo of thought for a chaplain."

"Yes, thought", he mumbled.

"Are they aware that you're a subversive?" she asked mischievously.

"A subversive! There's a judgmental word for you. No, they don't know, and what they don't know can't hurt them. It's for their own good, you see. They're part of an ancient structure, a rotten tree. It needs tearing down to . . ."

"To fuel the fire of a revolution?"

"It's a tyrant, an oppressor!"

"Does it have an army, a secret police?"

"Well, no, but—"

"Lethal weapons, torture chambers?"

"It used to, in the past!"

"But now? I mean now?"

"No!"

He was very irritated.

"Look here, Anne, you're doing that again! I never quite can grasp why you of all people must defend an archaic system that you don't even believe in. You are a perverse woman!"

She smiled.

"It's true that I don't believe, or at least don't believe in the way my husband does . . . like people who have seen something and are forever after changed. But you're wrong about me if you think I'm trying to be contrary. It's just that . . . well, I can smell lies, and there is a very strong smell whenever I hear that old institution being hated and feared. Usually what is hated and feared is in the imagination of the beholder."

"But listen, we're educated people! I have a degree and I know!"

She looked at him compassionately.

"I knew many brilliant people back home who couldn't tie their shoelaces properly and who maintained with absolute conviction some very bizarre ideas."

"Thank you very much!"

"Edwin, what I'm trying to say is that even the best and the brightest of your revolutionaries are steeped in their own mythologies. An ocean of facts can be colored by your opinions and your need to get rid of the old way."

"So you're saying I have a prejudice. I'm a raving lunatic!"

"That's precisely what I'm *not* saying. I think you are simply normal. We all judge, and mostly that means we misjudge. You told me that this Church you so detest is a tyrant. Of course to hate tyranny is good. But what if a child going through the turbulence of adolescence were to say that his mother and father were tyrants because they wouldn't permit him to do as he pleased."

"But I'm not a child!"

"We are all children, Edwin Gunnalls, and very immature children at that!"

"Thank you so much for this astute assessment of my personality!"

"You're angry. I made you angry."

"Not in the least", he huffed.

"This Church, this thing that neither you nor I believe in—it has a very odd sort of power, don't you think? Doesn't its only power lie in being a voice in the consciences of men?"

"There you go again. Look, Anne, it's so primitive a religion. It's so pessimistic . . . so damn *critical*!"

"Maybe it's realistic. Perhaps there's something to criticize, something invisible in the atmosphere that's poisoning us all. Something that kills love."

"Love doesn't need rules. Love should be like the fruit in a wild orchard, free for the picking."

"I think there is nothing so powerful as love, and nothing that is so much in need of rules. Orchards need exquisite care, you know. Otherwise the fruit gets smaller and bland and the tree puts out a thousand new branches; then it dies prematurely. Only for a while do the beasts gorge on the fruit that lies rotting in the forest glades."

"We'll see", he said coldly.

At that moment she had glimpsed the difference between the minister and her husband. Stephen's strength was the long, silent labor of the orchardist. Reverend Gunnall's strength was a flash of theoretical passion, ready for any heroic destruction. He was the religious form of those young comrades described by Emily in equally passionate, equally theoretical letters. What fruit would the coming decades bear? Which form of strength would be vindicated?

* * *

She arrived home one evening after another meeting in town. With the help of the local magistrate, the teacher, and the new minister she was conspiring to establish a small public library in an abandoned cabin on crown land. Already the bureaucratic road blocks were becoming impassable, for even the lowest of functionaries must defend his territory. Somehow the subject of books and children's minds had been lost. Eventually there would be a collection, she supposed, but it could be years before opening. Her temper had been under control all evening with some success, but now it might explode if given an opportunity.

She stopped on the threshold of the front room, listening. The house was quiet, though she could tell by the breathing from the children's bedroom that it was not empty. The atmosphere was freighted. She smelled a residual tension. Something had occurred in the room. Where was Stephen?

She found him in the dark by the red glow of his pipe. He was seated on a stump by the river under the moon. She walked up behind him in perfect silence. Without turning he said, "Anne."

She sat on the grass by his feet.

"This stump here, this is the first tree I ever felled when I came to this place."

His voice was strained. She reached out and touched the trunk of his leg.

"It's twenty-four years I've been here. Half of that I was alone."

"What's wrong, Stephen? Something happened tonight, didn't it?"

He sighed but did not speak. In the opal light his face was the carved marble of a Greek hero. He sighed again, staring at his hands as if they held something.

"Tell me, please, Stephen."

Speak to me, oh, speak to me from your ocean of silence.

He put his head in his hands. His sighs deepened, deepened, and gradually became suppressed groans. She stared at his massive, shaking shoulders. She was perfectly still. The impossible was happening, and it was a terrible sound, wracked and broken, going on and on. He was fighting it back, but the more he did so, the more forceful it became.

"Stephen", she whispered.

"I am not a good man!" he cried.

What has he done?!

"Tell me, tell me", her voice urgent and fearful. He raised his right hand and looked at it.

"I am not a good father. I struck Ashley tonight. I am no good, Anne."

"No good!" She almost laughed in relief. She had struck the boy's hind end a number of times, and he was no worse for wear.

"I was ashamed of something, and I took it out on him. I disciplined the lad, but for the first time in his life I did it in anger. I felt a moment of . . . hate, Annie."

"Hate?"

"I love him so much, you see, but there was that hate like a rock in my hand or a knife plunged in my heart."

She recognized the metaphor as a release of unbearable emotion. But what had actually happened?

"We're broke. I didn't want to tell you. I didn't want to worry you, but there's no more money from the government this year. And maybe never. I've been fighting with them over my sheep. You can choose, they said, it's your sheep or your job! So I said sheep. With the fire-watching, sure there would've been enough cash to see us through these times. But I chose my dream over my family."

Why, why, did you not tell me about this? Why?

"When Ash was at school I found I needed a part for the

buggy. I took the little box where he keeps his berry money. I got fourteen dollars and thirty-nine cents, mostly in shin plasters."

She looked at him.

"When you were out at the meeting tonight I took the boy aside and told him. Before I could say we'd pay him back, he burst into tears and wailed at me, 'You took my money; now I have no money!' It tore me up. I felt sick with shame. I struck his face hard with my hand and roared at him. Sent him straight to bed. He cried for an hour, Annie, a big boy like that."

The large man began to cry again. The woman noted the irony.

"Well," she said gently, "these things happen. Was it hate, Stephen, or was it hurt?"

"For a second it felt like hate. I stared into his bawling face, and I hated whatever was making him do it."

She was yearning the revelation out of him. It was coming closer, closer.

More, more, let it all pour out.

"It was me, you see. It was my own face I saw in him, a face full of fear. And he showed me plain what I haven't given him."

"But money buys only..."

"Not money, woman. Strength. Strength."

"Stephen, this is a tempest in a teapot. He's a good, normal boy. He's brave. Sometimes he's selfish, and sometimes he's kind. Just yesterday he spent hours packing Emily around the house, cajoling her out of a tantrum. And he loves you. He wants so much to be like you."

"That's what scares me."

"Do you love yourself so little?"

"This country needs men who are strong."

"But what do you think strength is?"

"You don't break. You don't cry."

"Rubbish! What a big lie you poor men swallow."

But her pity closed him up solid. He looked away.

Come back! Stephen!

"I think I need to be alone for a bit", he said tonelessly. His face was composed now.

"There are things a man and a woman are meant to share", she pleaded. "When I am weak, then you are strong. Won't you let yourself be human just for once? Allow me to help?"

He stiffened.

"All this strength of yours," she cried, "it's the greatest weakness of all, I think. You said that we must forgive ourselves, but have *you*? Have you? It's something in yourself that you hate."

He stood and walked down to the river.

Do not leave me so alone, she whispered.

Several days later the man apologized to the boy and counted into his hands, one by one, fifteen crisp dollar bills. He would not tell the woman where he had obtained the money, but she eventually realized that there were two items missing from his possessions: his best gun and his flute. She did not approve, yet it was an act she could scarcely condemn. He had sold a part of himself for the boy.

* * *

The sheep milled at the bottom of the trail, their bells making nervous music. The man put final hitches on the pack horses. He was distracted by a hundred details, but if he was too occupied at that moment to look at his family, he was fully conscious of them as they gathered around.

"You will be down once a fortnight?" the woman asked, though she knew already.

"Yes," he replied, "when Ash comes up to relieve me."

The boy was as restless as a young colt. He was upset that he could not take the sheep up the mountain with his father.

But the man had explained, "Who'll look after this place when I'm away?"

"Mum can!" the boy had replied.

"Your mother can't handle the livestock, the garden, and the little kids all by herself."

There was an acre of potato in bloom, and if bugs and weeds got to it first, there would be little for the children to feed on over winter. The man had to leave, for the flock of sheep was now too large for their limited pasture. The results were inevitable: when Ashley was not weeding up thistles or digging the new outhouse hole, he would be condemned to wandering despondent along the river or drudging his way through Cicero's Latin, which his mother had prescribed as a counterbalance to the priest.

There were embraces and more reassurances from the man and howls from the youngest. The eldest boy and his mother looked grim. Stephen looked at each face carefully, memorizing. And mounted.

"Ho, Sally!" he called to a blue dog, one of Bluey's descendants. Immediately she began to dart and nip and bark the sluggish flock up the gentle grade of the trail. The man became all rope and whacking leather and horse sweat and golden hairs coiling on his arms. He looked back once through the filigree of sunlight and saw his family there at the edge of the field, watching him go. That small cluster of human beings and the patches of field were made by him, he saw, and they were fragile creations.

Alone I came to this place,
I was barren and who has brought me these?

A little farther along, when the sheep began to fan out into the underbrush, he rode up around the main body of the flock, dismounted, found the leading wether, and tied him to the saddle by a long thin rope. The others would follow, gradually pulling together, urged on by the dog.

As they climbed, the forest changed from deciduous to conifer, thinning and drying little by little. Moss replaced the fern and devil's club that choked the bush below. Occasionally, he would cross the narrow migratory trails of woodlands caribou, thin paths, thousands of years old, cutting through the fresh trails of man. From time to time there were breaks in the trees, and he could see below to the slash of river, the miniature buildings of his farm, and a thread of smoke rising from the house. He turned back toward the peak of the mountain, and they became memory.

Mosquitoes hummed. The sheep began to pant, lolling their tongues, and the man decided to rest them by the creek that was following the path up the mountain. He did not want to push them. It was a good flock now, over a hundred ewes and lambs, built from the dozen animals he had purchased years before. *Suffolk*. Sturdy and big. Open black face, able to rustle for feed on dry range. They had been shorn a few weeks ago in June and were now as light as they would ever be. The climb was still hard on them.

A slow, steady progression upward with plenty of rests was about all they could handle. *Like people*, thought the shepherd.

Routes to higher ground tended to flow most accessibly through ravines and valleys cut into the mountainside. It was darker here, but water ran down as well, quenching the parched animals with catapults of effervescent blue struck by sun from the snowpack on the peaks above. There was abundant feed too, nourished by the spray in the shadow of green canopy. Yet there were many perils: rock slides and too-narrow bridges cast down over the rampant creek, or sudden alpine storms even in July, freak onslaughts of sleet and snow that might soak the thin-skinned sheep and kill them with pneumonia. And predators—bear, coyote, wolf, and cougar.

Water flows only through channels, observed the shepherd. *So too, the river of life flows only through those valleys that have been cut by trial and suffering.* He did not relish the idea, did not love suffering, as his wife had accused. But the thought did cross his mind that their present pain might be a route to higher ground if they could hold onto each other.

They were close to halfway by sunset, and the man bedded the flock down in a glade by the roar of the creek. He set a salt block in the midst of them and a kerosene lantern nearby on a rock, and they settled around these two islands in the unknown. The man rolled himself into a sleeping bag by the fire. With the sun gone it grew cold. A coyote called. The dog slept with one eye open, owls hooted, and dawn came quickly.

The following day they reached the plateau at the base of the crags, a meadow that opened up beyond the last stunted balsams. The wind and the alarm of marmots filled the air; the perfume of white and purple heather was everywhere. From the height of the meadow the earth rolled over into a deep bowl of green, a hidden valley hanging among the peaks. It was lush with grass. A few stands of dwarf evergreen grew here and there, none taller than a man. A silver stream ran through it, murmuring over cataracts. It was utterly pure and still, save for the sound of sheep bells and the bark of the dog herding them down.

He lay sleepless but content that night beneath the giant's ring of daggers, the moon shining into his world beyond time. He could hear his thoughts in space, monumental thoughts that seemed to cry out loudly over his kingdom.

He began to remember his wife, but the ache of her recent unhappiness swelled within him, and he pushed her from his thoughts. He turned away from that part of her he could not understand and was the source of their pain, it seemed. But he did feel longing for the warmth of her body beside him, her arms reaching around him in sleep, and the moments when they climbed together the rocks of physical ecstasy and fell sated into peace, all of their secrets poured out. Those moments had been rarer lately, copulation being simpler.

In the moonlight he pitched the camp tent, stretched his limbs, and walked from one end of the glade to the other. Water boiled on the camp stove, which he had stoked with spruce cones and brittle sticks. There was a joyful brittleness to all existence this evening: the stars, the grass, the ting-ting of bells, the snap of wood in the firebox. The air cold and luminous.

Again the memory of his wife afflicted him, an unhappy face that appeared to accuse him over and over of failing to be what she wanted him to be.

Why is it she cannot accept me as I am? he questioned. *Why am I not enough for her?*

He did not ask why she was not enough for him, why he pursued solitude as if it were his true bride. He played his tin whistle up into the atmosphere, long lamenting notes he could not coax into a jig. He missed his flute.

Sleep came eventually. Or half sleep. And into that zone that stretches between the poles of stone and spirit there came a visitor.

Stiofain!

"Who is that!" he cried.

It is I, boyo!

"*Da*", he whispered.

Silence. The vision smiled, riding a white donkey under the moon.

"A mirage. A figment of my imagination. Or a deceiving spirit. Go! Be gone!"

I am none of those things, Stiofain. I am a wee hole in the cloud of unknowing that you have entered. I am a messenger.

"Why have you come?"

I am here to speak a word to you, a small poem . . .

"Words. More words? There are no answers in words!"

Ah, you are afraid of that, aren't you? Let me assure you that there is Truth, though answers aren't always what we would expect.

"Enough! I will awake now!"

Wait, wait until you have received an answer for which you once begged . . .

"God save us, and what might that be?"

> *The stone and the fire made battle,*
> *The sea and the sky were wed,*
> *City and forest were coupled*
> *And lay in the bridal bed.*

> *Freedom and faithfulness were one,*
> *And danced in the morning light,*
> *But darkness covered the face of the sun,*
> *And drove them apart in the night.*

The man Stiofain lay listening, daring to breathe.

"Is that all?" he said.

Not entirely. The verse is unfinished. It is you yourself who will determine how the story shall end.

"The poem has no meaning for me."

It will in time. Listen to it, follow it, and the severed weave of your hearts shall be woven together. The past, the blood, the woman . . .

"I think it's too late for the woman and me. It was a mistake, and there's only endurance now."

The face of the vision grew gentle.

I promise that you will one day understand. Then you will see—not a drop of spilled blood has been wasted. Forgive, forgive . . .

The vision rode closer.

I am sent, also, to give you this.

The messenger dropped a ring into the dreamer's hand. There were markings inscribed into the thing: a triangle flanked by stars.

He struggled to understand the images. Was it a symbol of the Holy Trinity? Did it represent his three children? Was it a mountain? It blurred, became a cup overflowing, blurred again. The dreamer, choked on imagery, could not catch his breath.

Hup, Betty, hup, and off trotted the vision into mist.

"*Daddo*, come back!" he pleaded. The dog, barking sharp under the moon, began to tear across the slope. The man awoke. He groped for his rifle and fired a round above the dog's head at whatever she was chasing. The peaks repeated his shot and gradually faded into silence, or a stillness in which he heard the shot echoing in his mind.

It was gone. Bears, visions, a dreamer's glutted thoughts, and the horrible sensation of falling, falling through nightmare into the contours of the abyss. He noted above all that in his hand there was no ring.

The shepherd meditated for a while on the power of that hard-mouthed horse, his imagination, which would not be broken to the bit. He heated ewe's milk in the billy-can over the fire, drank it hot, and shivered in the cold night air. He called the dog and crawled back into sleep.

14

Her husband slept beside her in the dark. She lay awake, staring into the night. Owls hooted. The moon shone blue on the snowdrifts. Then the ocean heaved beneath the bed, and she was swept away.

"I haven't taken a sea voyage in decades!" she said to the purser. He pushed back his white cap and smiled at her.

"Going home, Ma'am?"

"Not to stay. A short visit. I haven't been back to England since 1922."

"That's a rough go. Canada's a big country. Fairly rich too. But not quite our style, is it?"

"It's very different."

"England's changed a lot since the War. This is 1938."

"I suspect I will recognize it, after all."

"I guess you will, Ma'am. *Bon voyage!*"

"*Bon voyage*", she said, as he tipped his hat and strode cheerily away down the deck.

She gripped the rails and watched the north shore of the Saint Lawrence slide by. The Laurentian mountains were white. Thin shelves of ice still clung to the shore. It was early spring, or late winter, depending on one's perspective, and the water three decks below her level was steel gray with white caps. It looked miserably cold. There was some slight danger of storms on the Atlantic, they said, but the ship could take just about anything. It was a liner built in Belfast during the twenties (*while I was bearing my children*, she thought). It was huge, but the passenger list was short, about half what it would be by summer. Not many of those who could afford a trip like this enjoyed the illusion of danger. The middle class or prosperous middle-aged were not fond of icy wind as they rounded the decks on their constitutionals.

The afternoon was bright gray, as if the overcast were backlit by bursts of photographic silver. The gulls shrieked. The wind was bearable. Seals arched alongside like black commas.

How very kind of Papa to have sent the passage money. She did not long to see him as she did to see Emily. Of course, they would have jovial, informative conversations, which he would cut short, called by duty to the hospital or to the lecture hall. Sad as it was, the situation was entirely predictable, but it would free Emily and her for real communication. Poor old dancing bear!

Until then, she would have seven days. Seven full days of sleep, brisk walks, solitude. A chance to evaluate the past sixteen years.

She went below to her cabin on B deck, a small, cozy room painted cream. It held a bunk, washstand, toilet alcove, and a chest of drawers. Bolted to the bulkhead wall was a print of a landscape with cows and oaks. Bolted to the door was a framed list of rules and emergency measures. The window was a circle. Shards of Wedgwood blue raced past.

She lay on the bunk and pulled a feather comforter over her body. It was warm. It was perfect. She sighed to the very depths of her bones. She barely felt the thrum of the engines. The surge of the sea against the little toy boat was merely the embrace of a mother rocking her child to sleep. Before long, she fell headlong into dreams.

The supper bell awoke her at five, and she changed into a dark blue wool dress and white hand-knitted cardigan. Turid had presented it at the Swiftcreek station. *Open it on the train, Annie*, she had said gruffly. It was wrapped in newspaper, tied with string. Stephen had kissed her and looked grim. The children babbled and looked upset. Carrying good-bye gifts, handbag, and a satchel of books, she climbed up into the car. The conductor blew a whistle. Stephen waved, the children waved, the L'Oraisons waved. *My family*, she said to herself as the car lurched, the rails rattled, and she cried halfway to Edmonton from fear and loneliness.

The white sweater now appeared to be buff colored in the light of civilization. The hand-made wooden buttons were quaint. It was lumpy, and it bulged in the wrong places, but she hugged it to herself. The cardigan was warm. It smelled of wool and lye soap. A coral-colored porcelain rose that Mama had painted in the late eighteen hundreds was pinned to the lapel. She dabbed on some cheap scent (gardenia—a gift from Stephen—ordered from Eaton's catalogue).

Whom do I wish to impress? The admirable young purser, who has seen a thousand women like me and learned to recognize us for what we are? The Captain, with his charming script? Will I be asked to his table for dinner?

"How very kind of you to ask", I shall say. "I am actually looking forward to a little solitude. Thank you so very much, but I think I shall dine alone this evening."

Do I wish to impress the government clerks on their way back to Whitehall? The merchants? The failed adventurers? The young nannies seeking their fortunes? The grandmothers returning home from visits to the new world, treasuring last glimpses crammed in just before hostilities?

She descended a long wooden staircase, savoring each step of the thick, purple, imitation Persian runner. Colored glass refracted lights from a false ceiling. At the bottom she parted a jungle of potted palms that threatened to encroach upon the dining room and found there a small nook with a table set for one. Many such tables were scattered throughout, and seated at them were other travellers pretending they were self-sufficient.

The lozenge-shaped dining room was pillared, adorned with antique paintings of dubious artistic quality. But the linen on the tablecloths was the best. The electric candles were not harsh. The chandelier in the center of the room threw enchanting crystal lights over everything. A small string ensemble played Strauss waltzes. The waiters were gracious. The Captain's table on the far side of the room was full, raucous, distracting for a few moments only.

I was not asked.

Thank heavens! she answered herself. *Thank heavens, I was not asked.*

She opened her diary and read the several entries that made up the previous months' events:

Bryan's appendicitis—to Jasper hospital in the nick of time. Stephen having a good winter for mink. Emily is too brash for her teacher! I must drive in to town and have a talk with her after school. Austria may cease to exist. Von Papen is a treacherous character. Hitler's tirade was broadcast last night on national radio. I understood some of the German words, enough to make me shiver. There are storms brewing. Chamberlain is either a coward or a foolish idealist. I have been depressed a great deal this winter. Why does this emptiness persist within me when I am so abundantly blessed?

She read and reread her diary, wondering if it accurately related who she was, then decided it didn't matter. Over coffee, she penned new lines: *On ship to England. Alone. My pain surfaces like the humped back of a damaged whale. I stare at the waves where it appears for a moment, at the spot where it rolls over into the sea. I wonder if I really saw it. Was it an illusion? Or was it a brief parting of the curtain that covers the vast mystery play beneath the surface?*

Why am I never quite resigned to unbelonging? Why must I always stare across rooms at the charming female extroverts lavishing gaiety upon themselves and others? The doting European bankers and New York bond salesmen are captivated. The officers and crew are old hands at this kind of deck game, but they seem to enjoy it. I am an introvert. I look at life. I live within. But within me is a void. Is there no love in me? Am I cold? Oh, yes, I miss my family in the west, and

I miss my family in the east. But this ocean carries me upon its troubled surface as if I do not know where I am going, a consciousness adrift at sea.

"Attention, ladies and gentlemen!" said the Captain in a grand voice. "A warm welcome to you all. The crew and I want to wish you a most pleasant voyage during the coming week. The crossing should be uneventful. Some of you have expressed concern about the weather, but I assure you that the meteorology people report normal conditions for this time of year. There may be a few rough spots between here and Southampton, but nothing to worry about. You will probably fox-trot through it all. Apropos of that, there will be a dance this evening in the ballroom. . . ."

And so it went. The jokes, laughter, chiding, the good-natured tease at the expense of an immensely fat German businessman, who laughed heartily and waved, put a fork to his upper lip to imitate *Der Führer*, and won the affection of the entire company.

Even Anne smiled.

"Furthermore, between dances you are invited one and all to visit the Princess Alexandra salon, where there will be the added attraction of a reception and art exhibit. Come and meet the renowned artist, Peter. . . ."

She only half-heard the name. When the Captain gestured theatrically in the direction of the starboard side of the dining room, she saw a man rise and bow, then quickly seat himself again. The artist did not seem pleased by the attention, and he sat staring at his tabletop. He too, she noted, had chosen a table for one, in a poorly lit alcove.

A fellow introvert, she supposed.

After supper she went back down to her cabin and had a nap. She had hoped to settle into bed for the night with a Willa Cather novel that she had borrowed from the ship's library, but her eyes would not stay open. Two hours later she woke, rested and restless. She could not concentrate on the book and got up. She splashed cold water onto her face.

The thought of the dance was not appealing. The life of a professional wallflower was detached at best, parasitic at worst. Then the image of the reclusive artist came to her and piqued her curiosity. She decided to search for the Princess Alexandra salon.

A porter informed her that it was on the First Class deck, toward the stern. Waltz music from the ballroom near the bow drifted along the corridors.

On the way up she wondered what the pictures would be. Drivel? Ego? Real talent? Was he a Canadian, haunted, as so many of them were, by the cruel beauty of their native land? Or was he a typical Englishman landscapist? Splendidly competent and dull. Perhaps he was a devotee of the European philosophies, lavish Expressionism or cold Bauhausian engineer's art. Or he might be one of the new breed who preached abandonment of visual language itself. Would she find slashes of negation, color used as a weapon, a revolutionary lost within his own revolt, infatuated with his anarchy? A daring young man on the flying trapeze of his public image. This year he would be a mad bomber; next year a court portraitist.

Oh, but it was such a surprise. Such a very great and curious surprise.

He was standing in the corner being talked to by an aging couple. The male partner, an Englishman, was droning on about his art theories. The actual artist (of uncertain nationality) was listening to the lecture with some discomfort. His arms were crossed tightly, his shoulders hiked up high and a pained look afflicting his eyes. He was tall and awkward in a brown tweed suit, and he possessed a fine, guileless face. When he worked up the temerity to break the flow of talk, he stammered out his replies, which Anne knew went far above the heads of his admirers.

"We had something really extraordinary during the late Middle Ages", he said. "Maybe the West lost its soul after the Renaissance . . ."

"Ah, poof, poof!" interrupted the lady in a throaty French accent.

"Your paintings are most unusual. Most . . . *unique*", said the Englishman.

"Thank you", replied the artist uncertainly.

"Though I must say there's a somber tone to it all. Rather, well . . . how shall I put it . . . rather sad-making. The world is so depressed these days, don't you think? People need cheering up."

The artist nodded, then shook his head, then nodded again, and Anne decided that she liked him. She took a biscuit and cheese and a glass of sherry from the banquet table in the center of the salon.

She pretended to read the one-page catalogue and listened.

"You paint *le joli désespoir.* It will never sell. You will be un-known."

"I think my friend means—don't you, my dear?—that modern people need a breath of fresh air after all we've been through since the War."

"*Alors*, I mean this man should paint two lovers in a spring orchard, not the broken heart. The broken world. It's simple, no? You choose which one you want!"

"Not quite so simple, love", said her companion. "I was in the trenches at Paschendale. Just a subaltern, mind you, and I came into the game toward the end, but it was enough to convince me that we must never again have a war like it. People need to look to the future now. We need to negotiate, not confront. We need positive attitudes. And your generation has to lead the way."

"But is optimism really hope?" said the artist.

"Surely they're the same thing!" said the man, puzzled.

The woman pulled a pink gossamer wrap around her white shoulders and laid a gloved hand on the arm of the artist.

"What a lovely man you are, with such *serious* thoughts. You should go to the south of France and bask in the sun for awhile. Your paintings are good. Really very good. But so dark! I must give you the address of my cousin Henri in Montmartre. He has a gallery where you could get some exposure."

"Thank you, Madame, that's most kind of you . . ."

"But really, I must admonish you," she wagged a finger at him in mock solemnity. "You must get more sunshine into your painting!"

"She means it, old boy, you could be famous some day."

"Thank you, thank you", he said as he walked with them to the door.

He watched them go down the corridor, exhaled loudly, mumbled, "she means it, old boy", and went out. Anne found herself alone in the salon. She sipped her drink and glanced around the exhibit. Approximately twenty images. Not very well framed. Rich earth tones with flashes of warm complementary colors. Strong shapes, magnificent balance in the designs. Subject matter: human groupings, drama, uncertain themes. She would look closely in a few minutes. First the general sense. Whatever they were, they were beautiful. Exceptionally beautiful forms. And, well . . . *unique*. She put on her reading glasses and was about to inspect them when the artist himself walked back into the room. Muttering, rubbing his face with a handkerchief, he nearly stepped on her.

"Oh, I'm so sorry!" he said, stumbling. "Oh, please excuse me. Did I hurt you?"

"Not at all."

"How very foolish of me not to see you! I thought you were a piece of furniture. I mean . . ."

He flushed and looked dismayed.

"Insult to injury", she said with a smile, thoroughly enjoying herself.

"I really don't mean to imply that you're invisible, Madam. I merely meant to say that I wasn't watching very carefully where I was going."

"No apologies are necessary, sir."

With that he bent and began to pick up the broken pieces of biscuit and generally to tidy up. She saw that his hands were shaking and that his eyes were strained. His ears were burning a bright red.

To distract him, she said, "Your paintings are very beautiful."

To her surprise his expression closed in upon itself instantly. He said, "Thank you", and walked away.

"How unusual", she whispered to herself.

New guests had arrived, and he went over to welcome them stiffly. She did not wish to overhear any more strained conversation and went down to bed.

The following morning he came by her table at breakfast. He put Mama's porcelain rose on the table. It had been broken into three pieces. She groaned.

"I found this on the floor of the salon", he said gravely. "Is it yours?"

"Yes."

"It must have come off during our accident."

She carefully gathered the fragments into her hand.

"It's important to you", he said.

She nodded.

"Look, I think I can fix it. I have glue and paint with me. Will you trust me with it? I'll make it good as new. I promise."

"Yes, please. If you want to try."

"Come by the salon after lunch. The glue should have set by then, and you can give me some pointers on repainting the rose tints. Closer to pink than to red, I should think."

"Yes, that's exactly right."

"These missing bits here, I think I can put some mortar in."

"Would you care to sit down and have breakfast with me?"

"Thank you, no", he said doubtfully. "I'm not really good at socializing. Mad artist and all that."

"You won't have to be charming, entertaining, or informative."

"Charming? I don't even know what that is."

"Don't worry. I have three children, two of them adolescents. I miss my children. I'm a plain woman. I'm older than you are. You won't have to suffer any unpleasant pressures."

He sat down.

A waiter brought them coffee. The ship tilted slowly and they looked out a porthole to see rain blowing sideways.

"I'm sorry about your rose. Someone must have stepped on it. It might've been me. With a little paint it'll be good as new."

"That's considerate of you. It was an accident."

"It was my fault."

"Maybe you had too much sun, old boy."

He looked at her quizzically, then burst out laughing.

"Right. Too true. It was the damn French."

"And the damn English too."

"You're English, aren't you?"

"Yes, full-blooded. And you?"

"Me? I'm a mongrel. Half French, half English, half Spanish and Irish. Black Irish. A nasty combination."

"You're not very good at math, but you are a gifted artist."

"Thank you", he said tonelessly.

"Compliments are a burden to you, aren't they?"

"I suppose they are. But what else do I say? If I protest that I'm not really a talented artist, they say it's false humility, which is the worst form of pride, don't you think? If I say, why, yes, I really am quite astoundingly brilliant, then they say, what a pompous fellow. So you see, there's no winning."

"I see what you mean. A cliché dispenses with the matter altogether."

"It throws a scrap to the hungry lions."

"You don't like your art patrons, do you?"

"I don't *dis*like them. They live in another world than mine. The best of the lot really love beauty, and that's to their credit. The ones who want something to match their carpets are the worst. Almost no one really understands what it takes to make something beautiful."

"I do."

He paused and looked at her thoughtfully.

"Yes, I think you do." He touched the broken flower with his finger.

"My mother painted it about fifty years ago."

"It's good. Delicate and strong at the same time. Your mother has soul."

"Had. She died when I was a child."

"I'm sorry."

"It was a long time ago."

"So, where do you live?"

"I live near a village in the mountains of British Columbia."

"Hmmm. Exotic."

"No. Very ordinary."

"Ordinary? I painted in the Grand Tetons one summer a few years back. The American Rockies. It wasn't ordinary. Nothing's ordinary when you really look at it."

"I suppose that's true, when a person is given the chance and the time to look."

"Most people don't, you know."

"I know."

"I do landscapes for fun. The paintings in the salon are the real work."

"Most people would say it's the other way around."

"That's true."

"Is it because they think a real painting is for decoration?"

"Exactly", he said looking at her steadily.

"Your accent is the oddest mixture of Canadian and midwest American."

"Guilty as charged! I've spent the last twelve years in London and Chicago. After the Slade school I went to the Chicago Art Institute. Eventually I taught there. I had some shows in New York. Minor success. The more serious my subject matter be- came—the more *joli désespoir*, as the lady called it—the less it sold. My dealer dropped me six months ago. I'm on my way to Yorkshire now. My uncle has a farm there. He's got an empty cottage out back. I'm going to ask him to take me in."

"Do you think he will?"

"He will. He says I'm mad but he loves me anyway. I don't eat much. If I can sell a painting or two every year it will keep me in paint and canvas and help pay his bills."

"If you could go anywhere on this earth, where would you go?"

After some deliberation, he said, "That lady last night wasn't half wrong. If I had my choice I *would* live in the south of France. Provence. Maybe in Italy. Umbria. There's such a won- derful light near Assisi. I love the sun. I love the light."

"We live by light", she said slowly.

"And by beauty", he added.

The ship rolled again, and they saw the ocean churning far below.

"I'd better get moving", he said, "if we're going to save this rose."

"When should I come by the salon?"

"I open up after lunch. Come then."

"Would you show me your paintings and tell me about them?"

"All right."

She found him in the salon seated at the banquet table, squinting into his hand. A tray of watercolor paints lay open beside him.

"The underpainting's done. Most of it's dry. Color goes on next. After that, we varnish. It will take a few days. By the time we dock you won't be able to tell it ever was broken."

"That's wonderful."

The small thing lay in his palm like a miracle. Streaks of white revealed the mortared joints. A painstaking task.

"How much can I pay you for this?"

"Don't be absurd", he glared at her.

She gulped and said no more.

"Pull up a chair", he said gruffly.

She sat down beside him and observed the mixing of colors. There were several pools in his tray, beginning with a dusty rose that was almost brown, sliding up through the pink hues to a brash cadmium red, and culminating at crimson. He mixed in white to get the subtler tones. His large brown hands manipulated the delicate brush like a surgeon. Stroke after tiny stroke and the shattered rose was recreated under her eyes. Mama must have sat like this at its first making. Now this man, who had not yet been conceived at its creation, was restoring it to its true form.

His jacket was thrown over the back of his chair, and she noted that the body beneath the white shirt and knitted blue tie was lean, muscular. She looked away. His face, half hidden beneath a sweep of chestnut hair was, she also noted, alarmingly handsome.

In a split second she played out several dramatic scenes, all of them ending in tragedy. Middle-Aged Woman. The flash of youth igniting fire in an old rose going black at the edges. The gradual realization that beneath the aesthete there was perhaps only a moderately talented, insensitive boor. A nice selfish boy in an athlete's body. It was so entirely predictable, a shipboard romance, a dime novel written badly, expressing pathetic sentiments. She would have none of it.

She looked away.

"Let's walk a bit", he said, rubbing his eyes. "This needs to dry. We'll come back in an hour and do the highlights."

"Should we leave the salon unguarded?"

"Where would a thief run off to with stolen art? Besides, anyone who nabs these paintings deserves them."

After agreeing to meet on deck, they went to their cabins to get coats.

The sun was burning through thick overcast, and the wind was brisk from the east. Scraps of ice went by on the water.

"The sea is down", he said.

"A cold wind though", she replied, pulling up the collar on her dingy felt coat, the one her sons called *the horse blanket*. She wasn't sure if she resented looking like a dowdy bush-wife or was grateful for it.

They walked counterclockwise around the entire ship.

"Do you like the wind?" he said.

"I do. I've always loved it. It's like music, like strokes of healing. But, where I live, sometimes it's a cruel thing, ripping at the corners of the house, wailing, tearing through the valley like vengeance itself. It can toss over boats and tear down trees. It reminds me how fragile human life is."

He did not reply.

"There's so much evidence of that in the wilderness", she went on. "Life is short."

"Yes, life's short", he said, miserably, and stopped by the railing. He looked out at the water, and the wind began to whip his hair around.

They stood together for a long time. Finally he said, "Last year I found out how short it is."

"What do you mean?"

"Someone close to me died. Until someone close dies, you don't really believe in death."

"I suppose most things are an abstraction until they hit you in the flesh or in the heart."

He nodded.

"Who was it, may I ask?"

"My wife."

"I'm so sorry. My sympathies."

"Sympathies? The clichés come crowding in."

"I'm sorry. Did I say something wrong?"

"No. It's so hard to really talk about these things, isn't it, because words haven't been invented that convey the depth of it. So you reach for the tired old metaphors that tell the story without making you spill your guts." He laughed. "There, I did it. *Spill your guts*, another great American metaphor. So expressive, isn't it?"

"Very."

"Have you ever lost someone?"

"My mother."

"Ah, yes, you told me that. Sorry."

"And a child in the womb."

"Not quite the same, though. Not as if you knew it."

"Before I lost the baby, I would have thought so too. But death teaches many things. I didn't suspect how much I would grieve for a being I had never seen face to face. But that little person was growing inside me. We have ways of knowing that have nothing to do with our ideas."

"You're probably right. You get a sense of people's souls, don't you? Maybe you guess wrong about personality and their opinions and what their surface life is all about, but you can get down to the heart of a person. Faster than telling will do."

"Sometimes. With certain kinds of people."

"By the way, I just realized—crazy, isn't it—I don't know your name."

"Mrs. Delaney."

"Mrs. Delaney? That's a surprise."

"Why so?"

"I would have guessed a moderately famous name, such as Emily Dickinson or George Eliot."

"You're mocking me."

"I'm part Irish. It's a tradition in my family that we only tease—and tease mercilessly, mind you—the people we really like."

"You don't even know me. How could you possibly like me."

"I liked you when I saw you last night in the dining room. I noticed how you analyzed the Captain's table, and how you wore that wonderful lumpy sweater that looks like an aborigine knitted it with sticks, and how you wrote so furiously in your notebook."

"And what did all that tell you? What did you think I was?"

"I said to myself, there's a woman with a noble mind and a troubled heart. I'll bet she's a lady author from Toronto who writes anguished, sensitive, unpublishable novels, and she's going off to England to see if she can't find a sensible publisher, one who won't treat her like a . . ."

"Like a piece of furniture?"

They laughed.

"Yes, like that. But you've already told me you're not from Toronto. How close am I on the other stuff?"

"I'm not a writer. I sometimes have articles in our local newspaper. I make short poems as birthday gifts for my children. Ditties that rhyme and make sense. Once, long ago, it might have been possible to turn myself into what you describe. But my life took a branch almost fifteen years ago, and I haven't looked back. The truth of it is I'm married to a sheep rancher. I'm a wife and mother, and I live in a small decrepit house three hundred miles from the nearest city. The winter is six months long. Our life isn't easy, but I love my family very much. I do."

"Then why are you crying?"

"I'm not crying. It's the wind."

"I see."

"Perhaps we should get back to your exhibit. The thieves may have come and gone."

"Good luck to them. They have exquisite taste."

The salon was deserted when they returned. Not a single image was missing. The rose was dry. It took him twenty minutes to highlight the bloom on the edges of the petals. Once again she sat beside him and observed. Once again she pulled her eyes away from the form that was a solid metaphor of the presence.

* * *

Later she napped for several hours and woke only just in time for the last sitting at supper. She looked across the dining hall, but the artist was not there. Altogether it had been an intense day, and she rather regretted the lack of privacy. But when he walked into the room a few minutes later, her heart gave a jolt, and she realized that it was only a very small regret, washed away now in a surge of . . . Of ? Of joy.

"Why don't we eat together", he said. "There are a few things I need to ask you."

"You don't need my advice. You're the master. You've saved the rose."

"Not about the rose", he said, pulling back the chair and sitting down. "I need to test something."

"What?"

"Perceptions."

"Perceptions?"

"Yes. I'll tell you later. Can I tell you when we walk? It was so wonderful today out there in the wind. Would you like to go out on deck after supper?"

"Certainly."

"I'm really grateful for someone to talk to, Anne."

"How do you know my name?"

"I asked the purser. Mrs. Delaney is rather formal."

"All right. Anne it is. And you're Peter."

"Yes."

"Peter the renowned artist, the Captain called you."

"All public images are lies. I'm not well known. I applied for the position of ship's artist in order to get half fare. You know— the sideshow. Trained monkey in the Alexandra Salon. The steamship company gets thirty percent of anything I sell. So far they're out of luck. In a stunted circle of New York art collectors, I'm considered an interesting but unprofitable throwback to a vanished era. I tripped and fell during the steady march of the evolution of Art! I refused to stride into the glorious future. So I paid the price. Failure. Obscurity."

"Bosch and Breughel remained unknown for almost two hundred years after their deaths. Until someone really looked. The famous artists of their time are now forgotten."

"How would a sheep-wife know something like that?"

"Oh, you might be surprised by what lives way out there in the shadows, far from the lights of the city."

"Every now and then I hear the poetry in you."

"Don't be fooled. I'm perfectly ordinary. Just a little over-educated for my position in life."

"Nothing's ordinary, sheep-wife."

"Why don't we walk now?"

The stars were bright. The sea almost calm. The air cold but not unpleasant on their faces. He gave the back of the horse blanket some friendly thumps and said, "Is that thing warm enough?"

"Yes. Quite warm."

Her hands were hot in mittens. He thrust his bare hands into the pockets of his greatcoat.

"Perceptions?" she said.

"Yeah. Perceptions. First of all, tell me what you thought when you first saw me."

"I thought, *a fellow introvert*. I've since been proved wrong."

"No, there's where you're wrong. Your first intuition was the correct one. I really don't know why I'm being such a blathering idiot with you. Usually I'm not much good at conversation. I avoid it whenever I can."

"So you *are* an introvert?"

"Absolutely! Classical example. Exhibit A. But having to sell my own paintings has turned me into a fake extrovert. I have to talk *about* art to prospective customers, or there won't be any more art. I hate the talk part."

"Then why do you do it?"

"Why do I do it? To keep going. So I can paint. Painting's like breathing. I do it because it's life. It's love."

"Love?"

"I think a lot about love. About how we understand it. And don't understand it. One of the things that haunts me as an artist is the way we project so much onto the world. I'm down on my luck, and the world looks a wretched place. I'm feeling prosperous, so I think the whole international scene is too. I'm unhappy, so I look around and all I see is unhappiness. I buy a certain brand of car, and suddenly I notice them everywhere. Or I'm in love and all I see is love, the whole world in love."

"It's a question of focus."

"Right. So what intrigues me about this way we see things is the interpretation part. Most of painting is leaving things out. A good image selects for the viewer, you see. The artist is an interpreter. That's the genius of it, the true art of it. Mixing the colors is just technique."

"That makes sense. So what are you asking?"

"I'm asking if when a person looks at another person whether or not he ever really sees him. You know, really *sees* him. Who he is."

"Theoretically, it's possible."

"I think most of us almost always see some image or symbol in the mind rather than the real person. The *being*."

"That's really quite deep, Peter. Too deep for me."

"I don't believe you."

"You told me you saw a writer in me. I'm not. You were looking for something or someone when you came on this ship. Maybe you projected an image onto me. Maybe you hoped to find a cliché like me. Please don't try to turn me into one. I know what I am."

He gripped her arm

"You're not a cliché", he said fiercely. "That's what I'm talking about. I want to get past that to the real. I want to know what's real."

She turned to the water and said, "The sea is real. The stars. The trajectory of the ship. We can know these for certain."

"But can I know you? Can you know me?"

"I don't think so."

"Not with the mind. Not by the passenger list and the personal histories. But in the heart. One soul to another soul."

"What is a soul?"

"A soul . . . ," he said in a low voice, "a soul is a word spoken into the void. It pushes back the darkness. It defies the night."

"You're a romantic."

"I used to be."

"Not any more?"

"Not any more."

"Easy to say. Pushing back the darkness is easy to talk about."

"D'you think that's easy?"

"No, I suppose not. It couldn't be."

"And when two souls speak their word together, you get something so powerful nothing can defeat it."

"Theoretically I agree. But . . ."

"It's called love."

"I know what it's called. You asked about true seeing. Look at me, my young friend. My good, earnest Peter. I'm a tired, very tired woman, a farm wife. I'm married to a decent man. My life is quite lonely, but that's more a defect of my character and of the choices I've made. I live my life bearing the consequences of those choices. I hope to make good come from an error in judgment."

"Is that your assessment of yourself?"

"That's about it."

He laughed ironically.

"Then what could you possibly think of me?"

"I think you're a very nice young man. You're grieving and you're lonely. But you're journeying into a new life. This voyage is only a brief transition. In England you'll find love. A man like you will find love wherever you go. She's waiting for you there and doesn't even know it. In a year from now you'll recall our meeting as one of those curious encounters that life permits from time to time. You'll forget all the words spoken here, re-membering only the fact that they were odd. You'll say to yourself, *an eccentric woman, living the wrong life.* You'll feel a slight pang of pity for me, and perhaps even affection, whenever I come to mind. But the memory will fade steadily and become one of the countless events that sink beneath the waves of the conscious mind."

"I wonder if you're right."

"I expect so."

"Tell me, then, do you think my paintings are as shallow as you seem to think my character is?"

"I don't think you're shallow. Merely young. And you've just reminded me", she said with a short laugh, "that I haven't yet seen your paintings face to face. I expect they're unique, pos-sessing their own indefinable, inanimate *being.*"

They went back to the salon in silence and found it busy with visitors. He had to attend to them. He told her to go around by herself. She said no, she would wait. She wanted it to be with him. She said it should be just the two of them, alone. He agreed and went to greet the visitors. She watched his shoulders go up and the strained, patient look go over his face, and she listened to the commentary through his ears, and she felt sad for him.

When they were gone, she said, "I think I understand you better."

"Really? What shattering revelation happened during the past hour?"

"Those people. They meant well. But I saw what it's like for you. It's like a lover who says *I love you*, and puts his whole being into it, and all sorts of people gather round to listen and to make comments and to debate over just what the poor fellow meant by those words. And they kill it."

"A painting is a word spoken into the void. It pushes back the darkness."

"It refutes the night."

"Only to the degree that it's a true word."

"What is truth?" she said.

"Truth? I don't agree with Keats that truth is beauty and beauty is truth and that's all you need to know. We need to know a hell of a lot more than that. But I do know that truth doesn't do well without the help of beauty. It needs it so badly I think the world would collapse without it. Without it we couldn't grasp things intuitively, things we could never express by intelligence."

They stood thinking for some moments. Then the artist shook himself.

"Hey, we got stalled in our own turgid philosophizing."

"No. This is the real thing."

More visitors arrived, and he sighed heavily.

"See you later."

"I won't budge."

It went that way until closing time. She worked hard at

ignoring his paintings. She wanted to see them with him, just the two of them, alone, together.

When the last guest had departed, he came over looking haggard.

"Let's go get a glass of wine", he said.

"Can't I meet your paintings now?"

He sighed. "It would be better some other night. Do you mind?"

"Only a little."

"I want us to be strong and happy together when you see them. It's as if you'll be seeing my soul, you know. And I don't want to be a zombie when it happens."

"I understand. It means a lot to you."

"A lot."

They shared a carafe of dry red in the lounge. He did not speak. She did not probe. Eventually he said, "I'll show you my work tomorrow." Then they each went their separate ways.

In the morning she took unusual care with her appearance. She rubbed her cheeks to make them look red. She massaged some lanolin around her eyes. The gardenia scent went on too liberally, and she had to wipe some of it off.

"I smell like an old ewe that's broken into the flower patch!" she scolded herself in the mirror.

"Sheep-wife", she added.

The porthole told her that a storm was brewing.

"It's blowing hard out there", he said at breakfast.

"Is today the day you'll tell me about your paintings?"

"I'm not going to tell you about them. But I'll go round with you as you look at them."

"It seems I forgot everything we learned yesterday."

"Don't worry. I forget it sometimes too."

"So. We'll be silent and listen for the cries of being?"

"Yeah, something like that. You're really a poetess."

"Don't tempt me to false images of myself."

"My apologies. I won't make that mistake again. Sheep-wife."

"All right, renowned artist, let's look and listen."

"*Il silenzio è la voce dell'amore!*"

"Which means?"

"Silence is the voice of love."

"No more words, Peter."

He took her elbow lightly and led her to the left wall near the entrance, and slowly, wordlessly (except that the last word spoken—*Peter*—hung in the air), they went round the room.

The first image was a woman in a blue dress holding her belly and gazing inward. A huge lute lay at her feet. Its strings vibrated. The label below the frame said, *The Womb*.

In the next image a man (obviously a self-portrait) sat on a hilltop by a river and played a flute. On the opposite bank of the river, large, white buildings were in flames. The title: *The End of the World Was Long Ago*.

In the next, two children, a boy and a girl, ran hand in hand toward an ivory castle. They were chased by a red wolf that appeared to be closing in on them. Titled, enigmatically, *Europa*.

A naked youth slept sideways on the cold, ash-colored earth. A giant hand hovered over him. On the horizon a gash of red dawn tilted across the landscape. This was *Adam Sleeping*.

Then a crowd of faces, hundreds of faces streaming out of a garishly lit city into the wilderness. Every face reflected a different emotion: fear, hope, dismay, courage, determination, hysteria, grief, joy. It was titled *Exodus*.

Two women embraced against a background of a sunny olive grove. Both pregnant. Brilliantly colored dresses, joy: *My Cousin Elizabeth*.

A barefoot man walked in shallow water along a shoreline, pulling a boat behind him. On a distant peninsula a solitary figure, watching. The man in the water glanced over his shoulder, feeling the presence of the figure. He resisted the presence, troubled by it: *You Sought Me.*

A somber portrait of a middle-aged woman. Intelligence and grief in her expression. She stared at the viewer. Her eyes were like wells. Around her head flew semi-abstract doves: *Warsaw.*

A young couple sat on a blanket in a city park. They both had easels. They both held clutches of brushes and palettes. The woman was painting the man's portrait, and the man was painting the woman's. The woman was lovely and grave. The man was . . . Peter. He looked happy and naïve: *The Last Summer— Chicago.*

Mountains. Dazzling white peaks, valleys so dark they verged on the negation of light itself. Turbulent clouds like wriggling ointment. A small climber stood on a cliff over a precipice. Black shapes whirled around him in the air. Eagles, demons? It was called *Grand Tetons.*

Close-up of a man struggling in an unknown dark brown space. No other discernible figures in the image, yet it was haunted by the sense that invisible hands were tearing his clothing from him. His face was an agony of horror and dismay. He was straining to keep the last scraps of his dignity. His eyes were shocked at being betrayed: *Coat of Many Colours.*

A ship tossed on a cobalt sea. High realism. The sky vermilion, electric. A man stood alone at the bow. He stared ahead into a wall of night. *When Everything Is Taken.*

A landscape of undulating hills covered with autumn forests, brash yellows, rusty reds, charcoals plunging down to deep cold lakes of teal blue. A savage and dangerous land: *Northern Solitude.*

A desert. Semi-abstract, cyan blue over gray background. Crimson tumbleweeds, vines, berries like drops of blood tangled themselves across the field of vision. Just that. Thorns. Color. Suffering—ineffably beautiful. Behind the veil of creation a hint of some ultimate light: *We Begin Again.*

Two hands reached down from the sky to receive a man. He lifted his arms upward. A desolate winter landscape behind them. Golden light streaming into his confused face: *Birth/ Death*.

There were more. At each station she drank deeply of the sense of mystery and struggle. Light wrestling with darkness, hope with despair. In the end she saw that *joli désespoir* was precisely what it was not.

"Had enough?" he said when they had gone around the circuit.

"I'll never have enough of this."

"Let's go out on deck and get some air."

It was blowing hard, and they had difficulty walking into the wind. She clung to his arm, and he pulled them along by the rail. The deck tilted up before them and then down again in a long thrilling roll that repeated itself endlessly.

They staggered to an iron bench and watched the bleak horizon tilt back and forth.

"I now understand why people love the sea. It's so dangerous and beautiful."

"You don't need to talk, Peter. I don't want to go back to yesterday, to normal relations between strangers. I want to let your paintings be in me."

"All right."

"You said everything in them."

"They're a bit enigmatic, the subaltern says. Pretty despair, says his wife. What do you think?"

"*Il silenzio è la voce dell'amore.*"

"Please tell me."

"Have you forgotten your own lessons?"

"Let's suspend class for today. I just want to know. Perceptions."

"I think that subaltern was a peacock and his companion a silly peahen."

He laughed hard.

"But what do *you* think about the paintings?"

"You told me everything in them. About what you've just been through. You told me about your wife, and that you loved her very much. It nearly killed you, didn't it?"

"Yes."

"We don't need to talk any more," she said, "but do you think we could go up to the bow and watch the storm from there?"

"Why not?"

After an arduous five minutes fighting their way forward against the wind, they climbed over the steel mesh fence that prohibited passengers from entering the forecastle. They sat in the triangle under the stem and caught their breath. The wind roared; spray was now reaching them.

"It's pretty wild up here! Do you want to go back?" he shouted.

"Never!"

"You're a great soul, sheep-wife!"

"You too, renowned painter."

"*Silenzio!*"

"*Silenzio!*"

They stood side by side at the apex and watched the knife of the ship cut deep into the Atlantic. The wrath of the sea struck hard against them, but they clung to a cable and to each other.

After a while she began to shiver, and he said, "That's enough."

Dripping and red-faced, grinning madly, they staggered down to the lower decks. He brought her as far as her cabin door.

"Your lips are blue", he said.

He took her hands, and leaned over and touched her lips with his. It was swift and tender. It was the sweetest kiss in human history.

"Good night, Anne."

"Good night, Peter."

He turned and went away to his own cabin.

* * *

Anne Delaney lay watching the snow blow against the window of her bedroom. Stephen coughed, rolled over, and got up.

"What time is it?"

"Five-thirty, maybe six", she said.

"You're awake early."

"I haven't slept."

"Aren't you feeling well?"

"I couldn't sleep, that's all."

"How did you pass the hours?"

"I pretended I was on a sea voyage."

"Where did you go?"

"Home to see my family. My sister. It's been so many years."

"I wish I could send you, Anne. But you know there's no money."

His voice was burdened.

"There's Brownie bawling to get milked", he said. "I'd better get busy."

She kissed him, and he patted her shoulder. She told him where to find his clean patched work overalls. He struggled into them and went out to the kitchen. He put logs on the coals in the firebox. The wind screeched up the flue. Then she heard the clump, clump of his barn boots, and the outside door shut with a thud.

"This is dangerous", she said aloud. "This is quite dangerous and unbalanced."

But what could she do? Turn it off now that it had gripped her heart? *Peter.* The name itself burned into her. He was too wonderful. So gifted. Articulate. A beautiful heart to match his appearance.

"It's deadly. It's death to my marriage!"

But Stephen need never know. Perhaps I could successfully live in two worlds, the practical one of the farm, the children, and chores and the alternative life created in the privacy of my own thoughts. What harm would this do to my family?

"What harm? The harm of gradually living more and more in my fantasy until the day it becomes more real than my life."

But fantasy is a form of art, she argued, *it's a way of seeing beyond the limits of a small life.*

"Will this help me to love my husband and children better? Gradually, little by little, won't they come to seem flawed and drab and exhausting in comparison to Peter?"

Peter? As if he were real!

She threw back the quilt and quickly dressed. The kettle steamed on the fire. She got the oatmeal bubbling and put a spoon of raw tea leaves into the comfortable old earthenware pot.

She put on Turid's lumpy sweater and sat in the rocking chair by the fire. It gradually warmed her bones. Was it the illusory sensation of salt spray that had chilled her? A cup of steaming tea tamed by milk drove the brittleness from her hands. She felt the blue leaving her lips.

Ashley shuffled out of the boys' bedroom in pyjamas and mumbled, "Mornin' Mum."

"Good morning, son."

Emily tiptoed out in bare feet. "Ooooh, it's cold, it's cold, it's cold", she shivered in her long flannel nighty. She got up onto the window seat and set to scratching pictures in the frost. A star. A mountain. A boat on an ocean.

Bryan staggered out and stared like a zombie. He came over, draped himself across her shoulders, and mumbled, "Porridge ready, Mum?"

"Not yet, Bryan. Let it cook a while longer."

He fell back into semiconsciousness on her shoulder and

snored. He smelled of sleep and wood smoke and small boy's sweat. The dawn was blue. The sun rose like a bomb burst.

* * *

Peter rapped on her cabin door.

"Come on, Anne, get up. Let's have an early breakfast. The dining room's deserted, but the food's ready. Everyone else is seasick or asleep."

They ate toast with marmalade, poached eggs, and bacon, and sipped at rich, black coffee.

"The sea's calming down."

"I can feel it in the ship's movement", she replied.

"Today is our last day."

"Yes, our last day."

"It's going too fast. It needn't end at Southampton", he said emphatically.

"It needn't end. Not ever."

"You feel it too?"

"Yes, but differently. Not like you feel it."

"That kiss. It wasn't meant to compromise you or anything."

"I know."

"It's just I want to tell you that I . . ."

"Don't say it. *Silenzio.*"

"You're right. *Silenzio.*"

"I gave my life away long ago."

"I know. A woman like you would. A woman like you wouldn't take it back again, either."

"No. I couldn't. That's why we won't see each other again."

"Don't say that", he said, alarmed.

"I must say it."

"*Silenzio!*" he cried.

"You must listen to me and try to understand. You are a very dear man. But you are somewhat naïve about the human heart."

"This is a *friendship* of the heart. Soul to soul."

"Yes, now it is. But it would not, could not, remain that. It would change."

"You're wrong. You don't know me."

"I know myself. I'm the problem. I'm far too lonely with a loneliness that no human being could ever fill. Even a friend as wonderful as you could never fill it."

"Don't hurt me with such lovely compliments."

"I don't want to hurt you. But a surgeon's cut avoids the disease that would kill us both."

"Is love a disease?"

"Desire can be a disease."

"Lust-at-first-sight? Is that what you think this is?" he said bitterly.

"I know it's not. It's hunger of another kind."

"It's love!"

"Real love is a long apprenticeship."

"Love is love!"

"Love would kill love if it weren't purified."

"You're destroying everything we created here."

"No, I'm ensuring that we don't lose it."

"I don't understand you. Not at all."

"In time you will. Some day, perhaps, you will look back and remember me and you will say, *that woman loved me. She loved me without taking. She let me go. She gave me the best kind of love.*"

He got up from the table.

"I will never know where you are, Peter. I will never know how your life turned out. But I will always hold you here in my heart. I will know you are on the earth with me."

"It's not enough!"

"There would never be enough, you see, even if we gave everything."

"Paradoxes, enigmas, riddles. Love shouldn't be so hard to understand."

"It isn't hard to understand. You give your life away. And you don't play at taking it back. In the end it's given back to you in a better form than you could have imagined."

"You believe that?"

"I have risked my life on it."

He left without another word.

She did not see him again. But an hour before the ship docked there was a gentle rap at her cabin door, and when she opened it there was no one there. A package lay against the door frame.

Inside she found her rose, perfectly restored. And a note:

I let you go.
But I will never cease to carry you in my heart.
Peter

15

The woman's loneliness was not assuaged by the considerable goodness of her children. Her fear for herself, of herself, grew more or less intense in waves. During the worst moments she strained after a normality that always seemed beyond her reach. But what was normal and made perfect sense in Swiftcreek was not so in Bishopsford or London, those places to which she no longer belonged.

The elder boy disappeared up the mountain once or twice a month with an enormous gun under his armpit, and the man came down to accomplish his man-tasks. He would drag the harrow across the fields or butcher the cow with the gross hemorrhoids. Or possess the woman on their bed. She knew that these were right and customary things, and her flesh did respond, though her soul, that clenched muscle, remained distant.

In late summer, she was brought to a state of hope by a notice at the post office:

SWIFTCREEK FARMERS INSTITUTE AND IODE FAMILY PICNIC

TO COMMENCE AT 2 P.M., SEPT. 4, 1938
(under the auspices of the Swiftcreek Chamber of Commerce)
Ladies' Egg & Spoon Race
Slow Bike Race
Tug-of-war, Homesteaders vs. Townies
Pillow Fight
Obstacle Race
Greasy Pig, Catch-It-and-Keep-It!

$5 gold piece donated by J. MacPhale
ALL RESIDENTS WELCOME

★ Boats leaving for Yellowhead Island at 2 P.M. SHARP!!! ★

She tried to convince Turid to come along, but the hot blowsy woman batted off the suggestion.

"It's a gatherin' of the respectable," she said, "and I don't think I'd qualify."

She did appear suety and dank, with her fingernails black from digging spuds and dunging out the barn. Camille was away down the Thompson that summer with the crew that replaced old ties on the track-bed. He had finally left the bush for regular pay.

"It's not posh, Turid, and everyone's invited. And surely," she quipped, "surely with a lawyer son in Prince George, you do qualify as high society!"

"Get out of here," she laughed, "I got too much on me hands without flibbertigibbets dragging me off to a ball!"

Turid's presence was something rooted, as homely as turnips, and just as tough. She had a mean streak, too, and could fight. Anne did not know if she wanted to face the town in a social situation without the armored guard of Turid L'Oraison. But the thought of not going was equally repulsive—to refuse such an outing to her children simply because of the cold eyes and the tongues of her enemies would be to flee, and if she started to run now she would never stop running.

Enemies, she rolled the word over in her mind. *I never had an enemy in my life until I came to this little corner of paradise.*

She loaded up the L'Oraison girls as well as her own three and was about to flick the reins when Turid said something unpleasantly perceptive:

"Must be hard with Steve gone up the mountain half yer life."

"Not so hard. Sometimes it's simpler that way."

"What y'mean, 'xacly girl? That's a damfine man y'got there. I gotta say I never could get why y'ain't quite happy."

"There is always more than meets the eye," she answered defensively. "And there is more to life than . . ."

"Than love? Tell me what's more important than love?"

"Truth."

"Seems t'me if y'don't got one, y'don't got t'other."

To which there was no response.

"You should learn t'have a little fun, Annie. Life ain't sposed t'be all blood and thunder."

"Fun?" she replied bitterly, loathing her dour self, "Fun? I almost resent the very idea of it!"

"You're too damn serious for yer own good", Turid said, wagging her index finger. "Look at kittens and puppies and kids. Look at any guy and gal rollin' round in the hay, lookit birds and wolves and just about everything that ain't half-dead . . . whatya see? Y'see playin'. Real knock-down, drag-out playin'."

"I never learned to play as a child. I was too busy having *rewarding cultural and intellectual experiences of the highest quality*— that's what my father called it."

"More's the pity, more's the pity", Turid said, shaking her greasy head.

"It's just that the world is too confusing. I simply cannot catch my breath, you see. There is no time to think."

"If I told y'once, I told y'a thousand times, y'think too much, dearie. Why don't y'just sit back and enjoy it? Y'don't have t' figger every little damn thing that happens."

"I can't help myself."

"You read too many books as a kid . . . that's yer problem!"

"It's more than just books and ideas. The world itself is riot-ing with signs and words. But it's as if I can't read!"

Turid wiped her nose and pushed back a thatch of white hair.

"Now I know y'ain't asked me, but if you were t'ask me, I'd have t'say that I think y'read just fine. The real trouble . . . the *real* trouble, mind you . . . is that the page is blank and you're strainin' t'read somethin' that ain't there."

255

"Turid, it's there!" she said vehemently. "But I can't read! I can't read!" Her voice was pitched just below the level of hysteria.

Turid cocked her head sideways and gave her neighbor a long look. She had seen Anne in some odd moods before and had heard many a strange word come out of her mouth, but there had always been a scratch of sense in it somewhere. For the very first time it crossed her mind that Anne might not be entirely sane.

Anne read the look with perfect literacy.

As the buggy lurched away, Turid shouted something after her:

"Oh, by the way, you remember that revernd fella was here a few years ago? Well, he's back. Couldn't stay away!"

That was a startling piece of news, but it sank swiftly into the pool of her melancholy.

She pulled the buggy up to the banks of the Fraser just as the last boat was loading. The children stampeded in, and she followed along behind and set her body on a vacant seat. The pilot poled the white jolly boat out into the leaping water, where it was grabbed by the current and thrust toward the shore of the island.

The children promptly scattered into the woods or over to the clearings where games were already in progress. A hand-crank Victrola was playing croons and syrupy waltzes; there were shouts and cries and couples strolling, women gossiping in the sun as they shelled peas under wide straw bonnets, and men drinking quart-bottle beer. Everyone was engaged with others —making, cooking, wrestling, laughing, discussing the hay crop or the new playboy king, planning engagements or breaking them, the electric hands of the young intertwining, the small mittlike hands of the children cramming berries and grass into their mouths. Life flowing like the river . . . only that thin gray woman, Mrs. Delaney, moved about the proceedings, a piece of flotsam cast out from the current.

I am alone as always.

She attempted to move her tense body toward a group of women congregating by some trestle tables. She forced herself to approach, extending a tentacle of consciousness toward those others of her kind, the middle-aged, thickening housewives.

Several ladies pulled away before greetings might become necessary. Or erected a shield of intense conversation that no one would dare enter. Some became busy, busy at the table their men had engineered from planks and stumps. There was rather a lot to do with the pies.

She stood alone then, condemned politely. Was it a form of justice, she wondered. But could not decide just what she might be guilty of. Chicks, a broken step, passed through her mind. Or was it the ladies staring at her as she rode to *The Echo* office to deliver her column. Perhaps it was something she had written:

> The mobilisation for war of a nation's strength, her youth, is no answer to an economic blight caused in the first place by greed. . . .

Was that it? People were being rather careful about patriotism these days. Or was it:

> The threat rising in Hitlerian Germany is real indeed, but it must not blind us to the evils of the Soviet regime, which many of our public speakers are now lauding as a champion of freedom. . . .

Or was it more close to home:

> We must awaken to our communal guilt in the shameful death of Thomas Delahanty, keeper of the beehive burner at the mill. It is scandalous that an old man should die of neglect in our day and age, only a hundred yards from his neighbours. His body was found in the shanty only after the smell had. . . .

Or was it any number of things she had written in letters to the editor over the past decade, many of them too pointed. Couldn't they understand? She was crying out, not in condemnation of their mean and narrow ways, but to protest the state of their imprisonment, to call forth a civilization of love . . . more than a school-dream of Utopia that went with the field hockey, posture, and Greek. Had the townsfolk read these things between the lines and pronounced her cold and superior as she rode above them to the post or station where her husband's furs and bags of wool were loaded? Poor Steve, married to *her*!

The yells of her boys involved in contest with other young males appeared detached from the meaning of her life. She held her arms lest they fly out from the centrifugal force of the pain. The core of her being remained intact only by the strength of this grip, by power of will. Scraps of thought, movement, a few tentative smiles coming from some of the poorest bush-wives rallied to her assistance, but it was too late. She slid into suspended time, a slow dance through mud, *adagio*. She would have remained frozen in the middle of the clearing, staring back through absent time into the adagios on the pianoforte that her small fingers accomplished nightly after tea. Nana timed her exactly, pursing her harelip whenever she slipped off the keys. *Encore, ma petite! Encore!* Locked forever into an encore that could never be improved and from which there was no exit.

But Anne Delaney was saved by an unsuspected note of grace in the person of Miss Isobel MacPherson, who now emitted a high-pitched whistle to gather all the picnickers to eat. She was a small wizened lady, not unlike Nana, but brown and leathery, woolly with liver spots and blackberry eyes. Whereas Nana had been parchment and yellow cream. Regardless, she snapped Anne out of the very first stages of madness with a perfectly ridiculous opening of all vocal stops, a resurrected patriotic hymn used annually for public ceremonies such as this.

Anne shook her head and rubbed her eyes. Once, Isobel MacPherson had detained her outside of MacPhale's Store, where the old woman had been peddling her wild fruit.

"Where did you get those wonderful berries, Miss Mac-Pherson?" she had asked.

"In the bush . . ." she had replied, "in the bush!" growing sphynxlike with her berry secrets. The location of thick bushes was as hard a territorial right as traplines. But the old woman had not meant to offend, was merely protecting what was precious to her. She had given a basket of saskatoons to Anne, who had been touched to tears by the gift, though evidence of the emotion was strangled.

"Why, thank you, Miss MacPherson", she had said and invited her to tea sometime. Though the berry woman had never come.

So she was saved momentarily by the sight of Miss Mac-Pherson now issuing forth in the full strength of her art:

"God save our gracious King: God save our noble King. . . ."

That basically sociable woman, Anne Ashton, might have joined in, as she had never been entirely absorbed into the exile of Anne Delaney. But the overwhelming quality of her separation from any community did not permit this. Her thoughts grew brutal toward herself. She was nearly swamped by the unseaworthiness of her craft, and might have cried out unconsciously, alarming the neat and laundered company. But she caught herself just in time and walked quickly through the trees around a jog in the path, where convulsions might remain unseen. Weeping did seem an inappropriate gesture at picnics, though grim flint was an acceptable reaction to assaults upon one's being by nothingness, as long as one did not commit any social indiscretions.

Mentally she pulled out the images of her children to console herself but grew even more frightened as the pain increased. Her hands shook in the cold sunlight.

I will fail them, scar them, leave a legacy of insanity.

She might have burst into wails given a few more moments.

It's better for me to die. He'll find a nice, simple, loving woman, who's strong.

The wind blew in protest.

Kill me, God!

The trees reeled in shock.

"When in peril on the sea . . ."

Laughter.

Shouts.

"We cry to Thee. . . ."

Like waves lapping on a beach, like blowing leaves, pieces of song tumbling over decent applause, light clapping of hands, lap-lap-lapping of water on the gunwales. Children's sweet cries.

But drowners are occasionally not permitted to die.

"Mrs. Delaney! Anne . . ."

A man's voice calling. She could not bear any apparition or hallucination at this moment and tensed for flight.

"Hallo! The eating's started. Won't you come?" he said, approaching.

She turned away.

"Anne", said Reverend Gunnalls, his face compassionate. He touched her arm. They stood by a mast of poplar where she had run to hide. Her arms were wrapped around the tree apparently. Mortified, she did not know if she could abide the return of a gawky archangel with a prominent Adam's apple. She composed her eyes quickly, as in all probability he was real. Her shoulders adjusted themselves. She shook off the tree.

"It's nothing, nothing", she lied, *everything, everything*. "It's just summer blues, a passing shower", and laughed her most fabricated laugh.

He stood looking. A clean, foolish face that lies and hollow laughter would bump against. His brows were attempting a dignity or a depth he had not yet actually attained. By unspoken agreement they began to walk. Edwin, yes, Edwin, that was his name, she recalled.

"I suppose I should say something", she offered blearily.

"I was going to start by saying it's very nice to see you again."

"Yes, let's indulge in the customary remarks, shall we? Like the good automatons that we are."

"Automatons? It's just a courtesy to make pleasant conversation."

"If you insist, we could try these: Welcome back, Reverend! How nice to see you! How's your health? Are you having a cozy little life? Oh yes, and by the way, how's the weather?"

"The weather is a little chilly", he said, glancing at the hot sun.

"Are you curious about the state of my soul?"

"I don't expect you to unburden yourself to me after all this time."

"Aren't you a doctor of the soul?"

"Yes and no. Physician, heal thyself . . ."

"That's honest of you."

"You weren't in the congregation this morning. And I'd so looked forward to seeing you again."

"I've been investigating my husband's religion for some years now."

"People are free to come and go in *my* religion as they please. They're free. As the Creator made them to be."

"Oh, yes, I remember", she said wiping her eyes. "Your religion within a religion. Everything is freedom and lovely feelings and very little by way of content, if I recall."

But the sting in her tone did not restore her sense of power.

He looked and waited. He could not break open those dried bandages of hers, which had begun to seep. He had never been endowed with that much courage. And she could not open her soul in front of a man whose skin, despite middle age, had remained too vulnerable. He had always resembled nothing more than an overserious boy. So they quickly reached an impasse of conversation, although she did pick at consolation in his presence.

She recalled her wedding reception years before. On that day

Reverend Gunnalls had worn a large delighted smile. Too large. His eyes, she now remembered, had been strained.

They continued to walk. He was a walker. His stride revealed that. A tame man. She imagined that there would be trays of watercress on a windowsill of the manse, and spears of aspidistra in pots. A retriever on the porch. Books, papers. And slippers. Perhaps a harmless maternal housekeeper of advanced age. The man removed a pipe from his mouth and stoked thoughtfully.

Stephen is a rider. He looks into distances and goes there, devouring horizons. This man, Edwin, is a walker. He doesn't go far, but he looks closely at the things he passes. Though what he makes of them I cannot guess.

"Why do some people marry whom they do marry?" she asked, while he was busy getting the pipe lit in a breeze. It was safer that way, and her voice could not strangle her so obviously.

His smile was philosophical. It was a smaller smile, and those eyes contained a fugitive suffering. He was about to answer her when they were saved by one of the children.

"Mama, I caught the greased pig!" said Ashley, who arrived sweating and red with a thumping heart they all could have heard.

"And I have swallowed it", she said obliquely.

The boy looked from the woman to the man and back again. He suspected an obscure joke but would not be pulled off his triumph.

"Em and Bryan got him pinned down for me. I gotta go!" and he galloped away to gather the prize.

They were approaching a group of picnickers, some of whom would never be able to overlook seeing a preacher and that woman entangled publicly in some private pain. It was irresistible evidence of the hypocrisy of the religious.

He turned to her, reached out, took her cold damp hand, and shook it, pastorally.

"Why don't you come and see me when you're able, and we'll discuss it."

"Yes, I believe I would like, need, that. Edwin."

Then he was engaged suddenly with a gambolling group of youths jostling each other for a ball.

At that moment she recognized her beautiful daughter running through the crowd to find her.

"Mama", cried the flushed, delirious girl. "Mama", she said again, just to say, and merged with her mother's body. Candied apple had smeared her cheek. She was possessing the woman who desired greatly to be claimed. Turid's girls were banging in close as well. Blood flowed through her veins again.

"Emily", she whispered, just to say it, clinging to something so hot and well, so overspilling with light, for safety, while not appearing to.

"Mama, what's a hoor?" the little girl asked. "Them Sinclair kids said Auntie Turid is a hoor."

Her mother choked, knelt, and encircled her with arms.

"Emily, your grammar! You should say, *those* Sinclair children . . ."

"Yes, Mama, but . . ."

"A whore", she said carefully, gently, "is merely a good woman who has had a little trouble in her life."

Emily was satisfied, though the L'Oraison girls looked at her quizzically.

"Come," said Anne brightly, "let's find those brothers of yours and make our way home."

16

"Jackie Tobaccy, Jackie Tobaccy,
Yer Mama is queer and yer daddy is wacky!"

Ashley heard them screaming as he hopped down off the porch of the school. *The haters,* he called them in his mind. He knew who they would be before he rounded the corner of the building, but he was surprised to see their victim. Tough little Jack Tobac.

There he was in the middle of a ring of tormenters. He was small, dark, the possessor of a famous temper, with two fists raised in defiance, his pants unpatched with a half-moon of rear showing and boots through which the toes had lately appeared.

"Jackie Tobac, Jackie Tobac,
Yer Ma is a nut and yuh live in a shack!"

Brainless adolescent laughter, sneers, jeers. Someone threw a rock that clicked on the white of the boy's teeth, staining crimson. Another threw a fist that twirled him to the ground. A little wooden bird flew out of Jackie's pocket and fell to the earth. One of the tormentors stepped forward and ground it into pieces with his boot.

Jackie liked to carve things, birds, bowls, bears, and faces. Indian things. Now he too was an Indian thing. Objects being easier to destroy than human beings, it is necessary at times to turn human beings into objects. They were gathering round now for just such a degrading, though it was not exactly certain what would be used—more words or stones.

Ashley stood watching. He was fourteen years old and by no means the oldest or the strongest. But he hated the tormenting of the weak, be it a live insect that Bryan was dissecting in curiosity or a frog being mounted on a hook in the interests of fishing or a person who had somehow said or been the wrong thing. Ashley's slow, woodsy manner had definitely placed him outside the wolf pack. His own mother was despised and made his life difficult simply by being who she was. But he was bigger than Jack and had shoulders from tossing bales of hay. There was also a cool impulse of justice in him that was more instinct than principle and now directed him through the ring of assailants. He stopped in the middle beside Jack, who was picking himself up from the dust. Ashley folded his arms.

"Get outa here, Delaney!"

"G'wan, this is our business!"

They would have pelted him with more solid things had they dared, but there was something about him that refused to abandon his secret shape. Though his power was contained, it could be unleashed decisively upon themselves.

A prosecutor rushed in to face Ashley with the evidence.

"Y'know what that little bastard said?"

Ashley did not answer, merely looked at him. Rinty Mac-Phale, red faced, red eyed, red haired, ham fisted, the leader of the pack.

"He called my Dad a crook!"

At this, Jack Tobac mumbled something through his bloodied teeth.

"What you say, Tobac?"

"Your dad *is* a crook!"

Rinty tore into him, slap-smashing and ripping the charity clothes and any other tatters still clinging to Jack. But Ashley stepped in, hurling Rinty neatly to the ground. The boy groaned, wind knocked from him. Confusion scattered the mob into individuals. Some were filled with a sudden admiration for

265

Ashley, while others, sensing a disintegrating situation, whacked hands against their legs and ambled off in disgust.

"Go on, Rinty, get out of here", said Ashley and watched as the ruffled cock stumbled up and strutted away, filling the air with oaths.

"You're bleeding", he said when they were alone. Jack nodded and wiped his face on his sleeve.

"Old man MacPhale *is* a crook!" he repeated, allowing himself a little victory noise in the dust of retreating armies.

The other champion was silently removing his silver shield, drawing off breast-plates in the hot sun. Girls and small boys admired, though not as much as they would have had there been howling and more convincing blood.

"I got my horse, Jack. Want a ride home?"

"Okay." And a moment later, "Thanks."

It was one of those days when school approached a longed-for end. The sun was lowering in the west. Swallows darted after insects silhouetted against the sky. Ashley mounted the sorrel and stretched an arm down to help the other boy up. He urged the horse on with a gentle kick, and they were off trotting down beside the railroad tracks.

The line wound south out of town, then bent around the head of Canoe Mountain and entered the Thompson valley. A half-hour's ride brought them to a footpath striking off into the bush. There they turned into the deep green canopy of the forest.

They spoke little. The three bodies were joined in a grip of motion and balance. There was the sweaty hide and leather smell of the animal and its wet mouth biting iron. The clopping of the hooves was the only conversation. The thoughts of the two young humans were more complex but just as visual and instinctual as the horse's. There were no words passing through their minds, though the scene of violence did play and replay itself, and their own roles within it grew more heroic with the colorations that time will give to the simplest of events.

As they entered the blue shadow cast by the Cariboo range, they caught a glimpse of the valley dwindling behind them. The last of the afternoon sun illumined the yellow haze of jackpine pollen blowing against its western ridges.

The boys were absorbed in different kinds of silence. The older, Ashley, gathered his about himself, flowing inward to that central core where all things were pondered. Though his mother had taught him the power of language, he felt that it was a greater strength not to speak. In the absence of words he was free to absorb other meanings from between the hoofbeats, to find it in the bush rioting with warblers and robins, the *craw* of ravens, and the babble of water everywhere seeking liberation. These works had erupted from an immense stillness in creation, yet they spoke. Ashley began to hear the soundless words.

Jack's hands gripped his waist.

"Rinty hates me!" he shouted. "Always has!"

Hate tore the sheet of music.

"Why? Why does he hate you?"

"I don't know. Maybe he's just one of them bad boys that turned into jackasses in *Pinocchio*."

They laughed. Jackie looked dumb, but every now and then something like that slipped out of him. He was an expressionless cigar-store Indian boy, copper-skinned rather than brown. He hid a lot behind his wooden face.

Ashley had known him since early childhood. Their dads hunted together sometimes in the fall, and on occasion the boys met at church, though almost never now that Jack's mother was back in the hospital. In the schoolyard they had begun to gravitate toward each other, as outcasts will if they have not yet been taught to despise themselves.

"What's Sarah doin' these days?" Ashley asked with a vague tone.

He could feel the smile and the look behind him. Jack pulled Ashley's suspenders and let them go with a snap.

"Yow, that hurt!" growled Ashley.

"Sorry. Very sorry. Sarah's the same as ever, but she gets tired o' takin' care o' the kids all the time. Since Mum's gone there's no end o' work. Dad's workin' on the track now."

"Yeah, I heard."

"Mum was pretty crazy those last months."

Ashley remembered. He had seen the woman go from shyness to eccentricity to distortion in a long slide that ended at a mental hospital on the coast. No one knew if she would ever come home.

His last visit had been a few months ago. That day he had taken Jackie home on the horse, a ride much like this one, though snow still howled around the fetlocks of the mount. Jack had had a pair of beat-up shoes falling off his bare toes. The veins in his ankles had stood up like cords, and he had shivered and chattered.

"Damncold, Jackie!"

"Ain't cold!" was the curt reply. To change the subject he said:

"Hey, Ash, don't mind my Mum, eh? She's been different lately."

"What you mean different?"

"Well, she says things about white people. She just might say things."

"But she goes t'church, and she plays piano for the town dances."

"Does it fer money. Says she don't mind makin' white asses bounce if it puts grub on the table. Things like that she says, so don't get affended, eh?"

"Okay."

When they bustled in out of the storm with red faces and hunger in their bellies, there had been no friendly greeting from the woman. She had given Ashley a stony glance. Sarah, who was a year older than Jack, had smiled at Ashley and made fried bannock with wild currant jam. The smell of sizzling bear grease was overpowering. There was little by way of power out there save what muscle and water provided. There was a cooling box in the spring and a screened meat-house built over the creek where Thaddaeus hung his moose and caribou. But aside from the plentiful wild game, it was slim fare with so many kids, the youngest still in diapers, and no steady work. Fur was poor that year, the valley still climbing out of the pit into which it had been thrust by the trapper MacPhale. Sarah had been pulled out of school to help her mother through a bad winter. Weather, fur, town politics, it all seemed to grind over the Tobacs, and the woman had not been strong enough to survive. She was tough, as tough as boot leather, but she had not been strong. First her body gave in with influenza and pneumonia, from which she had barely recovered. Then her mind had sprung leaks.

"Welcome, son of the queen of the valley!" said Wanda regally and sarcastically.

Everyone in the shack stared.

"You're a nice kid, ain't yuh? Bein' kind to the poor Indians?"

"Mum! Mum!" came a chorus of voices.

The woman flung a dark braid. Sarah fled from the cabin with tears streaming down her face.

"I'm sorry, Missuz T'bac . . . I just."

"Yeah, you just . . . you just got born in the right place at the right time to the right color people."

"Seems like there's good and bad people in every race", he mumbled.

"Yeah, and some races get a bigger share than others."

She popped some pills back in her throat and washed them down with a bottle of orange soda, a luxury to which she was addicted.

"My folk are Slavey and Dogrib", she went on. "We're river people from the Territories. We look differnt, talk differnt, think differnt . . . we ain't like them Shushwap Injuns, drinkin' themselves to death!"

Thaddaeus had come in then, catching the last part.

"Wanda!" he pleaded. He was one of those Shushwaps whose faces appeared to have been flattened by a shovel. His eyes were wells of liquid suffering. He looked beaten, and Jackie stood frozen into his wooden Indian shape.

That was months ago. The pageantry of this day's battle had cleaned the memory.

"Yeah, Mum's gone now", said Jack, as if reading Ashley's mind. Then he laughed perversely.

"Things were so bad a couple o' years ago that she went out one night t'steal potatoes. Dad was down at the trap-cabin, and there wasn't nothin' left in the house. MacPhale said no more credit till we produced some furs.

" 'Okay,' says Mum, 'it ain't no crime t'steal from the crook that robbed you in the first place.' So she hiked all the way into Swiftcreek, middle of the night, a sack under her arm. She passed Mr. Parsons the magistrate ridin' home from the bar, and he pulls up and says, 'Evenin', Wanda, where are you off to this time of night?' real friendly like, and course he was all liquored up.

" 'I'm off t'steal p'tatoes,' says Mum real serious. 'Ho, ho, ho,' says Mr. Parsons, 'That's a good one,' and trots away home singin' like a bird.

"Well, she got t'MacPhale's and crawled under the fence as quiet as a lynx, downwind from the house so even the dog didn't know anybody's there. Along the rows she went, diggin' up a potato here and there, then coverin' over the hill each time so no one'd ever guess there's some missin'."

"Why didn't you ask us for help?"

"My mum's proud, Ash, and she don't like t'beg. . . . Besides, she don't like yer ma too much." He paused to catch breath in the galloping air.

"I know she wasn't too nice last time, but she's not mean or nothin, Ash. If some drifter gets off a slow train lookin' fer work or a place t'bed down fer the night, well, she'd share what we had with him and let him sleep in the shed. I seen her give our last loaf of bread to some guy in a box car."

In our house, thought Ashley, *Mother gets nervous when we're down to our last hundred-pound sack of flour. In this house they sleep well on the last loaf.*

The Englishwoman, moreover, expected drifters to split a half-cord of birch before a meal. It was employment of a kind and, being an amateur psychologist of the male ego, she believed this exchange was easier on their dignity than a dole. There were also the old solitaries she would sometimes invite for a free roast of tame meat swimming in dumplings and gravy. They would protest against her hospitalities through bad teeth, hiding their buttonless flies behind hats, hungry and glad that she would persist through their refusals. She would drag them home and pump them for stories by way of payment.

Some were not old. Ashley remembered one young man especially, for he became a regular visitor for a year or so. Nigel Lord Rockingham. A destructible person of skin and bones whose voice was pitched so painfully high that he was commonly suspected of sexlessness around town. A male Medusa. A willow switch who whipped and wobbled through the village, peering and probing. It did provide some carnival amusement for those members of the community whose only encounter with the exotic had been limited to the prostitute at Henningville and the visiting M.P. It was not that Nigel was a threat to her boys, Anne realized soon enough, for he was not interested in them at all. His passion was his poetry, his vocation in life was himself. His past was shrouded. His home in the woods was a makeshift hut that he had constructed from pilfered slabs destined for the trash burner at the mill. It was, after all, only another extension of his flesh, that improvised shelter with which he clothed his mystery and mission. A shell within a shell within a shell—the bothersome concerns of food and appearance had ceased to matter to one who dwelt in the radioactive core of self-absorption.

Their mutual Englishness had attracted them at first, and a reverence for the mind. Their love of books might have dragged them into an infidelity of the spiritual kind, but the poet was so engrossed in an affair with himself that this proved impossible. Nigel borrowed many of her books, returned a few, remained hidden away with others for months, or arrived at mealtimes with monotonous regularity. He was sociable in spurts. They enjoyed esoteric conversations concerning the contents of the British Museum, repository of their nation's past. The marble columns would shoot higher than the oppressive pines rupturing the black vault of heaven. Exile was defeated, and their world was momentarily elevated from the kerosene half-light in which it seemed perpetually plunged. They recalled together the manuscript of *Jane Eyre*, or the handwritten deposition of the witness to Beckett's assassination. Or Lady Jane Grey's Psalter, which had accompanied her to the chopping block. Or the Magna Carta, sacred talisman of freedom. And, with hushed reverence, the vast glory of the Great Exhibition Hall—the Crystal Palace—the ultimate monument to the unique spirit of their race.

As history flowed again through the woman's arteries, blood began to beat in her face. She would glow with happiness and wish that fine young man a godspeed as he doffed his cap and bid all within a good night and went out into the night like a wandering dryad in search of its hole.

She thought of him as Jason embarking on the *Argus*, calling his farewells to the shore-bound throng. At other times he was the archpoet of the barren lands, his style sere and clean. Alternatively, he would revert to the simply plummy, spouting a gush of verbiage that was rich to the point of affectation.

"He's a thirty-year-old baby", said Turid L'Oraison in disgust. "A man should be full o' piss an vinegar. He ain't no man!"

She had expected her husband to join the general scoffing, like most men. But he didn't.

"What is a man?" Stephen had asked in his quietest voice and perhaps knew the answer. Even Turid was momentarily silenced by the question.

At other times Stephen sat in on the obscure poetic conversations—usually he was carving something, listening from the safe distance of the rocking chair by the stove. From time to time he would join in with old Irish verse or a composition of his own, child as he was of the most remorseless storytellers and rhymers on the face of the earth. It was a little thing he offered once, something about a fire and stone and a darkened sun. Nigel and Anne listened patiently and indulged in a smile.

Despite his limitations, Stephen appeared larger at those times than she had supposed him to be. For this mercy she was grateful. Grateful, too, for a husband who was not threatened by his wife's male friend. Grateful, mostly, for the friend.

There was a conversation that she recorded in her journal and that was secretly read one day by her elder son:

Swiftcreek, 17 July 1938.
Nigel was here today while Stephen was down the Canoe. I believe N. is afraid of my husband, as he appears most conveniently while S. is away. Without any preamble he rushed into the kitchen and threw his (my) books down on the table.
NIGEL: I have begun what I feel shall be my greatest work!
ANNE: Tell me about it.
N.:   It is a long prose-poem of about two hundred cantos, set in mediaeval mode but enlightened by the empirical advances made by such men as Einstein.
A.:   What will it be *about*? (Apologising for my clumsy word).

N.:   What science is calling the bottomless interiority of matter!

A.:   The what?

N.:   There is no beginning and no end. And like Virgil I shall take my readers on a guided tour down through the atoms into pure being.

A.:   I see. (Enthusiastic but puzzled)

N.:   "Within its depths I saw ingathered, bound by love in one volume, the scattered leaves of all the universe." That's Dante, *Paradiso!* Do you see, Mrs. D?

A.:   Yes, yes, I think I do.

N.:   So that my readers, my little Dantes, shall come to understand the fantastic value of thorns, berries, spittle, wind, a mother's milk, the merest glance, the smallest word.

A.:   (After some thought) But Nigel, doesn't this strain to put too great a meaning upon the simplest things of life, a burden they cannot sustain?

N.:   (Looking crushed by my moment of doubt) No, no, don't you understand? It is precisely that thinking which blinds the human race . . . (He glanced at the ceiling in a spasm of agony that I thought to be quite theatrical, then continued:) "O human race, born to fly upward, Why at a little wind, do you so fall?" Dante, *Purgatorio!*

    (I was growing troubled by the messianic glint in his eyes. I truly did not want to hurt him, but I felt I must establish a pattern of frankness.)

A.:   Nigel, isn't there a danger of sentiment, that it might just be romantic poetry?

N.:   No! (truly angry now) No! Poetry is not sentiment.

A.:   Yes, I realize that, but . . .

N.:   Do you realize that? (He began to shuffle his papers together in preparation for an abrupt departure.)

As I write this I cannot contain my sighs. It was our first quarrel and leaves me distressed. Is it possible that exquisitely sensitive young men might be as draining as the insensitive ones? It is always possible that I could destroy him by erecting a cold barrier. But I am responsible for him in some way. He calls me "Mrs. D". I know that I am his spiritual or cultural mother. Imagination? A little vanity, perhaps? Shall I be Gertrude Stein to this unknown Picasso?

Strangely, he reminds me of Stephen. In retrospect I see that Nigel is saying much the same thing as my inscrutable husband. It is Stephen's affection for manure all over again. As for me, there is too much filth in the world. Events are shaping up for a great spilling of blood on the world's stage. Horror shall be added to other forms of degradation.

But perhaps I am misunderstanding my two poets. It is not matter itself that is good or evil, but the motives and the ends to which it is put. Yet I cannot accept their view . . . there is too much that is accidental and cruel; there are too many smashed nests.

To return to the question of sensitivity: there are those who are sensitive only about themselves, like N. And those who are sensitive to the earth, like S. Yes, deeply sensitive! Why, I wonder, can neither of them hear my cries or ask what word flickers in my womb?

Is it foolish to believe that I, an absurd and self-pitying exile, might enter into creation and be its voice, its guardian?

* * *

"They say he's a remittance man", informed Turid one day, "They say his family sends money once a month, long as he stays this side of the Atlantic."

"And who says this?" inquired Anne. Her throat could swell with indignation to defend those for whom she felt responsible or who were defenseless.

"Mrs. Sinclair, that nasty bird at the post office told me the gory details. He cashes in his bank notes with her, I guess."

"It's entirely possible, Turid, that he sells his writing abroad and these are commissions."

She had never actually been huffy before.

No one could remember having heard any of Nigel's verse spoken aloud. He was a rather secretive poet, and Anne explained that he wished to be revealed to the world only when a major opus had been completed. So the offspring of his fertile core remained hidden to any eyes save those of his mentor. He fed sheets of paper to the woman, his face raised hungrily to hers, waiting for an approval that invariably came.

One morning, as she stood on the steps of *The Echo* office, a passerby shouted:

"Have you heard, Mrs. Delaney?"

"Heard what?"

"A pity! That young English fellow. Dead in his bed with cut wrists."

The wind could have roared, the ravens screeching through the torn veil over the sanctuary of innocence.

Lord, God, No!

She might have screamed as she ran through the devil's club, her dress catching and tearing in the thorns, faster, faster, until she came to the smoke and orange tongues of flame. Good, normal men were purifying the rat's nest into which he had fled for his final inspiration. Fire was cleansing what remained of the dwelling. They had torn it apart first, as hermits are notorious, after all, for secret wealth.

"What a mess, missus. Packrats and fleas were thick as thieves. Weren't nothin of value, some rags and papers with mumbo-jumbo on it, and some mildewy books. We had t'burn it all."

For a second she grieved more for her lost books than for this child who had been thrown away for a few guineas a month. Where was all the labor, the nine months waiting for someone's miracle to take on a form and a name? Who could measure all the milk sucked? A poor broken child cast off across an ocean to that sea of forest where the weak tread water until they sink.

She had believed she was standing on the edge of an abyss, placed there to save whatever discarded child would stagger out toward the void to pitch downward through the wide spaces between the atoms. She had failed. He had fallen through her fingers despite the breast of culture on which they had nursed. She understood nothing then. And he was dead.

The village ravens quickly gathered around the corpse, pulling on strings and pecking at organs in a gluttony of conjecture. Their guesses at the dead man's flaws stretched imagination. They *knew*.

What grieving the woman experienced was performed privately, the state of gossip being what it was. The only thing that escaped from her was spoken in the presence of her husband some time later.

"This land is very hard on people", she said bitterly.

"This land, or the one he came from?" said the man.

All of which was witnessed by their elder son.

Thereafter, the shining, handsome, and strong Ash Delaney began to collect enigma as diligently as he pursued his collection of mounted birds' eggs. He was filled with as much wonder as he had found in those creatures that were born to fly upward, but a measure of pain and puzzlement was added. The unexplained, the tormented, that which had careened off its natural flight path, that which was lost, he wished to find and to restore. Or at least to fit together the broken pieces to see what they would form. Many characters were mounted in his specimen box. There, he now placed carefully, intended for future consideration, the face of Wanda Tobac.

"Jackie", he called, returning them to the present. He had to yell above the hoofbeats as they cantered down the forest path, "D'you ever wonder why?"

"Why? Why what?"

"Why things go the way they do . . . like your Ma. And today."

"That's life, Ash", the boy called into his ear. "There ain't no why, and there ain't no answers."

17

"What is a man?" his father had said.

No one had answered him. And no one had raised the question again.

But Ashley remembered the question and searched for the replies offered by the males of his world. He saw that in this valley men conquered by physical strength. They defeated danger and overcame obstacles. They did not complain about pain or exhaustion; they despised their human enemies and respected their natural ones. They learned to outwit the seasons, to harness them to their own purposes. They were suspicious of change, and they treasured time-tested practical skills. They had simple pleasures and small amusements. Most of all they did not ask, "What is a man?"

In the year of the poet, as he was ever after to call it, Ashley observed and pondered that fundamental doubt. Several times during that winter he snowshoed to the scene of the fire and stared into the black pit of the shanty—and repeated the question. And when the sharply etched world of charcoal and white gave way to the blurred shapes of summer, and the bush had become an impenetrable tangle, he kept the memory of the pit from fading.

He went up the mountain alone that year, leading his father's sheep. He had asked for permission to do this, and after a moment's hesitation his father had agreed. In the man's swift glance he saw an admission that he was no longer a boy and had begun to pass through the poorly mapped territory that led into adulthood. This gauntlet was no less painful than the passage rites of more primitive races. Perhaps more so because there was no precise moment when he could know for certain that childhood lay behind. Yet, sent alone to face the dark and predators, he might endure as many ritual cuts or symbolic thrashings as any boy in hotter jungles.

The undergrowth through which he led the sheep to higher ground threatened to entangle him in coils of buckbrush and thorn. The light, steeped in liquid chlorophyll, filtered through the overcast. Buckets of green were thrown on the canvas, shaken, poured, and flowing until even the ribs of the range were softened. Higher up, the lines remained hard and clear, a terrain of cold granite where the whistling marmots competed with each other and the eternal sliding of scree, pebble by pebble, rumored the fall of mountains.

Somewhere along the way his horse had picked up a limp, and Ashley dismounted. He could find nothing outwardly wrong, though the hock appeared swollen. He was condemned now to climbing the last few thousand meters on foot. He looked up to the peak and saw its massive resistance.

You are small, said the mountain.

"I'm strong", Ashley said.

You are weakest when you think you are strong.

"You won't beat me. I won't flinch before you. You have no power over me."

Then he laughed at himself for speaking with a mountain.

He reached the high meadow exhausted, soaked with sweat, stained green, and bitten by insects. He was burdened, too, by the giant's gun and by a summer that opened ahead like a valley of tribulation, a place where he might be worn down by attrition. He was not so sure about manhood. Would he be tried and found wanting, forced off the mountain to wander down more a child than when he went up. At this moment fatigue ruled his senses, threatening to overpower the courage that had drawn him out of the valley floor. Then the overcast broke, revealing bits of cerulean blue.

"Mountain, mountain, never will you bring me to my knees."

There was pride in having brought the sheep safely to the meadow, and as he watched them flock over into the grassy bowl to graze and drink from the creek, he felt some of his irritation recede. Armed then with his responsibilities and his freedom, with a dog and gun, he walked down into the hidden valley to begin what would be.

That night, as he stared through the small spaces between the wash of stars, he discovered some of what sustained the man, his father. Their enigmas were becoming intelligible now, not a question of meanings deciphered but an awareness of being. Pure being, like the planets in space, around which infinity ran like black water everywhere and always. Stillness filled him, and he almost feared it. His small fleck of being could have been crushed by the immensity or deafened by the chorus of stars.

"Mountain, you've drawn me up here. All right, tell me what I need to know."

You are proud. You wish to master the mountain in the way you master your horse and your gun and your dog.

"Is that so wrong?"

It is illusion.

"It's to be a man."

It is to be half a man, and not the better half.

At this, Ashley shrugged off the imaginary dialogue and snorted in disgust.

"The better half, my ass! That half would turn me into another Nigel!"

At this the entire creation grew completely silent for the period of a few seconds.

Long ago, at the bottom of the mountain, his father had told him, "The mountain is a place where you'll hear things. It's a place where the light is clearer. You'll learn poems."

He had laughed behind his father's back: Poetry! Ha! Poetry was for the weak. Well, maybe sometimes it was also for a certain kind of man like his father, who was undeniably strong. But a strength flawed by sentimentality.

"I believe in rational thought", he admonished himself. "I believe in what can be observed and proven!"

Now the stars erupted in noisy debate:

Observe, observe, they sang, *but you will never prove. Sing the ancient poems with us and you will understand.*

He felt a sudden shame for despising his father's flaw. For an instant he longed to be like him, longed for the freedom to trust in the waters, to plunge into them, to swim and to drown and to rise and swim again.

He resisted the impulse.

"I'm not like Dad. Life's on top of him. That's not gonna happen to me. I'm above it."

At this idea the stars fell silent again, trailing their protests away into the waters.

"The mind is the power and it holds the key to everything", he declared.

A last bird winging home uttered a protest:

The heart is the key! The heart is the key!

But the boy had returned to normal and could no longer hear. The stars, after all, were merely a flat theatre backdrop to his boring life. It was all too effeminate. He sighed and turned over. He wished to sleep, pleased and safe in the armor of his powerful muscles.

* * *

The summer passed. He came to love adversity as an unsentimental but beloved teacher. He was brave. He swam naked in ice water. He slew trees. He shot a coyote, lost only a few lambs, built a tent frame and corral from balsam poles. He defended. He guarded. He grew lean. He roared and delighted in his echoes. He especially savored the sound of his name—Ash Delaney—which was the slash of a rapier. He ran up murderous slopes toward the surrounding peaks. He scaled the giants' teeth, save for the spike of his father's mountain, the one that towered over the valley.

And yet, time grew long. He read many books, sucking the marrow from the carefully chosen volumes his mother sent up. They were books about the mind and the honing of its powers. There was little poetry in them. Since the death of young Lord Rockingham, his mother had little use for poets, it seemed.

He braided rope. He whittled a gun stock. He blew a quantity of air down a flute. That also was her gift. Last Christmas there had been those two instruments beneath the tree. A flute for himself and a flute for his father. Strange, the way the old man choked up and went out by himself to the river. No use trying to figure out his parents. The moment you had them pegged, they brought your theories crashing to the ground.

Throughout the summer there were occasional visits from family or rare vigorous hikers, but the most welcome intrusion came at the end of August. At first they were just two dots of color loping down the slope of the bowl. He saw them long before they spotted him. The visitors finally materialized out of distance: Sarah and Jack.

They stood staring at Ashley. He had changed into a tall, tanned creature, wind-burned, all limbs and rifle in a grubby bush jacket, with the dog leaping in ecstasy around his legs. He grinned. They grinned back. Jackie attacked. The two boys punched and wrestled, made faces, and braced their legs. The girl stood back, smiling but not looking too closely. While Ashley was busy letting his friend defeat him, his mind was wholly engrossed with the presence of the skinny girl who was holding her arms in the checkered jackshirt. A startled doe, her great luminous eyes absorbed the battle, the field, the creek, the sheep, everything except himself.

Sarah, the quiet one. He imagined her pulse to be that of the hummingbird, her skin like the soft tan of deerhide. What were her thoughts and feelings? Could she speak? It seemed suddenly important that she be able to speak to him. On his visits to their cabin it had always been silence. Silence and the bearing of burdens. Touches of her private self were everywhere in the shack, he remembered. Jam jars full of paintbrush and Solomon's seal. Darned clothing, multicolored yarn stitched into the worn heel and toe of the family socks. Little things, evidence of a heart that wished to mend the torn fabric of her family.

Nobody had liked her at school. She had been too shy, inviting oppressors. Dark skin, a solitary homestead, and a mad mother hadn't helped. It might have been the dress, on which the faded name of a grist mill could still be read. But many of the other children bore such names: General Mills, Robin Hood, Prairie Pride, or Purity Flour Company.

Whenever he saw her, there leapt into his mind the words *purity flower*.

Ashley had always liked her, from a distance, as one might admire a sunset through a window. But liking had broken down in time, and a form of awe with a constriction of throat had taken its place. Sometimes when he was alone with her for a cruelly short minute, he looked at his feet. And for this reason she had long ago concluded that he did not approve of her.

"I don't understand this", he said to himself often. "She isn't very pretty. But her heart is so beautiful. I can hardly stand to think of her. I won't think of her. It hurts to think of her."

One of their longest exchanges had concerned a book. He saw it poking out one day from underneath a pillow where it had been hastily shoved, and he asked her about it.

"It's Kateri's story", she had replied. "A Mohawk girl who died a long time ago." The longest chain of words he had ever heard from the lips of Sarah Tobac.

Now that he was pinned to the ground by little Jackie, he

begged for mercy and it was given. The boys then went to gather firewood for the stove, and Sarah set to unloading the packs. Their energy splashed happiness around the valley. The pans sizzled with grease. Eggs, milk, and flour sent up by Ashley's mother were transformed into batter, and Jack poured it onto the spitting black griddle, flipping as the circles cooked. Sarah set table on a boulder, and Ashley poured a drip of molasses onto each plate. Shrikes cried, a hawk moved high overhead. The sun passed through the peaks, and a blue light settled on them as they ate.

"You havin' trouble with cougars?" asked Jack, with a full mouth.

"Some."

"Thought so. There's tracks in the mud at the head of the trail."

"I've seen him", said Ashley. "Last month he started to pick off a lamb or two when I was sleeping. He's a fine hunter, and even the dog didn't scent him. Or wouldn't." He glanced down at Sally, his intrepid blue, who appeared fearless.

"I was walking the little lake at the head of the creek when I heard a whine coming across the water. Sal was running like a shot around the lake, with a full-grown mountain lion loping along easy behind her.

"She came yelping past me and tumbled into a ball, cowering behind my legs. That cat stopped not twenty feet away and just stared. Right in my eyes with his big yellow stare . . ."

"Were ya scared?"

"No, I wasn't scared", he said in a casual voice. "My gun wasn't loaded and, well, if he wanted to he could have brought me down in two seconds and had us for lunch. But he just kept looking me right in the eye, the end of his tail going flick, flick. But I wasn't going to bow to him. I just kept staring back at him."

"That wasn't too smart, Ash."

"It was like he was telling me this is his mountain and I'd better not forget it. After about a minute he turned and went off as casual as all get out. I loaded my gun fast and was going to nail him when something held me back."

"Y'let him go!" said Jack.

"Yeah. I fired a shot over his shoulder though, just to let him know."

He glanced across the fire to see if Sarah was following this account. Her eyes flashed away.

"Lose any more sheep?" said Jack.

"No. I built that paddock near the tent. I bring the flock in at night and keep a fire going. And my gun loaded."

"Cougars hate dogs."

"Yeah, and I think they hate men too. I bet it's because Swiftcreek's getting too big, too fast, invading their hunting grounds."

"I don't know, Ash. They might hate dogs, but I think they're scared of men."

"Hate, fear, same difference!"

In reply Jack took a lump of wood and a knife from his pack and began to whittle. Gradually a human face took shape. In the firelight its expression appeared to change continuously. At first mirthful, then angry, delighted, enraged, and then afraid.

* * *

Sarah was sleeping, rolled up in blankets on the other side of the fire, the sound of her breathing regular, the dog snugged against her back. For some reason neither of the boys could sleep. The night held an early autumn crispness, with the moon rising in a tangent, the bow curved to the west. It was a sickle of light slicing the heavens, while beneath it the creek twilled and untwined, and the swoops of night birds glanced silver off their wings. Farthest away from the moon's track the twins, the brothers Gemini, sparked off the northern peaks.

Ashley's sleeping bag was hot eiderdown. He felt himself beginning to drift into sleep when Jack said quietly, very slowly, as if addressing the stars:

"My mother tried t'kill me, y'know."

Ashley did not respond for a few moments, wondering if his friend was attempting twisted humor.

"What?"

"She tried t'kill me."

Jack had been eight years old. She had never been unwell before, but in recent months had been drinking and yelling. Each binge was a little longer, more violent. She raged about *them*. Who? the children wondered. English and Slavey mixed with a smattering of French, meshing and fragmenting into secret laughter and shouts of outrage, cursing and mumbling. The boy began to be afraid whenever his father went out to feed the dogs. His body grew tense whenever he heard the back door close, then the creak-creak as his mother's feet beat the worn path in the floorboards, cycling back and forth between the kitchen and the children's bedroom. She would stop at the door to their room, listening, listening to the listening within. He held his breath, praying that she would not enter to cradle his head and drop hot tears on his eyelids. Then she would begin again, the eternal pacing.

Her talk was fretted with words he did not understand, neither Slavey nor French, and there were names, too, Fort Simpson and Kamloops and other stations of her pain. Sometimes the boy would be afraid to ford the torrent of this anguish, to dash for the tin-can chamberpot in the porch, and would wet himself, lying ashamed in bed.

In the final months it seemed that his father would be sucked under in currents that had already claimed the woman. He was discouraged, single-handed with a sick wife and a small flock of kids. Around that time Sarah began to shoulder some of the burdens of motherhood onto her spindly frame. She did all the cooking and washing while Wanda sat and stared out the window all day long, rolling cigarettes and chain-smoking. The woman would not talk much and only when her family might take the parts she had ordained for them in the dramas of her imagination or memory.

"Thadee, I'm cold!"

"Wanda, it's boilin' in here."

"It's cold. Snow on the ground, and the guard says no soup t'night cause Mary Drygeese went through the wire! Why? Why we punished for her?"

"Wanda, come back! That was a long time ago."

"No, no", she cried, shocked at his blindness, his cruelty. "No, I wouldn't run through the wire. You think I want t'die! You're crazy, Thaddaeus!"

She was laughing and weeping, throwing back her mat of hair. She would not wash the tangled mane until all the evil had grown out.

"Mary was grinning. Her eyes were turned up white and her hands stuck on the wire. Froze. They carried her like a sack of potatoes. She was bent out of shape. They had t'thaw her body on the workbench in the tool shed."

"Wanda, that's done and gone. Twenty years ago."

"Twenty. I'm twenty and pretty too", she said glancing sideways into the mirror. "I look almost white, don't I?"

"No, you're forty! Look at your hair. Gray. Look", and he forced her to peer into the mirror. She pulled her face aside and glared at him.

"I'm *hungry,* Thadee. There's no soup t'night!"

He would sigh, bend his head to his hands, his collar revealing a band of copper skin beneath the dark sunburn of his face. A neck resigned to some axe. He would slowly shake his head in defeat. He poured soup for her, broke the bannock, and touched her forehead with his fingertips for an instant, as if amazed that no healing would flow from them.

287

"Eat, Wanda", he said and went out to feed the animals.

"Why'd this happen to my Mum, Ash?" her son now asked. His voice trembled, and all traces of the tough little brawler were gone. He was a child hiding in blankets.

Wanda. Mum. Raised through the kindness of the State. She knew Québec French and Slavey and had her knuckles rapped for sneaking off to town in the beaded crow-boots her grandma had made—Grandma Bonnetplume, who died of TB in Campsell Hospital.

She had learned to play piano in the hostel. Miss Bock taught her. *Miss*, the thin woman with moles who stood watching with a tipped pointer as thirty little naked Indian girls doused under the nozzles in the cement shower room.

"*One little, two little, three little Indians, four little . . .*", they were taught to sing. Miss did not smile, though she was never cruel. She had brought Wanda to such a degree of facility that she could produce *The German Dance in F* by Wolfgang Amadeus Mozart, slowly, slowly, cautiously for the hostel concerts.

Through the chain-link fence Wanda watched the children of the other hostel, those Catholics. They sang and danced in the dust of their yard. Sometimes they fought with each other or kissed in the violet shadows of winter afternoons, while secular girls watched from the high, white windows of the other side. Leaning on the chain-link fence, staring through its holes, Wanda wished she were a Catholic and could kiss behind snowbanks and sing the hymns that came on the wind along with narcotic incense.

"What's that sweet smell, Miss?" they asked. The other playground was deserted, and music wafted through the links.

"They are inside worshipping idols", replied Miss with distaste.

Later, at the bedtime lecture, she said: "Religion is a primitive drug used by a majority of the populace to soothe its pain. You would do well to avoid its influence at all costs."

When she caught some girls observing the romances on the other side, she called them all to assembly:

"Senior girls! Sex is a normal, healthy drive. It is purely an appetite. When you are released from this Institute you would do well to pursue it in a hygienic, efficient manner, without the emotionalism that entraps so many of our gender. Sex is class warfare. You must understand your weapon if you wish to emerge the victor from the struggle."

No one knew what she meant, of course, for the entire world was worshipping and falling in love, kissing, and killing with absolute conviction. Passion was running wild through a hot universe like summer fire in the bush.

But the songs Wanda learned in Miss's own undefined chapel were a kind of icy fire. Full of robust sentiments, Miss led them in the singing:

"We are marching to U-To-Pia!" tromp, tromp, tromping around the gymnasium, grinning as Miss coiled and uncoiled their lines in a huge circle-dance.

"Just curious, Miss Bock, but what is that you are singing with the girls?"

It was the hostel supervisor, poking his head around the door.

Miss was charming. "We are marching to Pretoria, sir! Very good for the circulation!" And laughed with a wave.

"Carry on then. Well done!" he said, and left.

"Senior girls!" she said that night. "Do you know the meaning of the word *capitalism*?"

Much shaking of heads, no, no.

"I thought not", said Miss ominously. "And do you know the meaning of the word *socialism*?"

More shaking of heads.

"It is not necessary for you to know these words. But they will shape your future. You will hear them again when you are old."

She stared across the rows of beds like a shaman.

"The People are the will of the future! This is a force you must not resist. Some of you will live to see it. I will not."

Off went the light, and the last words rang in the air as precise steps disappeared down the linoleum corridor. Thirty seconds later, suppressed giggles blew holes in the dark to the tune of clanking steam pipes, while some of the younger girls entertained nightmares beneath the mantle of a cold universe.

Only on the piano did secret fires erupt. After a concert the audience gathered around to congratulate: wonderful what the administration is doing for these poor girls! The supervisor held Wanda by the chin and asked her name. He gave her a dime. She ignored the prize and gazed at the floor, wondering where her mum'n'dad were trappin' at that very moment and why she couldn't be with them. But long ago Mum'n'Dad had felt their hearts contort with conflicting desires, for they had wished her to rise above their poverty, to read and write and master the white alchemy. They had wept as they let her go but were consoled by the fact that many other girls had been combed out of the bush along with their daughter. They knew she would not be alone. Though she was alone. Each of the girls was alone.

So Wanda Bonnetplume was ejected when complete. She wound up in Kamloops eventually, learned to sit in cafés and suck on Black Cat Plains, to blow saucy clouds from her bright red lipstick and bounce her crossed legs. She thought that she might rob the spice jar of her senses or dump it out on some lucky fella to see what it might contain. But didn't. During the nights she was paid to play hot stuff on the piano at the Leland Hotel Bar, and some of the customers listened with interest. They thought that she was hot like her music and her costumes and were angry when they found that she was cold. Even that young guy Thaddaeus Tobac had to look twice when he came to town for an illegal beer.

Eventually she went to court for smashing a bottle over some white cowboy's head and sending him to the hospital with ten stitches and a concussion. She should have smashed it over his hands, said Wanda to the judge. Those hands had accosted her in the alley behind the bar one night when she was plodding home from work. Something had snapped in her when a policeman came running and discovered the screaming, bloody cowboy and tried to arrest Wanda for assault and battery. She went to work on the cop, too, and in time resisting arrest and contempt of court were added to the list of her crimes.

When Thaddaeus heard that she was in jail, he went to see her. Across the visitor's desk they began to talk, and the girl felt for the first time in many years that she was not a useless ward abandoned on the tundra.

"There ain't no love in the world", she told him.

"Sure there's love", he said.

"I got a friend in here that told me lots. She been lookin' for years and ain't never found a man yet that doesn't just want t'take and t'hurt."

"What's yer friend's name?"

"Mary Drygeese. She's a hooker from Edmonton."

"There *is* love", he said emphatically. As she looked at his clear eyes, his clean dry jeans, and cheekbones whipped red by wind, she thought for a moment that he might be right. His hands did not grab but reached across the vast expanse of the table and waited for her to reach across the other half. His fingers touched with a question in their surfaces, gentle, though they had been scarred by calf-rope and firewood. He was a nice guy—strong.

For several weeks they traded stories, holding hands, learning to look at each other without flinching. It was then that Wanda sobbed out the tale of her friend Mary, who had died in barbed wire during an escape attempt.

PROSTITUTE DIES OF EXPOSURE, said the headlines. Included in the columns was a vague, laborious explanation from the director of the prison. It was true what they wrote, but it was a lie, too, because it was not the real Mary Drygeese. The photograph showed a fat, pockmarked prostitute, but the real Mary was a spotted brown dove who battered her wings on the bars of her cage.

Thaddaeus helped Wanda to live. She suspected him at first of being the kind of nice guy who starts out good and gets worse with age. But in the beginning he was shining and unmaimed; he was willing and capable. He was also a Catholic, and when she was free he kissed her in the violet shadows. Gradually, she came to believe that he might be the kind of sheltering rock against which the occult forces would smash. She hoped that he would prevent her from ending like Mary, dead from exposure to life.

He did take good care of Wanda Bonnetplume. He intended to make her whole. She studied his faith and converted. They married. Children came, and the Tobacs moved north to places with no memory. For years their life was ordinary. They bought a trapline and settled in the North Thompson valley, near where it broke into the Canoe valley. They were strangers, except for the one or two trappers in the region who took an interest. There was an Irishman and his family. There was the occasional Mass said by a visiting priest. There were the cycles of the seasons and the harvest of fur.

But in the early 1930s Wanda began to drink. The first major collapse had come one night during a heavy storm, when all the trains from Jasper to Hope had stopped, the snow falling so thick that local historians pronounced it the worst since one in the twenties when there were only tunnels between the buildings, shoulder deep to the tallest man in town.

That night, Thaddaeus was fifteen miles down the Thompson at the trap-cabin by the glacier, across from the switches where the men of the section crew were dismally shovelling snow. The night was a menace—twenty below zero Fahrenheit and the snowfall heavy. They had been shovelling as fast as they could to keep warm and didn't know whether the plow train would clear the line sufficiently for their small speeder to make it back to Swiftcreek. Around midnight the gang broke for sandwiches and coffee. Thaddaeus yelled an invitation at the six men. One by one they took turns bending to enter his tiny shack, to drink the Indian's hospitality, hot sweet tea, laced with the railroaders' rum. Eventually they all crowded in and huddled shoulder to shoulder.

As Thaddaeus was eating with them, he began to feel an anxiety that had nothing to do with the storm. He knew, without knowing, that it was Wanda and Jack. There was a desperate trouble looming, and he knew that he must move fast. Camille L'Oraison, the foreman, told him to take the speeder. The other crew-men were half-liquored and did not bother to ask why the Indian was taking their only transportation back to town. When they had lifted it onto the tracks, Thaddaeus jumped in, revved the engine, pulled the brakes, and slowly began to push off into the snow.

Camille stood and watched the lights of the speeder disappear into the blizzard, wondering why he had done it.

"Well, if he don't come back," he said to himself, "we'll catch the wayfreight in the morning."

Thaddaeus wondered if he was crazy, doing such a thing on the strength of a feeling. The machine wedged through the solid mass of white caught in the headlights. Time and distance melted into dread. Only the signal light sailing by his left eye eventually warned him that he was approaching the bridge at Canoe River. He cut the engine and wheeled the speeder onto the next siding. He strapped on his snowshoes and set off into fresh snow that was waist deep, travelling by instinct toward the blind wilderness of the southwest, the earth and all orientation swallowed. His terror for the family must have acted as a homing beacon, for within an hour he reached the clearing by the creek that he knew was home.

It was about four in the morning when he arrived, but the lamp glow from the cabin windows rushed out through the snow to meet him. And along with it came faint cries. He was exhausted, and the final hundred yards seemed longer than the entire journey up to that point. He ran on his snowshoes and bashed through the door into chaos. The cabin was torn upside down, and it echoed with screams. He grabbed a butcher knife out of Wanda's hand, her face twisted and questioning, and pushed her across the room, where she slumped onto a kitchen chair. He pulled Sarah down from the rafters, and he hugged her, held her, touched her until she stopped screaming and grew quiet, trembling in his arms.

"Where's Jack?" he asked.

There, she pointed, *there*.

His father found him coiled under a bed, physically unharmed. He carried the cold ball of the boy's body to the bed and uncurled it slowly, embracing and whispering words of comfort until at last the blood beat color into his face, and the child was freed to scream and scream.

She was shipped away to the hospital that time, the first of many. And though she improved off and on, returned home, and was seen to perform the necessary tasks, she was never to become entirely well. Her children eventually forgave her and understood her as best they could. She did not repeat the violence, and they recalled it only as a faded nightmare.

"I'm sorry", said Ashley.

"Yeah, me too", said Jack.

* * *

In the night a dream:

The boy rose from the sleep of youth to float over the dark meadow, the muttering sheep, the bears and cats and other presences prowling around the edge of the encampment. He arrived at the glacial pond that fed the creek. He leaned out over the glass of the pool in search of his reflection.

Who am I, he asked the water.

The water stirred, then settled. A face appeared, his own. He cried out in alarm for it was a torn image, sewn together in ragged patches.

No!

He awoke shouting, his heart thumping.

"What the hell, Ash?"

Jack grabbed his arm. Sarah sat up. The dog whined.

"What is it?" Jack shook him.

"A nightmare. I was looking at my face in the water and it was all cut up."

"Just a dream."

"It was too real. Too real."

18

The power of her insights, though more prosaic than the mountain visions of her husband and son, could induce a trembling in the nervous system of Anne Delaney. The thought of Joseph Stalin or Adolph Hitler would do it. Or Chamberlain, or Mackenzie King. Or Belfast Realty and its speculations—for Jonah MacPhale had developed new appetites—buying and foreclosing on discouraged homesteaders, stuffing farms, treelots, and hotels into his never-satisfied mouth. Oh, there were any number of things she could fight.

Dan Cox, her editor, was more at ease railing against the price of timber than the rumblings of dictators. Over the years he had bought down from a feisty paper on the coast through a succession of small-town ventures to this final sheet, the woodsy *Echo*, in which he desired to live out his last days printing proclamations of birth, natural death, and church socials. It was a stubborn contrary streak in him, however, that permitted the inclusion of a lone warrior on his team, the unexplainable Mrs. Delaney. He was forced to warn her from time to time that her text was almost unreadable when she plunged beneath the surface account of events, her handling of the issues too subtle or complex for the average reader.

"Get rid of her, Dan", he had been warned a hundred times. "She's just spoilin' yer paper."

"Nobody loves a critic", he said to himself, and resolved not to lose her. She added precisely the right amount of controversy to the paper and a certain interest to his rather dull semi-retirement. Besides, he reminded himself, she was always so damn right about things.

Yes, there will be a war. It will be more devastating than the last one, and more terrible in its disdain for life than the atrocities now being experienced by the people of Spain.

How can there not be a war? Can we keep feeding the totalitarian beast small pieces of the free world and expect it to refrain from gobbling us whole one day? This, surely, is the slow, painful, and fatal method, as Mr. Chamberlain shall certainly discover.

Of twenty-seven European nations, only ten remain democratic in the sense that political groups are truly able to compete for public office and their citizens free to pursue life much as they please. The promise of the 1920s that constitutional democracies would flourish has been broken, and the average man, finding himself no longer a citizen but a cell in a vast organism, must pay the penalty.

The very idea of truth has boiled away in the political rhetoric, and this is only the logical outcome of a philosophy that is violent and pagan. The theoreticians of the new social order have declared thought and art to be the flabby activities of a pampered elite and attempt to replace it with a juvenile worship of the body and power.

It is only natural that the religious institutions should be experiencing such universal persecution. The treatment of European Jewry is an obvious example. In addition, the new despots are not only anti-Semitic, anti-intellectual, and anticlerical, they are explicitly anti-Christian. Should we be defeated in the coming war, it may be that the only remaining truly human communities will be found in the caves where such victims have fled for shelter.

The woman found it necessary to penetrate the home-front mentality as she went to and fro on her errands of wool and fur, eggs and manuscripts. Cold walls greeted her as she rode down Main Street; cold eyes assessed her as she went about her cabalistic purposes.

"Did you read that article last week?" someone would say as she trot-trotted by in the superior rig.

"Yes," another would reply, "yes, and didn't it sound almost as if she were a Jew?"

"She is dark, you know, and no one really knows where she came from."

"That woman could destroy the country's morale!"

"Some people are too clever."

"Yes, they really are too clever for words."

* * *

Journal Entry:

Swiftcreek, 30 Sept. 1939

So, the great season of fury begins. My own terrors are mixed inextricably with the universal fear and loathing that is now grabbing the tools of death. Fear! The fear that human beings have of everything, of enemies and friends, the opinions of men and the shadows in the forest. Especially their own reflections. For to see ourselves as we are would be to discover the tyrants and heroes raging within the battleground of our souls. Prowling around everything is the assumption that enough power is all we need to conquer our fear forever. Our greatest fear: absence of power, helplessness, nothingness. There is no one left on the face of the earth who would agree with this statement. Except one:

The war has swept even the clergy into uniform, for God, it seems, must serve the country's morale. During the past two months, however, in place of the regular visiting pastor, a strange young priest has been sent. No doubt he is someone neither army nor city parish will have. He is a refugee, a central European, I think. His English is heavily accented but quite clear. He walks with a broken gait, and his face is half-paralysed. He smiles rarely and then only crookedly because of his handicap. He limps about the village, haunting it. He is not social, speaking only if spoken to, a "Yes" or "No".

Totally unattractive. A stranger on earth.

I went to him after Mass one Sunday, I'm not sure why. My heart was drumming for no apparent reason. He is not an imposing person, and indeed he is only more or less tolerated around here. I managed to find out that he lives in a shack by the edge of the railway, halfway to Prince George. He serves the little missions up and down the line by hopping freights. He survives by begging, or should I say receiving, for he never makes his wants known. My news gatherers along the track say he is called "the hermit".

I gave him some eggs and milk, for which he was suitably grateful. I introduced myself, and he told me his name is Father Andrei. I was repelled in the beginning, remembering Nigel. But my reluctance was dispersed when he looked at me, into me, so steadily that I had to step back. I saw grey-blue eyes and strength, a kind of strength I have never seen before, not even in Stephen. He is like still water. I asked him to clarify a minor point in his sermon, which was a ruse on my part, for his sermons are utterly lucid. He speaks with humility and authority—an extraordinary mixture. He answered my question. Then, looking at me in the gentlest manner, he said,

"You are afraid, aren't you?"

What could I say except to stammer some assertion of my strength. He waited until I was finished and said, "Don't be afraid. You don't need to be afraid."

I was speechless. When I attempted to produce more words, they died on my lips. They were falsehood. I must say that he in no way exercised any psychic or spiritual power over me. If anything, his power lay in that he had no power. He merely looked deeply into my soul.

A tension broke within me, and much to my horror I began to weep. The tears quietly drained the hurt and terror from me and replaced it with peace.

"I cry out, I cry out, but there is only silence!" I said.

"Is it silence or deafness?"

I felt quite hurt by the question, but he went on:

"We are all deaf. The way of emptiness teaches us to hear."

That is the essence of what he said, though I cannot recall the precise words.

"The world is full of hatred because it refuses to be poor. It wants to conquer fear with power. But you will conquer in another way, the unknown way. First, perhaps, you will forget. You will not see. You will not understand. Later you may see, and then you will know that the false self must die in order for the true self to be born."

I stared at him, astonished. Was he a prophet, a saint, a mystic? A fool? A liar? Fears and doubts crept in even as I stood looking at him. The peace left. He smiled sadly and said:

"When you turn again, you will know the emptiness is your friend."

He never came back. My informants say he was transferred. And true enough, this week he was replaced by a newly ordained boy stuffed with theology and good will.

I digest the words of my hermit this way and that. I recall them at the oddest moments, and they are surrounded by silence.

Yesterday, as I was leaving the schoolhouse after Mass, I found myself avoiding Wanda Tobac's eyes. For once she was looking back, and it caught me off guard. I pretended that I hadn't noticed. We are strangers it seems, and I have not learned to love her. The wound in her eye terrifies me precisely because it is my own image I see reflected there.

* * *

Throughout that autumn she woke often to listen to leaves falling and drifting around the cabin. Then winter came. Molten lead skies poured over the earth. The blitzkrieg of snow began. Wood-smoke rose against the mountain in a peaceful Christmas-card village where war and evil are bad dreams and the better aspirations of men remain possible. Elsewhere, Hitler's armies had overrun Poland and were settling into the silent phase of what the city papers were calling a phony war. Stephen was away a great deal that winter, and during his absence the woman felt her old fears eating away from within at the shell of reason. The wood-smoke, on an afternoon, might rise up taking animal forms of bear, wolf, leopard, and serpent leaping into the sky or rummaging through the forest on the wind. Sometimes she thought she saw the shape of a monstrous animal roaming around the edge of the woods, though it might have been only shadows or the tricks played on the mind by the moon.

But one evening she was sure: a bolt of terror shot through her when she saw a malevolent shape heave out of the woods by the river. It was that beast she had seen in a moment of hallucination on her first day in this land, years before. Only now she knew that it was real. It was larger than a horse, and murk hovered about it like an absence of light, like the shadow of a shadow.

It stopped in midstride when it saw her and stared up the meadow to the cabin door. Time instantly froze. She ached to disappear, to flee inside and bolt the door. But images of her children came before the eyes of her mind, and a sudden outrage boiled up within her. She clenched her apron in her fists and took a step forward. She tried to shout at the thing to drive it away, but fear was a stone in her throat and she could not utter a word.

It hissed at her and spoke into her mind:

I will devour your children.

"You will not!" she cried at last, but it sounded like a croak.

I will destroy each of you.

Cawing angrily, crows burst across the meadow between

them. The woman quaked, but her gaze remained fierce, and a current of absolute defiance shot from her eyes back into the eyes of the beast.

For a moment it continued to stare, then sneered at her, turned, and moved away into the trees and disappeared.

She sank onto the porch step and buried her face in the trembling apron. She knew now that she was mad. Where was Stephen? Oh God, where was he? Why had he left her so alone?

All that night and the next day she missed him terribly. His habits were infinitely stable. His smell reassured, that resinous firewood and sweat smell, and his hands, his brown comforting hands, their nails spatulate from his forty or more years of labor.

He had been swallowed by empty valleys, extending his trap lines farther into that realm of silence which other men seemed to desire less and less as the season of fury intensified. But there was something about her memory of him, their incompleteness, that continued to haunt. Her emptiness was relieved only by the children. She read to them most nights or wrote long letters to Emily across an ocean that had become vast and filled with deadly hunters. Her children, the man who lived in tandem with her, the work at the paper, these were a frail defense against the forces now gathering in the world. It did not seem possible that even tiny valiant England, her soul's shrine, was teetering at the edge. If England was to fall, how could anything else be kept from pouring over into the bottomless interiority of matter?

The children were in school that morning when she went to the frame manse beside the new church and knocked. There were foot steps within, a creaking door, and then he answered.

"Anne", he said in suspenders and socks, with a big crumpled newspaper he had been reading. Spectacles. A coffeepot boiling over somewhere inside.

"Come in, won't you?" He seemed delighted but flustered.

"Yes, yes, please, Reverend Gunnalls", she said formally, and entered.

"Edwin", he corrected.

"Edwin."

How gray they had both become. They had been acquainted for how many, twenty years? And hardly knew each other at all, though he had seen her tears and her children and the *Echo* things, which was about all there was to know.

But of himself there was nothing revealed. As he poured two cups of coffee, she looked carefully at the interior of his dwelling but could find written there no highly personal statements. No housekeeper, dog, or aspidistra. No photographs of cathedral spires or rugby teams, in which robust males stood arm in arm in a confraternity of eternal idealism and youth. She had half expected to find photographs of swamis and bodhisattvas such as decorated Papa's study. Or perhaps the pamphlets of a veiled Marxism such as those Emily once mailed from home, the products of her own pen or those of her Oxford friends, she would never confess which.

She had supposed that Edwin Gunnalls was like them, but curiously his lair revealed nothing of the sort. There was a certain simplicity. The bare walls were accented only by a barren cross formed of two birch sticks—how very odd! A desk teetered with old letters, tracts, magazines, open books, the disarray of a full but scattered interior life. There were two easy chairs flanking a wood heater. A cell really, the home of the kind of soul who had made a certain truce with the demands of the flesh. Clothes, food, objects were only tools—functional, uninspired, necessary, and good. She suspected that somehow they were important to him only as the vehicles of his search.

Why had he never married, she wondered. He was certainly virile, in a thin, puritan fashion. And handsome. Age had silvered him and left him lean. He looked at you now, as once he had not. Perhaps he was a lake over which she could bend to quench her thirst and smile, finally, at her own reflection. There was a depth beneath the surface that had not been there before.

"I've been meaning to come for some time now", she said by way of opening, "To claim that offer of discussion you made once. At a picnic."

"Oh, yes", he said vaguely. "You were a little troubled that day, if I recall."

She was about to stumble all over herself to explain the incident but refrained, as she saw that it would probably make no difference. He appeared to hold her in some respect, despite the humiliation and the harsh banter of their previous meeting.

"I've been reading your articles in *The Echo*, and I must say I'm impressed."

"Impressed? By what?" She was suddenly stern, though secretly pleased.

"By your vision. By the way you see beyond this war to what will probably be left in its wake."

"Oh, it's only what anyone would conclude if he gave the matter some thought."

"No, not anyone", he said, clattering his cup on the saucer. He went to get the coffeepot.

"People don't always understand a lack of patriotism", he shouted from the kitchen.

"Then I'm fortunate to have found at least one", she called.

He was smiling when he returned. He could read the bird-script of her humor.

"I *am* a patriot", she went on. "But my country is an invisible one, populated by poets and painters, novelists and thinkers who are interested, above all, in truth."

"That's a very fine nation of yours! Is there any room in it for cads and simpletons and country parsons?" He smiled again over the rim of his cup.

She took the comment far too seriously and was groping in her mind for a reply.

"Anne, how are you?" he asked, getting down to business. There seemed no answer to that except a lie or the truth.

"I'm fine", she lied.

But somewhere in the past twenty years he had learned to see. He looked steadily at her without commenting.

"No, I'm not. I'm wretched, actually."

"I know."

"And I don't understand why."

His face grew gentler. She hoped that it might be a friend's face, not a professional's appropriate response.

"Sometimes the unhappiness we experience is actually the pain of being born, of labor", he said.

"And what about shelter? Where is that? I call and call, but there seems to be no answer." Her face became cruel with feeling.

"Human beings are not noted for being good listeners", he said.

Yes. True. But she felt slapped. The hermit had also said that.

"None of us hears properly", he went on. "Every one of us is tied up in our inner noise."

"Then why, if God is there, doesn't he speak louder? Why doesn't he shout?"

"I don't know. But I wonder sometimes if it's because deep down we want to be deaf. If he raised his voice, would we maybe just make ourselves that much deafer in order not to hear? He wouldn't want that."

He pointed at the crossed birch sticks.

"Didn't he already shout very loudly a long time ago? How many heard? How many hear?"

"It's the strangest feeling in the world", she said, barely audible. "I believe what you're saying somewhere down in the poorest cellar-room of my heart. But my mind says no! I cannot believe."

"The mind says, I *will not* believe!"

She put her head in her hands: "Am I two personalities? Am I splitting in two?"

"No, I don't think so. Do you? Do you really think you're going mad?" And smiled again, touching her secret fear.

She straightened herself. "No, not really", she said. No, not at this moment she actually did not, suddenly reassured by the articulation of the fear, by a smile and a cup of coffee.

Though at times she was convinced that she would join Nigel and Wanda beneath the crushing weight of this forest. Or be eaten by that beast.

"There's a dialogue between the self and the soul", he said. "They aren't enemies. More like two lenses trying to get in focus."

"Lenses", she said, remembering that she had once used that exact word—a lens through which to view the dangers of existence from a safe distance.

"Like a camera. And you know what comes out of cameras when the lenses aren't focused."

"Yes," she said, "tears and gibberish!"

"And fear," he added, "fear of annihilation."

There it was. Another haunted word from her past. That word with which they had begun their first dialogue so long ago, a conversation stretched out over two decades. She was still gripped by many of the questions that had troubled her back then. But *he* was different. What was this new thing in his eyes? Wisdom? If so, it was a cool gray version of the fathomless, bluer depths she had seen in the hermit's eyes. It was a coloration of the soul, a stroke of the brush accomplished only by an affliction patiently borne.

"Suffering has never struck me as a desirable path to God", she said. "I've always hated pain. It seems only to lead to despair. Is despair permissible?"

"Well, no, if by despair you mean that final rotten luxury of self-destruction", he said slowly. "But those plunges into hopeless feelings that at times afflict us all . . . maybe they're God's quiet shout."

"A quiet shout? What an odd thought."

"To wake us from the subconscious despair that saturates our entire world and our times."

"These times! I wonder if I will ever find peace. Is there any peace possible for people like me?"

"What do you mean by peace? A lack of trouble? Listen, a life without trials may be truly more hopeless than one that's constantly struggling with despair. One is dead, Anne, and the other is being born through blood and tears and agony."

"You sound uncannily like my husband. He, too, has great respect for unpleasant bodily functions. Stephen would approve of your imagery, at least, if not your conclusions."

"He's an unusual man, your husband." He began to stuff a pipe with tobacco.

"Stephen? He's a mystery that hasn't been explained."

"No? Tell me why he's a mystery to you."

"Tell me first", she countered, "why an educated woman from a highly cultured milieu should choose to marry a man so vastly different in background."

"Perhaps you should tell me."

"I don't believe I know", she replied, her chin becoming firm against a temptation to tremble.

"When I first came to this place it was a sort of expedition into the hinterland. I would teach. Write my poetry, experience what was not built on thousands of years of history, not tamed. I intended to collect the flora, make watercolor records of lichens and fungi . . . any number of similar projects."

"Some of which, no doubt, happened."

"Yes, but I didn't mean to be trapped here. I had dreams. And ideas."

"Seems to me that you still do", he said, picking up a newspaper from the floor, finding one of her articles.

"Those. But they're not what I had thought they would be."

"Dreams are changed by life", he said. "Does it really matter what shape the dreams take?"

"Yes, it does. It matters."

"Perhaps it does, after all. But there are times when one is merely glad to survive with one's faculties intact. With a little dignity."

She sensed that he was referring to himself. Could a terror of madness afflict the comfortable and positioned? Could this pious functionary who was equally at home in the Kingdoms of Swiftcreek and of Heaven be, like her, a stranger?

"Love is a dream", he continued, "that assumes strange shapes."

She looked at him steadily, irritated by his pedantic style, a possible condescension she thought she heard beneath the surface tone of his gentleness. In a mysterious act of vengeance, she wished to probe into his past. Ancient discussions flooded up from memory to provide the material.

"Are you still two people in one clerical garment?"

"Whatever do you mean?" he said, startled out of his thoughts by her abruptness.

"I mean the country parson and his alter ego, the revolutionary who was determined to tear down the old, rotten tree of his faith."

He smiled ironically, understanding.

"Ah, yes, so that a new sapling could rise from its ruins?" he said.

"Yes, that one. Which of them did you become? To which of them am I now speaking?"

"I thought that would have been obvious, Anne." He puffed furiously on his pipe, and his brow was heavily furrowed. "I found that there's no good sapling without the tree that bore it. That old tree is still an oak flourishing in winter. Battered, scabby, broken limbs here and there, but a heart that's sound and true."

"So you chose."

"I chose. Ultimately, everything's choice. I went through a few things during those years I was away. Out of curiosity I got involved with a . . . a society, let's call it, a group of people who meet regularly down on the coast. Together with them I ate the fruit I'd talked about so long. It was sweet, sweet on my tongue, this new religion. But it made me very sick and selfish, and I felt a malignancy growing in my mind."

He looked distantly out the window.

"And in the process I ruined someone's life. I destroyed a family. I hadn't meant to, of course, and it was all done in the name of love. But, you see, I found myself one day lying at the roots of the wild tree, and I was bloated on the last of its rotten fruit. I couldn't understand how I'd got there."

She was listening intently and did not dare a reply.

"I thought truth could look after itself", he went on. "I had this absolute conviction that, because I was a nice guy who meant harm to no one, I couldn't make mistakes, I couldn't possibly be deceived. But I was wrong. There's something in us, in each of us, that doesn't want the truth. And that thing, whatever it is, has to be seen and understood before its power over one is broken. Eventually, I began to use my head and to look closely. I found that the brave new church is a myth, a beautiful illusion. Maya!"

"But if all religions are the same . . . ?"

"I found, you see, in a long crucible of pain, that all religions aren't the same."

"So, the parson—you chose him."

"In a sense, yes, I chose. That foolish country dominie, bumping over the hills on a donkey. You know the image. Well, I'm beginning to suspect that he's got more reality packed under his silly hat than the revolutionary does. I could have risen in the world if I'd pursued my original follies. Revolutionaries aren't exactly in style yet, but they soon will be, and in the coming generations they'll be all the rage. I could have been a forerunner, even better than your garden variety rebel, a *father* of the revolution! Pretty intoxicating stuff, and I almost fell for it. In fact, I did fall for it. But it cost a ruined life to pay for my eyes to be opened."

"Good heavens, have you killed someone?"

"No. Nothing so uncivilized as that. I . . . well, one can kill the thing one loves in a thousand ways. You can be on fire with passion for its beauty and ignore the hidden truth of a being, a soul. You can do all kinds of permanent damage thinking you're making a beautiful creation, a free relationship."

"So, you ran back here."

"Not immediately. We walked away from each other in a most tasteful style. There were no unforgivable breaches of etiquette. But in the squalor left in its wake I did some real thinking. I asked to come back here. The powers-that-be said Swiftcreek would never merit its own resident minister. It was too poor and washed up for that. It just couldn't support one financially. It would always have to be a mission of McBride.

"I thought about it for a while. And I wondered if I was even fit to be a minister. I still wonder. But I made a suggestion to them. I'd just received a small inheritance that made it possible for me to live at a subsistence level almost indefinitely. I asked them if they'd let me come back here and build this little manse, put up the log church, and stay forever if I have to. They didn't like the idea much, but there was nothing in it for them to lose. So they gave me the go-ahead."

"I wondered how you'd survive."

"The little scraps that are left cover my food and firewood, and there are a few coins in the collection basket on Sundays. In Vancouver I was comfortable, respectably employed, influential . . . and quite wretched. In Swiftcreek I'm poor, but there's a curious joy in this poverty."

"Is this not," she said carefully, pausing, "is this not just, per-haps, another romantic dream, this heroic poverty of yours?"

He laughed.

"Romantic? Nope, it ain't romantic! It's reality, and most of us don't like much reality. Exotic images, impressions, good feelings, and, above all, the illusion of being in charge, that's what attracts us. Poverty is helplessness, vulnerability. You discover you aren't God. You learn to live with certain kinds of pain that won't go away."

Pain, what pain? she wondered, for to all appearances his well-ordered existence, though simple, was now devoid of stress. Could his vague infidelity have left so deep a wound?

"What pain have you suffered?"

"I will always carry the pain of that woman and her family."

But his eyes contained something else.

"There's more, isn't there?"

"I know now that I'm capable, given the wrong set of circumstances, of doing anything. I could very well repeat my first error."

She looked piercingly into him. His eyes looked down, then away.

"Tell me", she whispered.

"I don't believe it would be helpful to discuss it."

This angered her.

"I see. I'm merely a client after all! You cannot discuss with me any of your personal matters. Yet you are perfectly at ease giving me recipes to apply to my most intimate anguish!"

"No", he said looking down.

"No, what?"

"No, I am not at ease." And then slowly: "You see, your most intimate anguish is my anguish."

He spoke the last few words in a voice so hushed that she barely heard it. His meaning was unclear, and she mistook it as a mere declaration of sympathy. And quickly returned to her own cares.

Men so seldom disclose their hearts, she thought with a tincture

311

of resentment, *but women are always and everywhere ready to give everything.*

She thought of the man, her husband, who had seized her heart so many years ago. It was his beauty that had seduced her. Not just his strength and passionate grace, the animation that quickened physical desire, but that door which opened through his eyes into something infinite and . . . and!! She knew what it was, but there were no words for it. Knew it and was completely frustrated by her inability to express the full dimensions of her quandary.

"I did love my husband once. And still do. There's some gift he's been given to bring me, which we haven't yet learned to open."

Quiet, as they both thought. Geese in someone's backyard set up a racket; a car went by on the road, honking back—noises from a distant universe.

"Each of us longs to be known," he said, at last finding his voice, "to be recognized and loved in the core of his being. You felt it from your husband, and your truest, deepest self went searching for more."

"I was a fool. Can you build a life on a look, when so many other things separate you?"

"You weren't a fool. You built your life on what is the most fundamental need of the heart . . . to find a permanent home in the heart of another. The other things, well, maybe you should delight in the differences. How rich those differences make your family."

"Rich?"

"Yes, rich in gifts. And while we're on the subject, Anne, may I ask what gift it is that you were given to take to him? Have you learned to unwrap it yet?"

She had always assumed that it was her body that had been given to the man. That his passion might be allowed to climax itself upon her. Not through her eyes and what she might have seen in him. There were her sacrificial labors too, the butter and the stews and the babies, begetting a new generation of little Celts in his name. Oh, she loved them, loved, loved them. If only they would be theirs, not hers or his.

Had she missed something? Had she accepted a sort-of-life as a substitute for a real one? But what was a real one? Long ago she had thought she knew. Somewhere along the way she had abandoned a vision of their oneness, an explosion of two lights pouring into a chalice that they would drain together, consuming each other in joy.

Gone now. It was all bank statements and the monthly issue of blood, and silence. Silence and habit. Which they had lost the reason for.

"Thank you", she said on the doorstep as she was leaving. "You've reminded me of something I had begun to forget."

He stood gazing into the clouds of dust churned by the wheels of her buggy, long after it had turned the corner and had gone.

That evening, floating in a pool of amber kerosene light and lulled by the guttering of wood burning in the heater, he sat and composed a letter:

Dearest Anne,
If you could see my heart, would you ever return? That would be an unbearable pain for me.

I am torn between love . . . and Love. I am thinking that a great love will never come to fruition until the lover is willing to abandon his claims on the beloved, especially when those claims are without rights and usurp the rights of another.

I will never make claims upon your heart, as you unknowingly claimed mine so long ago, though for a time it was eclipsed. You never suspected, did you, that you had conquered me so completely? Had you known, I think you would have fled permanently from any association with this fool. I have learned that only fools can give their hearts totally, but only a certain kind of fool, a wise fool. Without that wisdom, no passion would ever mature into . . . Love.

Dare I send you this? I wish us to be friends. I wish to love you and be loved by you, without betrayal of your vows or destruction of the path God has mysteriously ordained for you. I . . .

At this point he stopped writing, sat upright, and stared at the sheet of paper for some minutes. Then, swiftly, he crumpled the paper and threw it into the firebox.

* * *

"She is so brazen!" said Mrs. Sinclair.

"It could be quite innocent", said her friend, Mrs. Parsons.

"Though there's the question of her first child, which was never satisfactorily explained."

"Whatever do you mean?"

"It was always suspected that she had to be married."

"No doubt she learned her trade at Mrs. Gunderberg's Rooming House", said someone daringly.

"And who's Mrs. Gunderberg?" said Mrs. Sinclair. The postmistress found it necessary to know about things, even those that had occurred before her time.

"She's Mrs. L'Oraison now, that ratty woman with the wild daughters."

"Her son's a lawyer, though!"

"Ah!"

"Ah!"

"But it could be quite innocent", the most innocent of the spectators suggested.

"Oh, yes, yes, very innocent!" said one of the more sarcastic ones. "Adele MacPhale has told me many *innocent* things it would be unkind to repeat."

"But if they're true, they're true!"

The group of women at the window were so convinced, they remained unconscious of the picture they presented to passersby. Three faces like fierce disembodied threats crowded out the curtains behind the glass.

When Anne Delaney crossed the street from the manse to her parked gig, she noticed them. She gave a startled laugh— they looked so much like hags waiting for children to boil or kings to accost with prophesies. Then she decided to ignore them, though she did see as a kind of omen the dog on Sinclair's porch stripping a bone and chewing its red cud.

She had been consulting regularly with Edwin for several months now and had begun to notice the consistent presence of observers.

"She saw us!"

"Then let her look, she knows her own guilt!"

"Let's not judge too hastily", someone said, because it had to be said and ignored.

"It's every week she comes. For months now and stays an hour or two."

"Which is enough time, don't you think?"

"I can't say as I would know, leastways not from experience!"

"My husband happens to know that her husband is away down the Canoe on his trapline."

"Still, that's no proof. Revernd Gunnalls may be tryin' *t'save* her."

"It's many a decent man got lost tryin' t'lift up a doomed woman."

"Ah, they're all hippercrits, them pewsitters!"

"He's a manly man", observed one. "And there ain't a man alive that isn't an animal at heart, even if he's decked in a dom- inie's gown."

There were some in the room who felt that might be going a bit too far. Though perhaps there was something to it, as smoke always does come from fire.

There they are again, looking, thought Anne. *And they're judging too, no doubt!*

Oh, yes, she knew that they had no more faith than she had. Perhaps less. But they had noses for sniffing out any odd behavior that offered the possibility of something to hate and envy. She knew those faces. Some of them were educated, and some were merely ignorant. If the winds of society were to change and infidelity or infanticide became acceptable, even normal, they would not hesitate to despise any deviation from the collective's revised judgments. Their sour, belligerent faces would have new prejudices and improved ideologies, but it would still boil down to lovelessness.

Their malice came from lack of hope, a despair deeper than her own. She saw this in the split second when her glance swept across the blind glass circles of their eyes.

She clicked her tongue at the horses and flicked the reins. It was better to ignore those women and whatever plots they might be hatching. They could not begin to understand the goodness of Edwin Gunnalls. She knew his intentions. He wished to bring her to that more public thoroughfare where she would have to press forward shoulder to shoulder with the saints, the dear Miss MacPhersons and their berries. That would be no problem, but he would have her forgive even the coven of witches in the window opposite. It would take a swallowing of pride to do that, she knew.

"Forgiveness is the key", he said. "Especially forgiveness of enemies."

"Is that entirely sensible, Edwin? Do you not run the risk of confirming an enemy in his errors?"

"Oh, yes, there's always risk. But forgiveness of an enemy turns things so utterly topsy-turvy that even if he goes on hating you he can't help but think and wonder and perhaps reconsider."

"It might be faster and a little less painful simply to demolish his pompous convictions."

"Fast? Less painful? Maybe. But brilliant demolishing victories usually just drive the enemy deeper into his prejudices."

"Are you speaking from a theology textbook or from experience?"

"From experience. I began to find it more important to forgive my enemy on the day I found out that I *am* my enemy."

"What a dreadful view of existence."

"Not really. It's actually quite liberating."

Strangest of all, he smiled when he said that.

Could she bear accepting such a proposition? The answers he had been producing from his hat and his book might make it inevitable.

"Answers are temporary things, Anne", he had said. "There will always be more questions."

"And shall we dispense with our minds?" she had countered.

"No", he said carefully. "Just be aware that rational answers aren't necessarily what we're looking for when we produce our questions."

Now what did he mean by that? He had looked at her so directly when he said it. Not a reaching-taking look, though it did attempt to instruct. He had lately grown more detached in his manner. He was no longer self-preoccupied but concentrated instead on throwing as much light as possible into the twilight corners of her life. She was thankful for this return to professional distance, though she had felt a stab of resentment at first.

An image of her father flashed through her mind. That kindly but distracted and evasive man. How few were the times he had ever looked into her eyes, she realized with an ache, remembering green and the paths that skylarks take in the English spring.

19

In her forty-sixth year, Anne Delaney was touched again by green, dispelling the frost of her suspicions about the meaning of existence. She was expecting a child. The language of tenderness she was learning to speak with her husband, the memory of the hermit, the ministry of Edwin Gunnalls, and, most of all, the swelling bud of life within were signs to her that benevolence might after all be the purpose of things. She was strangely reassured, less and less afflicted by fear.

She and Stephen longed for this child together. They explored new dialects of the heart and became more conscious of each other's burdens. Occasionally, he would grab the broom from her hands to sweep the cabin while the other four humans watched, amazed. It was a purely symbolic act, for there were more pressing, traditionally feminine tasks she would have been happy for him to commandeer. Nonetheless, she was pleased and from time to time would take a mug of rum and a pan of biscuits out to the ring of iron and fire in the blacksmith's shed, where he was hammering horseshoes. She took a new delight in such surprises and was equally surprised when he diligently read every one of her articles and understood them, though she had to explain a word or subtler ideas.

The children laughed at her as she preened the nest of the cabin, fussing and rearranging everything that was not nailed down. Despite her gray hair she appeared younger than she had for close to a decade. Three months into the pregnancy, she had knitted all there was to be knitted, was unable to write, and was driving the family mad with her restless moods.

"Anne," said Stephen one evening, "there's a position coming open at the school. They're desperate for a kindergarten teacher to start in September. Would you consider it?"

She peered up from some tangled darning she had been damning.

"But, Stephen, the baby."

"Yes, but this time round you seem so strong, with nothing to do on your hands."

"Nothing to do!" Snort!

"I mean, it would be a way of making time go faster and of helping some of the little ones hereabouts that don't have a book or a song to their names, like our kids do."

Yes, she thought, *yes*.

"And it will give the school board time to search around for a more permanent teacher. You can quit when the baby's getting close."

He brought it up repeatedly in the following days, and she began to think about it as a version of the future that might prove real. She imagined herself in gingham, moving gracefully between the rows of children, weeding, watering. She would bestow looks into eyes that had not been properly loved. Coax out visions in finger-paint from the most enclosed. Give challenges to the hungrier minds.

By midsummer she had filled out the necessary forms and handed them back to her neighbor, Camille, who was a member of the school board. He was delighted for her and said that, subject to a hearing by the board, he had no doubt that her application would be accepted.

Anticipation, she found, was one of those bittersweet delicacies not to be refused. She was sucking pleasurably on it as she made her way across the fields to L'Oraison's one evening not long after. The meeting had been held the night before. She was eager now to hear the answer, the *yes* that would open the door to a roomful of children.

Turid seemed out of sorts when they met beside the porch. She was hanging out her husband's legions of work socks and the daughters' many fancies. She seemed neglected and downcast.

"Well, c'mon in, Annie." Her eyes were strange, her jowls shaking, yawning, pretending that fatigue was the problem behind the disfigured expression. But the two women knew each other's faces too well, and such mummery only served to increase Anne's unease. Something was definitely wrong.

When they were seated across from each other at the kitchen table, Turid rolled and lit a cigarette slowly. Then she banged a kettle onto the stove behind her. The family scattered, leaving supper dishes everywhere. It was so different from home, where order ruled; this place was always grease spots and bosoms and dropsical geraniums. There were also crumbs to be cleared off the oil cloth and a brassiere strap that grew positively rebellious. Anne waited patiently while these introductory rites were completed and her friend was able to settle down to the gist of things.

"What is it, Turid?"

"I am sorry t'tell y'girl that y'didn't get the job."

"I didn't?"

"They said it was 'cause of yer morals", she added carefully.

"My what?" she breathed and could have been kicked. She was shocked to the core. When had her morals ever been in question?

"They're sayin' that when you'n'me was residents of my boardin' house, we . . . *entertained* men. Fer pleasure or profit they wouldn't exactly say!"

"How completely ludicrous! Don't tell me the board believed that?"

"Well, Camille didn't. But as fer the rest, it was their own wifes and some of the local women who convinced them. Which is crazy 'cause they don't give a damn about morals themselves."

"Those demons", she cried, her voice a hammer smashing on steel, her eyes a forge.

"They ain't devils, Annie. They're just people."

"They could accuse anyone of anything and find believers."

But Turid had grown strangely quiet.

"It's mostly my fault", she said looking out the window.

"Your fault?"

"Before I met Camille I wasn't always moral like. There was a feller or two, and it does get around."

The reddish geraniums appeared unconcerned. A fly buzzed. Anne recalled some moans behind a closed door, a dim memory. There was a judicious sipping of tea on the part of both human celebrants, the younger one concentrating on the contents of her cup, attempting to adjust to a state of affairs. She could not quite absorb the blow that had been administered to herself and turned the attention to Turid.

"That is the past", she said finally, sealing it.

"There are some who won't let the past lie", said Turid sadly.

"They would imprison a person there forever. But we mustn't let them. They are blind, and we are well off to know them for what they are."

"They're bloody killers!" said Turid. Her eyes became slits. She could have at that moment taken the axe from the kindling box and stalked purposely along the lane to town, to avenge the things that would reach her children's ears.

"It's done and finished. They can't hurt us any more if we don't let them."

"But Annie, they can! They just buggered up yer career, and that's a big chunk o' life."

"Yes," she admitted, "but life is *inside,* isn't it? It's inside of me, not outside . . ."

"Inside er out, it's buggered!"

"My freedom, Turid, does not depend on external events. And I shall never again allow those women to damage that inner chamber where peace and freedom reside."

"Ooooh, girlie, I hope yer right!"

Anne hoped that she might persuade herself of her own idea. Turid, however, was not convinced, though she was stopped by the sheer momentum of this dissertation. The younger woman had forged a sword, had mounted a war horse and might soon be ready to gallop off toward town.

"I hope yer right," Turid repeated.

"I am right!"

Her small fist thumped on the table, making the spoons jump. This was a hand that Turid had seen most familiarly up to the elbows in a tub of bluing or a vat of oak-bark liquor, tanning hides. This was a new Anne, who had found that anger could quicken the blood as effectively as hope.

"There's somethin' else, though, and I hope y'won't be offended at me bringin' it up."

"Offended? At what?"

"It's the matter of yer *affair* with the revernd."

"My what?"

Her little steed coughed and toppled. Her tin-foil rapier crumpled against the dirt into which she had been knocked.

"It was dragged out at the meetin' too. And the kid", she added, lowering her voice, pointing at Anne's belly.

Open-mouthed, speechless, she looked at Turid.

"Camille told em off. It weren't none of their business anyhow!"

When she found her voice at last, Anne could only bleat out her innocence.

"Turid, it's a lie! There is nothing to it at all. My . . . friendship with Reverend Gunnalls is . . ."

"Them that looks down their noses at others don't see far beyond it", said Turid, shaking her head, not listening.

"But Turid," she cried and could have panicked, "I'm innocent of anything they are accusing me of !"

"Of course you are", the old woman said, clearing the table without looking at her guest. "Of course you are."

Am I really innocent, she wondered, *Didn't I hope just a little in the beginning that Edwin and I might . . . but never did I want to do anything that might be . . . wrong. Just a look, a word of love—harmless, really—not betrayal.*

So a woman caught in an adultery of the unphysical kind might have resorted eventually to stoning herself. Another's sin, the more literal adultery, seemed less culpable, easier to forgive.

Her aloneness rose up in waves to engulf her and pull her back into a dark sea. Isolated by lies from even this one friend, cut off by culture and habit from her husband. Why had she come to despair of him and gone in search of a more complex man? Why? What had been omitted in her years with him? Speech? That total oneness they had attempted? The skills they had learned recently were swept away now as the old bitterness rose, and the drowning woman struggled deeper into its currents.

For an instant there flashed into her mind an image of the broken hermit, gazing at her, telling her to understand and to forgive. But a lifelong habit of self-pity surged up and obliterated it.

When she went outside, the mouth of night was crammed with sulphurous black birds, ravens or a murmuration of starlings. They jeered as the woman stumbled blindly along the paths that crisscrossed the settlement. The anguish in her heart was so intense that she retched. It was impossible to face the cabin with its lights burning, down by the Canoe. She stumbled upward on logging trails for hours, grappling with her own outrage and despair.

At one point she tripped over a log and her belly slammed full-force against a rock in the trail. For several minutes she could not move. Finally, she pushed her body up and staggered down to that robbed nest, her home.

"Anne", the man groaned, surfacing from work-drugged sleep, when she crawled into bed. "Where have you been? It's late."

"At Turid's. And walking", she said in a dead voice, drawing the quilt over her shoulders, back turned from his innocent body, which she had once wanted to hold.

"Good night", he mumbled.

"Good night."

* * *

In the same week of June when the armies of the West were thrown off the edge of the continent at Dunkirk, she bled copiously and delivered a stillborn child, a female. She was a miniature opalesque thing, startlingly perfect. They wrapped her in a piece of silk and laid her in a dovetailed pine box, which Stephen made silently in the shed.

When the earth had performed its task and the man and the woman walked back to the house with the three living children fanning out behind them, quiet for once, he tried to take her hand. But she did not respond. Death had once again thrust her light into a blacksmith's bucket. There was a hiss of steam, then darkness.

Disaster comes most often in packs, like marauding animals in a winter that is too long; they arrive when the fire has burned itself out.

A telegram arrived the following day:

DEAREST ANNE FATHER DIED THIS MORNING OF SUDDEN CORONARY OCCLUSION. GRIEVING WITH YOU EMILY.

20

She stood on the station platform looking lost and troubled, a small plump woman in tweeds, situated between two suitcases and a large trunk.

Anne, Stephen, and the children knew immediately who she was by the mixture of timidity and expectation on her face. The stranger could not immediately identify the family, however, though soon enough she was confronted by an aging farm wife with violet eyes who claimed to be her sister. The Irishman stood watching while the women clung to each other, sliding up and down the scales of emotion like two children wrestling over a harmonica. They sobbed and laughed with such abandon that Anne's offspring began to look over their shoulders nervously. The man was grateful for suitcases to carry and a heavy trunk that challenged his body.

"And this is Stephen!" said Emily, looking up, surprised at what she saw. The mythological trapper appeared to be a self-effacing sort, with uncommonly kind eyes.

The man also observed. The communist suffragette had become a conservative matron. The cartoon characters portrayed in letters would never be more than rough profiles, and they were now being filled in remorselessly. The man wondered if he should kiss the stranger, or merely shake hands, or leave her to her own devices. She was a handsome woman, like his wife, with silver hair in a bun and keen, birdlike eyes. She was a widow whose husband had recently crashed into the fields of Kent during the Battle of Britain.

"Emily," said Anne, who appeared to be glued to her sister in a very un-English burst of intimacy, "I'm so glad you are here!"

"And so am I", said Emily. "It seems that we're the last of our line and shall have need of each other!"

She spoke in exclamations, as if each of her observations was a victory she had wrestled out of the grip of ignorance.

"Yes. Yes we shall", said Anne. "I had forgotten just who I might be. That somewhere on this earth I had actually emerged from a living, breathing family."

She laughed, tearful, holding the tweed arm of her miraculous sister. Her family, the man and the children, were startled by this last remark, wondering if they had ceased to be her life, her religion. They looked more closely at the intruder.

"You were brave to come", said the man.

"Oh, I barely breathed at all crossing the Atlantic, what with U-boats sinking countless ships each month. They would never attack a Portuguese freighter, we were told, but most nights I lay awake listening for the whine of torpedoes. My cabin was at waterline, you know, and I thought surely I would be the first to go."

The children were warming to their mother's sister. So, this was Auntie Emily, a quaint creature who had become their own by a quirk of fortune, the first full-blown relative they had ever encountered.

"I can tell you", she continued, "that there were times when I actually heard that noise. I'd been warned and I heard! What brought us finally up the Saint Lawrence to Montreal I can scarcely guess!"

Her accent was more sharply bevelled than their mother's, who had acquired a few slurs in her voice and a patchwork vocabulary for common use. The letters had revealed nothing of this, and the public English of her articles had remained elegant.

"There's plenty we have to catch up on", she said. "So, so much . . . twenty years' worth!"

The carriage jostled, and the children shouted with glee.

"So, so much!" said Emily, looking closely at the aging woman, her sister, who had once been a girl, a stem of iris.

"As I told you in my last wire, it's more than grief that brings me here, though I would have come regardless. There are *matters* to discuss!"

"And what are these matters?"

"I shall tell *all* later, when there's time enough and we cease to bounce!"

When they were home, the giving began. The aunt asked the boys to open the trunk latches, a task at which they leapt. When they threw back the lid and began to scrabble in tissue paper, she interfered with an upheld hand.

"Slowly, slowly, boys", she admonished. "Treasure must be opened with care, like tombs and parchment!"

It was of utmost concern to her that they realize the significance of what they were about to see.

"Yes, slowly, slowly now", said their mother, who was just as eager as her children and atremble for the unveiling of her past. But as the aunt was in control, it seemed that the amulets and funerary relics must be opened one by one.

"This is for you, Ashley."

It was a mahogany box in which the boy discovered a high-power microscope, old, hopelessly expensive. Cases of slides came with it. His grandfather's. The boy whistled with emotion.

"And for you, Bryan", she said with a smile. He received evenly the ancient hand-made tools, intricate wood planers and carving instruments that had come down through several generations of Kingstons from some cabinet maker whose lacquer secrets went with him to the grave. There were also many books.

"We mustn't neglect you, Bryan, as you are the last of the litter, the scrapings of the pan, and might be overlooked!"

"Scrapin's of the pan?" laughed Bryan, who caught on

quickly to her queer humor. But he did not know quite what to make of her gifts.

"These were your grandfather's books", she said solemnly. "I understand you have a passion for trees."

He grimaced. His mother would have told her that. He was *interested* in trees, he corrected. Nevertheless, she placed into his arms nearly half a hundredweight of volumes concerning trees from acacia to yew, tree diseases, and orchard husbandry. There were volumes of specialized biology and insect life as well. An enormous, dusty *Mammals of the World*. Ornithological texts such as *The Birds of Wales*, entomological texts such as a very old *Insects of the English Isles*. A veritable mountain, which the boy began to scale at once.

"For you, my Emily", said the aunt to her namesake. It seemed incongruously small compared to her brothers' gifts. It was an alabaster jar, a carved ointment pot, thousands of years old, explained the aunt. Her great-grandfather had brought it home from an archaeological dig in Egypt. There was a brass hanging lamp from Palestine as well, smaller than a girl's hand. It had been found by that same forebear in another excavation near Jerusalem.

"For you, Stephen." She offered a lump of objects wrapped in burgundy velvet and tied with a golden cord. "These were Father's pipe things." There were rows of silver tools for preening and fussing over the pipes, which were handed to him in a small oak case. There were briars, cherrywoods, stone, clay, corncob, a ceramic meerschaum, and even a hickory carved with the head of a horned bull.

"I'm honored", said Stephen. "And I thank you."

"There are other things", said Emily. "More, more than I can explain tonight, and we have weeks to unwrap them, don't we?"

She turned from Stephen to Anne.

"There's half of Mother's jewelry, which I want you to have, and the first editions of the Brontës—and so much more!"

She handed Anne a velvet box. Inside there was a porcelain rose.

"Mother painted it herself when she was young."

"I remember. When I was very little, no more than three or four, she showed it to me. I wanted it so badly."

"Now it's yours."

"Mama said to me, 'Anna, when you are a lady, when you are all grown up and have a husband and children of your own, I will send you this rose. I made it. I made it for you', she said."

"How lovely, Anne. I didn't know. A lucky coincidence. To think that Cousin Beatrice almost got it!"

They all laughed.

Aunt Emily drew breath.

"There is another matter, which I couldn't entrust to the post, considering the state of the world!"

She handed a large buff envelope to Anne and waited as she opened it. The man and woman read together silently from the flimsy piece of paper they found inside. An international money order issued by Lloyd's Bank in London:

PAYABLE TO MRS ANNE DELANEY
TEN THOUSAND POUNDS STERLING

"It's your half of Father's estate", said Emily, having difficulty with her voice, for the transfer of money, she knew, is a liturgy charged with the highest reverence.

The family reacted in various ways to sudden wealth. The boys instantly were obsessed with fantasy adventures involving coupes and roadsters. The daughter pleaded for a sequined gown. Or else a big fancy car in which they might make the grand tour from the banks of the Fraser at Tete Jaune to the dirt track down the Thompson. They could have the car shipped in on the train, like MacPhale's, she urged, jumping up and down—for alabaster jars contained only transient pleasures.

Their mother remained absolutely silent.

Their father wandered out into the evening air. He wished to be alone and strolled along the river bank in search of some tranquillity of motion and permanence. The flow of waters consoled. The river blanketed all sound. The sun had set, though the sky plunged from deepest blue into emerald over the peaks, deeper black fields stretching away toward the lights of Swiftcreek. More and more settlers had come in recent years to push back the bush, and the road to town was stippled now with their improvements. By this umbilical cord of farms and cabins the Delaneys had become connected to that painted, luminous body of commerce that claimed to be their mother. Though forest remained in all other directions. The man had ridden alone into this solitude to slay the first tree, to lay the primal stones and erect the brave folly of his dwelling in the midst of the unknown. He looked at it now. And looked away. He found an old rotting stump at the edge of the field by the river and sat. His horses nickered at him.

The man lifted his eyes to the constellations wheeling around the axis of the polestar, points of light inscribed on the plate of blackness, their colors running, the orderly spin of harmonies faithful to themselves from generation to generation.

The man wondered what legacy, if any, he could hope to impart to his children. What would their paternal grandfather ever have been able to give them? Nothing, nothing but a pair of dirty hands, a hoe, and maybe, in the end, a poem.

* * *

"Tell me about Mum", said Ashley, "when she was a girl."

He was guiding his aunt around the lanes in search of yellow lady's slipper and forget-me-not.

"There's so much that's different here in your flora and fauna", she observed. "It's truly delightful, an entire world existing distinct and independent of what one has always known!"

330

The woman seemed to have forgotten his question.

"Mum says there's robins in England, same as here."

"Oh, yes, though they are much smaller. Someone once wrote, and it may be in one of your grandfather's books, that approximately one-third of our birds are the same as yours, another third are similar, and a final third are totally unique!"

"What was Mum like?" he asked again, worming it in between birds and flowers.

"Oh, yes, your mother! Well, she was always delicate, you know."

His mother, *delicate?*

"Especially in her feelings. That's perhaps why she forced herself to do so many difficult things."

"Like what? What did she do?" He wanted to *know*, walking backward through the scrub, bobbing and chafing at her slowness, which was too gentle.

"There were causes for which she fought. And she was a battlefield nurse during the First War."

"She was?"

"Oh, yes, she was. Also, she published a little collection of her poems when she returned from France. I thought that was really the bravest thing she ever did. It received some criticism, you know—self-publishing was very much frowned upon in those days. Most people thought it poor writing, but there were some touching pieces in it, mostly about the war. Didn't she show it to you?"

"No."

"There was one I liked especially, about someone in a canoe who was singing to ice, if you can imagine. It was really quite enigmatic, but charming and . . ."

The boy saw that his aunt was about to embark on a tangent of musing.

"What else did she do?" he interjected.

"She raised particularly fragile kinds of orchids, went to

teachers' college. And then she brought herself, finally, to this place."

The woman furrowed her brow, realizing that the boy might not understand the difficulty of his land. Its poverty, its crying emptiness, was a certain perverse wealth, an oppressive lavishness of green and black and white. She was astonished suddenly by the reality of his wiry limbs. Little English boys tearing around cricket fields did not have muscles like these. She looked at his dark, clear eyes and realized that they would not exist if a certain Anna Ashton had not been possessed by a whim to exchange sanctuary for the unknown. He was, she saw, the wild harvest of her sister's determination to conquer fear.

"And then she met Dad."

"Yes, then she met your dad."

"Look, Auntie Em, it's a busted lark's egg."

He was darting and distracted by something more real than history. He knelt on the grass with fragments of spotted grey shell in his fingers.

"Look," he said, "look, Auntie Em."

She might have stooped to investigate the crime had not the boy's busted grammar distracted her. The poverty of his education was much more important than the fact that there was a savagery at work among the small jungles where shelled embryos are smashed and eaten. Among that carnage the incandescence of language itself might disintegrate. Or she herself might be plunged into the reign of innocent terror. If there was a bite on every leaf and a dance of death seemed to be going full sway in the natural kingdoms as well as the unnatural ones of man, she was not one to question why. It was the state of things, she knew, and father's books confirmed. It was even fascinating in a lurid sort of way, though she might be tempted to draw back sharply when the little wars among the roots and branches threatened to shatter the shells of understanding.

She was not eager to probe any further into boyish investigations, and her time was limited. She had already approved his collection of eggs and brittler shells of insects. Her own language might disintegrate the most brittlely of all should they tarry any longer in the scenes of violence. But, being a considerate person, she did look quickly at the twisted, hairy fetus before the boy laid it away in the grass. Her nephew saw a flash of feeling and read compassion in it.

"It's those starlings", he said. "They're always robbing nests."

* * *

The two women walked arm in arm by the river one day, while across from them the mountain rose high and white above them, straining up from its roots on the valley floor. The river flashed in the sun, running through the kingdom of stone and air with abandon, gashing the forest.

"Emily, you must forgive me for probing", she said with a half-smile. "But I'm curious to know if you're still a Marxist."

The older woman laughed.

"No. I learned in the thirties that politics is the opiate of romantic intellectuals. And I was a typical romantic intellectual."

"You never wrote about it. But I guessed you were afraid to commit anything to paper, anything damaging."

"Yes. Afraid of both sides, I suppose."

"In one of his letters Father hinted at your trip to Moscow."

"They invited a mob of our intelligentsia to come and view the new Soviet dream, you know. The Webbs asked me to go along with them. Of course, I leapt at the chance. Beatrice and Sydney saw only what our hosts wanted them to see. But the trip tore the last scales from my eyes. I spent a lot of time looking at the faces of ordinary people."

"You were allowed to talk to the ordinary Russian?"

"Of course not. We were led through staged conversations and a carefully orchestrated tour. But now and then the stage managers would miss a cue, and the curtain would part to reveal the horror backstage. I saw a nation of people being turned into things."

"What did you do? Did you leave the Party immediately?"

Emily turned and looked slowly at her sister.

"No. It takes time and a little courage to shed the habits that indoctrination breeds. But I began to understand that my idealism and my loathing of Western materialism had blinded me. It became obvious that the East had merely replaced one form of materialism with another. And a more lethal one at that."

"But what happened then?"

"When I left the Party I was an empty shell. Then I met a good man, and he loved me. His love healed me. And that taught me everything. It's why I think, Anne, that the world can only be saved person by person, one by one. It's the slow way but the true one."

"You must miss Colin very much."

"Yes, very much."

She faced Anne, touching her own heart. "But you see, I have him in here, always."

Anne looked up at the mountain.

"I too have a good man. He loves me, my husband. But I'm not healed. Can you tell me why?"

"I don't know why. But I know this; the healing begins when you abandon your demands for love and choose instead to give love, no matter what the cost. Madness, isn't it? But a madness that works."

"Perhaps for some, Emily."

"No. For everyone. But first you have to forgive. Can you forgive Stephen for failing to love you as you wish?"

Anne opened her mouth but was unable to think or utter a word.

They walked on in silence. Presently, they came upon two of Anne's children lying on the clay bank of the river. Their heads were submerged, sucking in water. They did not detect the presence of the two women, who quickly sat in the deep hay at the top of the meadow, linked arms, and watched what was happening below. The boys bounded up suddenly and plunged with a yell into a pool. Their voices were like trumpets. The horses grazing nearby startled and trotted off to safety. The boys splashed, laughed, and shouted, hucking clay at each other, the horses, and the grinning dog, who snapped and chewed the gift but glanced sideways with amber eyes at the madness of her masters.

The two women remained unnoticed up above, though the aunt was having difficulty controlling her mirth. Anne smiled. The sun and the murmur of bees soothed her.

"You have wonderful children", her sister said, squeezing her arm. "And you live in paradise!"

At that moment their conversation was rudely broken by a bombardment of clay and shrill yells. Two savages with smeared bodies were running up the hill toward them at top speed, yelling, "If we catch you, Auntie Em, you're in trouble! We're gonna get you, Mum!"

"Quickly," said Anne, "run, or you will have much to forgive my wonderful children!"

The women threw bits of dried cow-dung at the savages and ran back into the woods. When their escape was certain, Anne slowed to catch her breath, while Emily ran on ahead. She realized then, for the first time in years, that she was still capable of joy.

* * *

Shortly before Emily's departure for England, the sisters sat down one evening on rocking chairs. The view from the porch toward the first stars over the mountain was restful. The clicking of their knitting needles rejoined their severed life. The pressure lamp hanging above them hissed softly.

"So peaceful here, Anne."

"Yes." Click. Click.

"London is a terrible place right now. You're a very fortunate family."

"I suppose we are." Click. Click. "It's so hard for me to imagine. It seems like the end of the world in a way. London burning. Children dying."

"It's quite real."

"But it seems impossible that such a thing could ever come here. Total war is a phenomenon of the Old World."

"One thing I have learned, Anne, is that totalitarianism is everywhere. Here it's masked. And one day, after this war is over, the mask may fall off."

Click, click, click, click, click, was the reply.

Emily, she saw, still had traces of the political opiate in her blood and was about to begin a lecture. Anne had listened to not a few of her theories about the world. She quickly changed the subject:

"Have you been to the Great Exhibition Hall lately? We saw the Queen there once, didn't we?"

"No—we saw a transparency of her visiting the Hall. The Crystal Palace is gone, you know!"

"Gone!"

"Burned. Didn't you hear? In '36 it went down. I always considered it a rather foolish exercise in national vanity. Architectural revolution and all that! Ingenious, of course. But it always seemed to me that a pack of little boys with rocks would make short work of it."

"Gone", said Anne in a whisper. She could not understand the ache in her throat.

"A palace made of glass! No doubt a very nasty little boy named Adolf would eventually have put a stone through it!"

Emily did not notice her sister's silence. If she had, it would have been incomprehensible to her. She chatted on:

"You were only three or four, I think, when Mama and I took you there. You were enchanted. You kept saying, 'A Fairy Palace! A Fairy Palace!' You were such a sweet child, Anne. How everyone loved you! But that day you cried all the way home and cried yourself to sleep into the bargain, you wanted so desperately to live there."

Emily smiled.

"Childhood!" she said.

Click. Click.

When Anne found her voice she said, "I have been rethinking many things during the past few years."

"What sort of things?"

"Oh, human accomplishments, ambition, greatness . . . "

"Yes? Pray tell what conclusions you've come to?"

"Emily, I think there's a thing gone very wrong in us. In humanity, that is."

"One doesn't need to meditate overmuch to come to that conclusion. Hitler . . . "

"No. I mean in all of us."

"Explain yourself, woman."

"It's a good thing to build a shelter that's beautiful and fits our human dignity. But it's another to build a vast monument to some architect's ego, or to a nation's ego."

"Papa used to say that a city is a replica of the brain."

"I remember. I never was quite happy with that idea. There may be some truth in it, but I say that a brain can be diseased. Why are modern cities so cold and hard and geometrical? They are terribly clever, I know, but ever so much like a brilliant mind without a heart. A city without a heart freezes the soul."

"But what sort of thing do you think makes a heart? Cities have parks and museums—"

"Yes, yes, I know, and song and theatre and . . . and especially its places of worship."

"Wasn't the Crystal Palace a sophisticated kind of temple?"

"Yes. A good point. It *was* a temple. But what was worshipped in it? There's the question."

Emily bent over her stitches, counting.

"Oh, damn, I have dropped a few here!" she cried, and started to undo the errors.

Into the gap Anne inserted a thought:

"Suppose there really is a God, Emily, and let's say that he knows full well that this *hubris* of ours, this damnable pride, is a thing that eventually destroys us. Would it not be an act of kindness on his part to bring down the temple in which we worship an image of ourselves?"

"*Tsk,* I shall have to do this whole row over again!"

"It says somewhere that no flesh may glory in his sight . . ."

"I would be very upset, Anne, if you were to tell me that you have lost all the advances our circle of friends made. To see you—you of all people—succumb to primitive religion. That would be too unkind."

"But you have abandoned the politics of our set. You learned and grew, you came to see deeper into matters with the accumulation of experience and time."

"I have merely discarded a theory of politics. It was a detour on the path of social evolution. It was something we tried that didn't work. Before the end of the century we will have thrown it off entirely. But religion is a different matter. It's the most potent drug of all. Very difficult to throw off an addiction of that sort."

"Didn't your former mentor say something to that effect? Opiate of the masses and all that? Who was it—Lenin? Marx?"

"I don't recall. But, look, back to our subject: Where's the harm, really, in a city that's an embodiment of our power? The world is changing very quickly, Anne. A city . . . well, a city is like a great portrait of a society. It needs ambition. It needs to look at its own greatness in order to grow."

"And its sins in order not to destroy itself."

"Sins?"

Anne nodded.

"Sins? An odd word on your tongue, dear. Rather Roman, isn't it?"

"Rather."

"I don't mean to be critical, but you have been away from civilization for quite a long time. One's perspectives can narrow."

"I know how difficult it is for you to understand what I have come to believe. I'm not saying it very well."

The two sisters glanced at each other with troubled eyes.

"Believe?"

"Oh, not in the sense of Stephen and his coreligionists. But in another sense. I believe there is a world beyond our proud intellects."

"Madame Blavatsky and Mrs. Besant believed that too, and so did the mediums who communicated Mama's messages to us."

"I know. I understand what you're saying. But there's a struggle going on in the transcendent realm. Some of it leaks through into our own world. Some of it's false and some of it's true. You don't solve the problem by saying it's all codswallop."

"It may all be a projection of our brains."

"Some of it. But not all of it. I've seen too much. And so have you."

"I've seen very little that I can say for sure has definite meaning."

"Which of us is the primitive, then?"

They looked at each other and smiled.

21

Journal Entry:

Swiftcreek, Sept. 1941

Emily has gone. There is time to think. Time to digest the incident of my questionable morals. And Father's death. During this period I have been unable to write a word. Oh, yes, I am suddenly quite wealthy. But my child and my reputation are dead, murdered by the tongues of gossips. I had hoped to give life, but that, it seems, is far too ambitious for the times.

I have groped through the cloud of this experience, trying to understand the mind of my detractors. They can hardly see themselves as such, for they are convinced of their position, confident that they carry the truth in their handbags.

Why do they hate? Why do they despise? Is it because they know the helplessness of their creaturehood, know that a random virus or a bullet can snuff out in a moment all the securities they have worshipped? So we find, each in our fashion, a way to transcend life. And those who cannot transcend through creating will eventually discover that one can also transcend it by destroying. To kill is to be above life, is it not?

To be a victim of their form of creativity is an honour it has taken me all these six months to accept. They cracked the glass of my being and in a curious way have set me free. A victim's pain is real. Blood is authentic. I should be grateful.

A few nights after Turid had given me the news, I was close to hurling myself into the river but chose instead to sit down alone in the shed and cry it out. The results were unpleasant to say the least, composing it was an act of retching. The title: "Gift for Hard Women". It was hatred mostly, and I tore it up, though a fragment of words remains with me even now.

> Conspiracies of despair take shape on the earth,
> and all that is beauty is killed before birth.
> Fire soon falls from out of the skies,
> And those who cover themselves with lies
> Shall never know beauty, shall die before birth.

Are they so different from me? We are all alienated in a most dreadful numbness. Is violence an attempt to deny our nothingness, our emptiness? They have chosen to deny by wielding their pathetic provincial power. And I too am guilty. I wished to preserve power over them through superior insights. I did not want them to despise me for the shack in which we live. I did not want to be lonely. Oh, blind, blind, blind, I have been so blind. And so proud!

How different life would have been if Edwin had courted and won me in the beginning—a decent orderly life, devoid of despair. Instead, I have been plunged into Stephen's mysterious universe and lost forever to the middle-class existence of the witches of Swiftcreek. I wanted to be something. I have become nothing. I shall try, once again, to love it.

This is a form of faith, I suppose. But faith in what? Faith, perhaps, in the unexplainable poetry that runs through all things. It needn't be there, if all of this is merely a cold race for survival and only to the fit go the spoils. Nothing whatsoever needs to be beautiful. But it is. Why is it? I have been very blind to the sustained plea of beauty and deaf to the cries uttered in all creation, as if the ear and the eye were covered by invisible screens.

If I am to write of the blindness of this people, it must be as one of them. Not as a voice of despair, but as a voice of protest.

341

Should I be communicating "happy" thoughts to a depressed world? Must I present a grinning countenance and speak of sunshine and daisies? Such symbols, along with the much-abused butterfly, have been totally exhausted. They can no longer communicate real joy because for so long they have been used to express false joy.

The world is in anguish at present. The reigning emotion is lust for victory, for enough power to crush our enemy, who desires the exact same thing. Certainly Mr. Hitler is real enough and monstrous enough for us to engage him in battle with easy conscience. But what of the war within us? We can scarce recognise the tyrant raging in our own hearts, just as we deny a whole range of inner realities, especially in the West, where every sadness must be dispelled by a pill or a toy. Unpleasantness, we think, is the archenemy. Eventually, we too will begin to kill the innocent in order to "free" ourselves. Emily is right: when this War is finished, there may be a worse war plunged into our interiors, only to surface again in new social projects. The witches will be more dignified, better educated, and very sincere, but they will not fail to destroy many a good thing in their efforts to improve mankind. I hope that I do not live to see it.

Emily's visit has helped me a great deal. She suffers much yet is quite a joyful person, for all her quirks. She has taught me that the rejection of suffering results, not in joy, but in depression. Depression, I have come to see these past few months, is the reaction of my inner self to a lie, to a false concept of the self, to self-delusion. It breeds a profound discouragement.

My grief—that I could not grieve for those who had been given to me, now gone. I have feared the pain of grief and thus have multiplied the suffering a hundredfold. Fear has been my constant companion. Two things, and two things only, can come from fear: courage or hatred. It is not the witches who are my enemy but the toxin of hatred. That is my tyrant. There stands my foe—within me! And in the fight, and in my search for courage, I will find deeper still a basic faith in existence. Not in Man or Society, or even that ubiquitous goddess, Art.

Courage? A word we use now only in connection with the Battle of Britain. The poet, the writer, the painter will not be born until the day she decides to engage the enemy within. As the artist wrestles life-and-death at the core of being, she will choose to take the step-by-step journey into the dark territory of faith; she will choose to celebrate a presence of which her own life is a sign.

This hypothetical "she"! It is I. It is I alone who must teach my own heart to play and to rejoice beyond the confines of my glass chamber. I must choose. I *will* choose, and choose again. Becoming a victim is a great gift. For the enclosure is smashed open, and through the breach one may at first crawl, pull oneself erect, then dance out into the darkness. This is not the darkness of denial. It is the darkness of absolute trust.

I am so tired! Still, I have seen. I am allowed one weapon only—truth. But a truth that has been purified in combat against my own impulses to despise and to kill. This generates light. To pierce the darkness boldly can never be a morbid act.

It is very clear now what I must do.

* * *

"Yer outer yer bloody mind!" said Turid.

"You may be correct on that matter."

Both women sipped tea over Anne's kitchen table.

"I mean, dearie, you just been handed a mountain o' cash, and you want t'throw it away!"

"No. Not throw it away. Use it for some good."

"Good?" snorted Turid. "You're pokin' a stick into a real hornet's nest, girlie, and you won't like the results. Just yesterday them Sinclair and MacPhale women and their followers stopped me in the street in town. They says, 'The spirits are not happy, Mrs. L'Oraison.'"

"'Not happy?' says I, all nice and sweetsy-pie, 'Why not, ladies?'"

"'The spirits are concerned about Mrs. Delaney, your neighbor.'"

"'And just who are these spirits?' I asks."

"'Oh, the spirit of the planchette! The Ouija and his advisors never lie', they says. Then, wonder of wonders, they invite me to one of their séances. 'God, no!' says I. 'You'll never catch me leapin' inta that pit of ooze.' The whole thing makes me itchy. Them women make me itchy!" And she began to scratch.

"What's got me stumped is I'm the last one in town they'd ever ask to their cozy little teas. So why to a séance?"

"Because of me. You're their only bridge to get at me."

Turid thought on that awhile, then grunted.

"Annie, you know I ain't religious like, right? But them old birds remind me of when I was a little gal."

"What do you mean?"

"My Mam used t'scare us good about Ol' Gooseberry. Ol' Scratch. And I get the same feelin's talkin' t'those ladies. Itchy. Y'know?"

"I think of it as a smell, Turid. A rotten smell in the mind."

"Yeah, like a dead hog."

"A Gadarene hog. But not so dead. Stay away from them."

"Y'don't need t'tell me that!"

So ended their discussion about Anne's big project.

Her husband was surprised but not dismayed by her purchase.

"It's your money, Anne, and it's your decision."

"But I wish to have your support, to know that you and I are together in this."

"Why do you need my approval?" he wondered, and there could have been hurt hiding behind his even tone.

"There will be battles, Stephen, and I cannot make them alone. Will you be with me in this?"

"I'm with you", he said soberly.

The only other person she told was Emily, before her departure.

"What will you do with your inheritance?" she had asked.

"I wish to do a little good in the world."

"Good? Just how do you propose to do that?"

"I might try my hand at writing something more than my columns."

There had been a strained pause before Emily replied:

"Anne, after everything that has occurred in this century, you still believe in words?! You and I were raised in a stew of language. Look how it deceived me for so many years. Look at Papa's life. Remember the eternal discussions in the parlor with the leading lights? Words, words, words—that's all we had after Mama died."

"Perhaps I should say that I still believe in truth, though I can't claim to have it totally and perfectly. And even if I did, yes, even then I would be incomplete. But it's all I have to give. I have learned some things. And so have you. Shouldn't we speak of these things when the world is awash in nonsense?"

"Yes, I suppose so, but . . ."

"And I'm not saying that it will achieve anything, only that I must try. Though," she added plaintively, "though there are times when I have almost lost confidence that man is interested in knowing truth."

"So why the big gamble, love?"

"If there is a glimmer of hope that we can be better than we are, shouldn't we try to be so?"

"Eliot says that human beings can't stand very much reality."

"Then all the more reason to begin."

* * *

When Dan Cox finally admitted to himself that he was no longer able to run *The Echo*, he decided to sell. It had been taking two and three weeks lately to get the issues written, type-set, and printed. The doctor's verdict made the move inevitable. He was more than pleased to sell to Anne Delaney, payment in full, real cash. He admired gumption in a woman, like spirit in a quarter horse. Though he did wonder if his pride and joy would ever resemble itself once she had put her hand to it.

"Do you realize the size of the task you're taking on?" he asked.

"Yes", she replied, with more bravado than realism.

There was considerable alarm as the news spread. It was a rock tossed into the calm of their community, shattering the surface, for *The Echo* had been the flattering pool into which the community had gazed and found itself the most beautiful in the land.

The convoluted logic of spite could convince just about anyone. Those tale-bearing creatures who hurried from house to house knew that she had bought the paper for no good purpose. That sister had gone back to England and left a pile of money behind her, and money is power, and someone with power will use it. Might even punish the town for its honest opinions, for only saying what had to be said, wasn't it the truth anyway? Oh, she was a superior one with her new toy, that English snob. Proud, despite the fact that she had been turned down by the school board because of her morals. And surely they would know.

"The spirits are very unhappy", said Mrs. Parsons in a hushed voice to Turid. "They say there will be punishment. That Mrs. Delaney will regret her decision."

When this message was transmitted back to Anne, she replied, "Please tell Mrs. Parsons to inform the spirits that I observed carefully their effect upon my father, and I know them for what they are."

A few people stopped her in the street to offer congratulations, but she was most moved by an encounter in the lobby of the post office.

346

"Anne", said Edwin Gunnalls. "It's the best thing that's happened to Swiftcreek in a long time."

"Thank you so much, Edwin."

There was a constriction in her throat. She began to cough, and such convulsions will often bring water to the eyes. He stood looking at her. It was written across his face that he did not understand why she no longer came to visit. How could she explain? There was no way they could talk in the street, as this would ignite a smoldering scandal and could be interpreted as a public proclamation of their guilt. It helped little to remind herself that they were, in fact, quite innocent. She attempted to justify her absence in whispers. They were alone in the lobby, but the keyholes did tend to funnel all information beyond the letter-boxes to the postmistress.

"Edwin, do you understand why I can't come anymore? I seem to be starving half the time for the kind of insights and encouragement you gave me. But it would be foolishness."

"No, I don't understand."

"I cannot compromise your reputation or my husband's feelings. Or my own health. The children, too, have heard things."

"Lies!"

"Of course, of course, but . . ."

"Will you allow the enemy of truth to rule your life? Ignore them, Anne. Not everyone believes their rubbish."

"Edwin, sometimes in my lowest moments, even I believe their rubbish."

"Are you the same woman who has just purchased *The Echo*? Who writes those articles that have for years dignified an insipid community news-sheet? Are you? Are you?"

He was angry. She had never seen him angry before. They were both rather too silvery to be standing there arguing over her identity.

"It is simply that I do not have the strength to fight a whole town!"

"I think you do! You have the strength to take on this whole province if you'd only believe in yourself!"

There was a click on the other side of the rows of boxes. The minister became furious, rattled his keys, and threw open his own slot.

"Mrs. Sinclair!" he bellowed through the square hole.

There was a sharp gasp from the other side.

"Mrs. Sinclair!" he shouted, "Repent!!!" and smashed closed the little door.

He was flustered and red.

"Forgive me", he said to Anne, fingers trembling as he wiped rage off his face. "I really don't know what came over me."

She laughed. She laughed in such delight that bending over double could not cure it. And he began to laugh, too, until they had drowned together the indignant muttering beyond the walls.

22

Heat simmered in the valley. Slag heaps of cloud rumbled over the rim of the western ranges but did not fulfill their threats. Golden bolts shot through the canyons of black thunderheads to the steaming earth.

It was cool on the mountain, and the older sheep were content to be back in the bowl of meadow with a new generation of lambs. The young shepherd watched them meander across the slopes as they fed on the grass. How small their lives, he thought. Perfect circles in time: birth, fruition, a brief life, then death. A whole giving of self: wool, lambs, meat. A sacrificial life.

Ash Delaney thought about his own life. In the fall he would be leaving for the coast, where there was a university, his journey financed by the remains of his mother's inheritance. At times this version of the future seemed unlikely to him. He anticipated studying, living in a residence, rubbing shoulders with other independent human beings in search of larger destinies. He shook his head at the feeling of unreality. It would be good, like scaling a mountain for the first time. But it would be strange, for he had never gone to any place larger than Jasper. Not that he would be the first to leave or to submerge in the roar of the city. Maurice L'Oraison had left some years back. He returned for infrequent visits, and each time he was a little more changed. He was smarter and well dressed, with distance in his eyes, a huge success, the valley's first professional in the making.

Would he become like Maurice? It would mean leaping from one world into another, and he was both thrilled and apprehensive at the prospect. As he sat musing on the sun-washed outcroppings of rock, he saw that worlds are always cut off from each other until the mind crosses over from one to the other. It held true for those passages from farm to city, farm and mountain, farm and town, and also between himself and any other human being. To be Jackie Tobac and to be Rinty MacPhale were definitely two very different worlds. To be healthy or weak. To be strong and beautiful or condemned to the underbelly of society.

He shook himself. He could not go where his thoughts were leading, down into the machinery of fate. The afternoon was too perfect for that, the rain over, the light swelling, insects humming, lambs bleating, and the creek ribboning forever through a contented landscape.

Later in the day he heard a gunshot crack against the mountains, echoing back and forth in such confused waves of sharp and muffled sound that it was impossible to tell from which direction it had come. Probably lower down on the mountain. He wondered who could be hunting out of season, certainly not his father or brother. Possibly a poacher or someone taking potshots at a tin can. But as no explanations were forthcoming, he shrugged it from his mind.

The following morning he packed a bag of bannock and jam and set off walking down the trail to meet Bryan, who was due to ride up that day with supplies. He commanded the dog to stay and keep watch on the flock, took one sweeping look around the valley, and was lost over the lip of rock into the ravine that led down the mountain.

Ordinarily, he would have taken his father's .303 along with him, but he had left it back in the tent, thinking he would be gone only a few hours, expecting to meet Bryan about halfway down the trail. He had been walking for close to an hour when he began to slow, troubled by a sensation that he was being followed. He turned to look over his shoulder several times but there was nothing. He resisted the impulse to break into a downhill lope. Very few predators were slower than men.

He lamented his missing gun, something he almost never forgot to carry with him. It seemed suddenly a terrible neglect. But summer had made the forest innocent. The stalking of flesh by flesh belonged to smaller regimes of nature than his own—the death of man being wholly abstract.

There was a snort from behind, and he whirled around to see a huge brown grizzly barrelling down the trail.

Yells leapt out of his throat.

Don't move, his father's voice rose up from memory. Sometimes if your will was firm you could stop the charge with immobility. *Grizzlies are individuals, Ash, some just curious, some mean. But on the whole they've got a reputation I don't think they deserve.*

Too late, he saw the red mat of blood on the haunch and knew that this was no sow feinting to protect her cubs. He knew immediately what he had to do.

Run, run.

He yelled, ran full-tilt into the trees a few yards ahead of the beast, which was slower than it might have been because of a hunter's slug. He saw a likely poplar and jumped high, grease-poling up as fast as he could. And was safe. He sat there on a branch, heart pounding hard enough to burst, sweat rolling down into his eyes. Salt. He blinked it away in the heat. Golden flies bit his arms.

Grizzlies can't climb trees.

"Stupid bear!" His breath came quick in sobs. "Stupid hunter!"

The bear reared on its hind legs. Yellow claws ripped green blood from the pungent skin of the tree, mixing with the beast's own blood and musk. Its snout was piggish and the silver-tipped collar was bristling. It grunted onto the ground, looking up. Hate would tear down the hive suspended in the tree and crush the paper skull with teeth and lick the flesh with a long rasping tongue. Its eyes smouldered. It sat, loathing.

Grizzlies don't eat man-meat. Can't stand the smell.

Though blacks were known to gorge on carrion, old dead trappers and lost kiddies alike, so said the campfire tales.

"What do I do now?" Ashley asked aloud.

The bear had no acceptable suggestions.

They waited. The boy's arms were scratched by bark and the small spikes of branches he had broken in his upward plunge.

The bear began to pant in the heat, complaining loudly about its pain, pawing at blowflies, which convened around the wound. Malice rose like clouds with the mosquitoes.

Ashley was sore and stiff, clinging to the tree.

What about Bryan, he thought suddenly.

Bryan with a harmless .22 and a dreamy apathy about danger. Laughing Bryan, the family jester, who tied knots that came undone and left gates open and generally could not be relied upon by older and wiser members of the family. He would be no match for a wounded bear that wanted nothing less than revenge.

"Bryan, Bryan", he shouted. Surely his brother would be well up the trail by now. It was almost mid-day. He had to warn him. He maneuvered his body around the column of the tree, supporting his feet on the springy rod of the branch, and cupped one hand by his mouth to shout louder.

The branch cracked. In a split second of error, he thought he was falling, reached for another branch, missed it, and plunged to the ground.

He fell at the bear's feet. The animal was astonished that it had been able to drag down the quarry by sheer force of hate. It roared and batted the unconscious sack; it worried the flesh and tore, and the disgusting man-blood poured out to stain the forest floor. And when the man-thing seemed dead, or vengeance was slaked, the beast ambled away into the peaceful sun-shafted trees.

* * *

Voices. The shaking and roar of a train. Pain. Unutterable pain. A woman weeping.

352

"Daddy, will he be okay?"

"I don't know, Bryan."

"We'll have him in Jasper Hospital by midnight", said a man's voice.

"It was a terrible mess, Daddy, his face all ripped up and the ribs showin'."

"Hush, lad, hush."

"I can't bear it, Stephen", a woman's voice cried. "He's in such pain. And his face, his face!"

His beautiful face, cherries split on a bowl of snow, raspberries smeared on brown skin, boys tripping and falling through the hoops of summer, girls tangled in their skipping ropes, larks ascending into the talons of eagles, water lapping on the white enamelled ribs of fractured boats.

Sinking, sinking, she cried inwardly and could have broken into wails. Her private passion for her son's beauty, though platonic, might become visible in the circus ring of pain, an arena where every indignity was possible. She remembered the sight of him when he was born, as pure as if he had been carved from blue ivory, wet from her body.

For what did I bring you into the world, Ashley? For this? For this?

His face was torn in crisscrossed flaps, swollen purple beyond recognition, shiny black pools of blood congealing around shreds of moss and pine needles.

"Oh, God, Oh, God!" groaned the distraught woman, not so much praying as acknowledging a greater mystery of struggle in which they had become unwillingly involved. It was not right that the shape of her creation be so wantonly damaged. Her permission had not been granted.

The family clustered around him in the lamplit caboose. Only the fireman was distanced somewhat from the clotting of bodies that sought to console the tortured flesh by grief and presence.

A conductor put his head in at the door to the next car. Anne startled. It was Monsieur Charon.

"Jasper in an hour", he said, and disappeared.

The journey into eternity rumbled through the bowels of tunnels, then stars again, and blackness, clouds, fangs of peaks against the milky way, then blackness. Light, darkness, victory, defeat, an endless cycle of futility. Wholeness, breaking apart, dying, being born, violence and hope circling around each other in the bearpit of existence. The shattered metaphors swarmed into her consciousness; her perceptions unbearable. She desired to hold the body of her son, but could not. Her love would have multiplied his agony.

"Oh, God, I loathe this country!" she sobbed. Aloud.

"Might as well hate the sea then, too," said her husband, slowly, "for men drown in it."

"Be quiet", she replied. "Please just be quiet."

It was this reproach, above all others, that stung the man, the father, most bitterly.

Death, death, death, said the clacking tracks. *Birth, birth, birth* they replied to themselves. Two silver moon-rails converging into horizons of black.

Time unwound and coiled up again. Lights from cabins. Then the long footprint of Moose Lake. More forest, and the lantern swinging on a hook. Coffee perking on the oil-heater. The fireman offered.

No, no, nothing, said the woman with her fierce hands.

Yes, said the man, her husband, *thank you*.

Their eyes were committed to the body before them in disbelief.

"Who'll do the milking?" asked Bryan, because silence and the collapse of order might be the vacuum in which his cells would explode.

What does it matter, thought the woman. *Who cares any more. Let them die, Stephen's damned cows. And those sheep! I hate those damned sheep!*

And hated herself.

"Emmie will milk, and Camille", said the father. The girl had stayed behind at Turid's, too terrified to see. Though she had bawled loudly enough, believing.

"If he hadn't dropped his knapsack on the trail, I never would've found him," said Bryan, who was desperate to talk. He was still shaken after several hours, as white as spoiled milk. He was also cold, sitting by the dead heater in the corner of the caboose.

"You remember that time, Dad, you were down at the farmers' meetin' at Golden? That time a few years ago when we had the bad winter?

"It was Sunday, and Father was supposed to be coming from McBride for Mass at the school that week, and everything was snowed in like crazy. There was no way anybody was goin' anywhere with a foot of new snow and the wind blowin' so hard it filled in your footsteps to the outhouse before you were finished your business.

"Ash was up that mornin' at least five o'clock. I heard him goin' out in the dark, and even the rooster hadn't sounded off. I watched him, Dad. Remember, Mum?"

"Yes, I remember." She was staring at him.

"He started shovellin' a path through the snow and got a quarter way up the lane by breakfast. Wouldn't even come in to eat, so Mum sent me out with some hotcakes and jam all bent up like sandwiches and he ate them on the run. By noon he'd got to the gate just in time to meet the town snowplow goin' the other way down the road.

"By then the wind had filled in everythin' he'd dug out that mornin', and there was no way Jesse could pull the cutter through that stuff. Ash just turned around and shovelled himself a path back to the house, didn't say a word. If the priest ever came, it was too late anyway.

"I remember how tired he looked, like a bull trampled him. He couldn't even lift his arms. I know 'cause I had to put him in bed; he was so worn out he just fell asleep with his long johns on. He kept mumblin'.

"Over and over he said, *Try, try, have t'try*, and when I shook him, he just looked me in the eyes like he didn't know me, and said it again. Try what? I asked. And he said, *For Daddy, for the kids.*

"Y'know, I think he knew we'd never make it to Mass. It was like he had to show us little kids somethin' about what he believed in. Course, we didn't care about missin' church, just words was all it meant to us and Dad's hand makin' y' sit up straight."

The boy's rattle-gun story kept unwinding too fast for anyone to follow exactly. And some in the caboose wished he would desist. But the menace of mystery would expose each one in various ways. Some chose silence. Others embraced their own bodies in search of stability. Others, like Bryan, would huddle around their stories to calm terror and to raise hope on high.

Storytelling was almost, but not quite, enough to enshrine the life that was about to drain away into memory. The boy began to cry, and his father, who had been listening, opened his arm and hugged him, hard.

"Yes, son, that was Ash for you", he said.

"That *is* Ash", said his mother. "He's not dead yet!"

Until the train rolled into Jasper many aeons later, she kept the spirit of her son enclosed in the torn bag of his body by the pure force of her will. The man, employing the only instruments at his disposal, prayed.

23

When the doctor informed them that their son would live, the mother experienced an instant scrambling of her emotions. Part of her exhaled in relief, another part felt the dull knife-thrust of regret.

"It's amazing that he survived those long hours and the rough trip down the mountain on a stretcher. And a shaking up on the Canadian National. An almost critical loss of blood, too, though I think the ice packing is probably what saved him. His youth helped, and the excellent physical condition."

"Can his face be restored?" It was the woman wanting to know.

The doctor looked down, embarrassed.

"I'm afraid I can't promise anything", he said. "Your son will be scarred for the rest of his life, but there are wonderful things being done with plastic surgery these days."

It was then that regret had broken through relief. Detesting this duality in herself, she began to feel ashamed. But the thoughts continued to bother her. At least in death he might have been preserved from evil, admittedly against his will. And what kind of future could he have, what possibilities for love? Were there really women who could see past the face to his interior beauty? The young were never that deep! Who could help him to love himself and discover his identity, not in the mirror, but in the eyes of another human soul hungering for him? Was his being enclosed in flesh like a spirit trapped in a jar, or was his being expressed by flesh, as much him as the words and music that escaped his lips from the invisible portion of his self? She could never decide what human beings really were, and now the answer seemed more elusive than ever. Were they no more than a race of Cains set loose on the earth to ravage and alter its face forever, the only consolation being their awesome power to name the things they destroyed, wandering like lost children through a wasteland, naming everything, knowing everything except their own faces? It might be better for Ashley to slip quietly away from this interminable carnage, to go gently into some unknown and possibly kinder universe.

But if he was not to die, she wondered, would pain and the sentence of life make him bitter? Would he feel cheated by this cold magistrate God, this absence or silence? Would he become destructive, deprived of the joys of union and procreation, go down to the arenas of the war? Would he kill and thus take a legal revenge on life? Or robbed of hope, would he curl up like a wounded animal to die?

Or will you, she wondered as a last resort, *will you become more wise?*

This remote possibility sent shivers across her breast. A haunting, timeless feeling. As if she had not thought it herself but merely received the idea on the screen of consciousness. The despair departed, though anguish remained.

Could he, could he find a measure of love? She knew that goodness and strength were only slightly less marketable commodities than beauty, which must fail in the end anyway.

But the black shadow erupted into her thoughts again:

Will your face ever be capable of joy? Ashley, Ashley, better to die than to endure all that is coming.

The woman found that she had only an experimental faith in life. She who could not bear the snuffing out of beauty in any form. She who had pleaded for her own death in the past. She turned now to that silence or presence which had permitted them both to suffer.

Complete your work, let him die!

And she burst into public sobs at her dreadful thoughts.

No, no, I didn't mean that! Live, Ashley, live!

Her husband held her, and the doctor remembered some pressing business on another ward.

The broken hermit knelt beside her. He was invisible, but she felt his presence. Functioning as an unseen icon in her heart, he said: *Do you think the heart of love does not hear your cries?*

"He is silence. Silence! And all the world is in agony!"

He is waiting for your cries to be still. He holds you. He is with you in your agony. For he too was once where you are. And where your son is.

To this she had no reply, and a strange inner calm permeated her. When she looked up there was no hermit, nothing, only a quiet corridor and a husband who held her and dropped scalding male tears noiselessly upon the back of her hands.

* * *

Eventually the boy's face began to knit itself together. The man and the woman told lies to him when they came to visit, assuring him that the healing scars appeared almost normal. He issued his own lies in reply, pretending a certain acceptance of the situation, putting on a mask of hope for them. He was responsible for their emotions. But when they had gone, he would lapse into a stare that could have burned holes in the wall.

He came home after some months and dwelled deep in his room, refusing to go to town with his father for the mail. His face was no longer a huge purple bag. It was gray marble shot with verdigris. It had returned to an approximate human shape. But he could not even endure the swift glances of his brother and sister.

"Go to town, Ashley. Get it over with all at once", said his mother.

"No."

When she badgered and pleaded, he blew up at her:

"Shut up! Shut up, will you!" he shouted. "Just leave me alone. I'll go when I'm ready."

"Ashley, you must learn to live with it. People won't notice if you don't make such a big bother. Nothing has changed, just a little skin."

"Nothing's changed, Mother! Nothing changed!? Look, look at me! I'm Ashley the dog-faced boy! Ashley the town freak!"

"You are neither of those things."

"I am so, Mother, and none of your words are going to change it. The moment I go to town half the village will be hangin' out their windows with their jaws dropped. Little kids will run away."

She looked grim, searching for the right chemistry of words.

"It's very hard, I know, but there are hard things in everyone's life, and if we were to allow them to overwhelm us, where would we be?"

"Please, I can't stand any homely old saws right now."

She became ramrod straight, her face severe.

"It's up to you, my son. Linger here, let your soul shrivel and die, or go out and face those people!"

"Why should I?" he whispered. "Why the hell should I?"

"For your sake, not theirs. Human beings don't just happen, Ashley. They are made, and it takes courage and suffering and damn hard work to give something life. You can be anything you set your mind to, but I'm telling you, if you lose courage, you will never be anything!"

"But I have lost courage!"

"Then find it again", she said, shaking his shoulders. "It's there inside of you."

He turned away.

"Ashley," she said, choking, her eyes fierce, "if you turn away from life because you can't face people, you will surely die. It would have been better had you never survived that bear!"

She left him with that.

He made a sullen truce with fate, and it did seem that a sort of life might be arranged around the barn and fields, tending the livestock and garden. University was out of the question.

"Then what do you want to be, Ashley?" his mother asked at one point.

"Nothing", he said coldly. "I don't want to be anything."

Occasionally Bryan was awakened in the middle of the night by Ashley's fists pounding on the mattress and groans escaping from clenched teeth. He would lie staring into the blackness as his brother fought. He would feel gratitude that he had not been scarred by the bear, that Ashley had taken his place in the slaking of the beast's rage. He would long to say something to comfort his older brother but knew that such words had not yet been invented. He would roll over and, after silence had crept through the scene of struggle, would sleep.

The question *why* had become so unanswerable that it was pointless to ask and only incited a degree of desperation that resulted in the smashing of objects. Sometimes the man and the woman would hear him stalking around the toolshed like a dismantled soul in search of missing parts. Bottles would shatter against scrap metal and chains banged on the anvil in a frenzy of destruction, but the scenes of such crimes were always found to be fastidiously cleaned up afterward.

"Speak to him, will you, Stephen?" she pleaded.

"He will take none of my words, Anne, nor my touch, which he throws off."

"I'm frightened for him."

The man paused, thinking, perhaps remembering.

"Don't be afraid. He's angry. He hates life right now, but it's far better than if he had just turned in and was crushed."

"I hope you are right."

"I hope I'm right too."

* * *

361

And so, to the family, he had ceased to be Ash Delaney and had become Ash Who Was Scarred by the Bear. He was the brother who could only bark when you asked him a civil question. Or worse, he was Poor Ashley Our Wounded Son. This, though it rarely appeared, was an attitude that infuriated him, and he quickly taught them never to express it. To those other human beings, the curious callers, he had become The Boy Who Is Scarred for Life, a monster living in their imaginations, for he was actually the boy whom no one outside the family had yet seen. He hid himself from the eyes of the greedy.

But one winter day he was captured. He was bucking up the poplar that wind had brought down in the back field near the little cemetery. The roar of the chain saw was so loud that the approaching footsteps crunching in the snow were drowned until it was too late.

"Hi, Ash!"

It was Jack Tobac.

"Oh, shit!" He turned away.

Jack stood there watching, seeing the full extent of the damage. Words of pity rushed to his lips. He choked them back. Then he desired to flee this grisly imitation of his friend. And rejected that impulse as well.

"Leave me alone, please", said Ashley, pretending to tinker with the machine, over which he was hiding his face.

Jack finally decided on a plan of attack.

"Geez, you're stupid, Ash!" he grumbled. "Look what you're doin' to the gas cap, all stuffed with snow."

He grabbed the saw out of Ashley's hands, hefted it into the air and yanked on the rip cord. The engine roared. Jack sliced the blade into the fallen giant and let it eat, spumes of wood chips fanning out onto the snow. He wrinkled his brow in concentration. He was gambling.

Out of the corner of his eye he saw the red flash of Ashley's parka turn and head slowly off toward the house. His heart sank; it appeared that he had lost. He was about to shut down the engine and go home when, incredibly, he saw his friend stop in the middle of the field, turn, and walk back. He continued to carve up the tree in frowning concentration as Ashley stood a few feet away, hands in pockets, watching.

Jack killed the engine, then began to roll the smaller discs of poplar up a plank into the box of the cutter. The horse shook its bells.

"You hidin', Ash?" he said as he worked. There was no answer, and Jack wondered if he had lost him again. But the other boy made no motions to leave.

"I'm not hiding", he said eventually.

"Then let me look."

"Okay, then, look at the freak!"

It was a confused moment, in which he stood, feeling like a carnival attraction, angry, hurt, and perhaps a little grateful.

"You ain't no freak, Ash", said the boy, inspecting with open curiosity and a hint of sorrow. "Fact you don't look one half as bad as everyone's guessin'."

That finished, Jack turned around to look at the wood needing to be rolled into the cutter box.

"If you play your cards right, Delaney, you might get me to help you load this."

Ashley's face contorted into a feeble smile.

"What's it gonna cost me?"

"Nothin' much. Just a promise."

"What promise?"

"Just don't hide on me again, okay?"

"Okay." The word was barely breathed.

It had been a small incident in a winter field. Anyone watching from across a fence or two would not have guessed that a life was being saved.

* * *

The circle of initiates expanded in time, embracing the Tobac family and even an old trapper or two. Later, he permitted others to see. They reacted in different ways to the affront of his face. Some refused to notice and talked to him as if nothing had happened. Ashley was not sure if this wasn't the worst reaction of all. Others brought it out in the open to acknowledge and dispense with it. An old mill hand showed him the stump of his arm, offering an exchange of the curious wounds that life inflicts, chattering about it with that enthusiasm which collectors of the bizarre reveal when discussing their specialty. Other callers became prone to long discourses on their many operations and varied internal ailments. Some fled. Others just stared. And somewhere in all this reaction, he began to shed his fear of the opinions of men, ceased to be The Boy Who Is Scarred for Life, and began to emerge as the man who would be.

Jackie left one day for the East. He had seen pictures of Québec folk carving in a magazine, and he wanted to learn about it. He took with him some aged wood blocks, his knives, and several pounds of smoked deer meat—all packed into a battered typewriter case that he bought for two shinplasters at Mac-Phale's white elephant sale. No one could believe he was gone until after he had jumped onto a boxcar and was, indeed, gone. He was seventeen years old.

Although his friend was no longer there, Ashley continued to visit Tobac's. Their cabin was a place where scars were common, though mostly of the interior variety. Sarah missed Jack a lot, he could tell, yet her gentle presence was unchanged. She had grown taller and more beautiful, in spirit if not in face.

"Will you ride with me to town?" she asked him one day. "There's a boy who's bothering me whenever I go for groceries. He says things."

"Who?"

"Rinty MacPhale."

He thought it over. Beauty needed protection, and what better to provide it than an ugly beast.

"Sure, Sarah, I'll be your bodyguard. Let him say anything and I'll just give him one look. He'll shatter into a million pieces!"

She glanced at him unsmiling.

"You're laughing cruel at yourself, Ash. I need a friend with me is all."

So they rode into town on the cantering horse.

Are you my friend? his eyes asked, feeling the thrill of her grip, firm and delicate, around his waist. He wished that the ride would never end.

She couldn't love me. I'm harmless now; she can touch me because nothing will ever happen.

But touch like all senses imparts a message that can be misread. As they rode on, Ashley felt her hands move tightly around his chest and her body press into his back. She lay her head against him, and he knew she was discovering his crashing heart and the pounding of the hooves as one continuous pattern. He felt that she was absorbing him with her whole being. Loving him. He desired to gallop away from this emotion of hers, but she, too, was mounted on the animal, assigned at high speed to his flight path through the trees. His body yearned backward into hers but pulled away, furious at her pity, for he felt that she was only tossing the consolation of a moment of affection. Well, it was not good enough, he raged. Was there any real possibility that she might allow him to turn, to stop the horse, and to face her. No, this silent embrace was an illusion, and he would not believe it.

But as the trees thinned, and the cut through the bush became a road, and the smoke rising from the village chimneys came into view, she held on and held on.

She held him, and he allowed himself to be held, as he drove the frothing horse faster, faster upward into the clearing of the future. Gradually they slowed, still strangely united, not yet able to look at each other.

They were walking down Main Street past MacPhale's, where a porch-front conversation was in progress between the proprietor and a customer. A smaller, red-headed version of MacPhale darted into the interior of the store.

MacPhale was expounding loudly:

"Damn Japs! Send em all back to where they come from!" said MacPhale.

"The government's no fool. And all the better if we get some work out of them, too!" said the hunkering debater.

"I don't rest easy with all them slit-eyes so close. Camps at Tee-John and Albreda, and now Redpass, plus the ones down by Hellroar."

"Course, they're citizens, Jonah, and most of them was born here."

"Look, we got a war on, and sabotage is the best way to cripple the nation, from her soft underbelly, like."

"What can a few chop-suey artists do? Nothin', I say."

"Listen, they ain't white, are they, and who knows what goes on in those heads. They never been allowed to vote, and you can bet the government knows what's what."

"Hey, ain't that Steve's boy with the Tobac girl?"

"Yeah", said MacPhale, spitting tobacco juice. "What a bloody mess. Looks like that bear sure's hell tore 'im up!"

Ashley and Sarah passed by the store just close enough to catch the meaning of the muffled conversation. The boy bristled and stared back with hate and would have spat some word at MacPhale, but Sarah grabbed his arm and turned him diagonally across the street.

* * *

11 April 1943

> The jay picks amidst the ruins
> of a burnt skull.
> The child abandoned cries.
> Wind blows steadily from the east
> and armies move upon the
> wept-upon
> bled-upon
> earth.
>
> Then the stars move unsteadily in their traces.
> The fighting angels bronze and light
> their faces.
> Battle unto battle races
> the horseman on
> his mystery.

These are fragments for a provisional poem. It's all I have—fragments. Nothing systemic, nothing cosmic, nothing to knit together all the severed strands of the universe. It comes from somewhere inside of me, but I do not pretend to understand it. I suppose from the burnt core of the abyss there will sometimes burst forth a bird.

Yesterday, I observed through the kitchen window as Ashley and Sarah sat on the woodpile looking toward the mountain. They were not quite close enough to touch shoulders, though one could almost see the waves that magnetised them. They were talking, these two silent people. They conversed together for hours without moving, a sign that love's terrible force was in motion, for only love destroys time. As I watched them, I too lost consciousness of its passage.

Presently they walked back to the house. Their heads were

bent together. My heart ached, and I dreaded what may come of this attachment. I fear this girl and her needy, troubled family. I am not a racial bigot. But perhaps I am, just a little, a cultural one. I know the agony of alienation that spouses of differing cultures can suffer. How even a great love can be worn down by "irreconcilable differences". Still, my own story is not yet complete. And Sarah has something to teach me.

They arrived at the door with transfigured faces. Both of them hushed, saying nothing, gazing down at what rested in the girl's hand. They were *showing* me, like two small children.

"A cedar waxwing", said Ashley.

It had died last winter most probably. They found it in a chink of the woodpile, where it must have fled for shelter. Who can describe its beauty? Its terrible dignity? The body was perfectly dry, mummified, the buff feathers shot with yellow and a flash of red. In Sarah's hands it lay as light as the wind it had once played upon. Her face communed with the bird in a mysterious way, while I stared at the girl's plumage: long cotton print covering a spindly frame, worn socks, shoes with holes. Gangly arms, hair plaited in one rope hanging down her spine. A face as still as well water.

"Why are you here?" her eyes seemed to be saying to the creature. "Why did you not fly with the others when the north wind came?"

Her face was the face of compassion. Her eyes the eyes of pity. When she turned them on me for one burning instant, I knew that it is I, not she, who is in need of pity. Is there hope for me? Will the fear that burdens my heart ever be defeated? Shall I one day be released to play in the wind?

Curious. This morning I received a letter. The stamp was cancelled with the name of some northern outpost. I knew instantly that it was a message from my little crippled priest, even though the signature could barely be deciphered. The message, however, was printed in a simple script:

I pray for you. Your path is hard and full of confused signs. One always wishes to know before making the first step. A lifetime can be spent waiting to know. Instead, one must make the first step in faith—then another, and another. Later, you will know.

Yours sincerely,
Father Andrei

He and Stephen and Sarah stand together beckoning to me to leap across a wide bottomless chasm. "Believe", they call out, holding their hands toward me. "Leap!" they cry. But I cannot. I remain on my own cliff edge, paralysed, strangely companioned with the powers of my mind and with my son.

Summer 1943

24

The day that Anne Delaney first took over the shed and office where *The Swiftcreek Echo* was created, she had no idea what was in store for her. When Dan led her into the pressroom to reveal just exactly what had been purchased, she balked. There was a broken-down pony-press lying butchered in a corner and a secondhand Washington taking up most of the remaining space.

"This is the platen", he explained. "See, you can print two pages at once on it. Here's the lever handle, and you pull to make the impression squeeze. Now you put the sheet of paper on the frisket after your helper has inked the type, and away you go. Give her a stout pull, reverse the crank, and off goes the sheet! Simple, eh?"

"Oh, Dan, it's a Chinese puzzle!"

He laughed.

"You'll learn it soon enough, Annie. And with a couple of hefty boys on that lever you should do just fine."

The system did appear to be intact. Along with the press and tables, tools and bundles of paper, there was an old Mergenthaler Linotype in the corner. In time she learned the ins and outs of these machines, and with the help of Bryan or Ash as printer's devils she was able to produce her first edition of *The Echo*. She and her sons quickly acquired the various skills needed for a small-town newspaper, but the mastery of the machines was only a prologue to the core of her enterprise, the marvelous authority of print, the potency of ideas impregnating the minds of her readers through the word. There were two hundred and fifty copies of the first edition, half of them going to subscribers and the rest to be sold in stores throughout the town. They were sold out on the first day.

> So a nation of free men and women has decided to open its own concentration camps. Twenty thousand Japanese Canadians are now incarcerated under armed guard in work camps and ghost towns throughout this province, and the reign of fear allows nary a voice to be raised in protest. How can we excuse it?
>
> Not only their freedom but their property has been seized and sold for a pittance, often at a fraction of its real value. Those prosperous businesses and thriving market gardens were built up from nothing by a humble, industrious, and honest people. One must wonder who are the fortunate purchasers of this stolen land.

Several subscriptions were cancelled that week, and angry letters were addressed to the editor. Those which were not full of curses she printed.

> Dear Editor,
> I lost one boy in the Pacific and I'll not let you go unanswered when you aid and support our common enemy, the Japanese menace. I am outraged. Where is your sense of patriotism?
> Yours truly,
> A MOTHER!

> Dear Editor,
> Your editorial concerning the plight of Japanese Canadians deprived of their rights deserves our attention and support. Surely a nation that is at war to defend liberty must not compromise the very principles for which it is so desperately fighting. The end can never justify the means.
> Yours sincerely,
> Rev. Edwin Gunnalls, B.A.

* * *

When Ashley informed them at supper one evening that he was joining the army, there was stunned silence.

371

"No!" said his mother.

"Yes", said her son, eating a potato as calmly as ever.

His father declined to comment, though he did look up and sucked on a dry, cold pipe.

When they had been through the whole ache and argument, realization and loss, they stood finally on the station platform watching him go. The train swallowed him and coiled off down the valley toward civilization and its conflicts. What beast would then devour the whole tragedy, she wondered. Would it drag a third of the stars from the heavens with its tail? Lost within its belly would be the speck of her son, armed only with a rifle and his face.

"Ashley," his father had said to him that last morning, "if you live long enough you may find that guns don't solve very much. In life you will choose to hold a tool in your hand, or you will choose to hold a weapon."

"Why not both?" Ashley snorted. And his father did not continue.

There were no wails of anguish from the woman, no whys tossed to the heavens, no protests. All that was young and free was to be consumed by this demon-god. There was nothing she could do to fight it, except to toss a few neatly arranged pieces of type against its impervious scales.

* * *

War was not hell, Ashley decided. It was a farce, and only the regrettable death of the characters, as an act of high realism, flawed an otherwise hilarious performance.

When he was stripped and led to be inspected by the doctor, he began to have doubts about the good intentions of the playwright. The actors in themselves appeared to be incidental to the script, disposable creatures that swarmed around the machines that performed the major scenes. Eventually they all lay strewn about the landscape.

Those newsreels were to come later, Ashley supposed, and he wondered how it would feel to be part of it. In the meantime his flesh was being fingered and judged, rendered down to its most glorious or undignified to see if it would be found worthy to perform such drama.

Naked soldiers filed down the corridor, a line of restless muscle and shaven heads, humanized only by eyes and scraps of white towelling with which they hid their secret identities. The linoleum was cold. No one said much, their blue-veined feet smacking flat on the floor. The line moved forward.

Ashley's turn. A doctor sat on a stool scribbling information on a chart. Wire-rim spectacles, parchment hands. He looked up at Ashley's face and shuddered.

"Drop your towel. Bend double, spread your legs, boy!"

Then he probed, handling orifices and members like meat. Government inspected.

"Moo", said Ashley.

"What the hell", said the doctor.

"Nmoooh!" deeper and louder.

"What's this one's number?" the doctor inquired of a male nurse. The scribe supplied the information.

"Did he pass psych screen?"

"Yes sir. Just barely!"

"God, you look like you've already been through a war."

"Nghmooohhh!!!"

The line of cattle began to quake with disorderly humor.

"Well, you're as sound as a moose."

"Don't be surprised," said Ashley, "for I was born and raised in their company."

"I wish I was as certain of the soundness of your mind, young man!"

"Nghmooohhh!!!"

Rebellions of laughter broke out in the stalls.

"Get the hell out of here!"

The doctor refrained from the final customary smack across the buttocks, a habit he had picked up from a stint at obstetrics. Soldiers were not known to squall like newborn babies, but a few might give off a steerlike chuckle when slapped, to assure the doctor and any observers that they were regular guys. Never, however, did they moo.

Things became even more amusing in the following months. There was a memorable incident on the Rideau Canal in Ottawa. The squad had been ordered across Cartier Square past the armory to the guard rails of the canal, opposite Union Station. They were surrounded by the peace-tower of Parliament Hill and the green spires of the Chateau Laurier Hotel. The little army was loaded up in full gear, packs and ordnance strapped to their backs, faces young, shining, and acting grim for the pedestrians who had gathered on the bridge to watch His Majesty's loyal men.

"All right, buckos," shouted the sergeant, "line up along the canal."

Groans and protests: "Hey, Sarge, we're not gonna swim that in battle gear, are we?"

"Damn right you are, lads, that's exactly what you're gonna do. It's not over your head; it's only up to the chin on the shortest of you."

The water swirled beneath their feet, taking leaves and maple keys in a tide.

"Are you sure about this water, Sergeant?"

"Shut up, Delaney! Now, when you guys hear this whistle blow, you GO! Rifles over your heads. Now!"

The whistle blew. Twenty or so men poised with their boots over the concrete lip and hurled themselves out into the brown swill.

Ashley hesitated. The others landed feet-first in the water and were taken to the bottom fast by the weight they were carrying. Their heads submerged but did not reappear; their hands began to flail the surface of the water, desperately, from beneath.

"Oh, God!" yelled the sergeant. People on the bridge were shouting, running about helplessly. Ashley shed his gear and clothes as fast as he could and dived.

"What the hell's goin' on?" shouted the sergeant in a panic. "It's not that deep!"

One or two heads reappeared, grasping at the slippery edge of life, their packs gone: they had been able to struggle out of their boots, which were stuck on the bottom.

"You idiot!" roared one surviving soldier at an officer. "You forgot the mud!"

Hands drifted like leaves on the surface. Ashley pulled one up, then another. Bystanders dragged the sodden bags of half-drowned men under the canal rails onto the grass of the park. Water gurgled from some, breath broke into others in agonized gasps. Some were dead—drowned green youths, wet lumps, dead, dead, like the heaps of dead everywhere at this moment on the earth.

Ashley worked alone in the water, until a man in a bathing suit dove in beside him, and they pulled together on the bodies that remained. He was the lifeguard from the hotel pool and had dashed across the bridge traffic and plunged from a heart-stopping height. He and Ashley and a few other men were able to drag the remaining bodies from the canal.

When all were accounted for, it was finally known: eleven dead, their mouths gaping, black holes out of which drained green water.

"You stupid bastards!" shouted Ash Delaney, an amphibian standing with claws uncurled, as shocking to the tourists as the dead youths lying in rows in the garden of their capital. It was not certain whether he was addressing the officers who stood around in hushed consultation or the more political men on the Hill. Or those immense bronze creatures of the war memorial towering above them, who immortalized and glorified the dirty facts of war. Ashley bore little resemblance to the bronze heroes. Their eyes fixed eternally on the horizon, rippling jaw muscles, and into-the-valley-of-death postures had no effect on him whatsoever.

Death, death, death, death, death, death, death, death . . .

A war-drum of engines.

The North Atlantic in the autumn of 1943 was a place of many comedies. The wolf packs of German submarines were sinking unprecedented tonnage among the convoys attempting to cross over the mid-Atlantic *black pit*, the zone beyond the cover of land-based aircraft.

During November, the *Corinthian*, a troop ship of English registry, was bringing a load of infantry over, and among them was stowed Ash Delaney. As always, his face made people uneasy. He looked like a veteran. But they liked his name. It had dash and swashbuckle. He made friends with one of the crew, a short Liverpudlian named Andy Wheeler.

"C'mon up, mate, and see the moon, when yer can get away. It's right nice on a clear night. Loverly view. Bloody deadly, though."

During the crossing Ashley would often sneak up from the belly of the iron tub to smell the salt air and wonder what lurked below the sea.

"Here, put on my life vest, Ash. If they catch you up here, you'll be stuffed in the bottom of this sardine tin till we reach port. Try to act like a gunner, man! Look dangerous!"

Ashley smirked and struggled into Wheeler's vest. They shared a forbidden smoke or two in the gunnery cage, crouching low so periscopes would not ferret out their addiction. Wheeler was stationed there to fend off enemy aircraft, but the sky was empty now in midocean, and the watch was long. They were both glad to trade in each other's histories. Wheeler was intrigued by Ashley's life on the farm and by the totality of wilderness.

"You're a lucky bloke, you are."

"Yeah, very lucky—such a handsome bloke I am."

"No jokin', you 'ad it good, Ash. Woo'nit be gran' fer a fella loik me t'ave a ole bloody cont'nent t'muck about in. You'll never know what y'got, man!"

"You're probably right. It's a great place to live if it doesn't kill you."

"Gor, Ash, no bear's ever gonna tear me up in downtown bleedin' Livapool. But there's packs o' two-legged bears oo'd cut me good with knives, just you believe it!"

"That's most reassuring, Andy. Remind me never to visit your home town, please."

"There ain't no place whu isn't dangerous. But none as wild as yours."

"It's not as wild as all that. It always seemed tame to me— even out in the bush. There's cities in Canada, too, and millions of people . . . though most of the world thinks we're just ice and snow."

"Empty or not, it ain't like my 'ome-sweet-'ome, with smokestacks as thick as forests, and not a green thing growin' as far's the eye can see. Least not where I was raised. Mum was a widow and brought us up by cleanin' ouses. You can guess what our place was like. It weren't no 'eye society, I can tell you!"

"Go ahead, tell me."

"Me dad was a soldier stationed in Ireland and drownded on the coast about 1904, and I was born three months later, which just about says it all, mate, but things ain't been as bad as all that, what with the King's navy takin' me on, and me wife and boy—"

He was in mid-sentence when their sister ship, *HMS Thessalonika,* suddenly blew up in the water, her magazines erupting in an ear-shattering incandescence that threw the waves into rows of startled fangs. Fire and metal flew through the air. And particles of men.

Their own ship veered sharply to starboard and began to zig-zag through the seas as fast as she could make.

Wheeler gripped the firing pieces of the cannon, though this sky-gun would prove useless against the present enemy. But it was more reassuring to embrace a weapon, however ineffectual, than to admit helplessness. Ashley watched him. He was fascinated by the firm set of his lips, the metallic eyes in which fire was reflected. They stood together, cool and collected, on the big iron plate as if they were not about to be slaughtered. Training, he guessed. Would he be as certain when faced with the enemy's head in his sights? Would it be like exploding a bottle with a .22, or would it be like stabbing a brother in a cloud of psychotic evil?

The orgasms of the depth charges began, imploding the black ocean. Another troop ship went up in flames forward of them, and the smaller escorts went scurrying around the damaged whales in search of survivors. The purposes of death became suddenly clear to Ashley. When a body floated past missing its face, he understood for the first time that there was no magic to protect him, no exemption from the events now unfolding in the killing ground. War, that abstraction, had begun.

Fear struck the depth of his being, and his endangered self emitted the death scream of burning horses. The sound was swallowed by the concussion of tortured steel and violated air. He held onto the hot rails with both hands, their knuckles white in the Armageddon light, bleached as bones, as black and white as an old newsreel.

Wheeler stared at him.

"C'mon, Delaney", he shouted over the din. "Snap out of it, man!" He, who had more to lose, a wife and son sitting anxiously in rooms by the docks at Liverpool.

At that moment, Ash Delaney was struck from the ranks of those who may still scream—punched against the wall of the gunnery cage by a ram of air. A torpedo hit the ship, sending streamers of death across the deck where men lay all around in odd gestures, shuddering, while a rain of small hot shards of metal fell on them.

His mouth open, all cries stifled at the source, he lay unhurt, as pieces of men and machinery washed toward him in a soup of blood and brine. As if it were reality itself that was being dismembered. Parts of Wheeler sloshed around him in the well; only the entrails of bucks and wethers had ever been exposed in such a fashion. He vomited and hid his face in his bloody fingers.

He believed he had gone insane. It suddenly appeared right that he too should die, perfectly logical that the triumph of chaos be total. He smiled a twisted judgment on the mayhem around him. Below in the troop quarters they must be dying in the hundreds without any possibility of escape, while he, the one who did not care to live, had been offered through the hospitality of Wheeler a passageway into the future. It did not matter—nothing mattered. Living flesh was only a conglomerate of cells that could be ripped apart at a whim. He wished to be sucked into the vortex of fire and thus to end its tyranny over him.

Yet his mind contracted suddenly into those ropes of thought along which it is possible for creatures to haul themselves to sanity. Something in him did not want to die, would not let him die, would struggle and protest to the last breath. Was it the animal part, the stallion screaming and hammering its hooves at the burning barn? Or was it that suspected *spirit*, invisible but just as determined? Why did it not admit defeat until it had wrestled a meaning, a word, or its own true name from the void?

The ship is going over, he thought, five clear words. His body struggled uphill against the deck. Then he slid down through the red slosh to the gunwales, out, out, over into the slime of the North Atlantic.

The water was numbing. He swam, clutching a white ring—the diagram of the universe—*HMS Corinthian*, pushing it toward—away—around the circle of burning water, among the white dots of lifeboats that cowered before the drowning monoliths. The ring and the vest kept him afloat.

Help, he cried. His mind could manufacture that much, a lamb's bleat on the altar of sacrifice.

Introibo ad altare Dei . . .

I will go with joy unto the altar of God. O my God, I am heartily sorry for having offended Thee. . . .

Then the sharp crack of skull, a sudden pitch forward into pain. Silence sucked noise from the world. Light ran from his eyes. He no longer was.

. . . and I detest all my sins . . .

But in actual fact his body did survive. A sailor's oar had struck the back of his head in the firelit water. Someone else in Lifeboat 13 spotted the bobbing head drifting by. They hauled him on board and pumped water out of him, slapping life back into what had almost been the end of a short line of shepherds.

* * *

Journal Entry:

Swiftcreek, January 1944

These vile times, these times of chaos and despair, time of death and a world writhing in agony! Will the war end? Yes, it will end, and begin again, and end, and begin.

The generations to come will sink into mediocrity as the cries of victims and the cries of innocent blood become a myth. They will desperately pursue amusements. Promises will not be kept, and false peace will deceive many. Finally, the powers of hatred will exhaust themselves utterly upon our violated flesh. They will pull a blanket of fire over us all, as if to have the final word, the definitive negation of our common powerlessness.

Keep silence! Go mutely in grief for the lost children, the broken minds, the dead heaped up like vermin across an entire world. If human life no longer means anything, of what value is a word? Be silent then, be silent, and seek the ungenerated forms to refute this unspeakable darkness.

25

It is always the sons of other women who are struck down by war or bears. So when Ashley was returned to her with a repaired skull and a frightening look in his eyes—a permanent look—she was once again brought face to face with the arguments that violence makes against the earthly paradise. It seemed not only unfair but highly suspicious that a youth who only a few years previously had every possibility before him should be so disfigured, cast down, and left for dead. Not once, but twice. Even from the beginning, with that knotted cord around his neck, he had been forced to struggle for existence. Why, she wondered, why did life not wish to see the survival of her firstborn son?

She had desired to give him a perfect world, one that intelligence and faith in mankind could achieve. But the small gods of men had proved flawed, capable of the most profound depravity. The British armies now breaking through the last defense of a ruined Reich were discovering what Anne had long ago suspected: it is largely the innocent who come stumbling out of abandoned concentration camps, blinking at the light. Not the guilty, those orderly citizens who had invented such circles of hell and went home every night to their dogs and recreation and rose gardens. The camps now disgorging haunted eyes and secrets were a fitting testimonial to the age of enlightenment and to the twilight of the gods. Was there an obscure design in the madness, a determination to degrade the human being, not just to enslave or to kill, but to reach that core of dignity which is the refutation of absolute power.

Anne could have vomited at the first photographs from

Belsen but held in her bile and issued it eventually in the form of cold, hard print. At moments she found it suddenly easy to hate *them*, the enemy, as if they could be radically changed overnight from the victims of their own regime into a race of beasts.

No, the horror, she realized, was that they were ordinary people, a nation of cultured, sociable folk, song-filled and hospitable, and if in their *Götterdämmerung* they had failed to use these qualities to fight evil, it only proved all the more their fellowship with the citizens of Swiftcreek.

Several citizens angrily phoned *The Echo* that week to get a definition of the word *Götterdämmerung*. She gave it politely and was answered by loud clicks on the receiver.

She did not know what to believe as events unfolded, who was guilty, who was innocent, and was further disoriented when the victors, the just, dropped their message on Hiroshima and Nagasaki, ending the war and an age.

While her son wandered around in the innocent August sunshine, baling unreal hay with his father, his head crammed with imagery she could never hope or want to see, she watched the movements of his shirtless body from a distance. The old beargash was visible across a hundred yards. It did not seem possible that one person could carry the memory of so much suffering. But she realized that many were carrying greater sufferings as they walked around Europe and Asia. It added to the confusion she felt over the fate of victims and questioned further her silent God, the one who might in the end be no more than the *Gott* on whom the twilight had fallen.

Ashley's shoulders revealed a permanent tension. He had been taught that the world is a place through which one must walk with a loaded gun. Yet he was troubled by the memory of Wheeler. If life is only biology and blind fate, he wondered, why did Wheeler give his life for him. He saw now that it was the other man's body that had shielded him from the flying metal. It was Wheeler's life vest that had kept him afloat. It was Wheeler's friendship that had drawn him in the first place out of the deadly belly of the ship. The thought of Wheeler left a great interrogation mark in his mind, a question that could not be cast off. Nor answered. He did not mention the man to his family.

His mother agonized over him. Nothing she could do would ever correct his face. But surely there was some explanation that would put life back into those eyes. What? What could she tell him that would refute the evidence of his senses and the testimony of his own image.

"Sometimes, Mother," he said with a macabre smile, "sometimes I look in the mirror and say, 'There but for the grace of God go I!'"

The army had offered to pay for plastic surgery to attempt some correction of his face, which was generous of them, as they were in no way responsible for any surface damage. But Ashley had refused, had decided to keep his face in its present condition.

"It's just perfect", he said with a twisted smile. "It's the true picture of things!"

"Oh, Ashley!" she said, frustrated by his stubbornness. "You are spiting your own face!" then covered her mouth.

"It reveals so much about human beings, Mother."

"Whatever do you mean?"

"Oh," he laughed, "you'd have to be all scarred up to understand that."

She mentally composed a variety of meditations:

"Ashley, I have no explanations for the state of the world and the way people are, but we mustn't allow ourselves to be crushed by it, or seduced into the world's hatred . . .

"Ashley, I don't know about God either. I grope and grope through the darkness, the doubt, the despair that I see also in your eyes. We are different from your father, you and I. He is a simple man, content with the earth and its seasons, and simple explanations . . ."

These discussions never occurred. Though practical needs and chores were mentioned daily, objects being safer than thought.

Once, when Emily asked her brother what the war had been like, expecting to feed on heroics, Ashley emitted a short, ugly laugh and looked away, refusing to speak. Everyone learned then not to ask.

Her constant anxiety over her eldest son was eased somewhat when he announced toward the end of August that he was leaving for Vancouver.

"Why? Where?"

They crowded around, drumming him for more information.

"Teachers' college."

His mother beamed, relieved that he had chosen to live.

"Why didn't you say anything?"

"I applied months ago and just never expected to get accepted."

"I'm happy. Very happy", said his mother.

"It's something to do", he said, with a wary eye upon her.

The father sucked at his contemplative pipe, his eyes expressing everything there was to say.

Later, when Ashley had left for the coast, the man and the woman wandered arm in arm through the fields of timothy and clover in the evening light. Alpen-glow colored the peaks a deep rose. They stopped to listen to the river singing of nightfall. They became intensely conscious of their union, their long indefinable marriage. Stars began to appear. Birds called. The universe filled gradually with harmonies. But if the woman was entangled for a moment in the peace of this cool Eden and the warm, strong arm of her husband encouraged such trust, it was only a temporary truce with life. She wondered what would fall apart next. She buried herself in the shoulder of the man, and he held her.

"What is it?" he asked gently, knowing her.

"Everything", she whispered. "Ashley, the war."

"The war is over."

"No, it's not over. It will never be over."

His face in the shadow of the mountain became obscure, though the gray-whites of his eyes showed. It was a used face, wearing down with dignity, stolid, and, some suspected, somber. He had no answers for her, save those his hands could impart.

She wept finally, releasing into the sanctuary of his capable flesh the accumulated anguish of the years of war, of her whole life. And she was grateful for him.

* * *

Into that autumn of the tranquillity between the man and the woman there came a visitor. Jonah MacPhale was familiar to them, not only because of their earliest acquaintance, but because he was a cornerstone of the community now. Owner of MacPhale's general store, a small hotel, several desirable tracts of flatland, and the town's first gas station. He owned three cars, one of them a spanking red Packard in mint condition, which he used only on Sundays or for the Dominion Day Parade. He had prospered, grown fat and expansive, smiled his public smiles, and had begun to brave the teapot tempests of small-town politics. He was one of *The Echo*'s best advertisers. Whether he was peddling men's sock-garters, women's foundation garments, land speculations, or his own large porcelain grin, it was always cash on the barrel-head.

That afternoon, when the newly installed Mayor MacPhale drove through the dust and hysterical fowl of her front yard, Anne was doubly astonished. He had been fairly elected despite her lack of support, so it was not a vote he was after. And it was their habit to discuss his advertisements in businesslike fashion at the office. Was this a social call?

"Good afternoon, Jonah", she greeted, as he rolled his body out of the functional old Tin Lizzie he used for inglorious projects.

"Anne", he said warmly, coming over, confident of his ample belly, in a vest with a gold watch fob. He took her hands in his and squeezed them too tightly, as if curious to know their components. His face was uncharacteristically poised, subtle, sympathetic, affectionate.

"How are you?" said the gentleman caller.

"I'm just fine", she said coolly. "And how may I help you, Jonah?"

"And Steve? How's Steve?"

"He is well."

She was puzzled. What little drama was this man about to enact?

"Good, good", he said, patting her hand. He inhaled deeply, almost sighing. "May we talk, Annie?"

"Speak your mind."

"Can I do that precise thing over a cup of tea, girl?"

The gray-haired girl nodded and led the way into the front room of the cabin. Jonah slumped into an armchair as she banged cupboards and rattled the teapot. She inwardly groaned, for it would be at least half an hour before the wood burner heated up the kettle and boiled water. But she suddenly remembered what had befallen him.

"I heard of your bereavement, Jonah", she said. "I'm very sorry."

"Yes," he said, clearing his throat, "yes, Rinty was his mother's idol and my spitting image."

"It's a terrible thing, war."

"It is that."

His grief carried with it a measure of dignity and brought them as close as would ever be possible. There was something authentic emerging.

"How tragic", she went on, "that he should fall so many days after the armistice."

"They said it was a sniper in some little Nazi village that didn't believe the war was over."

His hand went across his brow to hide the eyes, and the woman felt a constriction of pain for him, those fat fingers suddenly more pathetic than despicable.

She became busy at the stove with cups and saucers.

"You'll fergive me if I change the subject now", he said.

"Of course", she answered gently.

"Annie, I'm wonderin' if you'n'Steve have ever thought of sellin' off the farm?"

She looked at him.

"Whatever for?"

"Well, you are gettin' older, and maybe the kids are not after carryin' on with the place."

She was caught off guard by this notion and could have pushed him out the door had not his grief humanized him.

"It's true that Ashley is at college and Bryan at forestry school. But there's Emily. She might want to run this place some day with a husband."

"Or might not. I can give you a price right now that's more than good."

"But what would you do with a little flock of sheep and some poor acreage? You're as old as we are, Jonah MacPhale!"

"It's an enterprise of mine, girl, like some fellas collect old colored bottles."

"Well, you would have to ask Stephen when he returns from Ptarmigan, but it's out of the question, I'm sure."

"But you own land, don't you, which you got by your inheritance?"

"Yes, those plots of bush south of our property line. We had thought to clear it some day. The sheep . . ."

"You're the owner, not Steve?"

"That's correct, the land is in my name."

"Would you sell? I'm prepared to give you, say, twice the market value."

The offer was tempting. She pondered this as she set out a plate of biscuits. He gobbled them down. The way he ate disturbed her and aroused a sense of caution concerning his ingestion of land.

"Sure now, you and the manno can't have much cash these days, what with the fur and wool. And *The Echo*, I've heard, doesn't bring in many pennies."

"It just breaks even. But we're getting by."

There had been nothing much left after the enormous extravagance of her purchase. Enough for some good secondhand farm machinery, those bits of adjacent bushland, and a little set aside for the children's education. Almost all gone.

"I would have to think about it."

"Good, good", he replied enthusiastically.

Oh, Lord, a little cash would help out now: the Lino needed parts, and there was Emily chomping at the bit to have a piano. Stephen never mentioned it, but a tractor would considerably ease his existence. More necessities, more extravagances. Why couldn't life be simpler? Things, things, things, crowding up their lives!

Though there were some books she was coveting.

But something in Jonah MacPhale's eye was on the march again. This time a different approach:

"I know you ain't a Catholic, Annie, and I don't got nothin' against micks, but sometimes they are stubborn as mules."

"Yes, sometimes they are that."

"Could you convince Steve t'sell this place?"

"My husband is a man, Jonah MacPhale, and has a mind of his own. I can promise you nothing."

He noticed her mounting a high horse. She noticed his greedy eyes. Why was he so desperate to buy?

"I don't mean t'be makin' light of a man's religion, but . . ."

"I shall never understand you Irish," she interrupted coldly, "hating and destroying each other over things you cannot see."

"Well, t'some of us there's things y'can't touch that are real nonetheless", said the metaphysical MacPhale.

She had never seen this side of him.

"Now me grandad, he was a religious type of feller. Had a bunch of cronies used t'meet of an evenin' in our parlor. I wasn't sposed t'see nothin' of course, but sometimes I'd twist meself round the bannister and watch the shenanigans. He was a real old-timer with his secret societies and a white beard down t'his gut and a fine twinkle in his eye.

"I'm a Protestant, y'know, though me dad was as republican as Parnell himself. He was a farrier and friendly with micks. Once he even borrowed a Catholic horse for King Billy's parade.

"But Grandad, he had no use for Catholics. He and his friends used t'have this big engraved scroll locked up in the closet that we wasn't sposed t'see. They read it every meetin' real low, all of 'em mumblin' the words like a prayer at church. It was an oath!"

"How do you know?"

"Grandad fergot t'lock the bugger up one night, and when they'd gone off t'bed I snuck down and pulls the thing out."

"And what did it say?"

"We shall not rest until we wade knee-deep in papist blood!"

"How ghastly!"

She almost giggled in her cup, an image going through her mind of a cohort of graybeards stalking out into the streets with their raised canes.

"Yep, papist blood!" he muttered to himself, staring at the floor with an odd little smile.

"Me dad wasn't like that. He'd as soon hammer a shoe onto mick hooves, same's a prod's, fair an' square. Now me, I'm one step better, got a little Catholic pumpin' gas fer me and another one cleanin' rooms at the motel. Fair as fair!"

"Why does it matter to you which religion they profess?"

He had no answer to that. She appeared ready to drag him into an argument he was not equipped to discuss.

"Ah well, who's t'know the answer to those hard questions? Now to return to the subject of land . . ."

But his benevolence had failed to convince.

"I think I can safely assure you right now that neither Stephen nor I am interested in parting with any of our land."

He measured her eyes. His face grew hard.

"I see", he spat, suddenly almost lean beneath the rolls. "All right, but you'll regret it!"

He stood and jerked his head good-bye.

"Strange", she said, "so strange", as she watched the dust of his car disappear around a bend in the lane.

It crossed her mind in a flash of anger that the visitor had indeed revealed the spitting image of his dead son. Complete with spit and hate, she thought cruelly.

* * *

Some months after the incident, Stephen noticed an article in the city newspaper. It was a habit of his to read these articles long after their publication, a delay caused by his overly busy summers. Winter, which it seemed to be outside the wailing window, allowed a little contemplation of the passing events of civilization.

He pushed back his wire-rim spectacles. "Here's a piece about our neck of the woods", he informed the woman. "The Prime Minister announced in Parliament that an international commission is going to survey the Columbia and Kootenay rivers with a view to flood control and harnessing them for electric power."

"Oh", she said, distracted by her daughter's hair, which she was plaiting into copper braids.

"And if this bunch decides a certain way, Anne, we're going to get our feet wet."

"Our feet wet?"

"It's a wild possibility and will probably never happen, but if worse comes to worst, this whole valley, my trapline, your land, this house, will all be under water and gone forever."

26

The years do accumulate. Like memories and old newspapers. A quarter century was a long time, but not as long as she had presumed. The tree of time was sliced up into twenty-five wheels or else a hundredweight of seasons and became measurable in this way. Through the translations of memory the past was reshaped into long, convoluted creations that were not always clear as to their meaning. But time will assist in the analysis. The woman began to understand her position, to hold a grudging affection for her exile, learning that while one may never come to love it, there are gifts that come with acceptance. She now possessed a healthy respect for manure. And for wind, which spoke gently to her but at times could rip down the greatest of the old cottonwoods behind the barn.

Her garden continued to grow as faithfully as ever. The perennials pushed and shoved for space and bloomed lasciviously into each other's tubes and hollows, thorns scratching at tendrils, runners strangling the bushes. Small wild-rose slips she had once pleaded with to grow were now thickets that could barely be held back with a hatchet. In a land limited to the somber colors of water, forest, and sky, the annuals were a welcome splash of warmth, gashing the landscape with their hot reds and pinks and oranges, zinnia and dahlia struggling out from under the bully bear-berry. In her spare moments she tried to prune back this riot of fertility among the drowsy bees or attempted to rip up the omnipresent chickweed. But there was seldom enough time for this because of her higher calling, the perennial *Echo*.

"Lordy, girl", her friend Turid L'Oraison remarked. "All that time and money and nothin' t'show fer it!"

"Not exactly", she replied from underneath a frayed straw sunbonnet.

"Such a shame, such a shame, tradin' that big pot o' gold fer a shed full o' machines and yer neighbors' curses."

"There are some who approve, Turid."

"And as many do not", she said drolly, with a butt dangling from her lip and eyes squinty from smoke. "But that wouldn't be nothin' new."

"It's a pleasure of words—of making."

"Expensive little hobby, Annie."

"Truth is always expensive."

"Oho!" said her neighbor, inspecting her dirty nails. "If it's fillersophicle yer gettin', I'd best be on my way."

"Do you see what I mean? Mention a heavy word, and people begin to look for their hats and coats."

"And horse whips!" said Turid.

Anne relaxed sufficiently to smile.

"I would look quite ridiculous running out of town with the girls of the I.O.D.E. on my heels, their buggy whips snapping after me!"

Every few years or so she was known to produce a little joke. She trotted up and down the bean rows now, twisting and turning, eluding the sting of whip or tongue, sweat rolling down the creases of her eyes. Or was it tears that salted the calico dance of flapping apron and run stocking. Turid roared her notorious belly laugh, in which the actual belly was fully involved.

"Hear us when we cry to Thee, for those in peril of the I.O.D.E.!" said the prancing burlesque queen, tromping the plantain and chicory with her holey running shoes. Collapsing finally in the sunlight. Laughter, they found, could stitch together the fabric that had been torn by lies.

They went inside, sated, for a glass of water and came out again drinking their giggles. They sat together beside the spears of mint that grew by the rotting porch. Hummingbirds attacked the droopy blossoms, dill and basil scents teased from the herb patch. Time was a muddy trickle. The two women slipped into that absence of words that heat and an accumulation of shared years will permit. Though the older one, the visitor, was tormented by a thought.

"It ain't so much what ya say in those articles, dear, as it is what people think they're readin'."

"I know."

"People could accuse you of thinkin' you was the only one in town knows the truth."

"They could accuse and be wrong, as both of us know from the past."

"They could think yer too . . . proud", she inserted delicately.

"On that point, Turid, they might be quite correct. Quite correct."

Which was not precisely true in the way it was meant. A strange word, *pride*, she thought, a strange language, her native tongue. Using one word to describe something and its opposite. Pride could be that healthy respect for what one truly is. It could also mean arrogance. The woman accused herself privately of many flaws of character, including the vice of conceit. Signs of this were ever present, though they might be only the bad seed flung on the good soil of her soul. What mattered most was not that it was there; what mattered was the weeding.

The problem entered in when she attempted to weed her neighbors' gardens through the tools of print. True, the risk of arrogance was great when one determined to set another straight. But they did not have to buy it or read it.

"Journalism is democratic", she was fond of saying. It was a useful remark. Enraged detractors were usually stopped dead in their tracks by it.

A strange calling, this. She had become poorer because of her pot of gold, divested now of many pointless pleasures. She was richer, too, stripped down to the treasure buried in the field of herself. That she had not yet fully understood this was only a problem of time. Life itself assured that she would learn to re-peat the joke properly.

Turid had long ago found that comedies are all the better for a tinge of tragedy, which can be chewed up with buns over coffee, though they do make a girl wonder. Annie's particular trials struck her as being a bit more than average but largely self-inflicted. Didn't she have a heap to be proud of? A daughter at school in England with the auntie, the son in forestry up north, and of course, Ash!

She remembered how on visitors' day he had stood before his desk, inspected by thirty staring kids and a scattering of parents. What a picture he was in his tweed suit and oxblood oxfords, a necktie and purple diamond socks showing under the cuffs of pants he had grown out of. He was chalking something on the blackboard in neat, white letters.

MR. DELANEY
GRADES 6, 7, 8

From the back he was a sight t'make yer heart thump, but when he turned around there was that face. Poor boy. Ash Delaney, that perfect alabaster infant she had pulled from his mother's body, a *mister* now, with purposes.

"I hear yer eldest lad is a right fine teacher."

"I'm happy to hear it", said the woman evenly, she who had wept and bled for the compliment.

He was no longer at home. He lived in the teacherage, a bachelor apartment attached to the school. He was a man, it seemed, with memories, things to attend to, and the opening specimen box of his future.

Stephen had asked him if he wanted the farm. No, he did not want the farm, he had replied, perhaps taking a good hard look at his father's life.

"You have stopped attending Mass, Ashley", his mother said to him one Sunday over roast beef. He came visiting on Sundays, for which she was grateful.

"Yeah, I've stopped. There seems to be so little point."

Stephen was hurt and puzzled by this, wondering how his son could possibly survive without some religion, be it worship of God or faith in the natural laws of the earth. The farm, then the Church . . . what would he jettison next?

"I have my books", their son said by way of explanation. "There are some very interesting men writing things now out of France who feel the way I do. Camus and Sartre and other guys . . . course you wouldn't have heard of them."

They hadn't.

So he, too, was swept down the river of life, gone from her hands. The house was empty these days, save for the man. And often wholly empty when he was off trapping. She was left alone at those times, with the animals and the garden, with pools of lamplight in the evening when crickets rioted or rain struck the rusting tin roof in torrents steaming in the heat.

She would rock in the kitchen and stare, trying to recall what it had been like in this very room so many years ago when she and the boy Maurice had burst in upon the delirious Centaur. She shook herself and turned to the future, to other tasks.

She attempted to read some of the books that the years of motherhood had delayed but found herself unable to concentrate. She would stand in the doorway looking out into the night, then would turn finally to her pen and paper and the abiding *Echo*. It, at least, was hers.

THE SWIFTCREEK ECHO　AUGUST 15, 1950
It is no accident that American Senator Richard Neuberger in a recent speech to the Chamber of Commerce ended his address with the words, "if you Canadians continue to delay building of water storage, we shall have to consider your behaviour an unfriendly act between nations."

The growing impatience of the United States concerning our hemming and hawing over the proposed water plan is most evident in these remarks. Yet the problem, as I have noted in editorials for the past year, is not so simple. Involved are provincial and state rights and the federal governments of two nations. There is private as well as public land to be destroyed for the purposes of a certain kind of progress that has not been fully justified.

There are, of course, arguments for a continental sharing of resources, especially in the world now materialising before our very eyes. The conflict in Korea is a sign of the struggle to come. And, despite its failings, the American Republic remains a human and free society that shall be in need of the strengths we can share.

But we must be cautious that in strengthening an ally we are not decimating our own civilisation. Though smaller in numbers, we have learned unique lessons from our portion of the earth, wisdom that might be easily overlooked by our southern neighbours in their desire to make us their water boy.

We now have the skills and ability to produce energy without devastating many thousands of square miles of good farms and forests. There are towns and mines in the Kootenays powered by water turbines built at the turn of the century and still operating today. The mines at Coffee Creek and Silver King operated for twenty-five years without major repairs or a single shutdown. The reason: engineers built them with care and genius, using the materials at hand. There are countless possibilities for such installations, and surely there is enough spine left in this country to harness the power of our creeks and falls without a wholesale slaughter of a considerable portion of the province's good soil.

If you and I as citizens see a situation developing in which our rights will be trampled in the name of a hasty, desperate progress, then we must fight now. If we do not, then it is without doubt that a portion of civilisation will die.

And so in the clash and cry of battle, the woman began to be who she was. She learned finally that to fight, one must know the enemy and must love passionately what is to be preserved.

She would wander around in the autumn light, after evening chores, her husband snoring in a chair with a blanket of crumpled newspaper. He was old, it seemed. She would hang her apron on a hook and go out softly into the atmosphere of whip-poorwill and thrush, slapping mosquitoes and smelling the balsamed air. She would rise up the western field toward the cemetery where two of her unknown children lay. She stood and wondered who they might have been. Paint was chipping from the crosses, the fence bowing out from decades of wind and snow. In the silence she embraced herself. She was a fullness of years waiting to be emptied. She was an emptiness waiting to be filled.

She came back toward the house and wandered between the order and chaos of her vegetable rows, consoled by the messages of the earth.

"The manure is beautiful this year", she said, smelling a handful that had become rich humus. "Good for the root crops, though I would be wise to leave the beans alone!"

And flung the sanctified dirt beneath a plant.

Many times she had awaited the attack of terror that had afflicted her earlier life. It had come, of course. But she had ceased to be ruined by it. She could not have explained what that silent deadly battle was: An atom of antimatter attempting to destroy flesh through its weakest point, the mind? Bad digestion? Or were there indeed presences that craved her soul, whose malice took the form of shadows? Perhaps, in the end, it was only a little child, Anna, crying out for a mother who had never stopped to explain her absence? She might have apologized for it and called it suffering. At times she suspected it was some abysmal testing or a forging by fire and anvil, so that her soul, her character, or whatever this thing was that was *her* might receive its true form. And this form was hidden in the heart of a mysterious love permeating the world. She simply did not know. It was equally possible that she was mentally ill.

She had desired to know many things and had been given

399

mystery upon mystery. She had longed for normality, content-ment, a permanent hearth, and had been given exile instead. Its roots were so deep in her that she had bequeathed it to her eldest son. For years, not suspecting what she was doing, she had sought a retreat from the battle, desired to have the comfort of humble human happiness and acceptance. It had taken most of her life to realize that she would never find refuge in this world, that she belonged to a small wandering race of protesters crying out against the extinguishing of light. In her sixth decade she was coming to know this, a woman weeding in the dusk among her flowers and peas.

PART THREE

The Sword

27

Journal Entry:

Swiftcreek, B.C., 11 Nov. 52

Wind from the north. Colder today.

My first grandchild arrived home from McBride Hospital this morning. Sarah carried him into the teacherage with all the grace of a queen. Ash is so proud it fills me with joy and increases my hope that his bitterness will someday be completely healed.

I drove Ashley's pickup. It was acting surly again, and the mud-ruts had frozen hard; we bounced and lurched all fifty miles. I ached for Sarah. Ash held her and the child as best he could while I wrestled with the wheel. I was worried about bleeding, but she appears to have survived without serious trouble. Wanda was waiting for us when we arrived. She had gone in by herself and made a cake and tea. God knows we needed it. When she saw her mother waiting there to greet us, Sarah's face doubled its emanation of light.

Wanda is only temporarily released from Essondale. I believe they wish to see if she can still function in what is known as a "normal" environment. But it is obvious she is not well and fades in and out of reality. I confess that my heart sank when I saw her. A mixture of reasons: perhaps we who stagger along the borderlines of sanity have a fear of being pulled over ourselves. It is curious that most people are quite afraid of the emotionally ill. They are tragic, upsetting, draining. They condemn us to a realisation of our helplessness, our fragility.

I was jealous too. I wanted them all to myself. I had not yet been permitted to hold the baby, but when Sarah saw her mother sitting there with a distracted look, playing with her hands nervously, she went over and knelt beside the woman.

"Mum," she said, "here's my baby. Would you like to hold him?"

It was then that I understood the quality of my daughter-in-law. She had gone to the heart of the matter. I would always be needed, competent, respected. I have everything. Wanda, whom I so instantly and deeply resented, possesses nothing. Not even herself.

Wanda's eyes were confused. She would not take the baby at first. She looked away; terror of her own unworthiness was written on her face. But Sarah insisted, smiling into her mother's eyes with such trust and compassion that I was very moved. My ugly emotions vanished. We were each united in a moment of perfect joy as Wanda's eyes cleared and she opened her arms to receive the child. She beamed down upon him with a toothless grin that would have appeared crazed were it not so very tender.

"Mary", she whispered.

"No, Mum", Sarah said gently, stroking the hair back from her mother's forehead. "He's a boy, Mum, and his name's Nathaniel."

It was at this point that I realised Ashley had been watching me. I understood immediately that he had been reading my reactions. I was tempted to stiffen, to turn away, because I knew he had judged the movements of my small, mean heart. But, amazingly, he looked into my eyes with a great calm, and I might even say tenderness, and smiled the most loving smile I have had from him since he was a boy.

* * *

Swiftcreek, 30 Sept. 53

Stephen and Thaddaeus were all day getting firewood with Jan Tarnowski. Sarah is ill with the flu. So I have my grandson for the day. He is sleeping now in the old log bed his father was born on. Yet I am not destined to possess him, for no sooner had Ashley dropped him off than Wanda arrived for a visit. The other grandmother! She had walked alone on the bush trail from Tobac's, all ten miles of it.

Her improvement in a year is remarkable. There is little slid-ing in and out of reality. And, thankfully, she no longer mistakes us for individuals from her past. Occasionally, there is a sparrow-like smile, and she will even make a shy comment about the weather or the state of her major concern in life, Nathaniel Delaney.

He has learned to walk from chair to chair in the past month, and I hazard a guess that soon he will be careening unaided across the floor on his own two sturdy legs. He is not much like my babies, though his hair and eyes are regulation dark. That, however, could be as much Indian as black Celt. He is narrow of shoulder like the Tobacs, thin and brown-skinned. Cocoa-coloured in the summer, burnt sienna in winter. A real little mixture. I love him to the point of distraction, as we all do. Everything stops when he enters a room, and the mite knows it. He is the sweet crisp fruit of time, wiping away so much of the pain from which he has sprung.

The morning went well. Usually I want to fill up the vacuum between W. and me with the noise of my thoughts. What often comes out is a gush of intellectual nonsense or a grab bag of clichés, anything to convince myself that communication is happening. Today, however, I experimented with silence and found it strangely peaceful. Wanda seemed more relaxed too. She spoke from time to time in her slurred English or sang to the baby in Slavey. She tried to tell me little things, about how good a man Thaddaeus is, about this and that. I suppressed my dreadful habit of translating her own words back to her complete with analysis. She looked at me several times. She is knitting a sweater so large it must be a Christmas present for her son-in-law, my Ashley.

By midmorning I realized with a jump that during this plethora of mothering I had completely forgotten to get my editorial in to the typesetter at the shop. I tore off my apron, made apologies to Wanda, and was about to waken Nathaniel, when she said, "I'll look after the boy. Let him sleep."

It was as if a knife pierced my heart. I had a sudden hallucination of her hurting the child. What if she should have a regression? How well was she, really?

I started to protest with a number of lame excuses, but she looked at me with complete understanding.

"It's all right", she said very gently, sadly. "You can go; we'll be all right."

What could I do? Destroy her? Risk the child? Two impossible choices. But something prompted me to make an act of trust, to go, to hope and believe. I was out the door in a flash. I must admit that never before in my life have I driven to town and back so quickly. The horse glared at me resentfully; he was lathered when we returned. When I burst into the house I found Wanda and the boy together on the couch, completely engrossed in his little animal books. Luckily, she didn't see the relief on my face. I am not a good liar.

* * *

Swiftcreek, 8 Dec. 56

A cold, dry autumn. Wanda returned to the hospital, casting a certain gloom over us all. Yet life persists, an oak flourishing in winter. Nathaniel talking a blue streak, asking where his grandmother has gone and finding none of the explanations acceptable. At four he is the proverbial questioner. Is it genetics or environment?

Thankfully, there has been much to distract us. Stephen, Thaddaeus, and Ashley have nailed down the last shake on Ashley's new house. It is a stout dwelling, built of rock and pine, not to mention a great deal of Irish inventiveness. N. has been underfoot for months, falling down excavations, tripping over lumber, bothering the men with a thousand questions, so eager to be one of them. They are very patient.

The house is completed just ahead of the snow. It promises to be a severe winter if the berries, geese, and the thick fur on the squirrels are any indication. Thaddaeus insists that they are infallible.

I walked through the birches by the river today. It is overwhelming there. The earth is stripped down to simple designs.

The land has become a visual haiku. Sun on the fretwork of twigs. Blood droplets of dried rose hips clinging to the bushes. The chatter of the creek against trimmings of ice. Hoar frost on barbed wire. A skiff of snow. My breath a white cloud like a departing soul.

I am coming to see that it is not so much a question of finding the right place, the right time, the ideal marriage. Neither life nor happiness hinges upon such things. It is wholly within. It is response to what is given. It is choice.

There was a small bird playing in the creek. I was impressed by its courage. It is not a species I recognise. Smaller than a robin, slightly larger than a sparrow, upturned tail. I was amazed at the way it dove and splashed so gleefully on the ice. It was a form of play, perhaps even a dance of joy. Surely, it should have been dead of shock. But no, it flew off into a safe tree when it spied me, leaving behind a ravishing tracery of warbling notes.

I have always been beguiled by birds. As if there was much they would tell me if they could, but they are only permitted to bear witness with their lives, their song.

What of Wanda's song? What of my two missing children? What of Nigel, dead these past twenty years? He was too fragile, his song too refined for this predatory world. I have romanticised him, of course. He was a disturbed young man. But the song was there. It was! I recall the time he quoted from the *Divine Comedy*:

> O human race, born to fly upward,
> Why at a little wind do you so fall?

* * *

12 December 56

A strange day. I thought of my crippled priest all morning. It has been years since he has come to mind.

Just before dawn I rose and put the oatmeal on to simmer while Stephen went out to feed the animals. At once I experienced an irresistible urge to go walking up the old logging cut in the woods east of the barn. Really an irrational impulse, considering how much work I had to do today. I actually trotted there, as if my being were joyfully pushed by a benevolent wind. As I ascended the trail an enormous raven made several soaring passes low over my head. I felt the wake of its wing-beat, I heard the great black sails flapping. It was looking to left and to right as if searching for something. Ordinarily I dislike these noisy carrion birds, but you can't help but admire their size, their colour (for which they make no apologies), and their dedication to being lords of the wasteland. Today I was struck by the majesty of their flight. They are like desert cenobites. If only they were more silent the metaphor would be complete. When the bird had gone I turned for home quickly, as if the "wind" had died within me. Yet this too was curiously peaceful.

Didn't a raven feed a starving prophet in the wilderness? Am

I a prophet? If so, then I am a blind, wounded one, groping like everyone else through the thick smoke of our times. How can I speak of what I do not know? But perhaps I do know and have not yet admitted the knowledge to that *tyrannos* of reason and ego I call my mind.

I cannot speak like a theologian or like my broken hermit, who has seen and knows. But the presence who comes to me at times is so gentlemanly. He does not hammer for entrance and possession like the shadow presence. No, this spirit is love, and it has utter respect for my freedom to reject it. I have tested it a number of times. It is silence too. And in rare moments it takes a visible form: I see it in the spiral of the lark ascending, the fierce descent of the hawk, the spaces between musical notes, and the purity in Nathaniel's concentration as he invents something with twigs and string. I believe I would have died in one way or another had I not been able to make (babies, ideas, words, moments of meeting). In creating we are made strong, we sort order out of the chaos of existence. We learn to play again, like the child. The bird, too, knows how to play. She rejoices completely in her song, in her dance upon the frozen waters, in abandoned seeds discovered on the snow. She is at home in homelessness.

I stood by my desk at *The Echo* today and felt the full impact of what my life has been and yet may be. Is it possible that a failed poetess, a lapsed child, may finally become what she does not dare to define—a truth-sayer. If self-appointed roles of prophecy are distasteful to the observer, then even more distasteful and downright tragic is a calling abandoned, a gift extinguished.

I will tell no one. Let any who read this journal after my death draw their own conclusions about my sanity. We are all a little mad, and if my madness allows me to sing and to dance, then I shall not be afraid. I shall be poor and possess nothing. I shall be happily mad and home at last.

As I stood there thinking this, I was filled with a most trembling stillness, so gentle, so good, like fresh bread, warm and steaming on the sideboard, like certain kinds of white light through glass in March. There were no seraphic wings, no heavenly trumpets, no words in my mind. It was very simple, just being and embrace. I was thirsting to leap into the air, but the printer's devil in the next room would have been scandalised.

For a brief burning moment I saw the depth of my call. In the dance there is an unknowing that strips us of arrogance. My powerlessness is necessary. There is much truth to be said. The world is crowding up with despair, with lies, with power. For most people, not only "*Gott*" is dead, but man too is dead. The reign of fear, the day of fire approaches.

I gathered my papers about me as best I could. With a mad grin to the poor devil I was out the door fast, for there was a meal to be made and an article to write.

Summer 1960

28

When partridge flew down the slopes to hunt in the dew and pigeons flew up against the sheet of dawn, the valley rested dark and serene in the lee of the unborn sun. They slept, the people, not yet awake to their lordship of creation and their follies. The birds would pipe the matins of warble and trill, like bells summoning the world to the morning praise of wisdom—but the humans did not attend.

On some mornings, however, the child Nathaniel Delaney would wake before all others and rise into the light spilling through the jumbled hair and elbows of his brothers and sisters. He would walk quietly through the sleeping house and out through the kitchen door to the back porch. There he would stand shivering in pajamas to gaze over the fences and chicken coops, ashcans and woodpiles of the village, inhale the air, and listen to the wind and the crowing of the roosters. He would hear the tock-tock-tockas of the woodpecker and observe the wing-beat of Mr. Tarnowski's pigeons wheeling in arcs, white, now black, now white again as they passed in and out of the shadow of the mountain.

Barely audible was the muted note of a distant piano announcing that someone else was awake at this early hour. It was his friend, Mr. Tarnowski, who lived three chicken runs away. Oh, Jan Tarnowski was not a kid, but he wasn't as old as Grandma Annie, who was very old, or his grandpa Steve, who was older still. He was Jan's friend because no one else would be his friend. Everybody thought Jan was crazy, but it was only because he didn't have many words and because his wife and baby had been burned in an oven by a bad man named Hitler. Nathaniel was a listener, and people told him things, the real things, the important things. He knew that Jan was not crazy.

He taught the boy secrets, such as when to transplant wood's lilies or the fast method of gutting a chicken. He showed him how to butcher rabbits, too, which he snared behind the cabbage patch. The boy held back a lump in his throat when Jan smashed the back of the skull with a lead pipe while the rabbit dangled upside down by its hind legs, and, oh, it was awful if the first blow didn't knock it right out because its screams were like a baby and your hands would shake with the badness of it.

"Jan," he said timidly, "wouldn't it be better to let the rabbits just go into the woods and be happy?"

"Maybe you no like dat scream of *kruliczyk*, eh, Tanny?"

"I don't like it."

"If I let dis leettle *zając* go inta dat woods he get caught by wolf or eagle and he scream lots. Only den you no hear im scream! Right?"

"It's better we don't do it. Let the wild things do it. We aren't wild things, are we?"

There was a long, slow silence while Jan peeled back the white pelt and ruby droplets sprayed onto the snow.

"We got to eat, boy. We got to eat."

The boy's silence was loud.

"Animal, he's not a porrson, he's a dumb beast!" Then he whispered "*Dziękuję*", thanks, to the next rabbit and smacked another spurt of blood out the nostrils onto the white garments of the yard.

But he showed him other things, such as how to whittle a whistle from willow or play "chopsticks" on the piano in his living room. His wondrous living room. It was a fascinating place for a boy, with its blue glass candy dishes full of mints and the portraits of Polish generals above painted cavalry charges, bronze eagles and medals on chests, and men dying beneath a red and white battle banner. There were icons, too, the somber charged presences beneath which there was always a candle burning as testimony of the power.

Jan's house was made of tin. He had assembled this contraption himself, put it together from sheets of rusty, corrugated roofing salvaged from the mill. It was snug and dry and quite sophisticated inside. Jan was content. He had no social aspirations. He was the gardener at the CN station park, a vocation of dirt and flowers that had left him healthy and brown-haired in his middle age. The job was ideal for him, as the winter buried his work beneath several feet of snow, and he was free to make his strange feasts of sausage and fermented cabbage, with sips of vodka like gasoline. He would drink and rock on his chair as he stared at the cracked photographs of a woman and child beneath the icon of the Mother of God.

If the boy urged him, he would play the piano. Jan was not greatly gifted, but sometimes he said, "Oh, Tanny, when I make the piano it is my heart get born again and my Itsak is not die and Gott comes here in dis room!"

His fingers bent sideways like a deformed chicken foot. But he used their edges to hammer out tunes.

"Does it hurt you, Jan?" he asked once in the beginning.

"A little bit it hurt my finger. I don't care."

"What happened to your fingers?"

"My fingers get broke by communist soldiers for pray Gott."

"Did they work for Hitler?"

"No, boychick, Hitler one kinda devil, and communist nother kinda devil."

"Oh."

Nathaniel was glad that Jan always had new secrets, as if he saved the better ones for rainy days or the steady progress of a friendship that might last, with luck, forever.

"Tanny, how old you now?"

"I'm seven and a half."

"You pretty big boy. This year I let you help me make my *enduvdevorldkluk.*"

"What is a en-duv-de-vorl . . . ?"

"*Enduvdevorldkluk.*"

"Yes. What is it?"

"Dis is very important secret. You no tell nobody. It's a secret for last days. We be here for dat, you an' me."

Jan took him by the shoulder out into the back yard. It was a maze of rotting piles of firewood, heaps of scrap metal, gears, wires, rabbit cages, dozens of canyons that wound between the teetering blocks of decades-old gray lumber, palaces of empty forty-five gallon drums, and three rusting automobiles from the 1930s—the latter bequeathed by the previous owner of the property. Much of the material had been hauled from the dump. Grandpa lent Jan the horse and cart whenever there was some good cast-off that he wanted to salvage for his projects.

"If I show you what I making for de end of de vorld, you promise no tell nobody."

"I promise, Jan."

"Good boychick."

In the center of the maze, invisible from any quarter, was a pylon of black railroad ties, interlocked, stacked to the height of eight feet. Scattered around it were wooden crates containing an assortment of clockwork parts.

"One time few years ago, I hear a voice from Gott. He tell me to make de *enduvdevorldkluk.* Den I say to him, why you want me make dis ting? He say, Jan, you hurt from de bad mans in de vurld, from de bad mans in de var like nobody in dis country. Dey not know what's come on de vorld soon. You start now and make de *enduvdevorldkluk.* When devil comes and it look like he gonna win everyting, dat de time Gott vill tell me, now's de time, Jan, now you ring de *enduvdevorldkluk* and make warning everybody. Get ready everybody! Gott is coming back for trow devil into lake of fire. But first, many people die, *many, many* people die—because dey no understand!"

"But I'd understand, Jan. I know I would."

"*Tak*, you'd understand dat. Wit my broke hands I be not make little parts of de kluk. I make big parts. You be my hands for de little parts. Okay?"

"Okay!" the boy shouted gleefully.

In the mornings, then, Nathaniel would often waken and run out into the dawn to listen to the music of the seasons as hungrily as the old man pushed his mystic rhythms from the untuned Heintzman.

"It's not like my beautifool piano get stole in Varsava", he would apologize. "Gone, gone, boornt in de var, but she's goot enough!"

The wooden medallion carved in the front board was a face, a brooding visage absorbed in the sound and fury of creation.

"You see dis guy, Tanny, dis is not Beethoven, dis is not Mozart, dis is not dos Germans. Dis is Chopin."

The boy nodded.

"Tanny, what you wanna be when you big like man?" Jan said to him when he was nine or ten years old.

"I think I wanna be a guy who tells stories to people . . . hmmmmm . . . or maybe I wanna be a guy who plays the piano all day."

"No, no, no, no, no!" said Jan ferociously. "You be teacher like daddy. Or be newspaper like gramma. You no be artist. Artist poor."

The thought of poverty or insecurity made Jan's face turn red. His own reduced state was acceptable only because the work was seasonal and he had chosen it. But fear and unknowing were the worst, and he tried to convince the boy of this.

He would say, "Tanny, you make monieee!" His face absolutely convinced, his bent index finger pointing and falling through the air before the boy's eyes like a message from God.

"You make monieeeee! Monieeee, Tanny! Make *monieeeeee!*" And his fingers would rub invisible coins as his voice rose to a pitch.

"If you got monieee, Tanny, no bad mans is boorn your vife an' your babies."

The face of Jan. It was so often involved in calamities. His dire predictions about the future of nations were just as impassioned as his anger at the rising price of bread. But his voice grew quiet when telling about the immolation of his past. He wept only once in front of the boy—when he showed him the photographs of Sara and Itsak.

"My Mum's name is Sarah", said Nathaniel.

"My vife's name Sara", said Jan. "You see, boychick, Sara there, Sarah here. Badmans there, badmans here. Boorning there, soon come boorning here."

Even though he appeared to have been carved from cherry wood by some clever and humorous artisan, his eyes were momentarily extinguished.

"Miney Gott", he said to the boy who sat dangling his legs from a stool in the kitchen. "Miney Gott, boychick, you no be soldier! No, never, you go straight to hell, moorder babies and go straight to hell like *devil!*" The last word was shouted.

It was not always clear what Jan was saying, but you knew that he meant it.

There was an uncommon amount of storytelling in Nathaniel's circle of people. He had two grandfathers as well, and in their different ways they could spin a tale to make you sit up straight and take notice. Grandpa Thaddaeus was always ready with a new one if you badgered him long enough. He would drop his axe and set you, when you were little, on the chopping block beside him. The exploits of *Eena* the beaver and *Kalakala* the bird were many and varied and filled with the dangers of the forest. Often the boy rode his pony back to town with his ears pricked up to every rustle in the bushes along the way, for there was, he knew, the anger of *Siamitchwoot*, the grizzly bear who had scarred his daddy a long time ago.

Grandpa Steve was a storyteller, too, with his little people and the banshees that lifted the hair on the back of your neck. He liked best the adventures of a boy who lived by the sea and tended his family sheep on the side of a mountain. This boy was always meeting strange folk who hopped in and out from one world to another. More delightful terror. His two grandfathers were alike in that way, black and white but carved from the same tree. His grandma, on the other hand, told a very nice little tale about the adventures of Rupert and Ameliaranne, and Coco the monkey, who rode on the back of elephants in a land far, far away. Elephants were as big as moose, he knew, and moose were big. He had seen one with its blue tongue lolling. Grandpa Thaddee cut it out and sent it home to Mum. And a liver as big as a dog. Nathaniel had another grandma, too, whom he visited a long time ago when they went to Vancouver. She had smiled at him, touching his face and singing. She did not talk to you or tell you stories, but she could sing in her beautiful little voice: *one little two little three little....*

His dad did not tell stories. No, his dad told him ideas and facts about places. He was the principal of the grade school and taught grades five and six besides. Nathaniel had become his student that fall, skipping two grades.

"Nathaniel," Mr. Delaney would ask, "name the capitals of the provinces starting in order from east to west." And so he would do, but if he didn't know the answers it would have gone better for him had he been somebody else's boy.

"Nathaniel," Mr. Delaney would ask, "can you recite the poem you were asked to memorize?" Everyone in the class would snicker behind their hands, but their eyes would show.

"Yes, sir."

"Begin then."

> O, inspired giant! shall we e'er behold,
> In our own time
> One fit to speak your spirit on the wold,
> Or seize your rhyme?

"Who wrote this poem?" his father interrupted.

"Thomas D'Arcy McGee, sir."

"Very good. And who is this McGee, can you tell me that?"

"He was a very famous Canadian who was assass . . . ass . . . ass . . ."

The class exploded. At the sound of the forbidden word, giggles battered the ramparts of order.

"Assassinated!" said his father.

"Assassinated."

"Correct. And what else?"

"He was an Irishman, a politician."

"Excellent. Now can you tell me the meaning of the word *wold*?"

Silence.

"No, sir."

"Then it can't be said with accuracy that you know this poem, can it?"

"Uh, I don't think so."

"A wold is an upland plain or rolling stretch of land devoid of trees. Grade six, you can write that in your notebooks. Nathaniel, you can stay after class."

"Sir", said the boy later when they were alone.

"It's all right, Tan. You can call me Dad after four o'clock."

The boy squirmed.

"Do you understand why I expect so much more from you than from the other students?"

He shook his head.

"You have been gifted with a very good mind, son, and I

won't have it wasted, even if we are hundreds of miles from a museum or a library worthy of the name. Everything you have, everything you are, has been given to you. Someone else has suffered for it, and what you do with it will be your return of thanks to them."

He went out laden with guilt.

In his secret place he found solace. Above the house, at the edge of town, a rocky outcropping of his grandfather's mountain jutted from the main body of stone. High up, it was a deserted place of wind-twisted balsam and pine, of marmots and brighter light. There were some irregular folds here, and behind one of them was a cave. He had discovered it while roaming several summers before. Over the years he had dragged up a considerable amount of gear and crammed it through the crawl space into the hole. Candles and cans of beans, pots, pans, boys' adventure stories, and even a discarded battery radio, which never produced more than static. The cave was the size of a small bedroom, and he could just stand upright in it. Originally, he found it fouled with bat droppings and the murky scent of a mammal's lair. He claimed it as his own immediately, shovelled out the guano and the dusty brittle bones, covered the entrance with a stone, and camouflaged the approaches with small bushes that he had transplanted. They hid his secret completely.

No one knew about it. If his mother ever questioned him concerning his great absences, he would merely say he had been hiking, which was true. But it was such a long climb to the treeline that he was seldom free to make the journey. Sometimes on Saturdays he went, and during the summer he was allowed to be gone for days at a time if the dog went with him.

"He's just a boy, Ash," his mother said, "and I don't like him all alone on that mountain without us knowin' where he is."

"Sarah, if we live our days in fear of what might happen, it won't be much of a life."

"Can we let him risk the bears, Ash?"

"Scars heal, and you come to live with them. But you can't live in fear."

Oh, her husband had a good point there, thought Sarah. She might just as well wrestle with the likes of a bobcat as match wills with one of those Delaneys. They were always going off somewhere alone. As if they desired it. Well, she had packed around a number of troubles on her back all by herself in her younger days, and she had enough of it. People were made to stick together, and didn't the Good Book say just that very thing! But there was no fighting her married kin, least of all her husband. *Stubborn as billy goats*, she thought. It had always been easier to wear them down with kindness than to lock horns: you'd have nothing more than a sore head to show for all your butting.

Even their courtship had been like that. Him pulling away, coming back, running off again, never a word of explanation. Just that hurt look in his eyes that everybody said was full of hate but only she could rightly read. The Savior knew what a long fight it was to convince the man that she really did love him.

He had been so angry about his scars, about the war, and about what he called *Pop's God*. Well, that Lord was her own, too, same's the old Irishman's, and He could do a powerful lot of wearing down on that stubborn Ash Delaney.

Long, long ago they went walking in the forest, and the light was spilling between the high branches. Everything alive was singing that day. But Ashley's mind was dark and his heart was burning in him, she knew—she could feel it. He was leaning toward her arm just beyond the edge of touching, looking straight ahead.

"Sarah, could a girl like you ever love a fellow like me?"

Her heart stopped. *Yes, yes, yes*, Ashley. *Yes!* She was about to say it, but her mouth would not open.

He misread her silence, and his face twisted up more than usual. He strode on ahead.

"Ash", she called.

"Forget it!" he said and began to run. The underbrush was thick, and he was stumbling over deadfall. She, nimbler, darting like a fawn through the saplings, overtook him, caught him by the suspenders, and swung him around. He tripped and fell into a drift of leaves.

Now he was furious.

"You, you . . ." he sputtered, sitting up.

She knelt beside him, smiling. She took up a leaf and began to spin it in her fingers.

He stared at her and mounted his high English horse:

"You may think it extremely amusing, Sarah, to break a man's heart, then throw him into a pile of leaves . . ."

She began to laugh her laugh, covering her mouth as tears of hilarity spilled over the brim.

He smiled against his will.

They were quiet after a while, neither looking. She twirled the stem of leaf in which millions of veins were illuminated by light.

"Ash", she whispered.

"Yeah?"

"Could a fellow like you love a girl like me?"

And then—no, not then but later—he touched her face. He forgot to cringe before his own image reflected in her eyes.

"I'm a plain girl, Ash."

"Neither of us is too pretty, Sarah", he said solemnly, barely breathing.

She had expected a courtly lie, but it seemed he had no use for such things.

"But the insideness of you, Sarah. You, *you* are beautiful."

From that moment he had never run again.

On the day they were married, Father Andrei came out of nowhere and tied them together forever. What a scene they made: Ash with his awful wounds, a priest with a limp and a few scars of his own, and she.

Mrs. Delaney made a beautiful white dress for her, full of lace and tiny pearls, oh, the most beautiful dress in the world. A gown for a princess, and she wore it like a hair shirt, for she knew it was so beautiful that it turned her plainness into ugliness. Yes, on that day they were the ugliest couple in the whole wide world. And the happiest. Now this amazing little boy they had made together. The delight of her heart. Just like his daddy, running off alone through crik and holler, never a word of explanation.

"Bye, Mum", he would shout, with a knapsack full of her robbed larder. Off through the leaves in the light to his grandfather's mountain. It was there that Ash had been nearly killed by the bear. No, she must not let herself worry. That indestructible old man was up there from July to September with his sheep. If there was ever any danger, the boy could call to him by a relay of echoes.

Nathaniel's mother did not know about the cave. It was his private place, an inner vault to which he could withdraw to ponder the small and large educations that life persists in giving. He had gone there when they returned from the Vancouver trip where he met his singing grandma who was sick and looked away but touched his cheek. He had come once after a bully's beating and the time the colt died. And in later years, after Jan moved to Swiftcreek, Nathaniel's trips to the mountain became more frequent.

The accounts the immigrant gave of his sufferings contained wonder and dread. Though Nathaniel absorbed them calmly, images of chaos were pressed into his consciousness like fingerprints into warm clay. He accumulated a variety of imprints at the feet of the old man:

"Hitler was devil!" cried Jan one day. "Stalin was devil! And soldier moorder baby got devil!"

"What you mean, Jan?"

"Oh miney Gott, whole world gonna hell. Devils everywhere, Tanny!"

The boy shivered.

"Dad, what's Jan mean when he's always talkin' about devils?"

"Devils, eh?" said his father with a sarcastic look. After thinking he said, "Evil's just a part of the mind, son. Like a shadow. You have to embrace it, hug it to take away its power over you. There's really no such thing as good or evil, except what we say is good or evil. Understand?"

"No."

"Suppose you're feeling deep down afraid, but you don't know about what. Ever feel like that?"

"Yeah."

"Well, you fall asleep and you dream of a snake, right? Then you kill the snake in your dream. You've given the fear a face, and you know what you have to do. You run, or you hit it with a stick, or you tame it—maybe you even befriend it."

"Grandma, tell me about devils", he asked the next time he saw her.

"Devils?" she said, furrowing her brow. "There are spirits abroad in the world, and I've met a few of the nastier ones. But most of the devils in this world sit behind big desks and make decisions all day long."

This was not much more helpful than his father's analysis.

Then he asked his grandfather Thaddaeus, who in answer was silent for many minutes.

"My people known for a long time about bad spirits", he said slowly. "Seems like nobody wants to believe in them no more. But I seen one."

Nathaniel leaned forward.

"One time at Kamloops a friend an' me got drunk with this guy, I don't know him. I never see him before. This guy he's real friendly like and comes from the States or somewhere. He's pretendin' he's gettin' drunk same as us, but not really. I seen him outa the corner of my eye put somethin' in my beer, my friend's beer too, little pill. I'm too damned stewed t'care an' I think it's a joke, maybe. So I drink it down. About fifteen, twenty minutes later everythin' starts t'go crazy, walls swayin' and meltin', weird voices, and this other guy's face like a skull. All of a sudden, I see the room fadin' just like a candle runnin' out of air in a jar. The light starts t'go out, slow. This big black shape comes in the window and drowns all the lights, and it's a mouth and it's gonna crush me in its jaws. This thing is real, Tanny. Like, my body is just this drunk guy sittin' at a table, with a bottle in his hand, but my spirit is on the edge of hell. One more second and I be crazy for good. Worse than Grandma. I'm so scared I wanna scream but can't scream. Frozen. My spirit gonna get eaten. Just then my friend stands up an' he yells loud, *Jesus!* At first I think he's swearin', but I see he's scared too, and he ain't swearin', he's *prayin'*. It's happenin' t'him too, and this other guy his face is a wolverine.

"*Jesus!* my friend yells again. An then I tell you Tan, strangest thing in my life, this black cloud just sucks itself out the window. This other guy—the guy who put stuff in our beer—he looks sick, just gets up and goes out quiet like, never see him again. Lights come back on strong. My friend and me scared, boy. Never let nobody put nothin' in my beer again. I don't drink too much beer neither, no more."

Nathaniel was speechless.

"Bad spirits and good spirits in the world, Tan. Dogs sometimes know a bad spirit, growl, get scared. Know a good one too. Animals know. Spirit world dangerous. Real weird battle goin' on!"

"Grandpa, d'you think there was a bad spirit in the bear that got Dad?"

"Nope. Slug in the butt. No devil."

When the boy reported this to his father, Ashley looked disgusted. "More devils, eh? Tan, you'll find it harder to dislodge a man's prejudices about the supernatural than it is to teach a dog to read."

Which ended that.

Except for a final conversation with his other grandfather. When probed, the old Irishman did have convictions.

"Look at the light, lad. Looks invisible, doesn't it?"

"Yep."

"Put it through a prism, and you'll get all the colors of the rainbow. Did y'know that a deer can't see the colors we do? He's color-blind, which is why hunters can wear bright orange without being spotted. Now, I think we're like the deer in a way. We're blind t'some colors, some spirits, to part of what's real. We're small and ignorant, but we got a whole lot of pride. We're blindest of all when we think we see best."

"You mean like somebody who says there's no radio waves because he's never seen a radio and never turned one on?"

His grandfather turned a keen eye on him and pointed his pipe at the boy's head.

"That's very good, Tan! I never thought of that, but it's true. The whole thing's very much like that."

"Dad says . . ."

"Ah, yes, lad, your dad says . . . but y'know, your dad has talked to a lot of people who say that there's no such thing as a radio and there's no such thing as radio waves. And the problem is that most of these people are pretty smart folk. And they and your pa would rather there not be any such radio waves to start with, so they got the whole thing solved, y'see?"

"Uh, maybe."

"Tan, we got something a lot more powerful than all the good or bad spirits in the universe, more powerful than all human knowledge. We got the right to decide if we're gonna do good or evil. It makes us something special, lad, and something dangerous too."

He puffed on his pipe. They thought together.

"Sure, there's bad spirits. I've seen 'em at work. I've heard them whispering in my heart. They're liars, they're bluffers.

But they'll run you if you let them. Resist them and they'll flee."

"But why? Why's it like this?"

"I don't have many answers, Tan. I guess it's the old problem of evil. When we run out of words, we call it a mystery."

29

There was a tale that Jan told over and over, asking each time
if Nathaniel had heard it before. The boy always shook his
head because each recounting filled in a little more detail. The
man's vocabulary was in such a state of disrepair that it took
many tellings before his listener was able to piece the story
together.

In 1939 he was Jan Tarnowski, a watchmaker of considerable
reputation in the city of Warsaw, a craftsman equally at ease with
his Polish customers and the Jews. His shop was perched on that
no-man's land between the ghetto and the gentile section of the
city. It sharpened his sense of being situated between two
worlds, as his wife and his young son were Jewish, though the
woman had long ago ceased to believe. But her racial origins
were continuing to cause some bureaucratic troubles at that
point. Jan would not take seriously the hysterical suspicions of
some that the worst was about to happen. A reign of terror in
his holy Poland! Yes, said his brother Bronek. He had been an
officer in the cavalry when the Germans swept across the country and crushed the Polish army in a few weeks. Bronek was in
disguise now, a laborer in masonry. He was laying bricks across
that same Swietokrzyska Street on which Jan had his shop. The
Jews within, *Tarnowski's* without.

Despite the evidence accumulating, Jan continued in a state
of ignorance for several months, believing that his gentile status
would exempt his family from the universal dividing of the
world into the clean and the unclean. His illusions were shattered one evening when he arrived home to find the street being swept out by a squad of Germans who dragged his wife and

screaming Itsak into the back of a van already crammed with citizens who had officially ceased to exist.

"Papa, Papa!"

Jan went running down the street after them but not fast enough to smash his fists on the doors or to get himself arrested. He went to the blue police that night to inquire, but a stone-faced officer informed him that there was no record of such persons as Sara and Itsak Tarnowski.

But for a significant sum the officer might be willing to overlook regulations and search for the names of the missing persons. It would be a great risk, you understand. The Germans were not sympathetic to anyone investigating "resettlement" affairs.

Jan scraped together savings and loans and deposited all he had into the hands of the helpful policeman. When he returned a week later, the man had nothing yet to tell him.

"I need to have more", he said. "The power of money to avoid fate is great, but the Germans are fate incarnate, and it will take a great deal of money indeed. You must understand . . ."

Jan begged from his younger brother, but Bronek refused.

"I need what I have for guns", he said. "The Bund needs weapons if we're to kick the Germans out of Poland. I'm sorry, Jan. Guns are power. Guns are freedom. A single gun may free a hundred people some day."

Next he went to his older brother, but Pawel had shrunk behind a wall of books and could produce little more than apologies:

"I have no money, Jan. Every *grosz* has gone to buy more stock. These titles are truth. We must keep truth alive if we wish to be free again one day. A single book may liberate many."

However, Pawel donated his gold wristwatch, inherited from Grandfather, and a small cracked painting from the seventeenth century. Jan sold them along with anything that could be liquidated from the clock shop and approached the blue policeman once again.

"You are my countryman. Please help me! Here, more *zlotys* than I can count. It's the best I can do. Find my wife and child, I beg you!"

"I have found out what any fool knows. Your wife and child, if they are Jews, have been taken to the ghetto. Now get out of here, you pig, before I turn you over to the S.S."

For weeks he hung around the entrances to the ghetto hoping to catch sight of Sara and Itsak, but the guards were too vigilant to allow him to enter. Children were shot in front of his eyes for smuggling potatoes. And the Warsaw ghetto at that time was choked with hundreds of thousands of people brought in from the surrounding villages and towns. Jan sent in numerous messages addressed to his wife, hoping that somewhere in all the confusion his messengers might find her. But nothing ever came of it.

Wohngebiet der JUDEN. Betreten verboten! proclaimed the sign over the barbed wire gate, but it could have just as easily read: "Abandon hope all ye who enter here." His other brother, Pawel, stood beside him one day and spoke the words in Italian, then translated. Pawel, so gentle and literary.

"Do you sell books to the Germans?" Jan asked him as they stood watching a street cleaner brush bloodstains toward a drain by the gate.

"Yes."

"God, Pawel, what kind of man are you!"

"The kind of man who hopes that a word of truth will change even an evil heart."

"What do they buy? Goebbels' love poems? Nietzsche?"

"No, they usually want Heine or Mann or some great work that's been burned in the streets of Berlin." Then Pawel ran away, as he had done all his life.

In the early autumn of 1942, when starvation, disease, and the continual deportations were taking a high toll among the population, Jan finally despaired of ever finding his family again, though the cries of "Papa, Papa!" worked deeper into him and revolved like a blade. His fate was decided for him one night when he returned home from the gates to see a group of S.S. standing at the door of his apartment looking bored and dangerous. Instinctively he turned and fled.

For months he hid in a cellar with Bronek and his underground friends in the Front for the Liberation of Poland. They worked together on the little pamphlets that they scattered throughout the city and tacked to the doors of public places in the middle of the night:

Will we, like Pilate, wash our hands of the blood of the innocent? The blood of children and Jewish martyrs as well as our own Catholic blood is running in our land. Brothers, Heroes, Catholics, let the Truth be our weapon, let us cry from the bottom of our souls. Protest, protest, protest. . . .

There were no protests that were not greeted by the disappearance of the protester. Their cellar was raided eventually, and Jan escaped down an alleyway and ran until he collapsed in the snow of a farmer's field far to the east of the city.

In the following weeks he moved eastward into spring, sometimes aided by the mercy of peasants or farm girls coming out to stare, astonished in the dawn with milk pails swinging in their hands. Like a charmed man who cannot be killed, he wandered from village to village, subsisting on turnips and milk stolen in the deadest hours from the udders of cows. He hid in the woods and hedgerows during the daytime and sucked at the melt-water in ditches as the salmon sun sank along horizons where smoke continued to drift and gunfire hammered on the overcast of dread. Sometimes he saw trains of boxcars pulling ever eastward toward the frontier, and he would stand watching and helpless, wondering if they contained his past, or food, or soldiers—almost anything in a world that had come uncoupled from sense.

One afternoon, as he slept in a heap of last year's birch leaves, he awoke with a start. Two cold metallic points were pressed to the side of his skull, and when he opened his eyes he saw that they were the muzzles of guns. Two men with red stars above their eyes were glaring at him and demanding an explanation in Russian.

* * *

When it was determined that he was not a German spy but only one of the myriad pieces of debris thrown up by the war, he was packed into a Russian freight car. It was the season of nationalist boxcars, it seemed, with every other nation cramming its dispossessed and unwanted into various methods of transportation, bound for destinations no one cared to discuss. Jan found himself compressed among an assorted collection of Polish soldiers, none of whom could describe his destination with any more clarity than the word *east*. They knew only that the train was heading east, ever east.

"Dirty besturds!" said Jan to Nathaniel. "Communists very dirty besturds. But Russian people goot!"

They rolled slowly for days across the steppes. They were starved and parched with thirst, overnighting now and then on the outskirts of small villages along the track. The train crew and guards took refreshment while the cargo huddled and quaked in the late northern spring. They would groan like one frozen mass in their fitful sleep, hoping for death, as the human mind will do when convinced that what remains of life is a slide into agony.

But it was not without some relief. In many of these villages the boxcars would be attacked by old *babas*. While the sentry walked around the long links of the train, one or two of these women would approach the cars, cursing and swearing at the foreign soldiers inside. They would toss rocks at the locked doors, screaming, "Wake up, wake up, you scum!" Then, when the smirking guard patrolled the other side of the train, the old crones would swiftly remove something from their bulky dresses, a loaf of bread or shrivelled potatoes, and hurl them through the breather hole at the top of the boxcar. When the sentry came round the nose of the engine they would revert to stones and curses. Over and over again this happened on the long journey through the legions of hamlets that sprinkled the infinite Russian soil. The goodness of these foolish old people baffled Jan. Their courage was probably what saved him, as the weeks of starvation were to kill more than half of the original transportees.

Food. Nathaniel knew that Jan now had three freezers, which he kept always full of many kinds of food. And there was a loaf of bread with him at all times in the battered haversack he carried. There were bags of peanuts and candy beside his bed so that if he awoke with a nightmare, he could eat. Food was his security and the coinage of his love. He was forever stuffing the boy with sausage, buns, cookies, and goat's milk.

The Polish soldiers discovered eventually that the State intended them for benign purposes. They were to be slave labor. The contents of the train were unloaded at a short siding and escorted across the fields to an abandoned monastery, which rose like fantasy from the steppe. It was an ancient Orthodox monastery-village, which had once housed many hundreds of monks, surrounded by several dozen peasant houses attached to the stone of the outer walls. At one time the monks and peasants had worked together in the fields to restore a small portion of the earth to Eden. But it had fallen back into the hands of the serpent. The remaining peasants were tattered and hungry looking. There were no young men among them, only the old and the crazed. The monks were gone.

Kamiyonka, said the hand-lettered sign beside the track, the gold-leaf Cyrillic script blistering with neglect. They entered a narrow gate, with ropes swaying in the breeze, where once a silver bell had called to prayer. The stone buildings, centuries old, were well preserved, but their whitewash was stained a rusty-brown color in spots, especially where hundreds of chips had been flayed from the wall.

The Poles were permitted to walk around under the pale sun, to wander through the compound and the ancient cells or high onto the ramparts of the church's blue onion dome. Its gold stars shone out over empty space, and the prisoners leaned against them in the twilight, scarcely willing to believe their miraculous liberation. With only a half-dozen guards to oversee them and pure water from the well and a bucket of turnips to boil each night, they suspected they might perhaps no longer be prisoners. They were too weak to run, and there was no place to escape to with a thousand *versts* of Russian void surrounding them. So they ate and waited and lay in the waxing sun, resting their heads against the painted stars.

"You, you up there!" screamed an apparition. He was dressed to his ankles in a muddy sheepskin coat, and he possessed no teeth. His long white beard was as fouled as his ankles.

The guards stood around him laughing.

"Give us a word of prophecy, old Fyodor!" they shouted.

One of the Poles on the dome translated for his compatriots.

"It's a madman", he muttered.

"Those stars", shouted the madman. "Those are the stars of the woman of the Apocalypse! They are her crown! You poor ones up there are her stars and her glory!"

The Soviets roared; the Poles looked bemused. Jan stared.

"You are the children of the last days", screamed the madman. "You don't know who you are! You don't know what awaits the world!"

Then the soldiers pushed him out the gate. They struck lights and blew cigarette smoke around the courtyard and laughed some more. But the voice of old Fyodor blew in through the walls, "Chapter twelve, chapter twelve is soon upon us!"

"You see, Tanny," said Jan many years later, "dis ol crazyman read nothing else. Just *Apokalipsa Swietego Jana*. Very strange and beautifool book. *Apokalipsa* is for saints and crazy peoples."

As the Russians made more jokes and cut sausage, Jan noticed one of them who had not laughed, who had not so much as smiled. Like the rest of the soldiers he was a conscript farm boy. He was not unkind to the Poles, who were also, for the most part, farm boys. Jan struck up a sort of pidgin friendship with the youth who did not smile. They progressed rapidly through "You Jan, me Vladimir" to more philosophical matters. The young lad reminded him of his brother Bronek, the same flash of courage in the eyes, the anger, the goodness. To see such things in an enemy's eyes was a revelation.

"War is stupid, officers very stupid, and Josef Stalin most stupid man of all!" said the Russian boy. It was a remark of astonishing trust. Such utterances were sufficiently criminal to condemn him to years of prison.

"You communist, Jan?" the boy soldier asked early on.

"Me no communist. No communist in Poland!" said Jan, insulted.

Vladimir gave him a look of pity.

"Who's that old Fyodor?" asked Jan. "Is he a monk?"

"No," said the Russian, "he's just a holy man, a peasant. He was born here, and maybe pretty soon he'll die here."

The use of the word *holy* spoke volumes to Jan, and he ventured to ask, "Where are the monks who used to live here?"

"You come with me. I show you."

He led Jan down the steps to the cellar of the monastery, down where water ran from the walls and slime growing on the ancient stones made their way treacherous. Jan was still so depleted physically he was forced to hold onto Vladimir's arm for support. It struck him that, although he was only a few years older than his young guide, he felt like an old man.

"Look!" said Vladimir. "Look in there!"

He pointed through the spy hole of a heavy wooden door. Jan looked in. At first he recoiled in shock, then looked again. Around the room, chained by ankles and wrists, were a dozen skeletons dressed in sacred vestments. The scene was not at first believable.

"Bolsheviks do this", said Vladimir. "These men metropolitans, bishops, *igumens* of monastery. Starve and rot here twenty-five years ago in revolution. Communists bring peasants to show what happen to blood-sucking priests. Poor people free now, say communists! Here, here," he said, pointing to a large dirt-covered pit in the center of the cellar, "here they shoot hundreds of priests, boy priests, students. Buried here!"

Nathaniel was motionless when Jan came to this part of the story. That it was true was beyond doubt, but it was hard to see it in his mind, to feel it the way Jan felt it.

"I see lots, lots", said Jan one day. He possessed a wealth of horrific memories, though he would not share them out all at once.

"I see too much, boychick."

Then he told how the Poles were transferred to a work camp farther north and east and how they had spent two years there.

"Oh, lotsa propagand' in dat place, Tanny. Not enough men in Russia, so dey vant Poles to do dirty work, stay dare after var and be goot communists. But I look, I look very careful. Dey no like Jews in dat place, dey no like Catoliks, and dey no like priests."

He choked.

"I see priests hang on hooks from tree, hooks through jaws, and dey hang till dey die. Many days to die."

The boy sat very still as he listened to this fantasy from long ago and far away.

Tears streamed down Jan's face.

"Oh, Tanny, Russian people goot people, but *party* it like devil. Make people into beasts—you talk bad, *bam*, you dead! No lawyer, no prayers! Just a big hole and dirt on your face."

The boy had never seen a man cry. The sausage and cookies appeared absurd in his hands. He placed them on the table, then slipped off the stool and went over to Jan. Taking a red, not perfectly clean handkerchief from his back pocket, he wiped Jan's face with exquisite care and a compassionate look in his eight-year-old eyes. The man was startled. He hugged the boy.

Nathaniel took the personal wounds of these stories up the mountain to his cave, where he could ponder them. His stone face, part Irish, part Indian, would crack and melt. He would hold his chin in his hands and ask why. Only nightfall would call him down the mountain, his heart wrapped in a melancholy that is the residue of suffering an unexplainable violence. Why, he wondered, why did people do those things? People could do anything they wanted to, all kinds of wonderful things, like those books in his dad's library and the machines at Grandma's paper. Maybe it would be better to be part of Grandpa Thaddee's world. He told adventure stories about the wild earth, not about hatred. But even in Thaddaeus' world, he remembered, there was killing. He too said, "We got to eat. We got to eat."

* * *

"Tan often seems a little sad after his visits with Jan", said his mother. "I'm not sure it's all that healthy."

"Jan's crazy, Sarah, but he's harmless. And from time immemorial boys have sat at the feet of old men, listening to them tell their stories."

"Well, I guess by the time they start to understand, they start to lose interest anyway."

"Oh, I think Nathaniel understands a great deal."

"That poor man, Ash, I bet no one else really listens to him. Probably more history behind those eyes than anyone'd guess."

"There's lots inside of him, for sure. But it's all mixed up with his fantasies."

"He's got eyes like nobody I've ever seen before."

"He says he was a watchmaker before the war and was married to a doctor."

"It might be true, Ash."

"I don't think so. Jan's a peasant through and through, honey. He makes up things to keep a boy's interest. He's lonely, that's all."

"But what about the piano? Do peasants play Chopin?"

"Who knows. Maybe they do."

"Jan loves that boy, and he loves music. That's two points in his favor."

"He bought the piano from MacPhale when they tore down the hotel bar. I think he was after some class."

"Maybe the piano just makes him happy."

"You hear him play? It's god-awful!"

"But his fingers. It's the best he can do. Maybe he hears something beautiful when he plays. Maybe he's remembering."

"Maybe", he shrugged. "Anyway, I think it's good for Tan to learn about other cultures."

"You're not worried about Jan's influence, then. So, what's that look I see on your face?"

"It's my father. I don't like his influence on Nathaniel."

* * *

"Listen, Dad, I'm going to be frank with you. Try not to let your feelings be hurt, okay?"

Stephen got out his pipe and fumbled with a match, trying to raise smoke by way of diversion. He glanced at his son through the haze. Anne wondered why she was not also being addressed.

"I'm going to ask you," said Ashley with eyes that meant business, "I'm going to ask you categorically not to inflict any of your superstitions on my son."

His father's face looked suddenly stricken. The hurt in his eyes did not erupt in a word of self-defense.

437

"If you mean the leprechauns, banshees, and things . . .", intervened his mother.

"No. I mean the devils, the Mass, and the sacraments and things."

His parents stared at him.

"God!" said Ashley. "I knew it would be like this! Damn it, can't you see how you've been brainwashed, Dad?"

"I don't quite understand", said his father. "Your own wife, son—Sarah's a believer."

Ashley looked momentarily taken aback.

"Sarah is a beautiful person, and I love her very much. But she keeps her religion to herself."

"I thought I did too."

"Not really. Nathaniel is drawn to you like a magnet. He's always quoting your little spiritual nostrums. I don't want his mind cluttered up with a dying culture."

"You are the product of a culture, too, Ashley", said the woman.

"My culture values knowledge, not myths."

"You think so? You think that having sloughed off religion you are now freed to be objective?" She groaned. "My own father spouted that nonsense a half-century ago, and I'm still recovering from it. . . ."

"Mother, you're the last person I'd expect an argument from about this. I want to know what Dad has to say for himself."

His father's eyes filled with anguish.

"Some things in life are real, Ash, that can't be proved in a laboratory. I've seen them, smelled them, fought them, and loved them. But try to catch one in a bottle, and it disappears."

"Imagination."

"You listen, Ashley", said the woman. "You think you have discarded a myth and now you are free to be objective? You say you believe in nothing. But I say you have just made yourself open to whatever new myths are flying about in the atmosphere. You will now begin to believe in anything."

Ashley looked sardonic.

"You defending him, Ma? You caved in, eh? Settled for the cheap old myth?"

"It wasn't cheap, Ashley. It never was cheap, not the real thing."

"It's a very narrow vision of existence", he said.

"It's a narrow gate", said his father.

"Narrow?" said Anne. "Yes, like a door opening into a vast palace, or a passage that leads to an infinite and beautiful garden. I'm only just arriving there myself, waiting, waiting to see if I may enter."

"Anybody can go through, Anne, any time they want to ask", said her husband.

Turning to him, she replied, "Stephen, what if I'm not wanted?"

"You don't understand yet. He is love. Everyone is wanted."

She looked back to her scowling son: "Ashley, in your arrogance, you would batter down the gate if you could. Are you so surprised that it remains resolutely shut?"

He mused on that, but his eyes were hard.

"This shut gate of yours, maybe there's nothing on the other side."

"You're afraid of that, aren't you?"

"No, I'm not afraid."

"Yes, you are", said his mother.

"No, I'm not. This is getting ridiculous! Now listen, I'll say it just once. Nathaniel is going to be raised free. Free to think and be whatever he chooses. No one is going to mold him."

"Everyone is molded", said his mother. "We choose what to mold our children with. Nothing grows in a vacuum. If you think you're making a free human being just by letting him grow spontaneously, you won't end up with a free human being.

You'll have a patchwork boy composed of whatever is prowling about in his culture. He'll be about as far from freedom as you can get."

"I rather admire our new culture!" said Ashley.

"You admire this culture! It produces very little art, literature, or solid journalism, don't you think, for all its talk of freedom. It does, however, produce an extraordinary amount of corpses."

"That's a debatable point, Mother."

"I think you admire its arrogance, its image of itself. You aren't really looking at the fruits of your brave new culture. It's a culture of death, Ashley, and you want to feed our grandson to it."

"My son! My son!" he roared.

The three of them sat looking at each other in stunned silence. Then all three said at once, "I'm sorry. I'm sorry, I'm sorry."

"Look, I'd better go", said Ashley. "I can't retract what I've said. But I do regret . . . well, *how* I've said it."

He got up and was about to leave. His eyes were wet.

"When I was a kid I used to worship you, Dad. I thought you were a king. In exile." He smiled sadly, "You know, each of you in your own way has made it very difficult for me. Look at you: a rationalist mother defending an irrationalist father. What a combination. God, no wonder I'm screwed up! Well, it's not going to happen to Nathaniel!"

After he had gone, his parents sat together in silence. The man wiped his eyes. The woman looked cold and angry.

"Philosophically, Stephen, I suppose I'm closer to Ashley than to you. But at this moment I have a very irrational urge to give his face a sharp slap."

"Anne," he said gently, "don't do it. You'd drive him deeper into it. We must be what we are. Someday Ashley and Nathaniel will see. It will take time. There's nothing quite as blind as a man who thinks he's got superior sight. He never learns to look into things deeply or beyond things. He sees only his eyes, his own seeing."

"What are you suggesting we do?"

"Be who we are. Make no apologies for ourselves. Hide nothing from the boy. As for Ash, well, God will teach him humility."

"If . . . if there is a God."

"God teaches each of us the things we most need to know."

"What, pray tell, is he teaching me?"

"I think he's been teaching you for a long time not to make a god of knowledge. He's been teaching you to believe in things you haven't seen."

"And what is he teaching you?"

Eventually he replied:

"To trust that the past is forgiven."

* * *

From time to time Nathaniel would head out to the farm by the long way, going through the bush along the overgrown path his grandfather had made years ago. It had been abandoned since the coming of the road. The trail led to the edges of their field just by the bend in the river, and there he would always find a few sheep nibbling and the barbed-wire coil on the corner post like a crown of thorns. He saw green oats in the fields and the rooster threatening and spreading its wings as he approached the lopsided cabin-house and the dog barking gleefully around his ankles. He loved these things. They had always been here, dependable and good. Why had his father left this place, he wondered.

If his grandmother was not involved in one of her many tasks, she would agree to go with him up the slope for an hour's stroll. There was usually a suitable excuse offered by one or the other, such as, "The pin-cherries by the dead birch are ready for picking!" or "There's coyote tracks in the path by the river."

They had come to know each other much better on these rambles, more a twining of solitudes than a communion. If there was a question he had not resolved in his cave, he would raise it with her.

"Gramma?"

"Yes, Nathaniel."

"Why is there so much evil in the world?"

She sighed. It had been easier when he was younger and was asking where thunder comes from and how do chicks know when to hatch themselves.

"Evil?" she said now, doubting his understanding of the word. "What kind of evil do you mean?"

"Like the war, those terrible things Jan went through, the Jews and all that."

"Oh." She was silent for such a long breath that he wondered if she intended to answer. It was the duty of grandparents to inform the generations of the conditions into which they had been born. Though silence itself might speak most eloquently.

"I have often asked that question myself, Nathaniel, and never arrived at a satisfactory answer. There are books at home I can lend to you, but they merely circle around the subject."

"Sometimes it makes me sick to be a human being!" he spewed out.

"Oh, Tan!" she said, shocked, stopping to look him straight in the eyes. She took his shoulders to hug him, and he did not resist.

"You have inherited my disease", she said. "How easy it would be for a sensitive nature like yours to be overcome with despair." She barely spoke the last word aloud, for fear of naming the thing that still haunted her.

"You must not, boy! You must not! Fight it!"

"How do you fight it?"

"Well," she said firmly, "you start with yourself. If you're going to be sensitive, you'd better be strong too! Otherwise there's simply no point; you become just one more victim. What this world needs is people who are strong, not powerful or tough, but made of something inside that doesn't give up and doesn't whine about how hard life is."

Though she did remember with shame her own plaintive cries of alarm. The boy was drinking it all in regardless.

"Nathaniel, there must be a counterforce to evil that unmasks it and shows it for what it is. There must be voices to proclaim the truth."

He was not sure if he understood her. And was doubly surprised by all this fervor from his skeptical grandmother. His father said that she only went to church all these years out of kindness to Grandpa. She still looked as if she had stumbled into the wrong place but just might stay if it could be proved that anything of merit would happen. His dad always said this with a derisive look.

"Why do you go?" Ashley had once asked her in that cold voice.

"Because I want to be with your father in the one thing that matters most to him." Pause. "And because there's something there that I do not, cannot, understand."

Ashley had grimaced at the reply but said no more. Nathaniel heard it and stored it away.

"Ultimately, evil is a lie", his grandmother was saying now. "It's bankrupt and you have to call its bluff. Oh, it has power all right, a terrible, terrible power to destroy, but it can never create. Only love creates. Truth and love are stronger . . . far stronger. But it takes a lot more effort to create than to destroy."

"You sound like Grandpa."

"Yes, I suppose I do on that point", she smiled. "He is a religious man."

The boy nodded. His grandfather, though, was of the species of religious who rarely speak. The preaching in the family was left to the skeptics.

"Your dad has been teaching you Latin, hasn't he?"

"Yes."

"Did you know that the root of the word religion is *religare*? It means to reconnect. You see, there's a gash in the fabric of existence, and the only way to bind it together is to make new life. You can't just sit there hating the wound, Tan, or indulging in bitterness. Whatever you become in life, always ask yourself, am I making more life or am I making more death?"

"Dad says we can count on nothing but ourselves, that we're alone on the earth with all our responsibilities, and we have no other reason to be here than the one we make for ourselves."

She stirred inside her sweater. She groaned inwardly. So, it seemed that her son had allowed a little radioactive material to escape from his core. He was now proclaiming his doubts as articles of faith.

"Dad says we have to make friends with the dark side, 'cause it's just a part of us and won't ever go away, so we should learn to love it, you know. It's like a shadow, he says."

Even as he said it the boy appeared uncertain.

The woman looked fierce and said with a small angry voice, "Rubbish! Unspeakably stupid rubbish!"

The boy's mouth hung open.

Calming her emotions, she explained: "If your house is full of shadows, it won't be fit to live in. A house of love should be flooded with light, child. Light. I lived too long in shadows to accept that nonsense about loving them!"

The boy looked troubled.

"I love your father very dearly", she went on. "But you must understand, Nathaniel, that he has been hurt and doesn't see as clearly as he should."

"Maybe, Gram, he sees more clearly." He said it gently, as he often would do when contradicting his elders.

She wondered about that catastrophe, the wounding of her son, the boy's father. Ashley had not forgiven life for being dangerous. He was blaming his father's religion for failing to arm him. And he had become a wanderer, like her, but the difference between them was his lack of hope in anything outside of his own mind. He no longer looked beyond the edges of the wasteland and had begun to make his home there, whereas she had never totally despaired of finding her bearings. She scented from time to time winds from a far country where life resounded and water flowed. Yes, she continued to wander as he did, but was looking forward to the unknown land with hope. Hope could be painful, she knew, and perhaps for this reason he was unable to believe.

Ashley believed in the possibilities within man. Well, she believed in them, too, but their ultimate purpose was a subject on which they would differ. Her son peered into the face of man in search of something, perhaps his own lost face. She looked there also and had begun, through the friendship of Edwin and Turid, to suspect a hidden and sacred image within the icons of their faces. Would Ashley one day see through the broken image to find the mutilated face of a poor man hung on a tree? If her son could come that far, then he might one day go beyond it to . . . to the narrow gate? Here she stopped, reaching the outer limits of her own passage through the wasteland.

She shook off this line of thought. Clearly, her main concern at the moment was for the boy. His father had already taught him that life is an ocean out of which one may expect at any moment the sudden disaster of torpedoes. Would he teach the boy to have faith in nothing? In anything? What did her son believe in, she wondered. His marriage, the love that Sarah gave him? And where did her love come from, if not from the springs at which she regularly drank? Did Ashley believe in books, in the mind, in culture? Well, she believed in them, too, as far as they could take her. But the fact remained that many of the men of Jan Tarnowski's world, the ones who had created Auschwitz, had been educated and cultured. But then, just as many geniuses and artists had died in it. The answer was some-where beyond the mind without excluding it. Could her son throw open a little dusty window of faith onto the brilliant light of the universe? Or had he come to believe only in his religion of shadows? Would he be condemned forever to the lamps of his laboratory? She knew well the stifling air of that place, its illusions of a superior light. It was Papa's world. How had it become her son's?

"Most people think the shadows are just something that will be illumined by knowledge. They think that mystery is just ig-norance that will be done away with when we get enough of the right facts. It's a very foolish modern myth, Nathaniel, and I hope you don't fall for it. Try to look as far and as deep as you can. Go farther than the new religion, which thinks it has evolved beyond superstition."

"But, Gram, haven't we? I mean, Dad says we don't need those old tales any more, if we know."

He has not heard a thing I said, she groaned inwardly.

"In life," she said, "there is good and evil perpetually at war. A very deep mystery. But it's not a myth. It's a battle of the spirit that manifests itself in acts of . . ."

"I know, Gram, I know, but . . ."

How could he know! He was too young to know!

"And we must choose, Nathaniel, at every moment, which isn't as easy as it may sound."

The boy was obviously not satisfied. Why had she embarked on this deadly discussion? A heavy-handed old woman, a foolish melancholic, that's what she was! She had beaten around the bush of the problem, just as the books did, never getting much closer to solving it. Why could she not control herself?

"There will always be men who take away what others have worked for. They will steal, burn, or drown it, but I will tell you one thing . . ."

He waited, looking.

"They will be the losers. They have power and knowledge, but they are unable to love anything. Whether or not the world is really as your father imagines it to be, or as I'm convinced it is, we are agreed on one thing: such men will be the servants of destruction. Nothing good will ever come from them, no matter how high their motives may seem. If they have lost respect for even one small human life, or one small freedom, they will not long retain it for this humanity they profess to love so well."

What did she mean, the boy wondered. He loved his grandmother, but he thought she might, at times, be a little extreme.

30

In the late summer of 1961, his grandmother invited him to accompany her on an excursion to Crow's Nest, where government hearings were being held to discuss the question of flooding the Columbia and Kootenay valleys. As they rode down on the train, she explained to the boy that should the international treaty be ratified, the project would probably flood the Canoe River Valley as well. Their farm might be perched on the edge of an enormous new lake. If worse did indeed come to worst, it would be lost under water.

"That's not the point, though, Tan, it's not just our farm. It's all those traplines, villages, and hundreds of homesteads that will be wiped out. It's the moral question of a government's right to take away the property of citizens. The excuse is that it's for a greater good . . ."

"What greater good?"

"More electricity, more revenue . . . more power and money, basically!"

"But won't they pay for the land they take?"

"Oh, yes, they will. But how can you really pay for a life that's been built up for generations in those valleys?"

Every hotel room was filled that day in September when they arrived, but thankfully they had wired ahead for a reservation. They were checked into their room by a harried porter.

"You folks here for the water?" he asked.

"The water? You mean the Columbia project? Yes, we are."

"You for or against?"

"Lost somewhere in between, I fear. Though I suspect I will be tending to the *against* side, sir."

"Good for you!" he said. He refused to accept her tip. "My mum'n'dad have a place near Arrow Lakes is gonna be under six hundred bloody feet of water this thing goes through."

"Well, as I said, I'm neither for nor against but merely wish to observe. I will be writing reports for my paper on the hearings as they move about the province."

"What paper's that?"

"*The Swiftcreek Echo*."

"Swiftcreek? Where's that?"

It seemed that few people remembered right away just where her town might be. She described its location to a number of worked-up citizens who without much ado were accosting every passerby for impromptu debates. The town of Crow's Nest was awash with discussions, and in the lobbies, barbershop, and cafés there was talk of nothing else: water!

As Anne and Nathaniel were eating a late supper in the hotel restaurant, they were interrupted by a tall, graying man with a briefcase and tired eyes.

"Mrs. Delaney."

"Yes", she said.

"It's Maurice. Maurice L'Oraison."

"My goodness, but I didn't recognize you at all, Maurice. You have grown!" Then she smiled. "I fear that may always be what little old ladies are condemned to say to handsome young men!"

"You'll never be a little old lady, and I'm not young", he said.

They laughed together, and he sat in to join them over tea. Nathaniel was introduced, and Maurice shook his hand warmly.

"My God, you were a baby last time I saw you!"

Nathaniel sat up, quickening to the attention.

"I hear you're a pretty bright lad too", Maurice smiled warmly.

"How did you hear that?" said Anne.

"Turid told me. She says this boy is destined for great things." He clapped the boy on the shoulder.

Nathaniel beamed.

"I'm sorry I didn't recognize you, Maurice", said the woman. "It's been a few years, hasn't it? And you've turned completely gray."

"They've been hard years. I've gone a long way in a short time. I guess it cost something."

"Have you come for the hearings?"

"Yes. I'm one of the consultants for the Power Authority. It seems we're going to have quite a fight on our hands."

"It seems that you are", she said pensively. "I'm puzzled that you would be working for a scheme that may one day wipe out your parents' home."

His face fell.

"Put it that way, Mrs. Delaney, and I am without doubt a heartless beast. But the Authority fully intends to compensate anyone it finds necessary to displace."

"Are you aware of your mother's thoughts on the matter? I believe they are quite strong."

"My *step*mother's opinions about many things are both strong and colorful. She expresses them to me quite frequently by mail, and face to face when I can get down for a visit."

"That's their home, Maurice, and a way of life that will disappear."

"Their life?" he said somberly. "That way of life killed my mother."

There was an embarrassed moment during which the woman remembered the boy's eyes on that day of cold blue flesh. She had been there with him. The beautiful child was now an executive. She wondered fleetingly what had been lost in the intervening years. She looked at Nathaniel, as old as Maurice had been then, and she hoped that her grandson's life might escape a similar destiny.

The boy appeared to be drinking in the visitor's every word, fascinated by the aura of his power. It was not the swaggering pork-barrel-politics variety but a more suave, dignified sort, accompanied by a scent of eau de cologne and money. Even she was attracted, though for other reasons: within this costly armor there continued to exist a pair of rather gentle, troubled eyes.

"You see, there's more to this than meets the eye", he went on. His voice was confidential. "There's the question of my future. I'm not sure I should be confiding this to a journalist." He smiled. "But you and I are old friends, and I trust your discretion. Promises have been made that I'm to have access to real political power in the years to come. With that power I'm going to make the world a better place to live in."

"I see", she said.

"The shape of the future is being decided now, not only in this province, but in the nation and beyond."

"By whom?"

"It would be premature for me to say."

"Is this what you need, Maurice? Do you understand what you're choosing?"

He shrugged.

"Does anyone really understand what he chooses? I know what I want."

"Do you?"

Why this confession, Maurice? What can I say that would be of any use to you?

He looked away, distracted by some men with briefcases who had just entered.

Is this, then, the child who shall lead us? Is this the shape that poets take when the poetry has been destroyed?

After the man had left, the boy turned to her and said, "What a neat guy, Grandma!"

"Yes, Tan, a very neat guy. But he's not a happy one."

* * *

The hearing was held in the gymnasium of a school, and somehow several hundred residents and visitors had packed themselves in. Facing the rows of seats were a head table and the chairman's empty seat. Adjacent to the chair was a table-load of advisors and a stenographer. Among them sat Maurice L'Oraison. Nathaniel and his grandmother were in the fifth row, far left side, and the boy was craning his neck to watch Maurice.

"Gramma," he said presently, "maybe we're wrong about this. Maybe people like Mr. L'Oraison know the big picture about things?"

"Sometimes the big picture is best seen in the little picture, Tan."

"Huh?"

"Maurice is a very nice man. And I can see that you admire him. But some very great mistakes have been made in history by the nicest of people. We need to ask ourselves if this water is going to feed more human beings. Is it going to make modern life more sane? Is it going to—"

"I dunno, Gram", he muttered distractedly. She saw that his mind was drifting. Like so many of his generation, he was a creature of impressions, and each generation seemed a little worse in that regard, she thought.

At last the chairman entered, clicked open a briefcase, and worried his files. The room was crackling with the electrified atmosphere of dissent as he banged down his gavel and the hearing began.

"Ladies and gentlemen, the hearing this evening will consider the licensing of the British Columbia Hydro and Power Authority to build water storage facilities on the Arrow Lakes."

He went on in official jargon to outline the proposed plan. Most of the people in the room had been closely following the treaty for some years. They were prepared. After a few introductory statements by witnesses for the Authority and various branches of government, the average citizen began to make his presence known.

Questions arose from the floor concerning the compensation for land seizure. The mayor of Crow's Nest on behalf of his city council stated a number of their objections, mentioning the widespread damage to personal property and the loss of recreational facilities that would result from the project. Other witnesses rose to describe their expected losses.

The director of the Power Authority replied:

"What we have in mind here, Mr. Chairman, is that if a family decides they want to sell their land, we'll pay the market price plus a bonus of 10 percent for what I believe the lawyers call a *forcible taking*. In those cases where it would be possible to provide alternate lands in the same area, we would help on a legal execution of that sort."

A woman stood, a Mrs. Davis:

"When these people go looking, they don't seem to be able to find anything that has comparable acreage."

Mr. L'Oraison (counsel for the Power Authority):

"I don't think we've carried on our investigations outside this area yet to find out what other land is available."

Mrs. Davis: "Land in our area hasn't the market value that any land comparable in other areas has. Where we are is extremely fertile, and when we look at farms in the Okanagan Valley, the land is not nearly so good as ours; we find that the market value is much higher there. When we go to relocate, we'll have to pay much more than an ordinary market value might be considered in our area at present."

A Mr. Lepanto rose and identified himself as a resident of Crow's Nest:

"My occupation is farming, sir, and I've been asked by the Farmers' Institute to present their objections to the granting of this water license."

Anne listened intently to this impressive figure. His arguments were wide-ranging and incisive, and among them she especially noted:

"The map of Canada shows that B.C., despite its huge land area, is second only to Newfoundland in its adverse ratio of good land to territory unsuited for development. It's important that it be clearly understood that the land in this valley rates among Canada's best. First-class land can be considered that which has good soil, adequate water supply, moderate climate, suitable elevation, and good location. Only 3 percent of Canadian land is considered to be truly first class."

His testimony went on for close to an hour and contained a number of striking objections. He concluded by saying:

"We also object on moral grounds. More than any other section of the community, farmers set great store by their indefeasible titles. Farming is a long-term business based on security of tenure. If this dam is built, an alarming precedent will be created, namely, that lands can be expropriated at any time if the government of the day wishes to take over lands as a means of collecting foreign exchange."

A Reverend Pellerin spoke:

"I'm well aware of the expropriatory powers the government has by statutory law, and I'm also aware that the Acts passed for the different crown corporations aren't entirely consistent, with the result that the rights of the individual are left sometimes virtually unprotected.

"Money can't compensate for the destruction of homes and a way of life. In times of national crisis we're urged to pay the price for freedom and self-determination and, if necessary, to die for it. You can't expect us now to give away what many have died for, just because this government feels that it's a convenient way of making some sixty-five million dollars."

In reference to the financial compensation the government was offering to the displaced, he said:

"You can't lump all these people together into some sort of

vital statistics to be dealt with in the cheapest possible way. They aren't chattel, to be moved about at will. They're individuals with all the rights, hopes, and fears that you gentlemen possess."

Anne whispered to Tan, "He's right, but it's not going to make any difference, I think. Most people would prefer a shiny new car and a crackerbox house to a quarter section of good bottom land."

A clamor of witnesses now began to voice their support of the project, and she wondered how many of them were speaking from conviction and how many from desire for the government check. She was surprised by one, though she should not have been. He rose and said:

"I want to state that I'm in support of the plan, and I'm speakin' fer a majority of my people when I do so . . ."

"Name, please?"

"Jonah MacPhale, Mayor of Swiftcreek, at your service, sir."

"Thank you, Mr. MacPhale. Your comment has been duly noted."

A Mr. Basil stood. He was the owner of a real estate business that would probably make considerable profit from land sales should the Columbia development be approved. Despite this he said:

"It's said that the root of patriotism is love of the land, not as an ideology or slogan, but as something that can be seen and felt. That's something well understood by those of us who have regard for the land. From intimate acquaintance with many of the persons concerned, I don't exaggerate when I put it to you that the issuance of this license will smother the initiative and spirit of many of our best people, and that's a serious matter indeed, and one that would be difficult to assess in terms of money.

"The many losses the project will inflict would probably be accepted by thinking people if it had first been demonstrated that, one, the resultant hydro power is urgently needed in the next five or ten years and, two, that there exists no alternate source of equivalent power at somewhere near the same cost. What would the director of the Power Authority have to say on that?"

The director: "Simply, Mr. Chairman, that this program is one of the most profitable programs of its kind that could be developed anywhere in the world. To the question as to whether there are any alternatives in British Columbia, the answer is, of course, yes."

Mr. Basil: "Mr. Comptroller, I would like to ask one more question of the director. How in the world does he arrive at the conclusion that this will be a very profitable business when testimony has shown there's no accurate estimate of losses that will be suffered in land use, water use, and other values, not to speak of the aesthetic qualities, which you can't value?"

The director: "Taking all these things into consideration, I don't see how anyone who has made a thorough study of the matter and isn't emotionally disturbed . . ."

The emotional disturbance of many in the room was quite evident and, considering the situation, it seemed a moderate reaction, thought the woman who sat writing furiously in the fifth row, far left. She stood up.

"Mr. Chairman."

"Your name, please."

"I'm Anne Delaney, editor of *The Swiftcreek Echo*. I would like to say that I believe the plan is a very clever one."

From the corner of her eye she saw Maurice L'Oraison look up and stare fixedly at her.

"And I'll grant you, sir, that a lot of canny men are involved from A to Z, but you'll have to explain one thing to me, Mr. Director." She paused.

"Explain what?"

"Explain the cleverness of a project that proposes to sell our water for sixty-five million but floods forever a lumber and pulp resource that is conservatively valued at eighty-eight million and would be renewed over and over again in the centuries to come."

"Those figures are in dispute."

"By whom?" someone shouted from the back of the room. "By those who want this plan shoved through no matter what the cost!"

"Order, order!"

"Mr. Chairman, the forest renews itself, providing employment directly and indirectly for many thousands of people. That eighty-eight million would be earned a hundred times over. How can we possibly assume any benefits from destroying it? Oh, yes, there will be a temporary boom in construction jobs, and there's the little dowry from the Americans. But look at what's being lost. A civilization, sir, a civilization that has been growing in those valleys for a hundred years. Excellent farmland, thick cedar forests that cannot be found elsewhere, villages with memories, old people who slaved to cut those fields from the bush. Shall the next generation learn that the government can seize—?"

"It's not the government's prime intention deliberately to allow—"

"Is it your accidental intention?"

Laughter.

"Madam, I'm not here to explain the position of any governmental bodies but to apply myself to the task at hand, namely, conducting a public meeting."

The room became quiet. Her voice when she spoke was like the first bird piping in the dawn, frail but determined.

"Sir, I suggest that no matter what's said here tonight or in any of the other hearings to come, the great earth-mover of this government will roll on over us regardless. These hearings are a token, a playacting at democracy."

"I will explain again that this hearing is a *hearing*, not a polling booth. You may cast your ballot at the next election."

"That would be fine! A hearing would be grand, if you

would only hear! I think even if the whole populace were arrayed against you, you would remain unaffected."

"Order! Mrs. Delaney, I will depart from procedure only to comment briefly and off the record that public opinion in this province and across the nation is extremely supportive. We sympathize with the farmer and homesteader, but really, you can't stop progress. Should a few thousand people be permitted to interfere with the quality of life of millions?"

"The quality of life you refer to is not a better opportunity for education, scientific development, culture, or any other human value. It is one step of luxury heaped upon another that is the question. The Americans, with ourselves coming quickly up behind, are the most electrified, gadget-ridden, spoiled brats on the face of the earth, and you are insisting that hardworking, honest settlers are to be dispossessed of everything they have sweated and bled for so that a civilization utterly devoted to selfishness can compound its sickness? Rubbish!"

"I think these remarks go far beyond our frame of reference", said the chairman, as calmly as possible.

"Yes, they do. And how pitiful are those frames. All your talk of progress! What kind of progress is it that throws out wisdom and respect for the individual?"

"The people need—"

"The people?" she cried out loudly. "What are the people? There is no people here, only a gathering of a few hundred souls, each one packaged up in a body and making his way alone through this land. Are we going to turn them into a mass of numbers and call it our god? And worship it?"

The whole room had been as if under a spell up to this moment. Even the chairman had permitted an unheard-of exchange of inadmissible testimony that would never in the end find its way into the transcripts. He sat up straight now.

"Madam, I believe this board has been more than indulgent with you. Your time is up!"

"Let her speak", someone shouted, and others joined in. The hall began to rumble.

"Order, order!"

"Fine, Mr. Chairman, I'm finished. But I would like to read into the record a final quotation."

She lifted up a large leather-bound volume.

"All right, proceed. But be brief, please."

"I quote: *You don't seem to have grasped the situation at all. You have failed to see that it is better for one man to die for the people than for a whole nation to be destroyed.*"

"You will have to identify your source, Mrs. Delaney."

"The source is the Book of John, chapter eleven, sir. And the speaker is one Caiaphas, chairman of the Sanhedrin, referring to a certain Galilean rabbi who was causing a disturbance among *the people* that year."

* * *

It was curious. The silence. The hearing ground down to a sputtering completion shortly after she spoke. It was all business and parliamentary procedure and jargon after that.

No one came over to speak with her, though many cast a swift glance in her direction. *Religious fanatic*, the look said.

She felt like running after them, explaining, *No, no, I'm not even religious, don't you see. It's the idea! The principle of the thing!*

Fool! Old woman! Don't even know who or what you are! You deserve to be surrounded by solitude! Her thoughts against herself were hard. But the boy clung to her arm and beamed.

Maurice sauntered past with his arms full of paper.

"Rather melodramatic, Mrs. D!" he said with a frown.

"Indeed. But no one need know you're associated with me."

He did not find her jest humorous and glanced over his shoulder.

"Look," he said intensely, "this isn't first-century Palestine.

This isn't Nazi Germany. Why make such a fuss? No one is getting hurt by this project. This is a democracy!"

"Yes. It is. And I wouldn't want any of the alternatives presently on the planet. But, Maurice, the seeds of tyranny are in every democracy. You mustn't fool yourself. Anyone, any one of us can be seduced into trading away freedom to defend whatever we think the common good is at the time."

He paused, and his eyes were still hard.

"Sometimes the people have to be saved from themselves", he said in a small firm voice.

"Oh, Maurice", she said, heartbroken, as he walked away.

* * *

CNR Station, Kamloops, B.C.   30 Sept. 1961

It is 2 A.M. The boy sleeps curled up beside me on a bench as we wait for the train. By dawn we shall be home for a short respite. Boxcars shunt back and forth outside. The Morse key rattles behind us. Yardmen yell and curse under painful arc lights. This is the noise of the modern world at night, the crash and grind of a progress that never sleeps. How I yearn for the forest's hush, for that place which nearly destroyed me.

He looks for all the world like a child, and so he is. But he has taken to using words like "relevant" and "expropriate".

He is alternately ponderous and delightfully naïve, more eager for the sensations of the conflict than for its implications. And I? Do I grasp the implications? Will they clarify in the months ahead?

"If I were a man," one of my inner voices asks, "if I owned a more powerful newspaper," another says, "then would my words carry weight?"

But I see that I have been given a hunger for the truth of the matter. Oh, not the truths of logistics, revenues, and vote counts, but the submerged heart of things.

Once again I am being invited to fight, not from my strength, but from my weakness. Not in the light, but in a gloom created by the desires of men for power. I must strike a fire of imagery from the flint of my mind to illuminate the strange concept here perpetrated: that we can flood the world with electric light by plunging a valley and a principle into darkness. It is a lie, and I will fight it. Whether or not it is a major lie is not yet clear. But certainly, if we fail to resist it, we will be defeated by greater falsehood in the years to come.

* * *

The voices of those crying out in the wilderness are inevitably consigned to categories reserved for the emotionally disturbed and eaters of locust. As she followed the hearings from town to town, the chair never again made the mistake of recognizing her, and there was always a swift-footed lawyer with a louder voice who could beat her to the floor. But her jeremiads went into her paper and thence found their way into the offices of many people of power to whom she had kindly sent free subscriptions.

During this period her grandson began to look at her in a new way.

"You're neat, Gram", he declared from a sleeping bag on the floor one night. It had been an exhausting day, and all they had been able to find was a single dingy room to rent in one of the towns where the hearings were taking place. She was almost asleep.

"Thank you, Tan", she muttered, not really aware of the fervent compliment she had just received.

In these days of conflict she found a fugitive happiness and wondered if this might indicate her true nature—woman of battle as well as exile. It seemed inevitable that the maker of words must at some point stride out to wrestle at close quarters with her enemy. But the hearings ended eventually, and the war was taken off to other arenas of combat, where the weaponry of dollar signs rather than ideas did major battle. From her parapet, where she sat tapping two-fingered on the dilapidated typewriter, she continued to harangue:

> This is a great nation, but if it is corrupted, great indeed will be its fall. As power extends its grasp into wider and wider rings of human life, it becomes more hostile to anything outside itself. As it becomes nearly absolute, it grows increasingly negative, because it must by its very nature oppose what cannot be extinguished in men's beings. Totalitarian power does not rest content with obedience and a passive populace. It must seek at some point to crush the spirit, to destroy the inner impulse that depends for its well-being on freedom from manipulation. It may take thirty, forty, or fifty years to bear its deadly fruit, but the harvest will come.
>
> Thankfully, we are not there yet, but let us not fool ourselves that we live in the age of individuality and freedom. The truth is that the individual has never been so endangered by that conglomerate of power we are pleased to call government. Let us not be deluded into thinking that over sixteen hundred homesteaders dispossessed of their land by a few strokes of the pen can be compensated. It is more than land that has been expropriated; it is the idea inherent in our civilisation that the honest citizen is an equal partner in a federation of free beings. That has ceased to exist.

Winter 1966

31

In writing she had found an antidote to the helplessness of the age. And Nathaniel had been observing her closely. This worried her greatly, for she recognized an affair with words as a symptom of profound unhappiness with the world. But to the boy there was no more intriguing model of existence than his grandmother. Her vocation of protest was gripping his imagination.

He was a solitary, brooding sort of boy. At the age of fourteen he had begun to smoke a pipe and dreamed of being a journalist, one of various heroic images of himself that he cultivated. He had no friends other than Jan Tarnowski, with whom he spent far too much time. They were building something massive in the backyard of Jan's place; they had been building it together for years—a tower of some sort. It had risen steadily above the teetering lumber piles and was now visible throughout the village.

"What are you making over there?" people asked from time to time.

"An *enduvdevorldkluk!*" Nathaniel would reply to all and sundry, employing that oblique smile of his.

The mayor himself stopped him on the street one day and demanded, "What the hell's an *en-duv-de-vorl . . .?*"

"*Enduvdevorldkluk?*"

"Yeah. What is it?"

"Oh, it's just an idea Jan got into his head, and I'm helping him."

"For seven years you been helping him with just an idea?"

"Yep."

"It's crazy. Maybe you're crazy too, kid. But that figures—some o' yer family are a few bricks short of a load."

"We sure are. We like it that way."

"You're a smart aleck, aren't you?"

"Yep."

"You little widget!" muttered MacPhale.

"You gobbler", said the boy pleasantly.

"What you say?"

"You gobbler!"

"As in turkey?"

"As in glutton."

"Glutton, is it? Is that what your grandmother calls me behind my back? Just because I like a bit o' padding on me tum? Well, you can just tell your grandmother for me that—"

"It's not because of your tummy. It's because of your mouth, because everything and anything goes into it and out of it without hesitation."

MacPhale stared at the boy as if he had not rightly heard. When the meaning penetrated, his eyes goggled and he barked:

"You little bucko, I should slap your mouth! You think that's funny?"

"Definitely."

"Well, I don't, and I'm gonna raise hell with your pa."

"That's a pity. My pa's so fond of you. He'll be mortified that I've been disrespectful to an upstanding citizen. He'll inflict upon me an appropriate disciplinary measure."

"Quit using those big words, you skinny half-breed."

Nathaniel indulged in a chuckle.

"And wipe that grin off your face. I'll bet you're a faggot, too!"

"No. I'm not. But I'd turn myself into one if I had to marry your daughter."

464

"I don't have a daughter."

"Then she's a lucky girl."

"Huh?"

"Never mind."

"Now you listen to me—"

"I've been listening to you for rather an inordinate amount of time. Now it's my turn. First of all, why don't you compensate my grandfather Tobac for the useless land you tricked him into buying? He's been your vassal for an awful long time, don't you think?"

"He bought it legal."

"Legal doesn't always mean moral."

"Moral?" mimicked MacPhale. He bent his head down fully two feet until his bulbous eyes met Nathaniel's. "Don't talk to me about morals, kid. You're the grandbrat of a two-bit drunken whore and a batty old adulterous schoolmarm."

Only a keen observer of human nature would have been able to detect that this struck deep and caused pain. Nathaniel did not flinch. He smiled pensively. He tilted his head and furrowed his brow.

"Oh, dear, Mayor MacPhale," he said cheerily, "my falsometer tells me that you're a liar. And a very fat liar at that. Moreover, it informs me that you're also a thief."

"What did you say?" MacPhale roared.

"A petty burglar. Why, your honor, my instruments tell me that you'd rob the false teeth out of your own mother's mouth as she lay in her coffin."

At which MacPhale exploded and made a grab for him. Nathaniel jumped back.

"Come here, you little shit!"

"No, thank you, you gor-bellied pickpocket."

MacPhale's fists swung through the air and clipped the top of Nathaniel's head.

"You cut-purse penny-snatcher, MacPhale."

"Who taught you to talk like that?" screamed MacPhale, turning purple.

"You mastadon!"

"I got no sex problems!"

"You intergalactic buffoon!"

"Shut up!" he yelled, chasing the boy around in circles in the middle of the street. A pickup truck, a car, and a one-horse buggy braked to avoid collision. A crowd began to gather. Two men lunged at MacPhale and pinned back his arms.

"Jonah, he's just a kid!"

"That's no kid! That's a maniac!"

"He's under age, MacPhale", said the other captor.

"He's a devil with a dictionary in his head!"

"You'll go to court if you hit him."

"Hit him? Why, I'll massacre him. I'll squash his family flat."

"Only if you sit on us", Nathaniel interjected meekly.

"You see what I mean?" MacPhale shouted to the crowd.

At that moment Mrs. Adele MacPhale came out the main entrance of the post office, two doors up the street. She stared and assessed the situation instantly. She steamed over and planted herself firmly between her husband and the boy.

"Calm yourself, sir", she commanded. The mayor shook off the arms of his restrainers, grunted and snorted, breathing heavily, and thrust his hands under his armpits.

Mrs. MacPhale glared at the boy.

"Where is your father?"

"He's at the school, engaged in a valiant, probably futile, attempt to teach your grandchildren to read."

"Why, you rude little snip!" she said. Turning to the crowd, she declaimed, "My husband has a heart murmur. If this delinquent has caused the Mayor any harm, his family is going to pay and pay dearly."

She snapped her eyes at Nathaniel and said *sotto voce*, "If I were your mother, I'd give you poison to drink."

"And if I were your son, I'd gladly drink it", said Nathaniel.

At which the yelling, physical restraints, and general tumult erupted all over again.

"Go kiss the Pope's big toe", screeched MacPhale.

"You go kiss King Billy's ass!" cried Nathaniel, leaping down the street, deliriously happy.

* * *

"Oh Tan, how could you?" said his mother.

"I think there was provocation", said his father, who refrained from exercising an appropriate discipline.

"Really, Nathaniel," said his grandmother, "that was self-indulgence, pure and simple. However, although I cannot applaud your lack of prudence, I must congratulate you on a certain aplomb under fire."

"Thank you, Grandma."

"And tell me, where did you learn terms such as cut-purse and gor-belly?"

"I read dictionaries for fun."

"For fun?"

"For fun."

"All right, have your fun, but be forewarned, you're probably going to get into a lot of trouble unless you curtail your intemperate affection for retaliation whenever you're in high dudgeon."

He flipped through his dictionary.

"Is that d-u-g, or d-u-d-g?"

"D-u-d-g-e-o-n."

"Here it is. Dudgeon. Deeply offended and aggrieved."

He looked up at her.

"Nathaniel. You must learn not to react when your grandmothers are called silly names."

"I'll try."

"And Nathaniel. What he said isn't true."
"I know that. My falsometer told me."

* * *

Though only a junior at the new high school, Nathaniel had been submitting precocious essays and book reports to his teacher. The man frankly found them beyond the boy's years and suspected plagiarism, or at best some unfair help from his father, the principal of the grade school. Or perhaps the dubious influence of the grandmother. But the quality of the boy's other work was so consistently high that the teacher came to believe that the writing was original.

THE OLD WAYS
by Nathaniel Delaney

Recently, I had an opportunity to visit a venerable gentleman of our community, a Mr. Camille L'Oraison, who for thirty years has worked as a section-man on the C.N.R. One of the early settlers of Swiftcreek, he arrived as a youth of twenty to assist in the construction of the railway. Over time, he worked at many occupations, such as mill-hand, faller, prospector, and breeder of chinchillas. His wife, also one of the early settlers, came to open the town's first boarding house and became very popular, raising many children, her own and others.

On a recent visit, Mr. L'Oraison generously agreed to give an account of his early days in the valley. This is what he said: "I don't know if I can explain it to you. It wasn't a better time at all, like some folks say now, specially young 'uns. It was a struggle. Nothin' was easy, 'ceptin' sleep maybe. And y'never got enough of that. Lord, we worked hard in them days, young kids just don't know! And how people died then! Death was as big a part of life as birth, not shut up in hospitals and old folks' homes like now. Long come influenza. Bang! Half yer neighbours are down, and a good number of em never gets up. Every year there's somebody killed in the bush by fallin' trees or gettin' careless with a buzz-saw. Or tore up by a grizzly. It was hard times. No T.V., no medicine t'speak of, and no supermarket.

Long dark winters and too much of yer own company some-times."

Mr. L'Oraison paused here to spit out some chewing tobacco in the snow. Then he continued:

"But I'll tell you, boy, and yer grandfathers will tell you the same, a fellow's mind was clearer in those days, simple like. Y'stepped out yer cabin door in the mornin' and smelled what kind of a day it would be, and so it was mostly, rain or shine. And things moved slow. Not all this rushin' around t'get done. It was good times then. And bad. Same's now."

The voice of the pioneer! Mr. L'Oraison's wisdom points up a popular misconception. We of the younger generation must not become enslaved to the idea of speed and progress. But then, on the other hand, neither must we become entrapped in a sort of ancestor worship and a blindness to the present. If we want to go back to the old ways we will be doubly lost, because we will have a distorted idea of what went before, this past that we profess to love. That past will teach the blind nothing. It will become a dream of golden days that never really existed.

Nathaniel Delaney   Grade Ten   B+

The teacher was of two minds concerning clever boys. The pedantic streak that sometimes marred his grandmother's news-paper seemed to have infected the grandson. He warned Na-thaniel about pretentiousness, an admonition the boy took up the mountain to his cave, where the wound could be licked.

The school's creative writing contest was held as usual that year, and the winning pieces were printed in *The Echo*. First prize went to a girl who wrote a long essay on the care of horses. Second prize went to a senior boy who wrote on the necessity of voting. The third prize went to a junior who wrote a rather odd little piece of fiction and who just happened to be the grandson of the editor:

CURTAINS FOR CLAUS
by Nathaniel Delaney

"Why of all places does he have to live at the North Pole?" wondered the dark stranger as he plodded through the sparkling, powdery snow. The moon shone down upon him as he crossed the ice fields and frosty drifts. He fingered the .45 automatic in his parka pocket. Pausing on the top of a hill, he glanced at the merry red glow of friendly Christmassy cottages.

When Santa heard the knock at the front door, he dropped his newspaper, puffed in his mellow way on an aged pipe, and slowly rose from his fireside chair.

"I'll answer it, Mama", he said, and shuffled over to the door.

"Thank you, dear", his wife shouted back from the kitchen.

"Mr. Claus? Mr. S. Claus?"

"Yes?"

"I'm from the Mafia."

"Well, well, well", said the genial old gentleman. "I'm not familiar with the name. But won't you come in and have some cocoa and Christmas cookies with us?"

Kicking the door wide open, the hoodlum gave Santa three vicious slaps and pulled him outside into the icy wind. He jammed a gun barrel into Santa's snowy whiskers and squeezed the trigger thrice.

Mrs. Santa chose at that moment to emerge from the kitchen with a tray of goodies. Seeing her husband twitching in a crimson patch of snow, she screeched and dropped the loaded tray with an awful clatter. Unhesitantly, the hoodlum grabbed her and slipped a noose around her plump neck. He pitched the rope over a rafter and gave a terrific yank. Soon she was dangling from the cottage ceiling. As Mrs. Santa squirmed and gasped, the thug munched on Christmas cookies.

"These are good cookies", he said.

He was rifling a drawer when a creak on the floor-boards caused him to whirl around. A group of tearful elves stood at the doorway, gaping at the tragic scene within. Snapping out his blackjack, the mug whipped his way through the little crowd and into the night beyond.

Later, plodding back south along the trail, he thought sadly, "Wouldn't join the syndicate, would he? Crazy old fool!"

* * *

December 22, 1967
Swiftcreek, B.C.

Dear Editor,

Although no one in Swiftcreek really believes that Santa Claus exists, most of us feel, I'm sure, that he is a popular symbol of the true spirit of Christmas, of happiness and giving. Young Mr. Delaney's story was obviously meant to be funny and possibly to be satirical of something or other. However, the general opinion of people I talked to about it was that it was sick and in very bad taste. The idea of killing Santa "in cold blood", although an impossibility, is a little upsetting to anyone at this time of year, unless he hates Christmas, and was not at all worthy of being printed in our town newspaper, where children might pick it up and read it. I know you are his grandmother, but I dare you to print this letter anyway.

Yours disgusted,
P.J., Swiftcreek, B.C.

The editor had a policy of publishing any letter that was signed and not overtly obscene. She printed it whole.

"I don't understand", said Nathaniel when he read it. "They didn't get what I was saying."

The grandmother looked long and thoughtfully at the hurt in his eyes.

"Ha, ha, ha", bellowed Jan when Nathaniel went for a visit. The old man was overcome with hilarity, having encountered many humorous situations in his life, especially in Hitler's Europe.

"Ho, ho, ho", he laughed, choking, slapping the boy on the knee with a big grin. "Leetol joke, hey, Tanny? Nobody shoot Santa Claus . . . like shoot Queen or Pope!"

* * *

On a warm afternoon in mid-October, Jan Tarnowski threw a party. He and Nathaniel had spent weeks preparing the site. They had dragged heaps of refuse away from the *enduvde-*

vorldkluk, so that it was surrounded by a wide ring of bare ground, on which they sprinkled a carpet of dry pine needles. Nathaniel, a master of chain-saw furniture, had made dozens of seat-shaped stumps for the guests. Two ropes of thick wild ivy, accented with plastic red peppers and ribbons, formed a passageway from the street to the interior of the maze. There, tables were set up and covered with checkered oilcloth. An icon shrine was hammered to the base of the tower, and a candle made ready. Christmas tree lights were strung around the walls of the lumber canyons and tested. Rabbits and chickens that had escaped over the years were recaptured, along with their numerous progeny, and put back into cages.

On the eve of the party Nathaniel went through the town and to outlying farms delivering hand-made invitations. On each, in Jan's script, was the following:

> *You come my plase. 13 Oktobr 1972, 2,30 okluk.*
> *Party for make start uv end uv de vorld kluk.*
> *Plese come Jan Tarnowski hous.*

Beneath was a crudely executed drawing of a Madonna and Child flanked by a trumpet, a bell, and a clock.

A poster on the bulletin board by the post office announced the same information and extended the invitation to the general public. In that week's *Echo*, courtesy of Anne Delaney, was yet another public invitation—slightly revised by the editor:

> Mr. Jan Tarnowski, of Swiftcreek, British Columbia, is pleased to invite one and all to an open house at his home, lot 7, Pine Street, on the afternoon of October 13, 1972, at 2:30 P.M. On this occasion, for the benefit of his neighbours, he will unveil An Invention. The event will be followed by a light luncheon and refreshments.

Although Anne had not the slightest idea about the nature of the invention, she was reassured by Nathaniel that it was an important one, worthy of attention and respect—perhaps as a work of art. And so, the following day she and Stephen hitched up the buggy and trotted into town. By the time they sighted Jan's tower piercing the heaps of his backyard, it was a quarter to three. Dozens of cars were parked along the street. They halted the gig and were tying the horse to a tree when a new red car roared by and screeched to a stop opposite Jan's gate. It contained Jonah MacPhale and three cronies who were snickering and sipping from beer bottles.

"Hey, Stevie," shouted MacPhale, "are y'off t'the ball!"

"I am indeed. Are you coming in?"

"What? Me join that bin o' loonies?"

"A good number of the people who voted for you last time are in there waiting for the festivities to begin."

"Well, in that case", shouted the mayor with mock solemnity, and staggered out the car door, winking at his friends.

"Stephen, I wish you hadn't said that", whispered Anne. "He could ruin Jan's special day."

"I regret it. I was certain he wouldn't put a toe across the threshold."

"He's full of beer too."

"Jonah," said Stephen, "on second thought you wouldn't enjoy it!" he said slowly. "After all, several of us in there are a few bricks short of a load."

But the mayor was topping off his tanks from a brown paper bag and didn't hear. Anne and Stephen left him standing there and hoped he would not enter.

They followed the ivy garlands and arrived at the center of the maze to find a crowd standing around the rim of the circle, looking amused. The more intimate guests looked properly expectant, though Grandpa Tobac was having trouble keeping some of his brown grandchildren from scaling the lumber piles and shrieking with abandon. Katie, the photographer from *The Echo,* was here too. Bless the girl—covering the party had been her own idea. She saw Turid and Camille with some of their grandchildren. Reverend Edwin Gunnalls wiping his bifocals and looking properly cheery. Standing beside him, the new priest, a young fellow named Bill Ryan, from the east. He had arrived in town last year to erect a small parish church and had become one of Jan's close friends. Ashley and Sarah were here too, with the children. She felt a surge of love for her family, who had all turned out in their Sunday best. The boys were getting their shoes scuffed and their shirttails were flying as they ran about with their Tobac cousins, but Sarah kept the three little girls standing demurely by her side, wearing white ankle-length dresses covered with lace and small pearls. Anne wondered if their mother had made them from a wedding dress. Most surprisingly of all, there was Father Andrei, standing quietly at the back of the crowd. No one had seen him in years. He had aged greatly, she saw, and her heart contracted with longing to speak with him.

At that moment, Jan Tarnowski and Nathaniel Delaney came center stage beneath the tower and were greeted by a sudden hush.

Nathaniel announced in his man-boy's voice, with large theatrical gestures:

"Welcome, ladies and gentlemen, boys and girls, toddlers and tots, humble laborers and careerist politicians . . ."

Jonah MacPhale and his cronies had shuffled in at the back of the crowd, whispering, nudging each other, clutching paper bags. The R.C.M.P. constable eyed them, then turned his attention to center stage. People began to grow a little uncomfortable. The boy was using some words that most of them did not recognize. He was a strange boy, and everyone knew that Jan himself was a little out to lunch. Listening to the jabber would be boring, but it would be a small price to pay for the sake of hilarious stories that could be told years hence.

"Welcome friends and foes alike. Today in your presence is unveiled to you an *invention*. It is a machine of brilliant conception, created by our valley's one and only true unsung genius. I give him to you, Mister Janusch Tarnowski!"

There was a smattering of applause and considerable signs of discomfort in the audience. They did not know exactly how much of this they could endure. Several glanced unabashedly at their watches.

Jan stepped forward, looking embarrassed. His face was flaming red, and his body looked too large inside a suit made some time during the Great Depression. His tie was garish.

"My frends und nayboors", he began.

"Speak up, Jan!" a few voices shouted.

"My frends und nayboors, I am so lucky man to live in dis goot land of Canada and wit dis goot peoples who are so nice to man from de far away country. When I come here I tink de whole vorld is a bad place. I see many tings in de var. I see many bad tings come out of people's hearts. In start dey vas goot peoples. But den dey vas bad peoples. When Hitler und Stalin und der udder bad guys comink to us, we have no plase to run, no plase to hide. Ve hungry. Ve have not nuff vood und coal for fire. Ve have see mutter und fatter kill, vife und baby kill. But after de var, I find dis land full of goot peoples. Und I say, never again, Jan, you see dese tings hurt de heart und boorn de soul. Und break de mind of de head . . ."

At this point a few onlookers drifted back to the street without being noticed and drove away. A good number in the crowd stirred and watched their feet or gazed over at the loaded tables on which a big coffee urn burbled, a crock of sausages and sauerkraut attracted flies, and a gallon of vodka was surrounded by many little glasses.

"Und one day I prayink when a voice he speak to me and he say, Jan I vant you make big *enduvdevorldkluk* . . ."

The utterance of this by-now-famous incantation recaptured the attention of most.

"Gott say to me [several people laughed at this point], dis

475

peoples is like de peoples of you country ven de Nazis comink, only dey is veak, veak, veak. Dey is blind. Dey is for demself first. Dey is boorn each other if dey not change de heart."

Jan's eyes were leaking tears and the rising grumble of the audience threatened to drown him out.

"Get on with it, Tarnowski!" a voice shouted.

"Some party!"

"No more speeches", yelled another. And so on.

"Den wit help uv my frend Tanny I bilt it so high dat de whole valley see dis kluk and hear dis kluk ven it ring."

"Bring on the ring! Bring on the ring!" shouted a few, and others took up the chant.

"You peoples are de childrens uv de last days!" Jan cried above the clamor. "You do not know who you are. You do not know vat is comink on de vorld!"

More shouts and groans. More *Shhhhh's*.

Nathaniel lurched around the circle yelling at the noise-makers, "Shut up, dammit, shut up!"

The parish priest tried to hush the crowd more diplomatically.

Anne glared furiously at the mayhem, and Katie the photographer kept snapping pictures at fever pitch.

Father Andrei appeared stricken by an old grief and closed his eyes.

"Dis bell und dis trumpet is to varn you ven de time is near", Jan shouted. He climbed the ladder that was leaning against the tower. Halfway up he stopped by a lever that jutted from the side of the scaffolding. He pulled the lever, and suddenly metal weights in the shape of giant pine cones fell zinging along their chains and set a system of gears muttering within the entire structure.

The crowd fell silent.

Jan began to sob at the top of the ladder. Nathaniel climbed up after him and held onto his legs to keep him from falling.

At precisely three o'clock (many in the crowd checked their watches) a bell rang. The sides of the mountains repeated it from north to east to south and west, and back again, round and round in ever-diminishing echoes. The sound was so loud and so pure that the people were shaken. The bell at the very height of the tower was covered by a small cupola, open-faced to the four quadrants. Twice more it pealed, and twice more the people covered their ears, and looked down or at each other. But Jan and the boy and the two priests and the minister and Sarah and Camille and Stephen looked up in awe at the reverberation of light that signalled the passing of a giant stroke of music.

After that, stillness fell, and Stephen went over to help Nathaniel and Jan back down the ladder. Jan, blinded by his weeping, was in no shape to inaugurate the party proper, so Camille made an announcement in a big voice that the festivities had begun: Would people please make themselves at home with food and drink. Gradually, human voices were turned on again, and a semblance of normality returned to the scene. A record player behind the chicken run blurted out rousing marches. Two rabbits hopped across the circle, followed by many small bunnies. All in all it was turning out to be quite a ridiculous day, and laughter erupted to the sound of clinking glasses. Anne went over and hugged Jan and held him for a minute while her husband pumped his hand. Without attracting notice, the parish priest climbed the ladder and sprinkled the lower part of the structure with holy water.

Anne stepped back and watched the blessing. Something in the rite was so primitive that her critical faculty switched on and her sympathy diminished. But in another part of her being she understood. The young priest reached the top of the ladder, climbed onto the structure itself, and went up higher. When the bell was baptized, she noticed that there were trumpets just below the plinth of the cupola. These too he baptized. She walked around the structure and saw that there were four of them, one for each point of the compass.

"What is it, Tan? What is this thing?"

"An *enduvdevorldkluk*, Grandma."

"I mean, actually, what is it for?"

"Just what Jan said."

"I must confess that a good deal of his introduction was unintelligible."

"It's a clock."

"But there's no face, no hands, no numbers of the hour!"

"He says it'll keep time from now until the end of the century. But it's not a clock for people to set their watches by. It's for something else."

"A clock with no face or hands? What could it possibly be for?"

"He's afraid for the people of the valley. He built it to warn and to protect."

"Warn? Protect? From what?"

"From fire."

"I see", she said, knowing that she did not see.

She looked around for Father Andrei, but he was gone. Curiously, no one recalled having seen him there.

* * *

For several weeks Jan's clock struck the third hour, and only the third hour. When the novelty of it had worn away a little, people found other things to think about. But at three o'clock every afternoon they fell into the habit of turning on their radios to listen to the Dominion time signal. Without fail, Jan's bell rang in perfect unison.

Camille crossed the field one evening just after supper, when the stars were too bright, promising the first snow of November. He came into Delaney's looking very angry, in the way that only a humble, calm man can look angry when aroused.

"It's the meanest thing I ever heard", he fumed. "His worship *the mayor* has called an emergency meeting of the city council for tonight. I'm sure they're plannin' some trouble over Jan Tarnowski's clock. I think if enough people turn out, we can match them trouble for trouble."

"You're an alderman, Camille. Didn't they tell you what's up?"

"Steve, they wouldn't tell me nothin' except it's over a new bylaw about loud noises in the town proper. And that tells me a lot, cause they know we're partial to Jan, and right now Jan is the biggest noisemaker in the region."

"That's not strictly true", said Anne. "There's Jonah's disco bar, for example, the most renowned noisemaker from Jasper to Kamloops. There are four very loud lumber mills and an awful lot of trains tooting their horns as they rush down the valley. Not to mention gunshots on the farms, and chain saws in backyards cutting firewood, and explosions made by the crews putting in the highway—"

"Yes, all that. But Jonah has a bee in his bonnet, and the powers behind the throne put it there."

"Adele?"

"Of course", he nodded. "And Mrs. Sinclair and the sewing circle. Plus a few guys in the Chamber of Commerce who want the city to look like a respectable place."

They coated up hurriedly and got the buggy ready while Camille went back to his farm in the dark to change out of chore clothes. They picked him up twenty minutes later on the road and went trotting in the direction of town. But as luck would have it, the buggy hit a frozen rut and the axle chose that very moment to snap. It took Stephen and Camille an hour to get a metal splint onto it, and they arrived at the town hall by 9:00 P.M.

"We're too late", said Camille, eyeing the cluster of people coming out of the front door. Most of them were definitely members of the Chamber of Commerce, and a few were devotees of the sewing circle.

Reverend Gunnalls and Father Ryan were in a huddle at the bottom of the steps.

"Steve, Anne", said the priest. "The mayor's tried to pull a fast one, but I think Ed and I may have derailed him. But only just."

"He tried to get a bylaw passed that would make the ringing of bells illegal. Can you imagine!" said Edwin Gunnalls.

"A disturbance of the civic peace, he called it."

"An invasion of privacy was the other term."

"He had the whole thing in a bag, every member of the council except you ready to vote for it, and every noggin in the audience nodding enthusiastically. So we jumped up and said, just a moment, Your Worship, there are a few things you haven't considered."

"So Father Bill here tells them that declaring an act of religious liturgy to be illegal is a violation of civic rights."

"MacPhale replies that the noise of the bells—notice that he didn't say which bell—is a great irritation to most of the population and an invasion of *their* civic rights."

"So Ed points out that at least sixty percent of the population attends one of the four churches in town, and all of them have little bells that call their congregations to prayer. Now, one or two people on the council attend those churches, and they were beginning to look uncomfortable."

"Then Father adds that the noise of the CN freight going through with its horn blasting is louder than all the noisemakers in town put together."

"Yes, and what are the legal implications if a child is killed going over a crossing because the horn has become outlawed? Will that not be an *intrusion* of the child's civic rights? And what if the mills have to shut down while they install noise-suppression equipment? Is that not a violation of the rights of the hardworking people of this valley to earn a living?"

"Yes, and what if some of our congregations were to feel very strongly that the noise from the disco is an invasion of their family life, their privacy, and their peace of mind? What if they were to press charges under the new bylaw?"

"At that point they became pretty irritable and started arguing among themselves, and it looked like we had won a tactical victory."

"But then, the cover blew off the whole thing and the mayor stated outright—God bless his soul for being such a forthright fellow—he says plain as day that the real problem here is Jan Tarnowski's bell. Then he said some hard things about Jan's state of mind."

"I can imagine", said Anne.

"So the whole question has been remanded to further discussion and will be decided at the next meeting of the council. The first week of December."

"At least you'll be there to fight for us at the meeting, Camille."

"No I can't", he said, downcast. "That's the week I'm scheduled for surgery in Vancouver to get my cataract removed. And those fellas know all about it."

He pointed. The mayor and the rest of the council were coming out the front door and locking up. Jonah tipped his hat at the group as he went past.

"Evenin', Annie, Steve. Sorry you couldn't have been here, C'mille."

"Me too, Jonah."

The mayor squinted humorously at the two clergymen.

"Well, I'll say one thing; it's a cold day in hell when two of you lads agree on somethin'."

"Ah, yes, Your Worship, we're very agreed indeed", said Reverend Gunnalls. "And we'll be very agreed at next month's meeting."

"I think not, m'boys. It's an *in camera* session, as they say in

Parliament. No visitors allowed. We'll settle things our way, democratic like."

They stared at him and at the cronies, who were smirking up their sleeves.

Anne went over to the mayor and took his sleeve. He tried to pull his arm away from her with a laugh and a grimace at his friends, but she held on. A small woman half his weight, half his height.

"I would like a word with you in private, Jonah MacPhale", she said quietly.

"Promise not t'hurt me!" he cried loudly, and his chorus sniggered.

"A little walk down the block and back, five minutes only", she said evenly, smiling politely.

"Lord save us, it's the dangerous lady editor. A little black widder with a big sting!"

She felt Stephen bristle beside her but quieted him with a look. She guided the mayor's arm away from the group.

"Now, now, Annie", he said all conciliatory, when they were out of earshot. "You got a soft spot for outsiders and weirdos, and your grandson helped build the damn thing, but it's a menace to the civic peace and it's an unsafe structure."

"To what are you referring, Jonah?"

"You know damn well what I'm talkin' about!"

"Why should a little bell bother you? The town is peppered with bells."

"Right. There's too many of them, and this is the worst of them all. It's undignified."

"Undignified?"

"A lot of folks have worked mighty hard to make this a respectable city and . . ."

"Oh, it's a city, is it?"

"You know what I mean. Legally speakin', we're a city."

"Of two thousand people?"

"And we're not goin' to grow if we get a reputation for bein' a looney-bin."

"But we are a looney-bin."

"What?" he said, looking at her as if she were, indeed, crazy.

"And proud of it, Jonah MacPhale."

"What yer talkin' about, girl?"

"It's a place where people who don't belong anywhere else can come and live a human life. It's a place where the beauty of the land surrounds everything. It's clean and strong, and it's got hope written all over it. People can dream on something here. Don't take it away from them. If you turn this into a miniature version of the big cities, where no one can turn around without getting a permit and all sorts of simple and wonderful things are made illegal at some lawmaker's whim, then I'll have your hide on my barn wall."

He looked at her, astounded, and laughed, disbelieving.

"By God, you're a tough—"

"If the word you were unwisely about to use begins with the letter B, I advise you to think twice."

He harumphed and hemmed and hawed and shook his jowls.

"Now look here", he said sharply, wagging his finger at her. "This country is about to make a big leap in land values. We could attract all kinds of industry. We got the potential for becomin' another Ruhr Valley like they got in Germany. But there's other valleys in this province that got the minerals and forests we got. If we get a reputation as a resort for layabouts and nut-cases and every damn bit o' human junk that can't fit in nowhere else, then the big money's gonna look someplace else. They'll want to set up where there's a population of steady workin' class folk, like over in Williams Lake country or up by Prince George or the Bulkley Valley."

"You've been buying a lot of real estate lately, haven't you?"

"What of it?"

"You've made offers on every lot on Pine Street, too, I noticed."

He gave her a hard look.

"The new CN bunkhouse is up for bids, isn't it, and I'll wager that your construction company has put in a low offer. Pine Street is cheap land, two minutes from the station. A perfect spot for the site."

"You get off my back, you . . ." he said through gritted teeth.

She pulled him to a stop beside her. Then she turned him toward her, and he did not know how she had done it.

"Listen to me very carefully", she said in a quiet voice. "I've watched you play your games for many, many years. I've not confronted you about your lies and your manipulation and the way you use simple people as if they were things, because I've always given you the benefit of the doubt. But from the very beginning little warning bells went off inside of me every time you opened your mouth, every time you made a new deal. Why was there always something odd and indefinable about it, Jonah MacPhale? Why do those warning bells inside of me just keep on getting louder and louder? Yet, not once in all these years have I indulged in that sport which is Swiftcreek's favorite pastime—gossip, slander, and calumny. I despise detraction, but I warn you, I may change my mind in your case. I've overlooked everything up to now. But I'm going to get very *noisy* myself if you don't do some honest self-examination."

He stared at her as if she were criminally insane.

"Furthermore, you will leave Jan Tarnowski alone, from now until there *is* a cold day in hell, and you will restrict yourself to the tasks that any honest mayor should be concerned with. You will cease to intimidate and foreclose on people who cannot defend themselves against you. If I see a hint, the merest hint, mind you, that you aren't doing all of the foregoing, I will make it my vocation in life to fight you. At the very least I will expose you. But I think I can ruin you. I will do it. I will do it if you make me do it."

He stared at her. The noise, the bluster, was gone.

"Do you understand?"

"I understand", he said tonelessly, with hatred in his eyes.

"I have a press that I will use against you to the maximum. I have some land that I will be happy to sell in order to raise funds for a lawyer to keep you in court for years. I am an unbalanced woman, you see, and I am angrier than I have ever been in my life."

"I hear you."

He hurried away to his car.

It was the last ever heard about the illegality of bells. From then on the *enduvdevorldkluk* rang daily at three o'clock, and the people of the region came to love it.

32

Order asserted itself, as order will when administered by powers. The machinery of government turned as inexorably as had been predicted. The earth was moved. Gears revolved impressively. By and large a measure of progress came upon the land.

"There's so many of them government clerks buzzin' round here, it makes me dizzy!" said Turid one day. "There's more damn paper bein' passed round than snuff at a wake!"

She was bent badly and waddled along with a cane. She was still fierce, though, and had gardened right up until the previous month, when they had moved. She and Camille now lived in a small gingerbread box in town.

"I hate the damn place", she told Anne. "It's too damn neat!"

"But it must be more convenient now, Turid, with your health not what it used to be?"

"Convenient!?" she snorted. "Who the hell cares about convenient. I liked it better hard. And I just don't trust them pale little government fellers. What do they do fer a livin' anyway?"

Over the years Anne watched as the valley was undressed as far as the eye could see, and the town was swollen into a miniature city with more than half of its inhabitants encamped in trailers and mobile homes. They had come to strip the valley or to man the mills consuming the ingathering of timber or to service the needs of the suddenly expanded populace.

The trickle of the Canoe gradually filled the trough of the valley, approaching its northernmost high-water mark precisely in the fields of Stephen Delaney. It came with that dreadful willfulness which is the mark of acts of God and government. The woman watched the rising lake with a cold eye, imagining herself up to the ankles in water and a shotgun in her arms, daring them to drag her off the land they said was no longer her own. It wasn't that way, of course, though she was tempted to create a scene. She knew what a good opera she could have made of it—a photo on the front page of the *Vancouver Sun* or even the eastern papers, laughing at the province's considerable population of eccentrics. The revolt of the lotus eaters:

B.C. INDIVIDUALIST BITES PREMIER:
HOWLS OF PROTEST

And the reporters in hip-waders sloshing out to interview the old mad woman of Canoe Lake.

"What is it, Ma'am? D'you want more money?"

"It's not the money, it's the principle!"

"You're not really going to shoot anyone, are you?" they would ask, smirking.

"I have a shell full of rock-salt here, and if the men responsible for this cesspool dare show their faces or rears, I will sting their fat hides."

More laughter.

Oh, yes, the possibilities for theatrics were unlimited. But it would be too easy. Every reader from here to the Atlantic would be reassured that homely grassroots individualism and freedom and all the other comfortable totems were as safe as ever. No, better to let those illusions drown with the land.

A polite letter informed them that they were the last property owners eligible for compensation, and if they did not promptly reply on the proper forms, they could not expect to be assessed. The lake was already covering her land south of the farm. The trapline, the trap-cabin, the hot spring, and the homesteads deeper in the valley had already disappeared. The water was now licking at the upper fields. And so they did the only thing they felt was possible, signed the forms despondently and received a check.

They used the money to build a small house on a piece of inferior land, higher up and closer to town. In a way, feeling her age and a creeping fatigue that would not be shaken off, she was grateful for the building. It was solid and easy to heat. There were electric power poles to the lane. Stephen bought her an automatic washing machine, an invention more fabulous than the space ships now orbiting the planet. The radio informed her that men were walking on the moon. This radio did not groan down on dying batteries but played and replayed the new cacophonous music with the pitiless dedication of monomaniacs. For the first time in her life she experienced her home drenched in unfailing light. A kettle boiled in minutes. Power, her enemy, served the woman.

Why then did she fight back an ache in her throat whenever she walked down the road to the old place to watch the rising of the lake? It covered the porch one month, the window sills the next. She went to the water's edge on the morning of the first big freeze. A sea of glass. She skipped stones across its surface. *Zing, zing, zing*, with a hollow *knock, knock, knock* beneath it. She had never done such a thing before, but the sound was uncannily familiar.

The following winter it clamped the cabin in ice up to the eaves. She took some of the grandchildren skating on an afternoon in January when a vicious wind had blown the lake clean of snow. She stood wobbling on her old strap-on blades as the young ones whizzed around the ice-locked roof. Round and round the building they went, giggling and shouting and cracking the whip and sliding a dozen yards on their backsides. She would have laughed, too, had not the metaphysical ache contracted with particular intensity: if only, if only she had been given a glimpse of this scene during her first years here! *Why is it*, she mused, *why is it we are only permitted to look around in the present or back into the flux of the past?*

There it sat, the poor old house with its two attic windows staring balefully back at her from its pointed head. Her past, sinking into the depths, but frozen precisely at the moment before its final plunge into subconsciousness. Memory storing itself away while pleading for one last moment of seeing. *Well*, she asked herself, *is this tragedy or comedy? Choose, woman!* She looked at the question one way, then another, back and forth. Choice. It always came back to that, really. She stared for the longest time until the sting in her cheeks forced her to move, and a line of grandchildren slammed into her, and they all went down in a heap.

"Comedy!" she cried aloud. The children stared at her, then laughed the louder. This sound, she hoped, would be the sound that returned when the burnings and drownings were no more.

All afternoon until the sky was burnished green she loved them and played with them. The ice cracked like a gunshot. She stopped and cocked an ear, hoping for the ice to sing, but it did not. She called the children to listen, but they would not. As they raced around and around the house on fast blades, the shadows cast by their passing of the attic windows made its hollow eyes appear to blink. When the first star was in the deep blue-black above the mountain, and then another appeared beside it, she knelt and crawled through the window. Inside it was dark, and the surface beneath her hands and knees was like perfectly smooth marble. She struck a match and saw the fossilized remains of old magazines, torn photos, and tobacco tins locked in the ice. Stephen had left a box or two up here when they moved. "Junk", he had told her.

Darkness. She struck another light and for a brief burning moment she read a few lines from a scrap of paper, a poem, in Stephen's handwriting, of all things:

> The rock and the fire made battle,
> The sea and the sky were wed. . . .

The light died again. She struck one more match, and now there was a different scrap:

> Freedom and faithfulness were one,
> and danced in the morning light,
> but darkness. . . .

The light went out again, and her knees were aching. "Grandma! Grandma!"

Yes, their poor grandma had better gather them up and take them home to hot chocolate by the fire. She might even coax Grandpa to tell them a story. But why had she never seen these words of his before? She must ask him sometime.

Summer came again. The house finally disappeared under water, and the wind scattered anything that floated to the surface. The wind had permanently changed its patterns. Stripped of its windbreaks, it now began to blow harder and colder up the valley. The rampaging air screeched through the town like Stephen's banshees or winnowed in its gentler moments ever northward, north, north along the big lake. The salmon had dwindled in numbers and were replaced by the cooler flesh of dollies and whitefish. The woman missed those slashes of red cutting upward through the jade of river to spawn and die. And she longed for the geese, which had ceased to land in her field. They turned corners in the sky, confused by the waterscapes that contradicted their ancestral maps. There was restlessness in creation and in the little arrangements of men.

* * *

Stephen Delaney and his grandson Nathaniel went walking in the new field. It was a sour, stumpy soil that did not satisfy the animals. They had to import hay because of the poor pasture and the absence of cleared land. It came by truck along the new highway that snaked east through the pass to Alberta. The government money had not accounted for such minor details, and the man regretted he had not fought harder. Worst of all, he had sold his sheep. There had been a very bad month after that decision, while he had grieved for them. There was only a goat and a horse left.

"I should have gone with your grandmother to Victoria", he lamented, "and camped on the Premier's steps. Or written a letter. But she seemed to be doing enough fighting for both of us."

They smiled together over that private natural resource, the woman. They moved closer, their arms almost touching. The boy was in his late teens now, a gaunt creature with dark skin, a penetrating eye, and a shock of black hair that fell over his brow. He moved slowly like the Tobacs and produced his words like rare coins, which was a trait of his grandfather's, the old Irishman.

"Tell me, Tan, how is *The Quill* doing these days?"

"It's well, Grandpa. Seven paying subscriptions aside from yours, Dad's, and Grandpa Tobac's."

"Not a bad start, lad. God bless all your efforts."

The boy shot the old man a look. He suspected his mystical grandfather of religious sentimentality and was cautious in responding to anything that smacked of it. He believed in ideas, not the supernatural. Moreover, he was a freethinker!

If the fledgling *Quill* was only a small, untrained tongue of his thought, it was at least a mobile one. He produced the little eight-page monthly on his grandmother's antique French Press, a hand-operated iron contraption not much bigger than a television set. She had brought it out of storage from a back room, and together they had set up the entire offices and industry of *The Quill* in a closetlike room where she had been storing ink. His grandfather Thaddee had carved a small sign that hung on the door, a wooden quill and the word of his dream cut into cedar.

The paper was full of his recently acquired ideas, his misconceptions and poems, short stories and obscure wit. It was pompous and nonconformist. Its editor was preparing to do battle armed only with a dictionary and a point of view. His view, simply put, was that man is a noble, innocent being who has been deformed by repressive systems of all kinds. He must by his very nature find himself at odds with power in whatever form it happened to take. When he groped through an explanation of this for his grandmother, she sighed and said, "So, you're an anarchist!"

"A what, Gram?"

By way of answer she gave him *Fathers and Sons* by Turgenev and *Crime and Punishment* by Dostoevsky. He found them hard to understand but read them tolerantly. When Anne probed his memory to see if he had retained any of it, she found a disconcerting vacuum. And sighed again.

He had not yet learned the distinction between tyranny and responsible authority, she saw. But she drew hope from the fact that he was not a conformist, had somehow escaped being trained to be a well-adjusted consumer. He was working out his vision of the world, in the privileged position of being paid to do so, although real paying customers were few.

His own father at times wondered where the boy had drummed up his subscribers but assumed that there would always be those who enjoyed the rubble left in the wake of youth, like the surprises one sometimes discovers in glacial till. He saw that Nathaniel had avoided any contamination by the old culture and was on his way to developing a brilliant mind. Then he had thrown over a promising future, quit third year university, and returned in search of a separate education. His own kinds of books, Kerouac and Salinger, and worse—the yarns of dying races, offered by both male grandparents. It seemed that his son was trying to collect the stories of Irish and Shushwap, and even from time to time pried a fragment of socialist history from the old woman. What a mess. But Tan worked hard; he had to grant him that. He was a joe-boy at *The Echo* by day, and at night he was busy scratching out his articles for *The Quill*. He used a real quill and an inkwell, his father noted with disgust. His own son, a romantic!

But Anne and Stephen were, for different reasons, pleased by Nathaniel's choice. The grandfather noticed that the boy was disciplined. And despite a tendency to preach and exaggerate, there was often a flash of illumination in those pieces he wrote. In addition, the lad appeared to believe in his foolishness, in his own self, which in time would convince a number of others. He was bleary-eyed from late nights in his closet; he was too thin and *too bleedin' serious*, said one of his subscribers, Mrs. L'Oraison, who bought the damn thing for the jokes. He was liverish-looking to some and a worry to all.

"Grandpa, I don't know how you can stand to do business with MacPhale when you know how he cheated Grandpa Tobac and all those other things he's done."

Stephen looked at him. They sat together on a rock from which they could survey the new house. Across from them the forest sank down into the lip of the artificial lake.

"Well, Tan, when you get older you get a bit more understanding about the faults of human beings. I've told Jonah Mac-Phale to his face many a time what I think of his practices. It's like water running off a loon's back. He just laughs and calls me a good old mick. But I don't believe you can give up on people, write them off, you know, like so many do."

"Why not, Grandpa? He's a bastard!"

"Ah, he'd be the first to admit it. He thinks he's being realistic. You know, the problem isn't really his greed."

"No? What's his problem?"

"Same as everyone else's, only a little worse. Fear. That's his problem. Under that fat belly and a half-million bucks in the bank is really just a little immigrant boy who's scared of being poor or cold or alone."

"That little boy's been climbing and stomping on people's heads for fifty years!"

"We don't have a right to condemn him. We can see what we see. That's honest and true. But hate isn't—"

"Grandpa, you amaze me. I could kick that heartless old pig. When I think of him trying to destroy Jan's clock or standing up there telling the government that he thinks he represents the people of Swiftcreek and isn't it a grand idea to flood the Canoe—"

"The thing is, he does represent Swiftcreek. It's the times, Tan, and that old laddo is a sign of them. Besides, I have hopes for Jonah MacPhale."

The boy raised his eyebrows. His grandfather was too kind, a wrinkled, old-fashioned man, sprung from the weeping-wailing Irish, the most sentimental of tribes. The old fellow was tough, though, in his way. Trapper and all that. One of his earliest memories was of his grandfather bent over the bleating lambs at docking time. One slice of the hot iron and off went the tail, then flip, over on their backs went the little rams. One swift slit of the razor-sharp pocket knife and the top of the fleecy scrotum was open. Then he would take the whole sac in his teeth and pull out the testicles on their strings.

"Rocky Mountain Oysters", that old monster, Turid L'Oraison, called them. She was always around at castrating time with her tin can to collect the results. She liked to fry them up for her man. She was another tough one, that lady.

Or butchering sheep, a sight he could barely endure. One hammer blow on the forehead and the sheep collapsed. Swift throat slit, hoist the animal up between the poplars with block and tackle, slash, slash, off came the hide, out went the steaming viscera in coils into the wheelbarrow. No longer sheep but mutton. And his gentle grandfather, up to the elbows in blood, with a patient, thoughtful look on his face.

Stephen tamped his pipe, lighting, sucking, sighing as the

494

smoke wafted across the field. He recalled an afternoon, not unlike this one, when Nathaniel was about eight years old. He had come running through the hay to his grandfather and handed him a gift.

"What is it?" Stephen had said, unwrapping it from tinfoil and ribbon.

"It's a thing", the boy said gravely, "that I made for you."

The man's mouth opened but no words came. The contents revealed. It was a crude ring carved from the stalk of a willow. Incised on the outer surface of the band was a triangle flanked by two stars.

"Where did you get this?"

"I *made* it, Grandpa", said the boy, sinking, afraid that his passionate giving had not been received.

"No, lad", he said softly, "I mean, where did you get the idea? Did I ever tell you about two stars or mention a dream?"

"No, it's something I just thought up today. Don't you like it?"

"I like it very much, Nathaniel", the man said, pressing the boy to him.

"It's a mountain. And the stars are you and Gram."

So childhood grows and departs. And boys find themselves in the loneliness of manhood, where gifts and embraces are not so easily exchanged. As the old man and the young man now sat together listening to the wind, it seemed to both of them that they might no longer understand each other. Though beneath the unknowing was a contentment of presences.

"Aren't you mad about losing the farm, Grandpa?"

"Yes, Tan. And no." He puffed a bit more on his pipe, which the boy suspected was the smelter of some thought.

"When your dad was born, I took him out into the field by the river and showed it to him. And I made him a promise that the earth, the water, and the air he saw before him was his, and no one would ever take it from him."

"Promises aren't always easy to keep."

"Very true, Nathaniel. In fact, when Ashley came of age, I was ready to give the farm to him, or work it with him. But he didn't want it. Tossed it back in my face as if I'd offered him a burden and not a treasure."

Nathaniel's eyes remained fixed on the horizon.

Stephen tapped his arm.

"Tan?"

"Grandpa, I would gladly have taken that land."

"Well, it's gone now. Though this little speck o' dirt and the house will one day be yours. There's some bush, too, which should be cleared."

"I could kill Jonah MacPhale!" Nathaniel said through clenched teeth.

For a long time his grandfather stared at him, his eyes contorted with anguish. He was silenced by this outburst, not because it hinted at a murderous tendency in the youth. His grandson was not impassioned with power or wealth or violence but with words. Stephen was disturbed by his own past.

"I killed a man once", he said.

Nathaniel looked up.

A long time ago, years before these generations had been born, in the lost decades, time had flowed like the tides that struck the beach at Dunquin. It had formed a child of the sea, son of a fisherman, who had run with terror and hope struggling in his breast, run up the hills to tell his wounded father that help was on the way.

As the boy Stiofain approached the height of the *croagh,* he saw from afar the cliff where the opening of the cave would be. But his heart contracted when he noticed a figure bending over the entrance. There was a strong wind blowing, and the boy was running into it. The soft grass cushioned his feet, and whoever it was failed to hear his approach.

"It was a terrible moment, Tan. When I came over a hillock I saw the whole scene in a glance. I saw instantly what had happened. While I had gone for help, this soldier had found my footprints in the mud by the cave. He had shot my father in the face and was dragging the body out."

Stephen paused and collected himself.

"I went mad. I took a big rock and smashed the soldier's head from behind. I smashed and smashed until the village men came and pulled me off of him. They dumped the body in the sea where the waves will batter anything out of recognition against the rocks. The authorities believed he was drowned. I was filled with horror that I had taken another man's life. In my heart I knew I was a murderer."

"But he was the murderer, Grandpa!"

"Yes, but as they went through his papers before burning them in the fire, I looked at his name and photos and everything. He was a person, Tan. He was about as old as my father. In this one photograph he was strong and smiling beside his wife in a garden someplace in England. Just a poor bloody soldier with a wife waiting for him. I often wondered what became of his family and were there any kids I'd made into orphans."

"So what, Grandpa! He made you into an orphan!"

"He was a human being, Tan. Caught in a moment of great evil, but still a person. I hated him for so many years it near poisoned my life. His name haunts me even now. Wheeler."

"Who cares!" said his grandson.

"It was only years later that I was freed from the blackness and the guilt when I met this priest who was a fine man for understanding human beings. A little crippled fellow who was here for a while before you were born."

"But it was war. Ireland and England were—"

"War? Oh, yes. Men are always at war with one another. But it doesn't make it right. You see, when I looked down at his face as they were carrying him off the mountain, I saw something that scarred me for the rest of my days. His head was all busted, but I saw."

"What, Grandpa? What did you see?"

"I saw my own face."

"Huh?"

"I looked at his broken face, and it was *my* face. Do you understand, lad?"

"No."

"I pray that you'll never have to."

The afternoon was lowering quickly, and what had been a shared contentment had turned into radical disquiet. They sat side by side, unable to move.

"All my life I've despised Jonah MacPhale", said the old man. "But, you see, I was wrong. Each of us chooses one form of betrayal or another. Some betray people. Some betray the truth. We kill or steal or twist things up with a gun or a word, and all because we're frightened little creatures. I can't abandon Jonah to his fate. He is me, if you can understand, boy. And someone has to be there if his soul ever opens up long enough to ask why or cry out for help."

"You're too good, Grandpa. He's a rotten, corrupt sort of person."

"I'm not good. And it may be he's not yet doomed."

The old man was upset. Was it with life or the boy's blindness?

"You're good", said the grandson.

Stephen Delaney shook himself.

"Come", he said sternly. "Let's go, the light is failing."

33

"I haven't taken a sea voyage in decades", she said to the purser.

He pushed back his cap and smiled at her.

"Going home, Ma'am?"

"Not to stay. A short visit. I haven't seen England since 1922."

"More than fifty years. Long time to be away. England's changed a lot since the War."

"Which war do you mean?"

"The second, of course."

He had obviously been a child during that event.

"I expect I'll recognize it, after all."

"I guess you will, Ma'am. *Bon voyage*."

"*Bon voyage*", she replied, as he tipped his hat and strode cheerily away down the deck. The conversation was vaguely familiar, like something once dreamed but unremembered, lingering at the edge of consciousness.

She gripped the rails and watched the north shore slide by. The Laurentian mountains were white, and thin shelves of ice still clung to the river bank. It was early spring or late winter, depending on your perspective.

> I'm dying, Anne. Please come and see me. There's no one left but you and me. The phone book is full of Ashtons, but they're no connection unless you go back to before the Reformation. I have a peke named Baskerville. I watch a lot of telly. Good company, the both of them. I'm getting around with the help of a walker, and a woman comes in to tidy up. I've sold the big house at Bishopsford and got a small bachelor flat in London—it costs an arm and a leg. I hope you won't mind

sleeping on the pull-out sofa. Please come. I've enclosed the fare, and you mustn't argue about it. Come by air, love.
 Emily

*

Dearest Emily,
How much time do you have? Are you in pain? Tell me the details.
 Love,
 Anne

*

Anne,
Lots of time yet. Only smidgens of pain. The chemotherapy is the worst part. I'll have a break from it in late March. Come then if you can.
 Emily

*

Em,
I'm coming by ship. It costs a bit more, but Stephen insisted I use the tax rebate together with what you sent. It's been so very long since I've seen the ocean. Soon.
 Love,
 Anne

*

She had dreamed or imagined this trip many times in her younger days. Then, knowing it was impossible, she had stopped the dreaming and the yearning and had accepted what was given.

This trip was a wholly unsuspected gift, a marvel, a miracle. She vaguely recalled a daydream, so many years ago, an imaginary voyage in which love had reached out across the abyss of human loneliness and touched her. Love that was neither possessive nor possessed. *The best kind of love*, she had said to the man. What had she called him, that character in her fantasy? Philip? Paul? No, *Peter.*

She turned her face up to the astoundingly bright sun. The gulls were screaming and the wind was brisk. A day for glad shouts. She would risk her arthritic hip and go for a walk around the entire ship. It was a big liner, fallen on hard times because of international jet travel. Still, there would always be people like her who preferred the sea. Not many, though, at this time of year. She was deliciously happy. The slow walk round the A deck left her tired but exhilarated. She rested on an iron bench, tucked a blanket round her legs, and watched the water.

The river was more than sixty miles wide at that point. It was probably half ocean by now. Land dwindled to the north and south. Stars came out and she shivered.

Time to go in.

The dining hall was nearly empty. It was outfitted in art-deco design. She was intrigued by this nostalgia for what had been so modern during her middle years.

"I'm old", she whispered to herself and laughed. "I must stop this giggling or people will think I'm dotty." Then she laughed again.

"I *am* dotty", she said aloud. "So what's to worry!"

A passing waiter thought she was muttering for more tea and filled her cup.

"There's a dance tonight, Ma'am, if you care to attend. In the ballroom, forward A deck."

"Thank you", she said.

But she was exhausted and went to her cabin right after supper. She busied herself for an hour knitting a sweater for her newest granddaughter, Bryan's Caitlin. She used their own raw wool, carded last fall. The sheep were gone now, and this was the last bag. From time to time she buried her nose into it and inhaled deeply. A clean ewish smell, like the scent of a baby's head, like tea and comfort in wood-fire kitchens, like the aroma of freshly washed blizzards beating at your window and the awe that falls over a winter field on Christmas eve, or like the smell of pine needles baking under the sun in a freak February thaw. An earthy smell, with love in it.

She nodded off sitting up. Then she shook herself awake, got into her nighty, and crawled under the blankets with an Agatha Christie novel. Before she had read a page she was sound asleep.

The sea was rolling under a wide, scrubbed sky when she went out on deck the following morning. There was no land in sight. They were on the Atlantic.

She walked and sat and rested, then walked again. She could not get enough of it. The wind was a cold, familiar thing, like a blunt but beloved friend, beloved for its lack of guile, its unfailing honesty. Her parka was warm, one of those new synthetic things that weighed nothing and for warmth was the equivalent of a polar bear's hide. Modern man, so amazing, so clever.

There were a few others out enjoying the early sun. Vigorous middle-aged types mostly. Young lovers, an occasional crew member. Noisy children chasing each other up and down. The old people were inside guarding against pneumonia.

"*Old.* I'm old. I was old when I was young. But perhaps I'm growing younger inside, now that I'm old."

She laughed again, and two small boys who were tumbling down the deck screeched to a stop beside her and looked.

"Hello", she said.

"Lo", they answered in unison. They were playing at being seamen.

"Are you sailors?"

"Yeah, we're sailors." They looked very serious.

"Where is this ship taking us?"

"To Inglan."

"Inglan? Where is Inglan?"

"Over there!" they said in unison and pointed to the bow.

"Why are you going there?"

"Our Nanna died."

"Ooh, I'm very sorry."

"We never saw her. My Mum cried."

"She's sad."

"Yeah."

"Daddy's takin' Mum and us back to see our dead Nanny in a box."

"What? Are you going in a box?"

"No, no", they shrieked with laughter.

"Our dead *granny*'s in a box", said one.

"They put her in a hole", said the other.

"Oh, now I see."

"We wanted to go in a plane, but my Mum's scared of planes."

"Me too. Ships are better."

"Yeah", said one.

"Yeah", said the other.

"Sometimes you see pirates when you go by ship." She pointed toward the water.

"Really?" they said, eyes lighting up.

"Oh, yes, I've seen pirates. I'm very old. I've seen many, many pirates."

"D'you think we'll see some?" the older one asked eagerly.

"We might. If we do, I know you'll be brave. Sailors like you will defend us, won't you?"

"Yeah! We will!" they cried. After a quick scan of the horizon with their brave eyes, they scampered off, waving back at her.

Nice boys. So good to meet nice children.

In the lounge she found a variety of social groupings. Scattered solitaries, most of them reading or knitting. Many of them elderly women like herself. Some had closed faces; others nodded and smiled. A few businessmen were reading the Montreal and London papers. Mothers, tired and harassed looking, chatted with each other, jostling babies. One or two old men, looking withdrawn, tinkered with pipes and crossword puzzles. Two teenage girls postured, striking excruciatingly bored and sophisticated poses. There was a solemn, fortyish woman in a wheelchair, staring at the others from behind thick glasses. She had a severe face that could have been warm if she had made the effort.

"Just my sort of person", said Anne to herself. She sat in a leatherette armchair beside the woman.

"Good morning."

"Morning", said the woman.

She was obviously an eccentric of some kind: the gray pony-tail perched atop a scowl, impossibly thick glasses, cool analytical eyes; a black and red plaid skirt, hot-pink running shoes, fluorescent green stockings over legs that looked like broken pencils.

Anne opened her Agatha Christie novel and began to read without retaining any of the words. She felt the woman staring at the side of her face, reading her. The woman opened a pack of cigarettes and lit one. They stank horribly.

The woman inhaled distractedly, holding the small blue packet in her palm. The flash of incandescent color caught the corner of Anne's eye. She looked up from her book and stared at the packet as if it were a gemstone, a cube of turquoise. The cigarettes were called *Gauloises* and the blue was a shade she had never seen before. It was obsessively beautiful. It was an artifact of all that was foreign and continental, of everything exotic she had missed during her years of exile. She loved the packet with a passionate love that was beyond all reason.

"You need a smoke, lady?"

"No, thank you."

Anne looked down at her book and tried to concentrate.

The woman blew her exhalations politely away, but the circulation in the room pulled them back into Anne's face.

"You mind if I smoke? I can move someplace else, if y'all want." The accent was American South.

"No, don't move. I'll go upwind of you." She took the seat on the other side of the wheelchair and tried to concentrate on the text of her book.

"How far you goin'?" said the lazy drawl. A delicious accent.

"England."

"Crazy question. There aren't any bus stops between here and the U.K., are there?"

"All too true. Don't try getting out before Southampton."

This won her a sardonic smile and a slight melting of the harsh look around the eyes.

The wheelchair woman extended her hand for a shake. Anne shook it.

"Call me Fran."

"I'm Anne."

"I'm from Georgia. I'm a southern belle. Where you from?"

"British Columbia. A small place in the interior. A town called Swiftcreek."

"You got an English accent. Goin' home?"

"A visit. My sister is dying."

"That's too bad. But we all gotta go sometime."

"Sooner or later."

"Yep. Sooner or later. Myself, I'm circlin' the drain real slow."

"Are you unwell?"

The woman doubled her sardonic expression.

"Yep! It's one of them mean things that take away all your *faculties*, one by one, before they shovel dirt."

She lit another cigarette.

"Are you on your way to England for a holiday?" said Anne.

"Business meetin'."

"May I ask what business you're in?"

"Prostitution", the American snorted.

"I beg your pardon?"

"Uh, literary prostitution."

"I'm sorry, I don't quite understand."

"I write short stories. They get into magazines. Some fog-crazed publisher in merry ol' England wants to make them into a book."

"How very wonderful!"

"Yeah. So, part of the agreement is I go over there for newspaper and T.V. interviews at *the launching*."

"You don't sound too pleased."

"Nope."

"Why not?"

"I gotta act literary. I gotta talk to a lot of people who'll feel sorry for me and tell me I'm a smart girl. Some Baroness wants to fund me for a year of writing, but I gotta meet her first and impress her."

"That doesn't sound too difficult."

"You don't know how difficult it'll be. I ain't charming, except in a sort of grotesque way. But you already got that figured out, I'll bet."

"I don't find you charming. But I am enjoying our conversation very much. You don't like falsehood, do you?"

"Right on!"

"Can't you put up with them for the sake of your books?"

"I hate that kinda stuff. Gag me with a spoon!"

Anne laughed, and the woman watched her.

"Hey, you're a nice lady. Let's be friends. Wanna have supper together? Don't worry, I won't become a pest. I'll tell you when I get bored, and you can tell me when I'm being obnoxious. Then we won't bother each other after that. Three more days to go on this pleasure cruise. My mom tells me I'm pushy. D'you think I'm pushy?"

"A little. It's only because you're really very shy."

"Shy? Hey, you're pretty sharp. Most folks never get past my disguises. Course, they usually get stopped by the Tiny Tim routine. I'm such a *handicapped* person. I'm a *wounded* soul."

She said *handicapped* and *wounded* like the bay of a southern hound dog. Several people nearby looked at her.

She lit another cigarette, and Anne coughed.

"So, wanna strike up a shallow relationship?" said the American.

"Well, not really. I'm afraid I don't have much energy. Let's just enjoy each other."

"You *are* a smart lady. Where'd you learn this stuff?"

"Oh, life has ways of teaching us a few essential lessons. If you live long enough."

"I guess so." She pointed at her legs. "There are short-cuts."

"Would you like to go out on deck? The sun is lovely and the wind isn't too strong."

"Sure. Why not?"

Fran struggled into a ski jacket and wheeled herself toward the lounge door. Out in the sun she seemed suddenly a thin, pale creature.

"Would you prefer me to push your chair?"

"Nah. I hate the pathetic cripple routine. I got biceps like a gravedigger."

"Shall we go around the deck, then?"

"Sure. Tally-ho!"

They went several times around the circumference of the ship, and Fran kept up a continual stream of monologue. It was thoroughly entertaining, but by the third circuit Anne was becoming exhausted.

"I must go in for a nap, now", she explained.

"Okay. Looks like I used you up."

"Not so. Elderly people need their naps, that's all", she smiled.

"Yeah. Well, I'll leave it up to you to seek me out next time. I don't wanna be pushy, y'know. People like you aren't strong enough to resist people like me. Sometimes y'need a little help to protect yourselves. I'll help you not feel too bad when y'back off."

"What do you mean?"

"I'll do somethin' gross or say somethin' insultin'. Somethin' cruel. Take your pick."

"You don't like yourself very much, do you?"

"I like myself."

"Then you despise me and people like me."

"That ain't true. You're okay."

"I think you're really very lonely."

Fran didn't reply at first. Her face went hard, and she said, "Ah, shaddap!" and fought to light a *Gauloise* in the breeze. She wheeled her chair to face the water. The back of her head was shaking.

"Go have your nap, lady. I gotta memorize this conversation and put it in a story."

"I'm sorry. I didn't mean to hurt you."

"You couldn't hurt me if you hit me over the head with a two-by-four. Watch for *The New Yorker* magazine in May or June. There'll be a savage depiction of you in there. Now get lost."

It was so nasty that Anne laughed at the novelty of it. But it stung. She liked the woman, though she could not have explained why.

There was no sign of her in the dining room at lunch. Anne ate a meal, then read all afternoon in her cabin. She took a walk on deck just before supper. The sea was rolling pleasantly and the wind had died.

At supper she scanned the dining room and saw Fran wheeled up to a table in an alcove, talking to an elderly gentleman who was listening with strained attentiveness.

"There you are, Fran. May I sit down?"

Fran looked at her with something like wonder and said, "Sure." Then she went back to addressing the man.

"So I says to Kissinger, 'Look, Henry, don't you ever get tired of burning little brown people?' Oh, boy, did he ever turn on his heels fast and stomp away with that Ozymandias look of his, and I chased him down the hall in my wheelchair, *screeeeeaming* at him. Ahhhh, it is *so* satisfying, so *deeply* satisfying to have that kind of power over a tin-pot tyrant."

She flashed her glasses at Anne.

"So, how'r'y'doin? Forgive me yet, sweetie?"

"Absolutely."

Fran made the introductions.

"This is Mrs. Something-or-other, a housewife from Kayannadah. She says she's from a small place in the interior. This is Mister Athelston. He's a widower gent. He's fragile."

"How do you do", said Mr. Athelston, getting up with a slight bow; "not quite as fragile as this young lady makes out."

"He's a *real* gent."

"I noticed. A pleasure, Mr. Athelston."

"Aaaargh!!! Caught between two Brits making delicate conversation. What a horrible way to die!"

"I suspect, Fran," said Mr. Athelston tactfully, "that you chose to engage yourself in this situation, and you may have entirely engineered it."

"I cornered him", said Fran smirking. "Just like I cornered you yesterday."

"You didn't corner me", said Anne. "I chose to sit beside you."

"No y'didn't. With my gaudy plumage and my penetrating look, I *commanded* you to come."

"Fran is a writer of fiction", said Anne turning to Mr. Athelston. "Perhaps she has already told you."

"Yes. Very early on in the conversation."

"She composes continually", Anne added.

"She's very creative", he replied with creases of laughter around the eyes.

"Hey," said Fran, "this is takin' a nasty turn! Don't gang up on a crip, you two."

"I think we should celebrate our meeting with a little wine, don't you, ladies", said Mr. Athelston.

"He's so dashing for an old guy."

"Real gentlemen are few and far between, Fran. Let's treat this one properly."

"Gag me with a spoon!" she cried.

All three of them laughed.

After her meal Fran opened a medicine case and fed herself a large number of multicolored tablets.

"Such a life I got", she sighed. "Living better chemically! Ah well, these things let me enjoy for just a teensy-weensy bit longer my dazzling career as a famous author. I've had a delightful time, darlings. But these literary salons are *so* exhausting. I must get to bed, or they'll be carryin' me down the gangplank in a plastic bag three days from now."

When she had wheeled herself off, Mr. Athelston threw his head back and laughed. Anne could tell that he had not done such a thing for a very long time. He poured another glass of wine for her and one for himself.

"What an extraordinary woman", he said.

"She is indeed."

"I think she's a rather talented actress."

"Some of it's acting, that's true. Some of it's that peculiar southern charm. She's very bright, you know."

"That may be so. But awfully self-preoccupied."

"I suspect that has to do with her loneliness. There's a great soul there. Maybe no man has ever approached, never looked close enough to appreciate what's inside."

"Yes, I dare say. She's quite bitter. Do you really believe she's a writer?"

"I'm not sure."

"Her grammar is appalling."

"That may be part of the various costumes she tries on."

"I say, Mrs. Something-or-other, would you care to get some exercise? A walk on deck?"

"Yes, I would. Please call me Anne."

"Right. Anne it is."

The stars were out in full force, the sea as calm as one could hope for.

"Forgive me for asking—she said you're a widower gent."

"Yes."

"Recently?"

"Last November." His voice trembled. "My wife hadn't been well all year, and the cold snap took her. It was fast."

"I'm so sorry."

There was no more to be said about it.

"You're going home?" he asked.

She explained her situation briefly. She probed him for more details about himself. He had an engineering firm in Montreal, modestly successful, he said. He and his wife had retired a few years before to a cottage in the Laurentians. She made quilts. They liked to cross-country ski. Their sons and daughters lived in Montreal. All professionals. He had some worry for a while over a son whose marriage was in trouble, but everything was all right now. The grandchildren liked to spend weekends with him at the cottage.

"And despite Fran's judgment," he added, "I'm not a Brit."

"I didn't think so. You have a faintly British accent, but not enough to be convincing."

"I was raised on Vancouver Island, near Victoria. Last English outpost before the Orient. Very snobby place. Totem poles and silver teas. Lovely weather, too."

"I was there once."

"Were you? It must have changed a lot by now. I haven't been back in almost sixty years."

"About the same length of time I've been away from England. You called it my *home*", she said. "But I must say that after all these years nowhere is home."

"I know how you feel. And I'll go you one better: I feel that nowhere is home even though I was born and raised in Canada."

"Like being an alien and a sojourner?"

"Yes, exactly like that. An exile within your own native land."

After that they wished each other a good night and parted.

* * *

She was basking in a pool of sunshine in the lounge the following morning when he found her.

"Hello," he said.

"Hello."

"I say, it's not my habit to burden strangers with my personal troubles. Sorry about last night."

"No apologies. It was a pleasant evening. I'm enjoying meeting people. I've lived a quiet life."

"You're very kind. I'm afraid I've been rather depressed lately. My doctor wanted me to get a complete change of scene. He recommended a sea change. You know, I made this trip a few times when I was a young man, so I thought I'd refresh my memory. I decided to visit my brother in Yorkshire. He has a farm there by the coast."

"How lovely. I've never been that far north. I was born and raised in Bishopsford, just outside of London. We had black swans in a park. My father . . ."

She described her childhood to him, and he listened attentively. Several times she wondered if he was bored, for his eyes were staring, watery, red-rimmed, rheumy. The tufts of white hair at his temples were astray. The bald dome was covered with liver spots and scars. But his suit was tidy, and his socks matched his tie. He folded his hands this way and that. And every so often, just when she thought his attention was wandering, he would ask a pertinent question.

"Were you happy there? There in the mountains?"

She was taken aback.

"I suppose it depends on what you mean by happiness. I've

known moments of ecstasy. There were many, many joys. There were years of desolation and blindness. Years when I prayed to die. But life doesn't let you do that, you know."

"I know."

"Life always asks us to forgive in the places where we've been most hurt."

"Most abandoned?"

"That too. Just when you think it's over, when there's no hope, there's some great surprise. There's always more. And then you realize that we humans understand practically nothing about all this. All this we live in—as if it were ordinary."

"Nothing is ordinary."

"Yes", she said, and fell silent.

"You were happy, then?"

"Yes. I was happy. But not with the kind of happiness most people want. It went much, much deeper. I can't describe it. It was a sense that just grew and grew over the years, a current underneath everything, a feeling, a form, a hand that was on my life. A sort of fierce, fatherly love that demanded everything from me but hid itself from me. It had given everything. It wanted total trust in return."

"What do you mean?"

"I don't know. It's strange."

"Like always being alone, but not alone?"

"The feeling was abandonment. It was emptying. No strength. No power."

"You seem to have survived in good condition, for all that", he said.

"I suppose I have."

"It didn't kill you."

"It made me stronger. I gave everything, you see."

"When everything's given, nothing's lacking."

"But not in the way we want."

"Right. Not in the way we want."

"Not in the style to which we would like to grow accustomed."

"Precisely, Madam."

"Later, after the worst of it, you begin to understand that you've survived. You grow old and you find yourself able to take a walk with a stranger and a sojourner and speak with him of the sea."

He nodded.

"Would you care to do just that?" he said. "Let's go and speak together of the sea."

It was a deliriously fresh morning. They didn't speak much about the sea. They walked together and looked at it and breathed it.

They ambled for a long time in silence. Occasionally, he was forced to sit.

"My back", he explained. "A little memento from the First War."

After lunch they went out again and made the circuit. Some gray weather was coming in from the east, and around three o'clock the sea began to rise and fall.

He chuckled to himself and pointed to the bow.

"I love storms. On one trip I crawled up there to the forecastle, right onto the stem. It was in the midst of a gale. I held onto a rope and some bolts. You talked about praying to die. That's what I was doing in those days. My first wife had been killed in a car accident. She was life itself to me. No one ever loved like we did. I thought life was over. I wasn't suicidal in any way. But my life was simply over. Something prompted me to climb up there and face the storm. I have no idea why. I could have been killed. It blew hard, and I was soaked and freezing. But—you won't think I'm crazy will you ?—what I felt up there was . . . joy. Pure joy."

"I understand."

His eyes mused, far away.

"I went to England and stayed with my brother. Then the war started, and I was in it till forty-five. I was in the R.C.A.F., liaison, flying a desk because of my back. After that, I returned to Montreal, got my degree at McGill, married again, and had the rest of my life. Here I am."

"Here you are."

Heavy rain gusted in sideways and began to freeze on the decks. They went inside for an early tea. When the last cup was finished, and the chill was driven from their bones, Mr. Athelston ferreted about in a pocket of his blazer and produced an envelope.

"Photographs of my family", he said with an apologetic expression. "Here's a portrait of the grandchildren." He offered the top item. "I hope you don't mind me forcing these upon you."

"Mind? Of course not. I'm delighted. What lovely children."

She pulled a similar packet from her purse. "You understand that I deserve equal time", she quipped. They laughed.

"Here's my daughter Emily, and her fiancé. And this is Stephen. They were burning the old barn that day. And here he is with our grandsons, building the new one by the south pasture. Now this is Bryan; he has three daughters; and here's Ashley's wife making pies for the harvest festival with some of their children . . ."

And so it went for an hour. A most pleasant hour. At the bottom of his pile, she came upon a snapshot of a landscape that was vaguely familiar, though try as she might she could not place it. A giant earthwork of some kind, carved on the side of a high green hill. A strange, animal shape.

"Is that a sheep?" she asked.

"No, it's a symbolic horse. It's a place in the White Horse Hills, actually, southwest of Oxford. An ancient people scraped the topsoil off the chalk hills, leaving this image exposed. I went there a few years ago with my wife on our second honeymoon.

It's a national monument, you know. Surely you've heard of the great white horse at Uffington?"

"I think I went there once as a very young child. It looks awfully familiar."

She felt a moment of chill but did not know why.

"It's a mysterious place, the guidebooks say. Prehistoric. Maybe Iron Age. Scholars think it might have been a tribal symbol. Possibly religious. There's an ancient earth fort up on top, and below there's a hill where the locals say Saint George slew the dragon."

"Oh?"

"The place is fairly dripping with history. But no one really knows who made the horse. Some say Roman, but of course it's much, much older than that. Possibly Celtic, but who knows; it could be even older."

"Wasn't there somebody named Alfred connected with it?"

"That's right. Alfred fought the battle of Ethandune on the valley floor just below the horse."

"I remember. A usurper, wasn't he? Alfred the Fool, they called him."

"You mean Alfred the Great, don't you?" he said looking at her strangely.

"Oh, yes. Of course that's what I meant." She rubbed her brow. "I wonder why I said that?"

"He was no usurper. He was the Christian king who defeated the pagan Danes when they invaded England. He won against overwhelming odds. That victory preserved civilization in England. It's quite a story."

"Yes . . ." she trailed off.

"I'm surprised you thought he was a fool." He smiled, still puzzled. "You're an English lass. Didn't you do your homework?"

"I must have forgotten. Besides, that place has other meanings for me. Not very happy ones, I suspect."

516

"Really?" he said intrigued. "Can you tell me about it?"

"No. I don't think so. You see, I can't remember it exactly." An uncomfortable silence ensued until it was broken by two small sailors gambolling through the salon. She engaged them in discussion for a few minutes, and when they ran off she made excuses and went below for her afternoon nap.

Despite a feeling of profound unease, she fell instantly asleep.

A skylark flew overhead, and a small cloth doll named Bea wept in the center of a ring of red roses, pressing a blue enamelled cross to her breast. Then a black shadow swirled around and sought to close in on her. But Bea was brave. She was very, very brave, and she cried out.

"Anna, Mama, Anna, Mama . . ."

An old man with wicked eyes stepped out of the shadows, and all around him there was a ring of hands, each marked with a black mark like a claw or a spider. Upon his forehead there was the same mark. He poised his foot over the ring of roses, intending to enter, to take Bea, but something held him back. When he realized that his will was thwarted, he flew into a rage and thrust his staff into the soil, bellowed at the sky, and spewed vile curses in an unknown tongue. A carved red dragon on the head of his staff unfurled its wings and roared like a lion. Bea screamed, and Anna ran to her and held her very close.

Then a horse and rider descended from above and came to rest in the center of the ring. The rider was very beautiful and strong, and the wicked man fled with the dragon. The rider's crown flashed in the golden light that came from his eyes. His eyes, his eyes—they were so full of fire, so valiant and sweet, so faithful and true. He was dressed in white linen, and from his mouth there came a sharp sword that pierced the shadows and scattered them. He bent down and scooped her up in his arms and held her firmly. He turned his horse, and it leapt into the sky, carrying her upward, upward into light. And she was not afraid.

She woke feeling indescribably peaceful.

"A dream", she said to herself. "But what a dream! How very odd."

She puzzled over it. Who was the wicked old man? Who was the rider? A king, obviously. Was it Alfred the Great? It must have been. Yes, of course. Her subconscious had produced a king on a white horse from the conversation about Uffington. But the doll and the wicked old man—where had they come from? She wondered if perhaps she had once owned a doll of that name but thought it unlikely.

She was dining alone when Mr. Athelston came over and seated himself across from her.

"Good evening. I'm worried about our friend. She's missed some meals. Maybe one of us should look in on her."

"That's a good idea."

They located her cabin number on the passenger list and went down to C deck together to find it.

A note was pinned to the door: *Genius at Work. Do not disturb if you value your life!*

They heard faint sounds of a typewriter being hammered furiously.

"Here we are, consumed with anxiety, and she's having the time of her life!" he said.

"Genius needs no excuses."

"Ah, these artists!"

"Well, let's go upstairs and be ordinary."

"Agreed."

There were young Irishmen in the lounge singing rugby songs too loudly. They had been drinking. When a crew member quieted them down, they began spouting poetry.

"You can't suppress the artist in man", said Mr. Athelston.

"The art can die quietly, though", she replied. "It can suffocate."

"I tried my hand at painting when I was young", he mused.

"It was the usual heroic quest for vision. I was a dreamer, you see, before I became an engineer. My dazzling art career was a flash in the pan for a year or two, and then it was over. My first wife died during that time, and art got lost in the general disaster. I never painted again."

"That's a great pity."

"Some things die, others are born."

"But perhaps some things that should have come into being will never be, because of it."

"True." He thought about that. He shook off the thought.

"Here we are being profound, Anne, and perhaps we'll never meet again. I've enjoyed this so much. Tomorrow is our last day. Would you care to join me for supper?"

"Fine, Mr. Athelston. I'll see you in the dining room about seven?"

"Agreed. Seven it is."

She dressed carefully for dinner. A hand-knitted tan cardigan. A white blouse with lace collar pinned at the throat with Mama's porcelain rose. A long, gray wool skirt and tan stockings, maroon leather pumps. She felt a trifle overdressed by her own standards, though it was subdued when compared to the standards of most of the passengers.

They had a delightful dinner, made small talk about their children, and went their separate ways right after the meal. They waved to Fran on the way out. She had corralled the Irish boys in a cloud of smoke and was making them fall, guffawing, all over the floor.

"Dear Fran", he said. "I expect we'll have a chance to say good-bye to her tomorrow."

"Oh, I'm sure we will. Good night then."

"Good night."

The following afternoon, when they docked, Anne went down to Fran's cabin, but it had already been vacated, and none of the crew members knew where she had gone. Standing in line at British Customs, she saw Mr. Athelston. He had been passed through and was going out the gate when he noticed her. He came back.

He gave his habitual slight bow, doffed his cap, and offered his hand.

"There you are!" he exclaimed. "I searched all over but couldn't find you. You're next in line, I see. Look, that agent is beckoning to you. No time for famous last words. But I do want to tell you what a boost it's been to have company on this trip. You're a lovely person."

She stammered the customary replies.

"Here's my card", he said. "If you're ever in Montreal, please do come and see me. I'd like to meet your husband, too. He sounds a very decent chap."

"He is. Good-bye, Mr. Athelston."

"Good-bye."

The card read, *Peter Athelston, Engineer.*

She had no time to think about this because a very tiny gray woman was staggering toward her, weeping, with open arms.

* * *

She returned to Canada in May of that year, after Emily's funeral. She did not contact Peter. She was sure he would not remember a delirious night in a tent near Ypres sixty years before.

She took out a subscription to *The New Yorker*. The stories were well written, contained art and insight, and generally did not apply to the reality of her life. Many of the tales and essays were about the existential struggles of handsome young people in New England. The politics of adultery. Or social situations in megalopolis. Ambition. Ego. Artistic sensitivity. Success according to wholly alien criteria.

It was a warm summer in the mountains, and the garden was one of her best ever. She grew far too many vegetables and enjoyed giving them away. Stephen was busy clearing bush on the edges of the new land. Not that they needed it, really, but he did like to keep himself occupied.

An issue of *The New Yorker* that arrived in late June contained a piece by Fran. It was about a cold-hearted American midget, embarked on the trans-Siberian express, who manipulated fellow passengers during the entire journey, notably a herd of Russian soccer players. She won their attention through her use of wit and the mystique of her deformity. She made them laugh and sing and pity her, and in exercising power over "these magnificent males", these "white-toothed Tartars lusting for jeans and Coca-Cola", she achieved "a fugitive union that was her only passion, her highest art form".

Anne shuddered and felt grateful that she had not been the object of this analytical eye.

In September, there was a long essay by Fran. It was titled *A Small Place in the Interior*. At first she did not realize whom the author was writing about.

The ship to England was my ferry ride across the Styx. I intended to leave some statements in a file on my cabin desk, stinging indictments of the modern age. I planned to disembark halfway across. When you are young and dying, when your heart was made for a love stronger than death, but your body wasn't, you get trouble in the soul. Buckets of trouble. Ages of grief. You want to get off at the wrong bus stop. Death comes like release.

I was born with a strong will, says my Mom.

"That stiff neck made you famous, girl, and it's gonna kill you too, if you ain't careful!" She was right, as usual. Always listen to old chicken breeders on the edge of the peanut lands. She cuts to the bone with her tongue. She's a prophet without pity. I like her, my Mom. She raised me single-handed, a cagey old peasant who distrusted everyone except the publishers of supermarket tabloid magazines. She never did find an antidote for the kind of misery I was born to breed. She never could understand why a school bus or a prom night were suffering for me. That pain began long before my legs quit without thirty day's notice, and my hair went gray, and my eyes never did have to resign, having lived a life of negligence since birth. So we raised chickens together, and she cussed my absent father, a man who maybe didn't exist—I never met the gentleman—and I wrote stories about sensitive, deformed girls who fall in love. I dreamed of southern boys coming up out of the swamp with their hounds, lost, looking for shelter, seeing my heart under the Coke-bottle glasses. I wanted to be a 1950s girl who could kiss and be good all at the same time. I wanted them to think my ponytail meant sass. But my hair went gray at twenty, and the swamp never parted, and the boys at the post office and J. C. Penney's never did notice, except to look sad or make side-mouth jokes 'cause they was real embarrassed by a girl with a broken body.

All of that goes through your mind when your life is over and you're too tired to enjoy being famous, being the kind of hip, hype, heroine queen who represents Modern Woman. Hell, I'd rather represent Sophocles. Or Queen Esther. I wasn't born to be a democrat. I hate our murderous democratic civilization that blames everybody else for its troubles. Now it goes without saying that we all know where the blame really lies. That's you and me, of course. We had the armies, and we guarded the borders, and we shot the bad guys, but practically none of us kept watch over the kingdom of the heart.

To get back to my story. I was no longer satisfied administrating the last suzerains of my once-vast territory. It had shrunk to the size of a wheelchair and an ego. A very big ego. That's all it would ever be. No *body*, no other universe, would ever fill my womb. I would be a note in a history of women. Nike victorious over patriarchy. Patriarchy, hell! Give me one good man who knows what it is not to be a woman. Give me a patriarch over a whiner of any gender. Give me a woman or a man with a pen and some paper who wants to make a world anew. And, Lawd, protect me from all social revolutionaries! Give me Ulysses sailing beyond the sunset and the baths. Give me Antigone, that brave lass. There aren't many like them no more. The best are only good for kindness or wisdom. Fair enough commodities when the fires have died down in folks who had a body and a heart that worked together for so long they were too full, needing only rest from all that surplus.

Oh, I was young and ugly, and they called me a genius, when all I ever wanted was a soda and a ride to the prom. And thus, on that cold March day, tossing on the ocean waves, I decided that I was going to wheel my perambulator out onto the deck of the ferry and do it. I said to myself, Yep, as my last creative act I'm gonna twist some gentle, dumb person round my finger, and I'm gonna make him or her pity me, and I'm gonna get them to open the iron gate at the ass end of this soul-barge. Then, starting at the bow I'm gonna roll down the deck at top speed and gather momentum, and—Yahoo!—fire this lil' ol' missile me out into the wide waters of the North Atlantic.

I was sitting in my cruiser in the lounge, looking for my victim. Just about everybody has a secret sentimental attachment for euthanasia these days, so I had my pick of the litter. But wouldn't you know it. Along comes this lady with a face. Now it was a pretty face once long ago. And she's got smarts and manners written all over that face. But she got sufferin' in the eyes like only you an' me and the cripples know. "There's somebody you can admire", I says to myself. "Dis lady, she got guts. She got *resistance*. Dis is somebody who be a real challenge, lil' Franny. But sooner or later I'm gonna make her throw me overboard. I got three and a half days to work on her . . ."

Anne stopped. Looked up. She took a deep breath. She made a big pot of tea and went out onto the porch.

"Oh, dear, what on earth is coming next?" she said.

She sat on the steps in the sun and read slowly, carefully, for close to an hour.

The essay was very long, convoluted, and heavily psychological, studded with references to classical literature. Fran did not wear her learning lightly. It was awfully self-preoccupied, to use Mr. Athelston's expression, but fascinating nonetheless.

In the end the suicide was averted because the author was moved by something immovable in the other woman, the woman with the face. The woman called Anne.

In the end I was defeated. In the end you find beginnings. They're always there, if you would only look. I went to Europe and got even more famous. My titanic willpower guaranteed that. The ideologues, the Marxist dons and the fem-fascists, the duchesses and the modern Toquevilles, they all just loved me. They made me into a seven-day wonder, a myth on crutches. They wrote their reviews, and they were so wrong I had to laugh. They preached bullets or ballots, or bombs or braless Tuesdays, or they hated men, or women, or democracy, or the self-righteous, or all the old variations on totalitarianism (bless their souls), and in its stead they proposed every new tyranny imaginable. They proposed everything under the sun except the only things that really count under the sun: they forgot about a boy and a girl walking through a field talking about the people they would beget in their flesh. They forgot about the poem. They forgot about old ladies who can flush out lies like a truffle-hunter. They forgot about children who play sailor. They forgot about the end of the world and the end of man, and in the forgetting they brought us a lot closer to the end of everything. That old woman, Anne, she told me this. She'll read this some day and say she didn't tell me it. But she did.

I know what I am, and I know what you think: I'm just another parody of the southern scold. A cornpone crosspatch with cosmic leanings. You all just listen t'me, now, you hear. I'm older than you, sisters. I'm older than you spoiled yankee revolutionaries. I'm older because I never was a child like you. I never expected anything as my due. I never got a carnation and a surge of hormones at the proper time. Listen to me, fellow *enfants terribles* of the literary world. I got rights on your attention. I got automatic credibility because I was born in a body that fought my ambition from the start. You never learned a child's wisdom. You hear me, you spoiled denizens of Greenwich Village lofts and fashionable colleges. I got degrees coming out my ears. I got degrees in Chicken Breeding. I got my Masters in Human Suffering. I earned a thousand credits on a thousand sleepless nights. I got a doctorate in Unrequited Love. I can spot a high-class Ph.D. Harlequin Romance a mile off and the wind blowing the other way. Just get this straight. Your ambition is gonna kill you, child. I know, I just know, that you gonna sell your soul. Hell, most of you is gonna *give* it away! And it's gonna take somebody's blood on a Friday afternoon to buy it back for you.

I have a few months left, maybe a few years. My faculties, one after another, are being taken away. Until then I tend the kingdom of my desk. I am a tyrant-queen of typewriters. I drink a Coke. Mom bought me a carnation last week for my birthday. She thinks it's unhealthy to be a recluse. She told me it twenty years ago and ain't changed her tune since. I tell her I'm never alone. I hear pickups go by on the turnpike. I dream dreams. I see visions. I make worlds come into being. I have a permanent small place in the interior, where coon dogs and sweet boys come up out of the wet woods in autumn. They sit on the porch and hold my hand. They tell me useless things that are worth more than all the cargo at sea.

All flesh grows old with knowledge and returns to earth. The fires of the heart burn down. The hot hands cool. The tale alone endures; telling is the abiding act of love. Thus, for my brief span I sit and rock and tell my tales. I am content. The autumn moon walks slowly across the sky. The pumpkins are cured by frost. The smoke of leaf-fires rises in the garden.

I have been defeated, and in the defeat I have won myself. It is a pleasure to die at the hands of Life. On its terms. Not mine.

We are not alone. The vast sea sends messengers to us if we wait. They speak, they speak, though we hardly ever hear.

* * *

To Fran,
c/o The New Yorker Magazine,
New York City, N.Y., USA
December 10th

Dear Fran,
I read your story about Russia. Months later I read your essay about our crossing of the Styx. It was a joy for me to be reminded that we are never alone on that voyage. If, in some obscure fashion, I was instrumental in telling you this, it was in spite of myself. I too needed to hear it. You told me. Peter told me. The small sailors told me. You will say you didn't tell me. But you did.

On a Christmas card such as this, there is only so much one can squeeze in between the star and the crèche. If you feel like writing, I would be so happy. Someday, perhaps, you could get on a train and come to visit us in the mountains. No one here but me knows that you're famous. I won't tell a soul. I would caution you, however, against striking up conversation with rugby players on our Canadian trains.

Love,
Anne Delaney

*

January 10

Dear Ms. Delaney,
Thank you for your card to Fran Symons, which you sent to our editorial offices for forwarding. It is with regret that I must advise you that Ms. Symons died just before the New Year. Thank you for your interest.

Sincerely,
Ms. E. Benton,
Editorial staff

34

She sat alone in her office, feeling the disease eat at her. Her heart continued to beat. She breathed. Her thoughts spilled out into emptiness as she sat numbly staring at the calendar. A few months at the most, the doctor said. Suddenly everything was changed. Even the weekly publication of *The Echo* had become an activity belonging to another universe. People assumed a distance in her mind, cut off from her by the imminence of death. She would not tell anyone. No, not yet, for most of them were afraid even of the word *death*, as if it were contagious. Death, that unreality. As if it weren't written into the code of every human being on earth. Like the presence of a predator one never thinks of until it parts the bushes and swipes a lethal blow across the face.

So I am going to die. Circling the drain, Fran called it.

The awards for journalistic excellence framed above her desk looked absurd. And her local fame merely a gaudy dress being torn from her back. Long ago she had learned to ignore the effects of praise or criticism. Now, they ceased to exist. Her position, her powers, had no effect whatsoever. Her pen could not cut out the runaway cells, her authority did not extend beyond words and paper, though there was no end to the resonances they might set up in the hearts of her readers. But those realities seemed remote from this drama of cellular war. She could not draw blue lines through it or type over the impending event with better news.

She attempted to continue with the editorial she had been writing all morning:

In the life of nations, as in the life of human beings, a great crisis can be a blessing, if it reveals in the outlines of the abyss the simple truths that men and women abandon only at their own peril.

Not bad. A trifle too ringing, perhaps. Was it good to capture the reader with stirring words? Words that would probably be abandoned after the first shallow flush of emotion? Or was it better to put down the idea simply and run the alternate risk of being ignored? An unresolved question, which was being swallowed now in the largest question of all. She rubbed her forehead. Her mind wandered a great deal these days. What had she been working on? Inflation, crime in the streets, the latest atrocity? It was suddenly impossible to write about such things.

But what had her own life been about? The revision and editing of her discouraged existence into a creative one, of course. That had made the difference between life and death. And she knew that it had not happened by sheer cleverness and force of will. No. She had discovered that all strengths would fail in the end and a beating heart exposed to eternity must come to understand its frailty. Only then could it begin to know its true dimensions, its simplicity and greatness.

I have been a stone buried in deep earth, which is taken up and placed on a fence post in the sun.

Was it possible that she would be returned now to darkness? The thought terrorized her. What if it was all illusion? What if . . . ? But she opened slowly her tightly clenched fists and became, in this almost unnoticeable movement, the victor. It was the first of many such skirmishes, but she had set the pattern of struggle and was determined to win.

I will believe that I have come finally to the gate of light, no matter what the darkness attempts to say in the next few months. I shall trust that what is being done to me is for a good purpose.

At that point her approaching death almost ceased to destroy her and was replaced by awe. It was a voyage she was about to embark upon. Had she desired it? No, but it could be the one journey for which she had been preparing all her life. An uncharted course, yes, but it had always been so for her.

I will not turn away from life. I will love each mote of existence passionately.

She looked at the trays of blue type as if they had assumed a sacramental quality, burnished and burning blue in the afternoon light streaming through the office window. A bluer fly buzzed and banged against the glass.

She sipped her tea.

I am to die.

Jan Tarnowski's mad clock struck the hour, and she knew it was time to go home. She took the long route through town, avoiding the modern streets, searching out the remains of the primitive village. She found the weed-shot lanes choked with memories. New children played there with games unaltered by a half-century of use. Everything else was crumbling. The roof had caved in on the log shed that was once her school. Turid's old boarding house was a hollow foundation, burned by the fire marshal last year. Then around the corner to MacPhale's supermarket, the false front listing slightly into the street, the violet neon of his name creaking in the wind.

Then, as if she had been brought here for this alone, all noise drained from the world. She turned in slow motion, gazing down the length of the street to a small figure dressed in black. It stood there looking at her. With failing eyes she thought at first it might be a raven, but then he raised a hand at her, turned away, and went limping out of sight.

Father Andrei, she exhaled, and in the next inhalation came a breath of sweetest peace. Mysterious and still. Was it, she wondered, a touch on the shoulder? Was he saying to her, time now, woman, arise, let us go into the new mystery you have never understood? Come, and see.

People passing by saw the eccentric editor standing quite

motionless, staring into space. They spoke to her, and she did not appear to hear. She always was unstable, they noted.

In the following weeks she began to detach herself from those humans who had become entangled with her in mutual dependency.

The boy. She cared for him far too extravagantly for his own good, tempted to swallow him whole, to re-create herself in him as best she could. And thereby perpetuate herself? If so, it was wrong, she decided. But she could leave him some tools with which to work out his destiny and a few scraps of paper on which she had scratched a record of her hard-won lessons.

Nathaniel, be a father to your people. True fathers and mothers shall heal a ruined nation. Be faithful to your foolishness and strong in your dreams.

Could he hear? Would he listen?

He had been a child once, a small presence waiting to be enlarged among the greater presences, listening with big eyes while they discussed politics and war. He had become a large presence now, never saying much, using sparingly his ration of speech. A hoarder of books and ideas that escaped through the valve of his writing. Slowly, slowly there was balance and insight growing in his more recent work. Was he wise enough yet to receive *The Echo* into his hands? Or was he still too much the child for such a burden? Would he take the sword of her press and use it like a cudgel? She knew that a surgeon's scalpel was needed here, but such skill was still beyond him. Sword-craft would have to do for now. Still, it was better than the axe.

She was thrown again into the dilemma that had occupied all her adult life, a question she had asked of each generation: Who are you? He was a boy no one could get inside of. Strange how they remained boys so late; clever, talking boys with the oddest inner zones of immaturity. Spoiled, she guessed. In her day a young man in his early twenties was just that, *a man*. There were depths in this one, however. His thoughts could not be read on his face, though they might be purchased for a few nickels by anyone interested. A reader might be surprised by what was written there, and he would probably like that. He felt that a stiff kick would do the bourgeoisie a bit of good. His wit was still in that state of immaturity that delighted in bitter sayings. He was clever and knew it, pleased to be exceptional in a world that exalted the banal. Though he was a sworn enemy of power, he had so far failed to understand his own power. If he were not soon taught something about life, he might become irredeemably, politically, righteous. A sociologist, or some such frightening thing.

People were so different these days, thought the woman. Was it any longer possible for them to understand about power? The land, her exile, had humbled her. Would her grandson be able to accept what her trials had shown her, that when power was without humility, knowledge without wisdom, then pride, the death-bringer, ruled the heart of the individual and the nation?

This offspring of my flesh, Nathaniel. He is myself. And not myself.

They went walking together one day soon after the news, before anyone else knew.

"I've made a decision!" he declared.

"What, pray tell, is that?"

"I'm getting my name legally changed back to what it's supposed to be?"

"To what?"

"O'Dulaine. I think it's much more genuine, don't you?"

"Well, that depends on how you look at it."

"Do you think I should?"

"If you want to, yes, go ahead."

"That's interesting", said the boy. "Grandpa told me I shouldn't, but I could see he was secretly pleased. You tell me I should, but you're not happy about it. Most peculiar!" he concluded with a flourish, imitating her accent.

"You are a very perceptive young fellow."

"Thanks, Grandma. Guess where I got it?"

She laughed at him. "In the gene pool?"

"Right on", he said, shaking his head. "And what a pool it is. You and Grandpa are so different."

"English and Irish. Man and woman. One human being and another. Yes, we're different."

"But how could you agree?"

"You mean, how have we kept together all these years? With so much to separate us?"

"Yes. How did you?"

"Well, it wasn't always serene. But many questions do resolve themselves without words. You stand side by side for so long and have other things to fight than each other."

Yes, she loved the man, her husband. But still did not know him. At least not with the knowledge of the laboratory. It was an inner kind of knowing maybe, an underdeveloped sense. In the early years she had hoped they would descend together through the currents of their cultures—down to the deepest waters where barriers dissolve, where all is one, she had thought. They had held hands, held breath, and plunged. But there had never been enough oxygen.

"When I was young I thought that the universe was one vast organic being", she said. "I used to think that it was all a one-ness, and the pain of separateness was just illusion."

He looked at her quizzically.

"You don't think so any more?"

"No. No, I don't." Then added, after a pause, "It's far more complex and beautiful than that."

From a rise of stone she looked back toward the valley of the Canoe, where the lake covered the fields and the old cabin. She felt a longing for it suddenly, that place she had once hated.

Nathaniel saw where she was staring.

"That damn lake!" he said.

"It's not the thing in itself", she answered quietly, sweeping her arm across the brooding vista of water. "Oh, I would fight it again to my last breath if I could. But Tan, it's not so much the lake as what it represents. What it says about the times and those who profess to lead us. They want to make everything into a oneness. To homogenize everything."

"Like milk?" he laughed. "I don't like to say it, Gram, but there're few people who'd agree with you."

"I know", she said carefully. "But truth must be spoken even if no one will listen, no one will hear."

Why had she said that to him, he wondered. Was it because of his toy newspaper and the things he was writing in it? Forty paid subscriptions now! Wise old editor ruminating for young cub reporter, he thought to himself. Pomposity? No, not Gram. Maybe she was a bit discouraged lately. Everything she had fought against had come to pass; everything she had promoted in her editorials had not come to pass. But had she forgotten that prime ministers and cabinet ministers from the Atlantic to the Pacific were now reading her little sheet? Most of the twelve hundred *Echo* subscriptions went elsewhere than Swiftcreek. From sea unto sea people chuckled over her wit and insights, reprinted snippets in the larger journals, and sat back, some of them, to think about what she said. Not too bad for an old lady. He wished he were as lucky.

"This lake is a warning, and a very serious one, Tan. Yes, it's beautiful in its way. But it's a beauty built on a deep and dark cynicism."

"But why?" he pressed, not entirely sure of her meaning.

"Why? I'm not sure. I may never know for certain. You get old, Tan, and come to accept that some questions may never be answered."

"But if we persisted, maybe the answers would come."

"You used the word *we*", she said, pleased.

"But wouldn't we find them?"

"You had better ask someone older than I."

"But the issues, Gram, don't you feel they're worth fighting for anymore?"

There was distress in his voice.

"You are the fighter now, Nathaniel. Yes, issues are important. But age will show you that they come and go and always remain the same: one man taking the wheat another has sweated for. Justice, it is the eternal struggle. Freedom, the eternal mystery."

Age had not diluted her habit of offering dissertations instead of chat.

She stopped to break off a branch of buckthorn, its red spikes pricking her palms as she began to whip the air before her.

"But I have other battles that you don't know of, and won't for a while." She would have wrapped herself in enigma had he not understood her so well.

"C'mon, lady, there's fight in you yet", he teased, taking her arm as they crossed the field. "And you'll be scrapping with the likes of MacPhale and the boys in Victoria till—"

"Till they bury me?" she smiled.

"Yeah, till they bury you", he laughed, making a joke of such impossibilities.

They entered the woods and went along the path that led to the house.

Nothing is certain, she thought.

The wind moaned up the drowned valley that had been named for some politician.

"Sharpen your quill, Nathaniel", she said. "My time is ending now, and yours has begun."

* * *

Carefully, as if by intent, life itself continued to pry her fingers, one by one, from her attachments:

My dear Anne,
Old friend! Sister of my spirit! The Board of Directors has informed me in a letter this morning of my retirement. I have

become an embarrassment to them. My conservative theology was tactfully mentioned. They are offering me a ministry among Victoria's elderly, if I so wish. The senile cannot be harmed by reactionaries, they presume. Ah, I do not wish to go, but this, at last, is the test of my submission to poverty, the test of my obedience. But I am compelled to go for other reasons. Should I linger here any longer, I would be beatified by the Ladies' Auxiliary, and I am too much the Protestant for that! New blood is coming with shining faces and social platforms that sound hauntingly familiar. Do you recall my feckless youth? How kind you always were to that boy-minister with his imposing voice and stopped ears, not to mention the nervous, roving eyes. Do I dare remember? Have I changed? Tell me, Anne.

I write this to you because the telling of it in person would be too difficult for me. I have written countless letters to you in the past forty years, letters that, as you know, you have never read. Destroyed before foolishly sent. I shall now miss you more terribly than I have for all these years. You said the other day (or was it the other year—I do misplace the past from time to time) that I had helped to save your life. I have never told you, but it was I who was saved. Saved by your obedience, your word, which you refused to break. And saved by your humility. I do not believe I have ever wept in front of another human being, as you have. And it is more than a half-century since I have been held by anyone. Even now I cannot bring you my news face to face for fear of my own emotions. But I have permitted myself a little prisoner's walk in the bright sunlit compound. Truth flies over walls.

You have been humbled, broken. But you have become strong in a way that the world cannot understand. I have remained intact because of your love for your husband and your faithfulness to him. We are flesh and blood, we are longing and loneliness. But we are also spirit. This sounds hopelessly confused, doesn't it?

I will write.

With love always,

Edwin

She was tempted, of course, to tell him of her own impending departure but did not. Better, she thought, to continue that

weave of distance and intangible union they had arranged somewhere in the past. Better to have no final scenes.

There were other moments of significance. She was to meet
with Turid often in the last months, and she treasured especially
a certain encounter among the vegetables.

"Yer weeds are outpacin' the good uns!"

Turid L'Oraison was as blunt as her fingernails, as right to the
point as ever. Bent over, supported by a cane, she had ten times
the power of young modern women. She was a beloved character now, town landmark, great-grandmother, surrounded by a
harvest of generations. She was still the queen of fullness and
fruition, and her eye was as keen as it had always been.

"You ain't lookin' too sharp, gal. Got somethin' troublin' you?"

Anne Delaney looked. And Turid saw.

"Is it fatal like?"

Anne glanced at the pea vines and nodded.

Turid looked at her. Looked at the ground. Looked up at the
mountains. And received an inspiration.

"Well, let's get the hoes, hey, honey, and scratch this dirt a
little!"

The visitor waddled to the shed, threw down her cane, found
a couple of garden tools, gave one to Anne and began to attack
the chickweed savagely. The younger woman stood watching.

She reached out and touched the old woman's hand, a liver-
spotted claw that was both ugly and excruciatingly beautiful.
The hand allowed itself to be taken.

"I am grateful for you, Turid", she whispered.

"For me?"

"When I first knew you, I didn't understand."

"There's little to understand. A sack of groats usually holds
groats."

"Though it can hide gold just as well."

"Gold now! Next it'll be the royal jewels. Close yer mouth,
girl, before more foolishness comes flyin' out."

"Turid."

"Eh?"

"I thank you."

"It's nothin'", said the frowzy woman, who had found an irritant in her nose.

35

It happened too slowly, like pond water pouring over the lip of a beaver dam. Sometimes she felt an ineluctable joy. At other times she experienced those ancient and too familiar plunges into depression and despair. Light was extinguished forever. She was damned. Her own churning soul, isolated, cold, unloved, and unlovable, proved it! God himself had found her unfit. Annihilation was arriving on the afternoon train.

It was feelings, of course. She knew that, grasped it in her mind, though she remained unable to force the knowledge downward toward the center of her fear.

To combat it she made acts of faith, which she called poems:

I am her sister walking in the rain,
To count time's tick and wait for sister death to come by train,
Shall go by pain through click of gate,
Round trip ever turning soon complete.

Like cripples leaping in a dream I'll hurl myself a ball-in-hand
Into the deep cold lake, suppress a scream,
Where take the measured strokes (down-up) in realm of air,
Will walk on weed and sand but not on wave,
Have never learned to save myself or dare.

The rhyming of the singing ice will keep
But rarely speak a eulogy upon a sea-grave of self.
It turns and moans like lovers' sleep or arc of whales who slide
From continental shelf into the deeper song
Or flee the last apocalyptic beat.

As drummers in the bush with speckled wing
Will thrum their feathers on a log, attempt to raise a mate,
I'll wail with wind in leaves and grieve as widows grieve,
And wait to see his hidden face.

As scythe and plow effect the cyclic race,
I'll be the wheat and thistle falling under blade.
Root and berry yielding inner selves are not afraid.
Seed and fruit are ground most finely into flour
Become a bread with leavening of yeast.
My singer asks me to be present at his feast,
So I shall say my yes and be released.

She used various other methods of self-defense: knitted socks
and soakers for her grandchildren, kept a secret journal of her
last thoughts, which she hoped to leave to Nathaniel, if she
didn't burn it first.

*O child of my flesh and my spirit. Do not be a success too young.
Postpone it as long as possible. Strip yourself down for the journey and
go without provisions.*

*Solitude is the natural dwelling place of truth, my Tan. It is there you
will wrestle. It is there you will be tested by fire and by darkness.*

*Oh, Nathaniel, Nathaniel, understand this: There is no longer any
sanctuary. The only indestructible palace is in the heart.*

She spent many hours with her eyes closed, listening to such
words as they surfaced. Occasionally she thought of her husband and something that was not yet resolved between them.
He knew now. He had told the family. Well, it is time, they
would say, she has had a long and interesting life.

From the perspective of the bed, where, she admitted, things
were a little more bearable, she was able to love passionately the
shades of purple, mauve, and violet in the wild bouquets
brought by her granddaughters. And the languid black commas
of tadpoles in jars of slime offered by the small grandsons. The

beauty of this could have wrenched her heart had she not been waiting an extinction of light.

Someone brought an orange moth fluttering about in a container. In order to entertain her, they would drag in all manner of unwilling flowers, neighbors, and flying things.

Is life a glass jar in which we are permitted to rattle noisily for a while?

When no one was looking, she got out of bed and lurched over to the bedroom window, fighting terrible pain. It took great effort, but she was able to unscrew the lid of the peanut butter jar, open the window, and shake out the small orange marvel. Instantly, it knew what to do and ran away on the wind.

Joy. Extreme joy to see it fly. In her memory she saw other things flying, birds and butterflies she had rescued over the years. A thrush thrown into the air with a mended wing, restored to its own true form.

When was that other time she had seen one? Oh, yes, a few months ago, while walking with Tan. There had been pain even then, and no one yet knew except the doctor. But she needed to be free to the last moment with no one nagging her for her own good. No, this was the real good, to bear your pain and to breathe deep the last few moments of free flying.

Tan had been with her that day. She was trying to tell him things that he could not possibly grasp, foolish old crone! But they were words she hoped he might remember years from now, and he would understand, and they would be together again. If he were alone, then he might not feel so . . . so alone.

"A life is a mysterious thing," she said, "mysterious and difficult to grasp."

"Mmmm", he replied. His face took on its patient look.

"Do you think, Nathaniel, that there are people who are led to the borders of the promised land yet aren't permitted to enter?"

"If there's such a thing as a promised land, Gram, and if it's worth a damn, then I think nobody deserves getting in more than you."

"But, you know, there was a prophet who led his people across a desert for forty years. They arrived and entered, but he wasn't allowed in. Moses was his name."

"Grandma Moses!" he laughed.

She stared at him until he began to feel uncomfortable.

She looked up suddenly, past his eyes, into the east and saw a flash of wings.

It's a thrush, she thought, but reminded herself that at some distance it is not easy to know. It might well have been a starling. She watched it cross the river and disappear against the background of blacker pines.

A mixed memory. Wings flexed in the sky could bestow a little time in which she would try to translate the rattle into song.

The disintegration began, and the drugged flight from pain. She refused to have anything to do with hospitals, would not let them drag her off where tubing and wiring would rob her of any last scraps of pride. That would go soon enough, she said.

"I will die when it's time to die", she told Stephen. "A body knows when it's finished. To hasten its departure or to delay it by machines is foolish." She paused, then added, "Until then, I shall fight."

"Good", he said. "You haven't given up."

He sat for long hours with her, waiting for some word that might be exchanged for an article of their love.

"Are you scared, Anne?" he asked, wanting to share in that private war she was determined to wage alone.

"Yes, I'm frightened."

He had to bend to hear her.

It seemed a neglect of justice that an old warrior should not be permitted to die in peace and that whatever was afflicting her should also smother her hope of attending the victory feast.

Admonition to myself: Anne, you will not deny in the dark what you have seen so clearly in the light!

"If you knew my thoughts, Stephen, you would be horrified. I could kill myself without a second thought at certain times."

He nodded and nodded, empty of any consolations to offer.

"But it would be wrong", she added. "If this is the last little bridge over the abyss, then I'm glad to be crossing it."

"Glad!" he said, not believing her. If the dirt under his nails was any indication, he had a fiercer grip on life than she, or still believed in manure.

"Can you understand that I might finally have something to offer?" she said.

"To offer? But what haven't you already given? All the things you've been and done, woman!"

She smiled weakly.

"Yes, a battle in strange territory. I have many ribbons and medals from my campaigns, don't I? But they are just tin, cheap tin, compared to this gift. The only one I have ever given freely, with no thought of response, with no certainty."

"What gift?"

"My nothingness, my emptiness."

"No, no, no . . ." he said, attempting to correct this sick child.

"You see, Stephen, if I had what you have, your confidence in the . . . your belief in the . . . the love, you see, then I would know, wouldn't I? It wouldn't be such a gift that I'm giving."

"I just don't understand what you're talking about!"

"Suppose there is a great Love behind creation, but the original unity of this vast work of art has been damaged, and all of existence as we know it is merely a brief moment during which the artist repairs his masterpiece. If he is that beautiful, it would be unspeakably shattering to have a glimpse of his face. Do you understand, Stephen? So what can I give him, really? Nothing . . . nothing except the gift of trust in what I can't yet see face to face. There is beauty in the world. There is no reason for it to be here.

If it's all biology, all eating and getting eaten and the strongest devouring the weakest, then it's madness. Nothing more than madness. It's dying and drowning, and all love is illusion. But there *is* love, you see. Poor, weak, and broken love—a sign of something from a distant land. Whoever made Sarah's heart and Nathaniel's mind and Jan's passion to invent and your . . ."

She had been about to say *eyes* but fell silent.

"Whatever or whoever made these must be very wonderful indeed. If I am to meet him, then I want to stride into the dark holding an image of beauty and the goodness of being right here in the center of me. Do you understand?"

He was silent.

"I am naked before God, Stephen. I have nothing to give him except this . . . faith."

"It's said that he loves best what's little and truly is itself."

"Well, I am small."

Another day he said, "I wish I could give you my belief, my certainty."

"You can't give another person such things."

"So there's nothing I can give you. It's always been that way." His voice was hurt.

"No, you have always given what you had to give. That is the difference, you see, between you and me."

Her breathing became labored. She drew out her words laboriously.

"It took me a long time to learn what I was, and until then I was a sour thing. You know. Of all people you should know. I see the scars I made in you."

"The past. Little things. Over now."

"Not so little. I hurt you."

"And I hurt you. There was something frozen inside me for too long. A part of my heart was dead, Anne. But I do love you." His voice choked.

"I do love you."

543

She saw the anxiety in his face. He became intolerably beautiful in her eyes, this humble beast of burden, her husband. A man who did not finish sentences. With cracked fingernails and a vein wriggling in his temple. The Centaur. Old.

"I love you too, Stephen."

He blinked, apparently alive.

"You'd better sleep now", he said, returning them to earth.

"You want to leave me?" she asked, suddenly disoriented. "You want to go where there's some peace, someone strong?"

"No. I want you to sleep. I'll be right here."

She desired this moment to flow on without end. She hungered for his eyes, needed him to hold her with them, to look into her the way he did with children and animals. She would have begged for it, too, if silence, the third partner of their long marriage, had not raised its voice.

Loss, loss, all that waste, thought the woman. *Oh, the times I did not love you.*

"I love you", he repeated foolishly.

He reached out his hand. She reached out hers from across a chasm. But as they touched and his grip was firm upon hers, she saw that the chasm was only a crack, and that it had always been so. As she watched, it closed and disappeared altogether.

They looked into each other now, and the woman's soul swam outward through the liquid black of his eyes. They were walking together in a garden on a revolving earth, eyes opening in a first seeing.

"Did you hear that?" she said, startled, looking toward the window.

"What?"

"Glass. The sound of shattering glass."

But he had heard nothing. Only the sound of their grandchildren at tag beyond the window.

* * *

The day following this conversation, a stranger got off the passenger train and walked through town toward the Canoe Valley road. He asked a few townsfolk for directions to the Delaneys' new property. They noted that he was foreign looking and walked with a limp. That evening he spent two hours talking with Anne. Stephen gave him supper, and then the visitor left.

Later, when Stephen brought Anne some tea and thin soup, she smiled radiantly at him. The room was filled with an extraordinary peace.

"You look wonderful", he said. "What did Father Andrei say to you?"

"Very little. He listened mostly. And then he said some ancient words. Latin words."

"Oh?"

"It was so simple. So beautiful. This should have happened many, many years ago."

She took his face in her hands and looked deeply into his eyes.

"My Centaur", she smiled.

"Come now, have some supper. You don't want your tea to get cold."

"Listen, my dearest. I want you to know that the shadows went away. They've gone forever. I'm not afraid anymore."

He made her lie back and proceeded to spoon-feed her the soup. Then he held her hand without speaking until she fell asleep.

On the following day, after many hours of physical pain, behind a wall over which the curious could not peer, she died. Stephen found her lying upright against the pillow. He stood looking at her face, which he did not recognize. Her body was empty, a shucked sack out of which grain or gold had been spilled.

He felt nothing. Oh, yes, that first distant vibration of the tidal wave of grief that would soon rise up over his life. He would begin to sense some of what he had just suffered. But he was momentarily numb.

He coughed. There seemed nothing to do. Except to tell. He stood in the absence absorbing silence as her final word. The only sound was Jan's clock pealing in the distance. He would ever after be able to say, "She died at three o'clock. Yes, my wife—Anne was her name—she died at three o'clock."

Then he saw that she had already laid down a large portion of her life long ago. Piece by piece she had given it away as she wrestled with existence, as her self was absorbed as nourishment into his life and the life of the children and the community. And laid down most piercingly as she abandoned, one by one, the shapes of the dreams she had planned. Only to take them up again in other forms.

He wandered out into the kitchen, where he had been serving coffee to a visitor only a few minutes before.

He looked at the fat woman who was massaging her tired feet. The woman saw his eyes and knew that Anne Delaney was gone. She looked at the floor, and her face was hard.

"Tis a wee visit we make t'this world", said Turid L'Oraison.

PART FOUR

The Stone and the Fire

36

There was an exceptionally light snowfall that winter, which left the fields exposed to killing frosts. The water lines in town froze and burst with regularity. It was a season of disruption, followed by a newer, hotter one whose possibilities were more terrible. The spring brought little rain, and the sun baked the earth mercilessly. The noises of insects cut the parchment air with razors as their wings snapped in flight. The underbrush withered into dried herbs, and the leaves exposed their white underbellies on the trees.

There was no rain that summer, though an occasional fog would lift by noon into thunderheads that moved eastward over the ranges to the plains beyond without dropping their burden. There had not been a summer like it since before the time of man in this valley. No one knew what the outcome would be. The snowpack, which usually gripped the sunless sides of the peaks, had become a dream that the creeks had ceased to run from, though here and there a little sluggish water trickled down warmly from the remnants of glaciers. Even the Canoe grew thin between the shrunken gums of its banks.

Many bear and caribou moved down from the high places to seek shade, to rummage with the deer in the bush, and to drink from the river in the night. Their patterns were disrupted, tempers bad, crowding up the forest with their complaints and moods so that it was dangerous to go walking beyond the fields or the town.

Stephen Delaney was a man who had begun to bend before life. In reverence or in defeat it had not yet been revealed. He was considerate toward it. He would place a salt block at the edge of the field for the wild things to come and lick. There was always a herd of white-tails or mule-deer gathered around the red minerals if the man rose early to look. He woke before dawn most mornings and got himself up eventually to wander through the kitchen in bare feet. He would be comforted by the recurrent newspaper and a cup of tea, the tick of a clock in the parlor and the patchwork coloration on a spread his wife had made for him. He would watch the passing of weather. He had an extensive collection of peeled twigs in the shapes of letters of the alphabet and a pantheon of political gods and goddesses whose activities he followed in the paper as if they were real. He read the large-print Bible his grandchildren had given him one year; he swayed and rocked as the sun moved around the kitchen floor, and he wept soundlessly as the words burned in him like sweet amber light. His life was occupied in this way, and with memory, which is the food we digest when life allows us to lie down.

In the mornings he would milk the goat and feed the chickens, then would wander around the garden muttering over those potato plants that had refrained from giving up their lives to the sun. He would pour a cup of water on each surviving plant as if it were an individual who must be encouraged, for life, he knew, does not thrive on water and mineral nourishment alone. He would sleep most nights after a lacing of whiskey in the goat's milk, would toss and turn in the heat, covered only by his white undershorts. No one came visiting much anyway.

He was older than old. His long muscles were slack and yellow, the skin rippled and spotted, his face and arms dyed a deep onion-skin ochre. He had lost all beauty, and the last reserve of his physical strength was departing as well, those admirable qualities that are so easily replaced by foolishness. People did smile over him a great deal these days. He did not care or perhaps did not think about it. He was the carving someone had left too long out in the elements. He was not especially good to look at, if you ignored the eyes. But if you saw them, you would notice something seldom seen on the faces of human beings. It was that transparency which is the property of the very young, to whom it is given freely, or of certain kinds of old people, who have earned it. His eyes were gray quartz, smiling, or thinking, or sometimes weeping. Or looking into middle-space as he rocked on the back porch, or gazing through the dust and flyspecks and spatters of red geranium, up the slope of dead grass to the cemetery.

Beneath a stone lay his wife's body:

WHO CAN ESTIMATE HER WORTH,
A GOOD WIFE,

ANNE DELANEY

1895–1976

There were two smaller crosses beside it, wood, painted white over their blisters, crosses that had stood above the graves of the children who had died before birth. The little girls. He remembered the time they had moved the coffins from the old place before the new lake drowned it. Oh, he was angry that day and expressed it in actual words to his wife, who stood apart, holding her arms tightly.

Anne, even the dead may not rest in peace.

When they unearthed the boxes, which were half-rotted and rattling with the tiny, holy bones, he had desired to pry off the lid to see what time does accomplish with things. But he resisted. The others would have found him ghoulish or at least too curious for his own good. But he continued to desire, wishing to know, to discover something elusive in the hollow sockets. Did it still flow in the hairline joints of the skull like a map of rivers? He had made them, he and the woman. They were intricate strokes of grace and spoke eloquently to those who would probe. He had yearned for them to reveal themselves, to enlarge and become presences that laughed, obeyed and disobeyed, and ran around his dream with warm limbs and futures, and cleaner pasts than his own. But they had emerged unprepared. Or was it that they had been blessed with simplicity and completion.

In any event, they were dead.

This is a place of death, his wife once said, shuddering in the wind, hating the valley. Oh, she was young and fierce then. She looked fit to kill death.

And life, he had replied. *It's a place of life, Anne.*

There were the three who lived, after all, and time does teach that death is defeated only by the creation of new life. But like some terrible prophetess she had glared at him, as if to say, *all flesh is grass that rises up in the morning and is slashed down at noon!*

Now his flesh could hardly disagree. The heat continued to destroy the remaining grass unabated through August. There was no work in the bush. People abandoned their gardens and watered the roofs of their houses so that sparks from cook-fires would not ignite the dry shakes. By Labor Day the grass was dust in the pastures and farmers had been forced to set their cattle loose in the bush to forage for leaves and underbrush. Children lay panting for breath in cellars, and patient, long-married couples began to snap at each other for various accessible reasons. Summer dried up the people as if they were stubble.

In his later years the old man became the boy once more, because there were so few to remind him of his more social identity. Age returned him to the tides of youth and a world full of missing people to whom he would always and everywhere be that laughing black-haired child, *Stiofain*. With hot soda bread or cockle juice dribbling down your chin, and joker's eyes that flashed at the mention of those exotic creatures, *girls*. Flesh had been the green grass blowing in the salt western wind and cold red hands on the nets, or the night under thatch when ignorant flesh first became informed, waking from childhood, wet with the riddle of his own body. Hot as the slippery olive seaweed flung for compost onto the barren earth. Or running the hares around and around the island till you had a wiggling bag full to take home for stewing—home, home over the moonlit water with your father in the curragh, sleeping flushed and weary on the canvas while the sea butted your head. And you were carried up the rocks to bed. That was when you were young, and the world was beginning forever. Now you were old, and the world was ending.

"How fast it has gone", said the old man Stiofain.

As he emerged from his house that morning, there was a knowledge that came upon him. He smelled it on the air though there was no definable scent. He recognized a vibration at the edges of awareness, as some will sense a distant motion of animals before they are seen. As the geese will know it is time to leave. As the fish will know it is time to spawn and time to die.

He walked slowly in underwear and boots up the slope to the cemetery, where he could see farther down the valley. He sat in the grass by his wife's grave and thought of her. He lay his head on the stone. He recalled rolling around in the hot passionate sun beneath the crab apple tree one summer long ago. He smiled as he recalled the woman's timidity, how she had refused at first to expose flesh to the light on the ravaged blanket. How she had said yes finally—the farm was far in the bush then, and no one to see except the astonished calf and the dog who ignored this particular commotion and the baby who slept beneath cheesecloth in the wicker laundry basket. The man and the woman had laughed together eventually, shameless and immortal under the apple-light. But from the vantage point of her grave, it did appear that life was shorter than had been expected and that flesh, like grass, must lie down at some point beneath the sun or the scythe.

Far to the south, where the Canoe should have been clear and shimmering, there was a thickening of the air, as if the valley had been poured full of saffron glass.

Smoke. All morning he watched it filling until the south

became a mass of dirty yellow, streaked with smears of brown, dwindling down at the floor to a line of terra-cotta. Tendrils of smoke were coiling upward, moving ever closer as the slow ticking hours poured out over the valley. From time to time he saw pickup trucks roaring by toward it on the dusty road. Bryan would be among them, he knew, directing the frantic activities of the suppression crew.

He went in for something to drink and eat about noon, judging by the height of the red sun. As he nibbled on a piece of mutton from the cooler, he listened. The whine of a small bird-dog plane went overhead, guiding in the droning water bombers to the fire line. From the window he saw them drop their tanks of red chemical, then turn southward to reload at the Blue River tanker base. All afternoon they hovered like bees over a ruptured hive until by four o'clock they had ceased to work, the entire sky choked with an impenetrable haze.

"Fire", he said, peering down the valley. He knew it was not slash fires lit by loggers, as no one had been permitted to strike a match in the bush for months. It was gun-powder dry, so parched that the merest thought of flame would explode an entire forest.

"Glannan teine", he said to the wind.

Yes, replied the wind, *fire cleanses*.

Still in his underwear, he went out to the pump house and started the gas motor, which would pull the cold earth-water up from its underground sources. As the water tank filled, he untangled the garden hose and began to sprinkle the walls of his house. But the wood panels merely sucked the water greedily, turned black, then returned to their original gray within minutes. The air was growing white, evaporating the man's sweat before it had a chance to ball and roll. Then the field filled with actual smoke. Rivulets of hot wind came in, at first small but urgent, then unceasing and mean, licking around the house before the first and final taste.

He watched as a bear ran out of the wall of haze, looked around, and went back in again. Deer crisscrossed the field in a frenzy, leaping. The mare whinnied in the field, shaking her mane, looking at the house, trotting sideways, stopping, turning around and around, then trotting again, her cries growing shrill. He tried to catch her, to throw a halter over her head, but she evaded his every attempt. The goat naahed angrily from the shed. When he untied the creature, it instantly bucked and bolted away into the bush. The fire could be heard now, crackling at some distance. Stiofain stared in the direction of the noise.

He climbed a ladder to the roof, with the hose looped around his arm, and stood in the suffocating wind, directing the water down over the shingles. The house was an island in choking fog that thickened minute by minute. Insects screamed at high pitch in chorus. Birds flew low in alarm, darting round and round in circles, no longer able to fly upward, because above them the layers of smoke were rolling over in thick blankets.

At that point a Ministry of Forests truck roared into the yard and screeched to a halt, still bouncing on its springs, raising a cloud of dust.

"Dad", yelled a man who jumped out. He saw his father up on the roof in underwear and groaned.

"Bryan, I'm saving the house."

"Dad, I've come to get you out of here. Looks like this fire is gonna let er rip, and Swiftcreek's right in the path."

"I'll stay and fight it."

"No, you won't! We're gonna lose the whole shootin-match, Pa! C'mon, let's get you dressed."

He came obediently down the ladder. They went inside. As Stiofain struggled into clothing, Bryan paced back and forth.

"It's that lake", he said. "Since the valley was stripped out it's become the damnedest wind funnel you ever saw."

"There's been a terrible lot of wind the past few years", said Stiofain slowly, fighting his suspenders.

"Well, it was just waiting for a summer like this. It's gonna be bad. Where's your money and papers?"

"I keep it all at Ash's place. Safer there."

He picked up a photograph of the woman, his dead wife, and began to look around the house for other treasures. He found her journals lying where he had placed them beside the bed months ago. He had intended to read them some day but had not yet dared to crack the faded silk-bound volumes. The pages fanned and flapped before his eyes:

> alone . . .
> a tidy universe . . .
> his mark upon myself and our children . . .
> God . . .
> alone . . .
> the geese south early this year . . .
> 1939 . . .
> his face . . .
> tested by fire and darkness . . .
> alone . . .
> God, god . . .
> Stephen . . .
> alone . . .

The old man seemed confused, searching around the room for something. He dropped the book.

"C'mon, Dad, let's go!" and the frantic son pulled his father out the door and into the truck. As they roared down the lane, Stiofain looked back steadily, yearning for a last glimpse of the tossing form of the horse.

* * *

Nathaniel Delaney went out onto the porch of *The Echo* that evening and soberly observed the progress of the fire. He grew alarmed when he realized that the tanker aircraft had given up bombing in the zero visibility and that the fire would now do what it had set out to do. The wind was rising. He looked around. The village was heavily treed and kindling dry. Only a few buildings were made of metal: the offices of the paper, the town hall, and Jan Tarnowski's place. Everything else would probably be incinerated.

He realized suddenly that his grandfather was between the village and the fire, lost in a world of smoke. After a few telephone calls he learned that his parents were hastily gathering the family into various cars. As soon as the grandfather joined them, they would drive for the Fraser and cross at the Tee-John bridge. It was unlikely the fire would be able to leap the river.

Bryan had left more than an hour ago to fetch the old man and had not yet returned. Had they lost their way? He knew that they should have been back long before this. Something must have gone wrong out there. He soaked himself under the garden hose, filled a water jug and stuffed it into a knapsack. He went by memory, following the barely visible streets toward the general direction of south-east. He passed Pine Street just as Jan was climbing his clock tower.

"Jan, Jan," he shouted, "get down off there! The whole town's in the path of the fire."

"It de time uv de *enduvdevorldkluk*, Tanny."

"Huh? C'mon, Jan, this isn't the time. You've got to get out of here right now."

"*Nie!* I stay until it de right time. Maybe dis is de time for de bells only. But maybe if dis is de end uv de end, den I have guard dis kluk for de trumpet blow. In dis trumpet is secret for de last end."

"For God's sake, this is no time to be crazy! If you've any sense in your head, get moving right now or you'll die here."

"I no die. I know my job. I know my place. I was borned for dis. All my life I be make ready for dis."

"Jan, I don't have time to argue. I gotta go get my grandpa."

"Hit's okay, Tanny. You make your part for dis *enduvdevorld-kluk* long time ago when you vas little."

"Please go!"

"I sad you no believe no more, boychick, in dis kluk."

Exasperated, Nathaniel plunged away into the deeper smoke toward the Canoe Lake Road. The bell began to ring as he went. When the road sign appeared out of the gloom, he turned south to follow it. He knew that a half-hour's steady jog would bring him to his grandfather's gate. Already he could hear the snap and rustle of the dying bush, though there was no flame to be seen. Where could the old man be, he wondered. He did not know that only a few hundred yards from town he had passed Bryan's abandoned truck. His uncle and grandfather had gone on foot by another street and were now joining the exodus.

Nathaniel began to run. The crackling grew louder, and great belches of acrid smoke burst through the wall of terrified trees. Tongues of fire darted out of the forest and climbed. The trees panicked and gesticulated wildly. A porcupine scuttled past yowling, the tips of its quills smoking. A rooster emerged out of nothing and disappeared into it again. Dead dog on the road. The air black, night falling. A red glow emerged from the pall, tendrils of fire swung down from the branches. The bell from Jan's clock kept ringing, and it began to sound as if it were the very voice of madness.

The mailbox. *S. Delaney*. The gate. He ran up the lane. The field was black, two tiny crosses flaming above. The horse was galloping in circles. Nathaniel banged through the house. No grandfather! He searched frantically through the field in case the old man had collapsed somewhere out there. Nothing. He must have gone.

The horse! Nathaniel upended his felt hat and filled it with water from the jug. He tried to approach the animal but she continued to scream into the wind with the universal scream-ing, racing madly about on burned hooves. As she went by once more, he flung the hatful of water into her nostrils and she trampled to a halt, wheeled, and trotted to him, tossing her head, wild-eyed and stomping, but under a measure of control. He grabbed her mane and pulled her to the water tank, unscrewed the bung, and let it pour out over the animal and himself. It splashed onto their burns and eased them a little, though the water itself was becoming hot. Nathaniel's arms and face sighed with relief. He tied the horse to the scaffolding of the tank and went inside the house.

He stumbled on the journals. He stuffed them, the stone cross, and the flute into his knapsack. That was it. He had to get out now. The roof was in flames. The air spat gobs of fire past the window, the door was smoking, the green snake of the garden hose bubbled and coiled as the plastic boiled.

"Up, hup, hup!"

He was on the horse, kicking her belly, forcing the animal down the lane to the road.

"Go, Go!"

He beat the rump with a stick, and the mare galloped. But she screamed again as they emerged into the road, reared back and threw him. Then she galloped off into the mouth of the blast furnace. Screaming.

The fire had curved around the field and was now advancing through the bush between the farm and the town. Trees had fallen, burning, across the road.

"O God", he cried, turned, and ran back up the lane. There remained only one way open. If the creek bed had retained a little water, he might be able to go up through it to the mountain.

Yes, at the end of the field he found it oozing down the banks, gray and clogged with floating pieces of charcoal, dead birds, and ash. But underneath the scum there were a few inches of sluggish water a man's body wide. He hurled himself into this wondrous muck and lay in it face-down, lifting himself only to breathe. Then, slowly, he began to crawl and stumble through the night and the rain of fire, up onto the darkened mountain.

37

It was well beyond midnight when he emerged from the burning universe. He was above the tree line now, and only a few charred patches and sparks showed among the moss, though smoke was thick. Below, the world throbbed, suffused in a dull red glow.

He lay exhausted on his back by the edge of the creek, his face a scratched mask. He drank the ugly creek water. He ached. He was alive.

Through a break in the haze he saw a few stars and a sickly moon.

"*This majestical roof fretted with gold fire*", he whispered, remembering a line from Shakespeare. He laughed, finding himself hopelessly literary even in the midst of disaster.

Oh, we are poets and would crawl through fire to say something moving.

Well, it could not be helped; it was in the blood. What had his grandfather said that time they buried the old woman? Something sentimental:

"I had a poem to tell her. Or the end of one, but I never got a chance. I was always waiting for the right moment."

Nathaniel felt a wave of condescension for his uneducated grandfather. There were things about himself that he did not like, and this very feeling was one of them, a streak of severe observance that might solidify into judgment. He was possibly cold. And proud. He might become harder still. He turned now and raised himself on hands and knees, then upright, and stumbled off toward the peak and the configuration of rock, at the base of which was the cave of his boyhood.

He found the hole eventually and stumbled through the

bushes, removed the stone, crawled in, and threw himself down on the dirt. The insane ringing of the bell was blotted out. The lightless interior cooled him. It was of purest black, like a fabric that reflects nothing. He touched the stone walls. They were warm.

His head began to spin. He was about to let his body suspend itself in sleep when he heard:

You are here.

A quiet voice in the cave, with him.

His hair stood on end. He shouted.

"God! What! Who . . .?"

Silence.

"Who's there?" he asked trembling.

It's me, the voice replied serenely. It laughed, or employed a faculty of pleasure that was not loud, not even sinister in an obvious way. It was a soft voice, tainted, neither masculine nor feminine.

"Who are you?" he cried.

You know me and I know you.

"I don't know you at all."

You know me.

"This is my cave. Get out of here!"

Again that strange laugh.

This is my cave. All the places where men crawl in are mine. And you are mine too.

"I am not yours, whatever you think you are!"

I have many names.

Nathaniel scrambled about, feeling for the matches he had always left stored by the lantern.

No. You will not do that!

"Do what?"

Do not try to make a light.

"I want to see you."

Not yet.

562

His hand struck a matchbox, fumbled it open, and lit a match. The incandescence blinded him for a moment, but beyond it he thought he saw a shape that melted and flowed, a hybrid abomination of leopard and wolf, a coiled serpent, a bear. Gradually his vision cleared. It was a bear. It was very old; its snout was scarred and its flanks matted with dried blood. Its eyes were black lodestones rimmed with red. It sat back on its haunches and opened its mouth.

You see me, and yet you do not see me. You know me, and yet you do not know me.

The match burned itself up. He fumbled for another, but his fingers trembled and could not obey.

"I want to get out!"

He panicked, crawled toward the entrance but found it blocked; the stone had rolled over it again. How, how?

He choked.

The darkness was a presence waiting. He realized that he had never before encountered darkness as a presence. Until now it had been merely an absence of light, a shadow. He had seen greed and hatred flowing from some incurable wound in the hearts of men who could still know shame. But this thing had no shame in its voice.

You have received an invitation from Maurice L'Oraison.

"How do you know that? What are you!?"

He wishes you to become his assistant at the Legislature. You want this position very badly, don't you?

Yes, he had wanted this job very much, but he had turned it down in the end. He wasn't sure why he had done so. A feeling. A hunch.

You will write to Maurice, and you will change your mind. You will go to work with him.

He felt a wave of power from the other, a force of will that was only weakly deflected by his own small will.

"No", he said.

But the wave increased and, with it, a surge of self-pity rose up within himself and a longing to be understood, to be accepted, to be known for his hidden greatness. The thing understood it too; its voice was sympathetic:

You have never been loved. How pitiful these people are who have spawned you. But I love you. You are different, you are beautiful, and in me you will become more beautiful.

"Let me go."

Go then!

He tried to move toward the cave entrance to push on the rock with the remnant of energy left to him. But his will was weakened by the struggle, and he could not make himself go.

You are alone. Come and join me.

"I don't know what you mean. I'm not alone!" The faces of his grandmother, his grandfathers, Jan, came before his eyes, welling up from within his heart. He felt strength return for a moment.

"You are sick", he said. "People may be ugly, but they're also good, and sometimes they're beautiful. They don't mean to do all those—"

Oh, of course they don't, can't you see? And that is why you are different from them. You are beautiful because you know. Come with me and know.

Nathaniel felt heat burning in his face, blood pounding in his temples.

"I . . ."

I will give you more than enough power to create a new world. It is not your little nightmares, not your childish image of "evil" that I offer you. It is goodness I give you.

"Goodness?"

Unlimited power to change mankind. You are going to become a very powerful man. And I am going to give this power to you.

His voice trembled, and his hands shook: "I don't want it. I want . . . I want . . ."

What do you want?

"I want truth."

There is no truth. Only knowledge. Only power.

"That's a lie."

Is it? Tell me what your "truth" is built upon? Tell me what I cannot blow away?

Nathaniel opened his mouth to reply but realized that he did not actually have an answer. What was his concept of truth built upon? Vague ideas of democracy and freedom? Belief in man?

This was getting too complicated, he thought.

"Let me go."

Go then, the thing said into his mind. It was boundlessly complying, no monster masks, no devil's faces.

Nathaniel turned to go, but stopped.

"Wait", he thought. "This is crazy. Who am I talking to?"

He stumbled over the pack of matches and a candle. He lit the stub and planted it in the dirt. The cave was empty. He laughed with relief. Imagination! Hallucination! He crawled to the entrance and found the stone rolled away, tilted into the junipers where he had left it. The atmosphere outside the entrance was no longer breathable. He crawled back in.

You have returned to me.

His hands shook. He tried to light the lantern, but there was no oil in it. Another match died. The candle stub burned down and was swallowed by the liquid shadow of the bear.

"Who are you? What are you?" His voice was weak and terrified, a child's voice trying to be a man's.

It is I who ask you that question.

"You mean who am I?"

You do not know, do you? Real people make the reality they want. I will help you to be real. I will help you to create your reality. I am the master of knowing, and I will teach you. Your brilliance is wasted on this little town. The town is dying. I will take you elsewhere. You must be lifted up over the heads of this generation to speak what I would have them know.

"The truth must be spoken . . ."

There is no truth. There is only knowing. Childhood is over now.

"No!"

Once more the thing sent a wave of its will toward Nathaniel. He felt it pushing for admission into his very being. He refused by an act of his own dwindling will.

The people need you to teach them to love the shadow, for the shadow is the fullness of knowledge, and the light is half-knowledge.

"No."

The people need . . .

"The people? There are no people", Nathaniel said, interrupting the overpowering voice. It was the first time he had done so. He felt a burst of strength. Then he remembered something his grandmother had once said about the people: there are only persons, each one a world, each one a nation.

But the shadow was changing subjects quickly now:

You are mine.

"What?"

It is a fact, and there is nothing you can do about it.

"What!"

It is not what you think. It is freedom from the Other. Come with me, and I will make you free.

"The Truth will make us free . . ."

There was silence for an eternal moment as Nathaniel waited.

Then the entire chamber filled suddenly with a choking smell that made him retch. Horror swept over him, as if he were blown in a hurricane of malice, an unthinkable force that would tear the hair, the nails, the flesh from his body. It was power. It was fear.

I own you, said the voice, with boundless certainty.

"No!"

You are mine.

"God save me!" he shouted from the depths of his being, a spontaneous outburst, a cry from his dormant spirit.

He could not move, he could not think, he could not pray. Prayer was the dust of Adam, the dry clay that fell from the ceiling at which it had been tossed.

Fear screamed over and through him. His soul became a shrunken twisted nub, holding onto itself only by the last resources of will.

"I believe in God, the Father Almighty, and I believe in . . ."

The bear staggered back from him, but Nathaniel did not know any more of the words. They were little scraps of paper torn from his mind, blasted away into the wind by the maniacal laughter. Even so, it was not laughter but a mimicry of it.

Words, words, words, words, words, the thing sneered, and began to approach again.

With the small consciousness left to him, Nathaniel realized that he was gripping the knapsack and within it the lumps of his grandfather's possessions. He felt the stone carving. With all his strength he commanded his fingers to move an inch, two inches.

The force of terror increased.

Your little trinkets and amulets, the thing jeered, *your pathetic medicine bundles and superstitions.*

The top of the bag opened. Nathaniel grabbed the stone cross and lifted it high. His entire being, past, present, and future, was suspended upon it.

I will burn you, I will burn you, I will burn . . . I will make you burn each other. I will . . .

Demented laughter, a self-loathing and self-destroying sound. The phantom bear, a cloud, a fume, a reek, a final lunge and recoil, was sucked out of the cave. Nathaniel collapsed in the dust. He wept bitterly and uncontrollably, his limbs trembling and cold, crying out from exhaustion. He knew now the taste of that fear which afflicted all mankind. It had taken on a shape. Its voice had come from the formless void to manifest its compelling arguments in his fragile mind. It had argued and come close to winning. But it had lost by the authority of one who, long ago, had carved a rebuttal with the sacrifice of his life.

Pale light sifted through the entrance. He moved his hand, and the small stone thing pulsed in his fingers with the warmth of his blood. He operated his pain-filled joints, then rose and stumbled out into the morning. Light filled the valley. Light and smoke. Below him he saw that in many parts the inferno had burned itself out, and the bombers were at work over what remained of the fire line. The front now extended from east to west and had swept north to the Fraser River. Behind its path he saw a vast area of black, the geometrical gridwork of the town, smoking heaps of ash in the mill-yard. Still farther south, the lake.

It began to rain, and he stood in the outpouring with his face turned to the sky, his body scoured and ravaged. The downpour washed him, and he stood with hands open, a child among the ruins.

"I don't understand", he whispered. "I don't understand what happened in there. Maybe too much smoke. Maybe heat exhaustion. Or the ghost of our family bear."

He breathed deeply. His lungs ached. He rinsed his clothing in the creek and dressed himself again. He looked around, a sleeper awakening. He began to walk down the mountain, holding the stone cross against his heart.

"I didn't know I was empty", he said to it. "I didn't know. I was blind. I didn't know I've always been afraid. But where else could I have learned this, except in the face of terror?"

He was empty, and he was full. He was alone. Yes, he was alone among men. He was an alien, a stranger and sojourner like all his fathers before him. He knew now the anguish of exiles, the depth of their loneliness. And he saw that this was a gift, for it was the state of pilgrims journeying toward their own true home.

"I didn't know I was alone", he said to the stone. "I didn't know I was *not* alone until you came unto my aloneness. And I was no longer alone."

The town was burned, the streets full of smoking foundations. A few tin buildings remained, *The Echo*—a paper without a city—the town hall, and Tarnowski's house.

He found Jan staggering about the *enduvdevorldkluk*. In a circle of giant smoldering pine stumps lay a heap of twisted gears and cracked bells. A melted trumpet jutted from the side. Jan went round and round, muttering to himself:

"De bombe! De bombe come and now doze besturds is gonna trow us all in de camps!"

"Jan! Jan!" he said. "It was a fire. Over now. You're not alone. Don't be afraid."

The old man stared.

"Itsak, you is comin' from de fire? The fire no eat you? Is you be pulled from de fire?"

"It's me. It's Tan."

"It's you, Tanny? But my *enduvdevorldkluk* is boorned!"

"We'll build it again. You and me. Together."

"My vife is boorned", he cried, tears streaming down his cheeks. "My boy is boorned. My kluk is boorned. My piano is boorned."

"Come, let's go see."

Inside, the contents of the house appeared to have been baked. Everything of wood was blistered, resinous. In the corner, covered with blankets and sagging ice-packs, stood the scorched Heintzman.

He took the old man by the arm then and set him down on the stool. Jan stared at the yellow keys. Nathaniel touched one.

A simple note sounded.

He played it again.

"Play, Jan", he said. "Make beauty."

Jan lifted his fingers and began to pick out a slow, tortuous path through one of the *valses* of his beloved Chopin.

"Make beeooty", he said.

"Yes, make beauty", said Nathaniel. "The fire is finished, Jan. Make beauty."

* * *

Always, the aristocracy of nature asserts itself. The burning of forests subsides into the weeping of rain. The earth grieves and is born again. The seeds burst in the hot soil and germinate. The men return, encouraged by their dreams and by their curious ability to endure. They build and build again what has been torn down and thrown onto the pyre. Some will proclaim their permanence in the face of all seasons; others will suspect their oneness with the transience of water and sky. These human beings are loyal subjects of the great ecology of hope.

The old man who lives in a tent and dreams of the sea will tell you about some of this. His eyes are full of stories that will not be heard. People will suspect him presently of losing his mind, Old Mister Delaney, who sits out there in the charcoal field, where green shoots are returning. He is waiting for them to grow and is encouraged, while his sons and grandsons rebuild his cabin on the ruins of the old.

People passing by suspect someone deranged by fire, and having looked into fire he might agree. He sits with his hands outstretched on knees, suspenders biting into the spindly frame. The palms are cupped to receive an outpouring of light, are drenched in a light as ordinary as dirt, as ordinary as fire. Observers go by on the road in clouds of dust, but the old man is too engrossed in his vocation to notice. He is speaking, which seals the matter of his dubious sanity. He is speaking to a more silent audience, a host of listeners who stand watching on the banks of the terrible and beautiful river of man. There is a dog that snores beside him in the sunlight. There are ravens that crack their voices in dispute. There are clouds that take the shape of white horses and white riders, galloping in silent formation above the mountains.

Stiofain's sons and grandsons call out words to him. He does not always hear. They drink beer and joke and are happy in their muscles, raising secure dwellings in the autumn air.

One of them separates himself from the others and goes to sit for a time at the feet of his grandfather. He asks questions. Stiofain answers. He is eloquent with silences. No one else hears.

Then he sings a word or two in a language that has almost ceased to exist, words that endure beyond forgetting, his face raised into the sky, an old man in a burned field, waiting for light.

Novels by Michael D. O'Brien in the series
Children of the Last Days:

A Cry of Stone *
Strangers and Sojourners
Plague Journal
Eclipse of the Sun
Sophia House *
Father Elijah

*Asterisk indicates a title not yet published, but forthcoming.